Cynthia Harrod-Eagles studied English and History
at the Universities of Edinburgh and London. Her
novel *The Waiting Game* won the Young Writers'
Award in 1972

Cynthia Harrod-Eagles, who lives in London, will
be taking the story of the Morland Family to the
present day.

Also in the *Dynasty* series from Futura:

DYNASTY

10

The Tangled Thread

Cynthia Harrod-Eagles

Futura

A Futura Book

First published in Great Britain in 1987
by Macdonald & Co (Publishers) Ltd
London & Sydney

This edition published by Futura in 1987

ISBN 0 7088 3160 5

Reproduced, printed and bound in Great Britain by
Hazell Watson & Viney Limited,
Member of the BPCC Group,
Aylesbury, Bucks

Futura Publications
A Division of
Macdonald & Co (Publishers) Ltd
Greater London House
Hampstead Road
London NW1 7QX
A BPCC plc Company

For Allen, with love

The Morlands of Morland Place

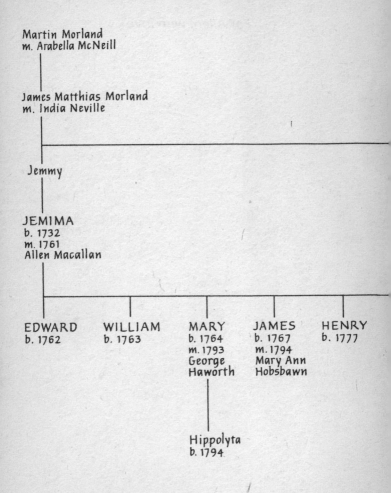

Martin Morland
m. Arabella McNeill

James Matthias Morland
m. India Neville

Jemmy

JEMIMA
b. 1732
m. 1761
Allen Macallan

EDWARD
b. 1762

WILLIAM
b. 1763

MARY
b. 1764
m. 1793
George
Haworth

JAMES
b. 1767
m. 1794
Mary Ann
Hobsbawn

HENRY
b. 1777

Hippolyta
b. 1794

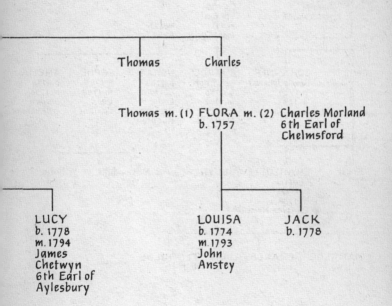

```
                        Thomas        Charles
                          |             |
              Thomas m. (1) FLORA m. (2) Charles Morland
                            b. 1757      6th Earl of
                                         Chelmsford
     |                         |            |
   LUCY                     LOUISA        JACK
   b. 1778                  b. 1774       b. 1778
   m. 1794                  m. 1793
   James                    John
   Chetwyn                  Anstey
   6th Earl of
   Aylesbury
```

The Chelmsford Family

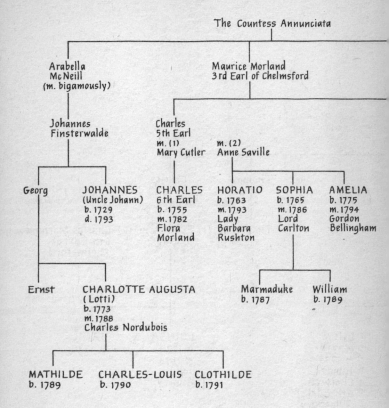

The Countess Annunciata

Arabella McNeill (m. bigamously) — Maurice Morland, 3rd Earl of Chelmsford

Johannes Finsterwalde

Charles 5th Earl
m. (1) Mary Cutler
m. (2) Anne Saville

Georg

JOHANNES (Uncle Johann) b. 1729 d. 1793

CHARLES 6th Earl b. 1755 m. 1782 Flora Morland

HORATIO b. 1763 m. 1793 Lady Barbara Rushton

SOPHIA b. 1765 m. 1786 Lord Carlton

AMELIA b. 1775 m. 1794 Gordon Bellingham

Ernst

CHARLOTTE AUGUSTA (Lotti) b. 1773 m. 1788 Charles Nordubois

Marmaduke b. 1787

William b. 1789

MATHILDE b. 1789

CHARLES-LOUIS b. 1790

CLOTHILDE b. 1791

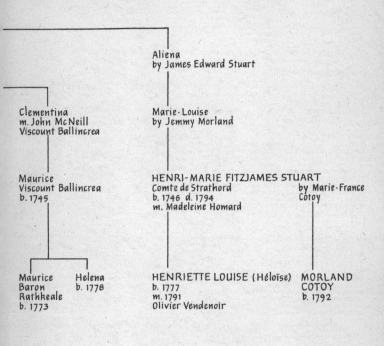

Aliena
by James Edward Stuart

Clementina
m. John McNeill
Viscount Ballincrea

Marie-Louise
by Jemmy Morland

Maurice
Viscount Ballincrea
b. 1745

HENRI-MARIE FITZJAMES STUART
Comte de Strathord   by Marie-France
b. 1746 d. 1794   Cotoy
m. Madeleine Homard

Maurice   Helena
Baron   b. 1778
Rathkeale
b. 1773

HENRIETTE LOUISE (Héloïse)   MORLAND
b. 1777   COTOY
m. 1791   b. 1792
Olivier Vendenoir

FOREWORD

Though I am sure there will be those who dismiss Lucy's adventure in this volume as pure romance, there are several well-authenticated accounts of women serving as ratings in the Royal Navy during the eighteenth and early nineteenth centuries without ever being found out. There was also the fascinating case of Dr Barry, who in 1809 entered Edinburgh University at the age of ten, disguised as a boy, qualified as a doctor and then served her whole life until retirement in the British Army as a military surgeon. Even after her death, when the woman brought in to lay her out discovered her secret, the military authorities were unwilling to admit how they had been deceived and continued to affirm that she had really been a man. I refer anyone interested in this case to June Rose's excellent biography.

Amongst the books I have found helpful are the following:

T. S. Ashton   *The Industrial Revolution*
T. S. Ashton   *Economic History of the Eighteenth Century*
John Bowle   *Napoleon*
Nancy Bradfield   *Women's Dress 1730–1930*
Capt. Edward Brenton   *Naval History of Great Britain*
Asa Briggs   *The Age of Improvement*
T. A. J. Burnett   *Rise and Fall of a Regency Dandy*
Hubert Cole   *Beau Brummell*
Paul Emden   *Regency Pageant*
John Fielden   *The Curse of the Factory System*
Joseph Fouché   *Mémoirs*
Dorothy George   *London Life in the Eighteenth Century*
R. Grundy Heape   *Georgian York*
William Howitt   *The Rural Life of England*
W. E. H. Lecky   *History of England in the Eighteenth Century*
Michael Lewis   *A Social History of the Navy*
Dorothy Marshall   *English People in the Eighteenth Century*

BOOK ONE

The Columbine

From you, Ianthe, little troubles pass
Like little ripples down a sunny river;
Your pleasures spring like daisies in the grass,
Cut down, and up again as blithe as ever.

Walter Savage Landor: *Ianthe*

I

On a sunny September day in 1788 a gentleman's travelling-chariot bowled through the gates of the Château of Chenonceau and up the driveway, between the ranks of magnificent, towering plane trees. The chariot was not new – in fact, it was a little old-fashioned in shape – but it had been recently refurbished with handsome black paint and crimson trim and a good deal of gold leaf about the shafts and cornices. It was drawn by four good horses; the postilions were in livery; and on the door on the near side was painted a coat of arms.

Inside the carriage, upon the new crimson velvet upholstery, with gold tassels upon the fat cushions, lounged Henri-Marie Fitzjames Stuart, Comte de Strathord, and his long, dark face softened into a smile as he looked at his daughter, Héloïse. The plumpness of the new cushions had been of no account to her from the beginning, for her whole body inclined forward in her eagerness to reach her destination, and her thin hands were clasped together so tightly that her knuckles were white. Her excitement had been growing since, four days ago, she had spent an entire morning packing and repacking her trunk in her small room in the Convent of the Visitation in the rue Saint-Jacques in Paris. Packing had taken an immensely long time, because her closest friend, a tall, buxom Normandy orphan named Marie-France, had insisted on examining and exclaiming over every new item of clothing with which Papa's money and Tante Ismène's direction had provided her. The item dearest to the hearts of both the girls was the new corset, made of linen and canvas, bound with white kid, and stiffened with real whalebone. Héloïse, at eleven, had never worn a boned corset before, and she hugged to herself the knowledge of it, nestling inside her trunk in the second carriage which followed behind carrying the baggage and servants.

'Oh, how I envy you!' Marie-France had cried wistfully. 'Such lovely new clothes – and a real maidservant to wait upon you, too.'

'Tante Ismène said that as Papa was to be a house guest at the château, it would not be proper for me to travel without a female companion. Though, of course, Madame Dupin wishes to consult Papa about refurbishment as well,' Héloïse said apologetically.

'And you are to stay three weeks. Oh Héloïse, you are so lucky – you go to so many places!'

'But I have never been so far, or stayed so long, before,' Héloïse offered consolingly. Indeed, she knew how lucky she was. She loved living at the convent, was fond of the nuns, and had many friends, but a restless spirit of eleven could not but be grateful for changes of scene. Papa designed interiors and advised the nobility on refurbishment, and had often taken Héloïse with him when he went to visit a great house in the country. He also took Héloïse out riding in the Bois de Boulogne every Saturday, and sometimes in an open carriage to watch the racing on the new course there; and once, as the carriages left, the Queen in passing had smiled and lifted her hand to Héloïse.

Then there were her vacations from the convent, when she returned to the house on the rue Sainte-Anne where she had lived most of her childhood. Madame de Murphy, whom she called Tante Ismène – though she was really no relation, but only a friend of Papa's – entertained all the most important people, and held regular salons where the *Philosophes* gathered to talk about the 'new ideas' and read from pamphlets and discuss how society could be changed for the better. Uncle Meurice, who was a colonel in the Écossais, sometimes worried that their republican ideas were disloyal to the King, but Papa only laughed at him and said that it was merely a new toy to Ismène and her friends, and far less harmful than basset or dice.

Papa knew and talked with real revolutionaries, in the Cour du Commerce on the Left Bank, where he had once lived incognito as Monsieur Écosse. He had a friend there, a lawyer named Danton, who kept his own salon of lawyers and students, poets, pamphleteers, out-of-work printers and renegade younger sons; and Héloïse, who knew far more than she should, on account of the servants not thinking she understood their gossip, knew that Papa still liked to slip away and resume his alias and sup with Danton and listen to the talk, and that he would return sobered and thoughtful.

Héloïse, of course, was not supposed to know of these visits, and was not taken into Papa's confidence about them, but once, when he had been quarrelling with Tante Ismène about what he considered a piece of dangerous folly, he had turned away and said quietly to Héloïse: 'Your mother would not have been so taken in.'

Usually, however, he merely smiled sardonically at Ismène's salons and her friends, and it was through them that he had met Madame Dupin, the châtelaine of Chenonceau. She was a bourgeoise, the wife of a rich farmer, who had the *entrée* at Court. The Dupins had owned a fine house in Paris, the Hôtel Lambert on the tip of the île Saint-Louis, and Madame Dupin's salons there had been famous, for the New Philosophies were her passion in life. Now a widow, she had retired permanently to Chenonceau, where she still entertained all the best of society. Some years ago Henri had been called in by her to advise about the restoration of the State rooms, a delicate and difficult task; and now she had invited him to stay for a house party, and had in her straightforward kindness extended the invitation also to the little girl.

'Depend upon it, she would not have asked you if you were not one day to inherit your Papa's title, *and* his fortune,' said Manon, the maid Tante Ismène had lent her as lady's maid, when she came up to Héloïse's room with a footman to carry down the trunk. But Héloïse only smiled and disbelieved her, for she saw good in everyone, and turned to clasp her dear Marie-France in a farewell embrace.

'I wish you could come too,' she said sincerely. Poor Marie-France never left the convent, except to go to church, and for walks in the Jardins du Luxembourg with the nuns.

'You will have a lovely time,' Marie-France assured her bravely. 'Be sure and remember *everything* about it, to tell me when you come back.'

'I shall keep a diary,' Héloïse said sagely, 'to be sure of forgetting *nothing*.'

Everything about the journey had delighted her: travelling with four horses, putting up at inns, being waited on like a lady by a real maidservant, the changing countryside around her, having Papa's company all day long. At first she had chattered – 'like a little monkey' Papa said – in her excitement; as she grew used to being in the coach, she and Papa had had proper conversations, and he had expressed himself surprised at how much she knew. 'You have your mother's head, my child,' he had said, which she knew was a great compliment. But since leaving Tours on the last stage of their journey she had been too excited to talk at all, and as the coach came out from under the trees and swung round on the gravelled forecourt before the château, she could only cast him one silent, expressive look before her eyes were drawn back irresistibly to the most beautiful sight she had ever seen.

In a moment the step was let down, the door opened, and she was helped out, and could stand staring to her heart's content. Before her the river Cher sparkled green-gold in the sun, its further bank a dark mass of trees, just beginning to be sparked with autumn; and from the middle of the river itself rose the château, small, delicate, graceful, its white stone honey-coloured in the sunshine, its long sloping roof and slated turrets gleaming blue-grey like a pigeon's wings. A stone bridge joined it to the bank, and behind the main building the gallery wing reached to the further bank, spanning with five graceful arches the river which flowed so tranquilly under the deep blue sky that it barely ruffled the perfect golden reflection of the château.

'Oh Papa, it's beautiful!' Héloïse said at last. 'It is the most beautiful house in the world.'

'Yes,' said Henri, 'I think it is. Most châteaux, you see, were built by men, to impress their friends or repulse their enemies; but Chenonceau was built by a woman, to be happy in.'

'Oh, one would be happy here!' she said, smiling up at her father. 'How could one be anything but happy?'

In the hall they were greeted by Madam Dupin with the greatest cordiality. She was in her eighties now, a small, very upright woman of great elegance with large, dark eyes and a pleasant smile. Héloïse could see that she must once have been very beautiful.

'And this is your daughter, Henri?' she said, extending her hand to Héloïse as if she were a real, grown-up guest.

'Yes, madame, this is Henriette-Louise, but we always call her Héloïse,' said Henri.

'Madame,' said Héloïse, taking the hand and curtsying deeply as she had been taught.

'Bless you, child,' Madame Dupin laughed. 'You should save such deep curtsies for the Queen! Rise up, and let me look at you. How old are you, my dear?'

'I am eleven, madame. And three weeks,' Héloïse said conscientiously.

'And you live with the good sisters – yes, I know convent manners when I see them. Well, I hope you will be very happy here at Chenonceau, my dear, and we must see how we can amuse you, while your papa and I are working.' She turned her smile on Henri. 'I hope you don't think it too bad in me to ask you to work while you are here? But there are still some of the State rooms in need of attention, and I would not trust anyone but you with a task requiring such delicacy.'

Henri bowed. 'It will be my pleasure, as always, to serve you.'

Madame Dupin laughed. 'Your pleasure, I hope, and your profit as well, my dear Henri! Now I am sure you would like to go to your rooms, before we take a little refreshment. Ah yes, here are your boxes. Caspar, see that the boxes are taken up at once.'

Papa's room was one of the guest chambers above the gallery. Héloïse thought it splendid, elegantly and thoughtfully furnished with everything one could require for comfort, and almost a superfluity of mirrors. There was a large dressing-room attached to it, with a couch on which his servant could sleep.

'So you may be quite private,' madame said to Henri, who laughed in a particular way and kissed her hand. Then she turned to Héloïse and said very kindly: 'I thought perhaps, as you live so simply with the good sisters, that you might be more comfortable in something a little less formal than this, so I have given you one of the turret rooms. Gilbert, take Mademoiselle de Stuart and her maid to her room.'

The white-wigged footman in his green livery preceded Héloïse from the room, held the door for her, and then extended a hand along the corridor with an 'If you please, mademoiselle' and a look that suggested he thought it a little beneath his dignity to be conducting a mere child. Héloïse walked behind him, along corridors whose floor tiles were patterned with royal fleurs-de-lis and salamanders, whose walls bore dim oil portraits in gilded frames of ladies and gentlemen in the costumes of half a dozen past ages, and Manon, the maid, trotted behind her. Following the broad green back, Héloïse noticed that his hair, of which a strand had escaped from under his wig, was fox-red, and that he had a boil on the back of his neck. It made him seem more human and less awe-inspiring, which was a comfort.

The room to which he shewed her was quite small and almost round, and seemed very crowded when they arrived, for two footmen were there putting down her box and valise, while a very small maid tried to squeeze in past them with a ewer of hot water. The footman Gilbert, to restore his self-respect, commanded the situation with loud and unnecessary orders, and after a few moments of noise and confusion they all withdrew, leaving Héloïse alone with Manon, free to run to the window and look out.

'Oh, but the view is lovely. I can see everything!' she cried. The turret was on a front corner of the house, so that the window looked back down the avenue of plane trees, on either side of which the woods stretched as far as the eye could see. Beyond the bridge which connected the château to the bank there was a funny little stone watchtower overlooking the gravelled forecourt, and to either side formal gardens set out in geometric patterns with clipped box hedges and gravelled walks. By leaning out and looking to the right she could see, beyond the tall slope of the chapel roof, the dreaming river, on which a small boat drifted while its occupant held a fishing-line. 'How peaceful it all seems.'

Manon sniffed. 'A paltry little room, mademoiselle, if you ask me. I wonder your father should let you be so slighted, when you will be a countess in your own right one day. It is not at all what I expected.'

Héloïse drew in from the window to confront the situation. The room seemed charming to her, with its stone-ribbed vaulted ceiling, curving walls and a dear little bed with a snowy-white counterpane and white cambric curtains. Manon had not seemed displeased when she had been chosen to accompany Héloïse as her maid, had attended her cheerfully on the road, and had even gone so far as to say she would like to see the inside of so famous a château; but now she stood with hands on hips and a sour expression on her face, eloquent of disapproval.

It was not long before Héloïse guessed what was upsetting her. Though she was only eleven she knew a great deal about the lives and opinions of the people around her, largely through her habit – which Papa told her was a reprehensible one – of chatting to the servants about themselves. She knew, for one thing, that a servant's status in the servants' hall depended upon the importance of the person he or she served. She guessed that Manon had just realised that here at the château she would be held in very little esteem, as the maid of a mere child, who had been given the smallest and meanest of guest chambers.

'I'm sure madame meant it as a kindness,' Héloïse said, and then added impulsively, 'Oh Manon, I am sorry you do not like to serve me, but I will try not to be a trouble to you, and it is only for a few weeks.'

Manon was only partly appeased, for she liked people to know their place, and it was not for the mistress, though she was only eleven, to apologise; but she was at least recalled to her duty.

'Let me help you off with your habit, mademoiselle,' she said briskly. 'The water will be getting cold, and it won't do to keep them waiting for their meat.'

Héloïse submitted to being undressed and washed and helped into one of her new gowns. The robe was of primrose and white striped cotton, the white stripes figured with sprays of blue and red flowers on green stems. The stiff bodice tapered to a long point at the back over a very full gathered skirt, and at the front the skirt opened over a plain white muslin petticoat. The ensemble was completed by frilled muslin cuffs, and a white muslin kerchief folded over the shoulders, crossed in front and tied behind the waist.

'You don't think it too plain for a château?' Héloïse asked, with only the faintest touch of anxiety. She loved the dress, but wished most of all to be correct. Not at all, Manon assured her. It was exactly the thing, and *très elegante*, which madame would regard more than anything.

'Now come to the window, where the light is best, while I

dress your hair,' she said. Héloïse was quite happy to stand looking out of the window, patient as a horse being plaited, while Manon poked and frizzed at her dark hair, and then at last she was allowed to look at herself in the mirror, which Manon held for her and moved up and down so that she could see everything.

'I wonder what sort of a woman you will make,' Manon mused, surveying her critically. Not a very pleasing one, Héloïse thought, to judge by her tone. 'However,' Manon went on briskly, 'you have good hair, and your eyes are fine. If only you were not so thin and sallow – but you will probably fill out when you are a little older, and if you don't, well, there are ways one can remedy that.'

'Are there, Manon?' Héloïse asked with interest.

'There are, but that's nothing to you for the moment. Here is someone come to fetch you, if I don't mistake.'

There were footsteps, a tap on the door, and there stood a footman, not the disapproving Gilbert but a boy hardly older than Héloïse herself, whose livery was too big for him.

'I am to conduct you downstairs, mademoiselle, if you are quite ready.'

Héloïse inclined her head graciously and swept out in fine style, only spoiling the effect by giving the boy not merely a smile – which would have been wrong to begin with – but one broad enough to be called a positive grin.

Downstairs, the company had gathered in the Diane de Poitiers salon to eat. The salon was one of those refurbished and restored under Henri's guidance, and he was pleased with the success of his labours, for the room was magnificent, and he ventured to think that even the King's mistress herself would not have been displeased if she had been able to return from the past and see it. The repairs to the massive marble fireplace were undetectable, the gilding of the cornices and ceiling had been done with a lavish but tasteful hand, and the portraits had come up excellently well after their cleaning. Flemish tapestries and fine furnishings adorned the room, but the company were much more interested in the buffet spread with a lavish array of cold meats and fruits, and in conversing with one another.

The talk naturally centred on the proposed calling of the Estates-General for the following May, the news of which had but recently broken. Everyone seemed to have his own idea of what the assembly was likely to achieve, and of what it ought to achieve, which were evidently very different things. Henri, ostensibly listening to two languid young men whose sartorial sophistication was pleasantly at odds with the down on their cheeks, let his attention wander in an unfocused way. 'Deficit' and 'Necker' were the two words most frequently employed, along with 'ministerial despotism', which had a fine ringing sound like a new-minted coin. There was considerable use of the rather more worn currency of 'liberty', 'justice' and 'privilege', and one or two coins of a new denomination and doubtful value: 'patriot' and 'nation'.

'One cannot be glad to see our country so deep in debt,' one of the young men was saying, 'and yet one sees that the American wars had to be fought. We could not leave our American brothers to struggle for liberty alone.'

Henri raised an eyebrow. 'I had imagined we fought to increase our territorial possessions in the New World,' he said. The young man blushed, and his companion came to his aid.

'That *was* a secondary aim, of course,' he conceded generously. 'But the deficit has had its use, after all. It has shewn the true colours of the King and his ministers in the high-handed way they proposed to raise taxes to pay off the debt, and then dismissed the *Parlements* when they objected.'

The other young man was heard to murmur something about despotism, Rome and Caesar; at any moment someone would say the word 'republic', Henri thought, and they would be off on the paths so familiar to him from Ismène's salons. Behind him he heard someone say to Madame Dupin, 'Is it true, madame, that the great Jean-Jacques Rousseau was once tutor to your children?' A great weariness came over him, and he was glad to be able to interrupt the young men by saying, 'Ah, here is my daughter. Gentlemen, you will excuse me?'

Héloïse's eyes were very wide indeed, with all there was to see: the wonderful room, the beautiful clothes of the assembled company, the variety and quality of the refreshments, served to her by a liveried footman on a plate of blue-and-gold porcelain so fine and delicate she could almost see the light through it. The footman had just offered her a glass of champagne when papa arrived at her side, and solved for her the problem of whether or not to accept it.

'Mademoiselle would prefer lemonade,' he said firmly.

Héloïse gazed at her father in satisfaction. He was, she thought, the handsomest man in the room, and he was wearing her favourite of his waistcoats, the pale blue one embroidered with blue and pink birds and almond-blossom sprays. All around her people were eating, and chatting in well-bred voices about people whose names were very familiar to her: Plutarch and Cicero, Voltaire and Corneille, Mirabeau and Lafayette and the Duc d'Orléans. She smiled at her father as he offered her the glass of lemonade he had procured for her, and said, 'Why, Papa, it's just like being at home.'

Henri laughed. 'Madame would be outraged to hear you say it; but I know exactly what you mean. They are so very like your Tante Ismène's friends, aren't they?'

Héloïse nodded. 'But everything *is* much grander,' she conceded.

'You wait until dinner, my marmoset! Madame's table is renowned.'

'Papa, am I the only young person here?' she asked him anxiously, in a lowered voice. Henri was about to point out the two downy-cheeked young men, and checked himself as he realised that though to him they appeared as children they were at least seventeen or eighteen, and would be indistinguishable from grown-ups to Héloïse. 'Yes, I think so,' he said, 'but you mustn't mind it. It is a great honour for you.'

'Ah, Henri,' Madame Dupin said, at that moment reaching them on her round of her guests. 'Well, my dear,' to Héloïse, 'how do you like your room?'

Héloïse curtsied. 'Very much, madame, thank you.'

'I thought that you would. I hope you will enjoy your visit, child. It is a pity that I was not able to procure for you a companion of your own age – '

'Héloïse is accustomed to entertaining herself,' Henri interposed.

'Well, she may safely walk about the gardens here, and my library is at her disposal,' Madame Dupin said with a smile. 'And – your papa tells me that you like to ride?'

'Oh yes, madame, above anything,' Héloïse said fervently. 'In Paris, where I live, Papa hires a white pony for me, and we ride in the Bois de Boulogne every week.'

'Then you shall not lack for amusement here. I have no suitable horse in my stable, but my near neighbour has a pony which is accustomed to carrying a young lady – his daughter, who is just married and gone away. I am sure he will be happy to place it at my disposal. I shall send to him at once and see what can be done.'

'Thank you, madame,' Héloïse said, her eyes kindling.

Madame Dupin, as practical as she was kindly, went on: 'I shall tell one of the grooms – Saultier will do – to hold himself in readiness for you. You may ride whenever you like; no need to ask permission, just ask one of the servants to send word to the stables, and Saultier will bring the pony up to the house, and accompany you. He will take good care of you.'

'*Thank* you, madame,' Héloïse said, and found nothing would express her feelings so well as the deepest curtsy she had yet performed.

During the afternoon, while Héloïse was being taken on a conducted tour of the château by the housekeeper, who had never had so attentive a visitor, nor one so rapturously moved by the romantic stories of poor Queen Louise and the battle royal between Diane de Poitiers and the wicked Queen Catherine de Medici, Henri mounted to the upstairs hall to attend Madame Dupin and discuss with her her plans for refurbishment. He found her there, but not alone, for she was, apparently, in the process of welcoming and conducting to their chambers two guests who had just arrived. Henri bowed and prepared to withdraw.

'I see you are not ready for me, madame. Pray send for me when you are at liberty.'

'No, no, Henri, on the contrary, I wish you to meet these gentlemen,' said Madame Dupin, stretching out a slender hand to him. One of the newcomers was a young and handsome man of twenty-four with the unmistakable look of a Parisian about him. The other Henri judged to be about sixty. He was tall but unstooped, and though thin to the point of gauntness, there was nothing displeasing or severe in his face. It was rather tanned, fine-featured and sensitive, and made alive by a pair of large dark eyes full of liveliness and humour which made Henri think – absurdly – of Héloïse. His hair was white without powder, which made a startling but pleasing contrast with his dark face. His clothes were evidently those of a rich man who was interested in his appearance, and yet there was something indefinably odd about their style. He looked at Henri with a frank interest which Henri found irresistible, and he found himself smiling at the stranger before they were even introduced.

'Henri, may I present to you Herr Johannes Finsterwalde of Leipzig, stonemason and architect. He has been kind enough to offer his services to Chenonceau. Monsieur de Stuart, Comte de Strathord,' Madame Dupin completed the introduction.

'Your servant, sir,' Finsterwalde said, bowing low. 'I have heard of you very often, Monsieur le Comte, and even trodden in your footsteps – I worked upon Monsieur le Prince de Rohan's house, only a week after you had quitted it, and of course I have seen what you have done at the Palais Royal.'

The strangeness of the clothes, Henri realized, came from his being German. He returned the bow, and a little social lie.

'Of course, Mein Herr, your name is very familiar to me.'

'You are too kind,' Finsterwalde said, and his eyes twinkled as if he knew Henri was lying. 'But I beg you, not Mein Herr. I am from Leipzig, it is true, but madame did not mention that I have made my home in Paris for three years now and shall remain here for the rest of my life, if I have the choice. I am to be a true Parisian, is it not, madame? I am to be *Jean* Finsterwalde from now on.'

Madame laughed at what was obviously an accustomed joke between them, and at Henri's enquiring look presented the young man, Charles Nordubois.

'Despite his apparent youth, he is the finest engineer I have ever met,' Finsterwalde interposed. 'He has further done me the inestimable service of marrying my favourite niece, Charlotte Augusta, and of giving me the perfect excuse to remain in Paris for the rest of my life.'

Madame Dupin gave Finsterwalde a wry look and said to Henri, 'He has never forgiven me for giving up the Hôtel Lambert, because when I lived there he was able to stay in Paris in the greatest comfort.'

'Such a lovely house!' Finsterwalde mourned.

'So as soon as his niece – who is also his ward, you understand – was fourteen, he dragged the poor child to Paris to marry her off to the first Parisian who would have her,' Madame said severely.

Charles Nordubois addressed Henri in a patient aside. 'Madame and my uncle like to talk nonsense, sir, and do it by the hour. The fact is that I fell in love with Lotti the moment I saw her, and begged her guardian to let me have her. He was not at all willing.'

'Only because she is so young, Charles; there is no one I would sooner see her married to than you,' Finsterwalde said, smiling.

'Your wife does not accompany you here?' Henri asked Nordubois politely.

'I was forced to leave her in Paris, sir. She is increasing, and I felt the journey might be too much for her.'

'Besides, we are here to work, not to enjoy ourselves,' Finsterwalde said sternly.

'Well, for you, Jean, it is the same thing,' Madame said, and added in explanation to Henri, 'Charles is an expert on bridges, and he is going to look at the foundations of the piers, which I am a little worried about; and Jean is going to design my new stables for me. I hope, Henri, that you will give him the benefit of your advice. I know you are passionate about horses – it is one of the things you and Jean have in common.'

'I am sure he stands in no need of my advice,' Henri said, catching Finsterwalde's eye and smiling, 'but I am never averse to talking about horses.'

'Well, to tell the truth, Monsieur le Comte, I have built many things in my time, but never a stable. I have some ideas, however, which I shall like to put into practice, for horses are my other passion in life – after architecture – and I saw some interesting innovations in England which—'

'You have been to England, sir?' Henri asked eagerly. 'It is a country I have always wished to visit. My grandmother was English.'

Finsterwalde smiled. 'A curious coincidence – so was mine!

It was from her that I inherited my love of horses, and the fixed idea that English horses are the best in the world. That was why I went to England, to tour the country and purchase some breeding stock to bring back. It was a most fascinating tour, I assure you.'

'And did you stay with your relatives? Are they interested in horses too?'

Finsterwalde smiled apologetically. 'Ah, I am afraid I have misled you a little. When I said my grandmother was English, I should have said I *think* she was English. She was a remarkable woman, sir, but a woman of mystery. I'm afraid she may not have been quite respectable in her youth.'

Henri laughed, thinking of his own chequered family history. 'One's ancestors, sir, rarely were.'

Madame Dupin's confidence in her neighbour's generosity was not misplaced, and the pony was brought over by a groom that same evening. Héloïse saw it for the first time the next morning when, thrilled almost speechless, and dressed in her habit of mulberry-coloured English broadcloth and a tiny tricorne hat with two white feathers, she came down the steps of the château for her first ride.

He was a chestnut with four white socks and a very long mane and tail, a showy little creature with a proud way of holding his head and lifting his feet. His name was Prestance, which Héloïse felt suited him perfectly. She loved him passionately at very first sight; and since she had the wisdom to greet him that first morning with a palmful of salt, he decided he liked her too, and by the second day was greeting her with a whinny as soon as she appeared. He carried her well, and had a light mouth, and though the first day he was very fresh and inclined to test her, he quickly learned that she knew what she was doing, and settled down to a happy relationship with her.

The one thistle in the flower garden was Saultier. He was an old man, kept on out of Madame's kindness to do odd jobs about the stables; but a lifetime with horses, which had bowed his legs like hoops, had done nothing to sweeten his temper. He let Héloïse know right away that he had been head groom in his time, and she rightly inferred that he disliked being the recipient of madame's charity in his old age. He considered it an imposition to have been put in charge of Héloïse, and since he had – magnanimously, in his view – agreed to take on the task, he expected her to give him as easy a time as possible by wanting nothing more than half an hour's amble up the avenue and back.

The dichotomy between his expectations and hers let loose a flood of complaint and rebuke on her head. She would damage the horses' legs – break their knees – break her neck – ruin her complexion, her health, her reputation. It was unseemly, improper, and unsafe for a young lady to ride all over the park all day long, and to gallop at full tilt and even jump ditches and fallen logs. At first Héloïse tried to argue with him, pointing out that far from being harmed, the horses were looking fitter and happier for the exercise, and that Papa thought exactly the same about her. In the end, there was nothing for it but to ride away, since he, having his orders, was obliged to follow her. She tried to sweeten him by chatting to him, asking him about his past triumphs as head groom and huntsman, and about his family and home, but he would not allow her to make a friend of him, and regarded her questions as impertinent curiosity. He remained obdurate, unwilling and sour, and since Héloïse could never bear simply to ignore people but must always try to make them love her, his presence, whether chiding or silent, marred her otherwise perfect enjoyment.

When she returned from her first day's ride, she insisted very firmly to Saultier that she wanted to take Prestance to the stables herself, to see where he was stalled, and to have a look at the other horses. She also wanted to rub him down herself, but seeing how savagely Saultier disapproved of the first half of her request, she wisely decided to defer mentioning the rest of it. Ladies – even diminutive ladies below marriageable age – did not frequent the stables; but when they clattered round the side of the stable building into the cobbled yard, hidden from the house by a fine stand of evergreen trees, she found Papa there talking to M. Finsterwalde.

And Papa, greeting her cheerfully, completed Saultier's rout by saying, 'Ah, there you are, Marmoset! I didn't think it would be long before you found your way here.' He came and lifted her down from the saddle, while a boy came running up to take the rein. 'Have you had a good ride, my love?'

'Very good, Papa. He is a *lovely* ride – much nicer than my dear old Snowball, though of course,' she added anxiously, 'I *ought* to love him best, because he has carried me for so long and . . .'

Henri laughed. 'Your soft heart is your trouble, Héloïse. Can you discard your old love for your new one?'

'I shall love them *both* best,' she decided. Saultier had taken the opportunity of her being preoccupied to gesture the boy to lead Prestance away, and before she had time to notice and protest, Henri said, 'I am glad you are come, chick, because M. Finsterwalde has been telling me of some wonderful stables he saw in England which I know would interest you.'

'Oh – have you been to England, sir?' Héloïse said, unconsciously echoing her father. 'Papa says I may go one day. I speak English – at least, I am learning it,' she added honestly.

'I saw a stable there that was like a palace,' Finsterwalde told her. 'The walls were of fine stone, and partitions of polished cedarwood, the manger and water bowl were marble, and the floor had the most beautiful patterned tiles on it, like the hall upstairs in the château.'

'Oh, it must have been beautiful!' Héloïse breathed. 'It must have been made for a very fine horse. Was it the King's horse, sir, that lived there?'

'No, there was no horse living in it when I saw it, but it had been built a long time ago for a beautiful stallion called Barbary. His name was engraved on a gold plate over the door.'

'What happened to him?' Héloïse demanded.

Finsterwalde looked apologetic. 'I'm afraid I never found out.' He saw her disappointed look, and reached out to pat her hand. 'But I have lots of stories about horses that I could tell you--'

'Oh, please!' Héloïse could not prevent herself from saying, and then remembered her manners and closed her mouth and curtsied, glancing at Papa for approval.

'I should be delighted to tell you every story I know, mademoiselle,' Finsterwalde said gravely, returning her curtsy with a bow. 'Perhaps if your papa would allow you to visit me in Paris – my niece, you see, with whom I live, is not much older than you and has not many friends. If you were to come and visit us one morning, I know she would take it very kindly.'

'I would like that, sir, thank you. Papa, may I?' Héloïse said. Finsterwalde looked at Henri.

'My Lotti has big dark eyes just like those, and when she looks at me so, I can refuse her nothing. We would both be honoured, Monsieur le Comte, if you would allow your daughter to visit us in the rue Montmartre.'

The district was unexceptionable; and Henri had for some time been seeking some more eligible friend for his daughter than the Normandy orphan of somewhat dubious antecedents. Besides, he liked Finsterwalde and was not averse to the notion of furthering their acquaintance.

'I will not only allow it, I will do myself the honour of bringing her myself,' Henri said, 'if it will not inconvenience your niece.'

'Ah, I had hoped you might, sir, I had hoped you might,' Finsterwalde said, and Henri had the novel experience of finding his hand heartily shaken in the best German manner.

Later, when Héloïse was in her chamber, waiting for Manon to come and change her for dinner, a knock at her door heralded not the maid, but her father.

'I have something for you, Héloïse,' he said, smiling. 'I went into the town this morning, and saw it, and hoped it would be what you wanted. Here, with my best love, child.'

He gave into her hands a book, bound in the finest leather, decoratively tooled, and held closed by a leather thong and brass lock.

'There is a key to go with it,' he said. 'Here.'

Héloïse looked up at her father in astonishment, and then down again at the book, and with careful fingers she inserted the tiny key, unlocked it, and opened it. Inside the pages of beautiful cream-laid paper were blank – enough pages, she thought with dawning joy, for her to keep a diary for five years, if she were careful.

'Oh Papa, it is beautiful! Oh, and just what I wanted! How kind you are – thank you, thank you.'

'Just a trifle, my darling. I should not like you to break your

31

promises to Marie-France,' Henri smiled, accepting her fervent kisses.

'I shall write *everything* in here, about the château and Prestance and everything, so that I shall never forget. I am glad that my journal will begin with a visit to Chenonceau. What could be better, or grander?'

'Quite right,' 'Henri said and, smiling, made his escape as Manon entered the chamber to dress her mistress for dinner.

Héloïse's desire to be loved by everyone made her in general not only an obedient child but a surprisingly patient one. Five days of Saultier, however, were enough to drive her to an act of rebellion. It was not difficult to escape him: she had seen enough of him to discover that he hated jumping, and would do anything rather than put his horse over an obstacle. The avenue, which was bordered by the fine plane trees she had admired that first day when they arrived, had ditches to either side beyond the plane trees, to divide the road from the woodlands which stretched away, shady and sun-dappled and inviting. While Saultier was delivering his most tedious lecture on the proper behaviour of young females, his attention was not fixed on her, and it was the matter of a moment to dig in her heel, swing Prestance off the path, over the ditch, and away at a canter into the trees.

Saultier's cries diminished rapidly in the distance, and Héloïse smiled, thinking that even if he decided to follow her, he would never dare to ride so fast through the trees as she did, so he would have no chance of catching her. After the first few moments the wood became more dense, and she was forced to slow Prestance, and keep a sharp look-out for low branches, and at last pull him back into a walk, to thread a way between the closely packed trunks.

The wood stretched all around her now, mysteriously quiet, like an enchanted place. The first fall of leaf rustled under her pony's hooves, and the ring of his bit and the creak of the saddle were unnaturally loud; I might meet anyone here, she thought, a witch or a bear or an enchanted prince. It was an adventure, she decided, though she was not at all afraid: the sunshine filtered through the canopy above her, making a green-gold, underwater light, and horses always knew how to find their way home.

She rode along in what she thought was the direction parallel to the river, allowing Prestance to pick his way through the trees on a loose rein, for there was no proper path here. He walked briskly, as though he knew where he was going, and after a while he came out from the density of trees into a clearing. It was so pretty, with its circle of blue sky above and green grass below that she halted him, and at once he tugged at the bit, wanting to get his head down to graze. Such a pity, she thought, that she could not dismount and sit here for a while, but once down she would have no way of getting into the saddle again.

'Oh, very well, just for a minute,' she said aloud to him, yielding to the urgent tuggings and letting the rein slack.

'I beg your pardon?' said a voice, startling her so that she gave a little shriek and made Prestance flinch, and then was ashamed of herself as she saw a boy sitting in the shadows under a tree on the other side of the clearing.

'You startled me,' she said. 'I didn't see you at first. I didn't expect to find anyone here.'

'I didn't expect anyone to find me here,' he countered.

He looked at her enquiringly, as though she ought to explain her presence, so she said simply, 'I didn't like the groom, so I ran away from him.'

'Which groom?' asked the boy.

'Saultier.'

'Ah, yes, Saultier. I'm not surprised you ran away. I often wonder how a man who spends his life with horses can be so disagreeable.'

'Oh, but that is just what I thought! How very strange!' Héloïse cried. The boy stood up – no, she could see now that he was more than a boy, almost a young man – and came towards her.

'How did you find this place!' he asked. 'I have always thought of it as *my* place.'

'I'm sorry if I disturbed you,' Héloïse said. 'It was Prestance who brought me here, just as if he knew his way.'

The boy had reached her, and was caressing Prestance's neck, and the pony lifted his head for the second he could spare from cropping the short, bright green grass to nudge him in a friendly way.

'He does know the way. I thought it was Prestance even

34

before I saw him, from the sound of his hoofbeats. He's a real little stepper, isn't he?'

'Have you ridden him?' Héloïse asked with interest.

The boy, unaccountably, blushed a little. 'No, of course not. He belongs – or did belong – to Mademoiselle de Brouilly, from the next-door estate. I used to ride with her sometimes. It was me who shewed her this place. I expect Prestance remembered it. She's gone away now – married,' he added gloomily, as though it were a sad and slightly shameful fate. Héloïse could think of nothing to say to that, and after a brief pause he looked up at her as if on a sudden thought, and said, 'Do you want to get down?'

'Well . . .' Héloïse hesitated.

'I can help you up again afterwards, don't worry. Isabel – Mademoiselle de Brouilly, I mean – used to like to sit on the grass over there and talk. It's two months since she went away.'

Héloïse felt challenged not to fall short of Mademoiselle de Brouilly's standards, and nodded assent. 'If I won't disturb you, then.'

'I was only reading.' He reached up his hands to her. He was tall, a little gawky, as though he had only recently shot up, and had not had time yet to adjust to his height. His skin was brown, as though he spent a lot of time out of doors, and where his shirt-sleeves were rolled up she saw that his forearms were strong and brown, with a little fine dark hair upon them. His face was straight-featured and rather stern, his eyes a curious yellowy brown under fine dark brows, his hair chestnut and very thick. The hands that had placed at her waist were long-fingered and strong, and she leaned forward with complete confidence as he took her weight and lifted her down. He released her and watched critically as she rearranged her skirts, and then turned to the pony, hooking the end of the rein under his stirrup.

'That way he won't tread on it and break it,' he said. 'No need to tie him up – he won't stray while there's grass to eat. Come and sit over here. The grass is quite dry.'

'It's all right, my habit is very thick,' she said, following him. He indicated the place where he had been sitting, and she sat obediently, making room for him beside her so that they could both rest their backs against the broad trunk of an oak.

'What a pretty place this is,' Héloïse said, looking around her.

'In the spring it's full of bluebells,' he offered, and then relapsed into silence. What a strange boy, she thought; having asked for her company, he did not seem inclined to talk, so she looked for some polite way of starting a conversation.

Her eye fell on his abandoned book. 'What were you reading?' He handed her the book in silence, and she took it and read the name from the spine. '*Le Contrat Social* – Jean-Jacques Rousseau. Do you like it?'

His face lit with enthusiasm. '*Like* it? It is the most wonderful book I have ever read! He is a genius – he shews the way for us all. There never was such a mind. He makes one see . . . However,' he checked himself, 'if you haven't read him, you won't understand. All I can say is that he spoils you for other writers. You never want to read anything else once you have read his books.'

Héloïse thought this a very poor idea. She loved to read, but to read the works of one writer only would be dull indeed: however, she said politely, 'I have heard that he is very good, of course, but I have not read him myself.'

'You are a little young, perhaps,' the boy said kindly, and added proudly, 'My father was taught by him, you know. Jean-Jacques Rousseau was my father's tutor.'

Héloïse's eyes opened wide. 'Ah, then you must be Madame Dupin's grandson. I am her guest, you know, staying up at the château.'

The pride faded from the boy's face. 'No, I am not related to Madame Dupin,' he said shortly. Héloïse was confused.

'Oh – but – I am sorry. I heard that Rousseau had been tutor to Madame's children, and here you are in the park . . .'

He gritted his teeth. 'Madame Dupin has always been very kind and generous. Rousseau was tutor to her son, and at the same time, she asked him to teach a boy from her estate who was very bright but could not afford schooling. She said he could teach two boys with no more trouble than one.'

'That was your father?' Héloïse asked carefully.

'My father,' he admitted. 'When he grew up, she employed him as her estate manager.'

Héloïse looked at him enquiringly. She thought it was a

lovely story: just the sort of thing Madame Dupin would do, to provide the poor boy with an education. Had she invited him to come and live in the château? she wondered. She would have liked to ask, but saw that the question would not be a welcome one. Carefully she asked instead, 'Why do you *mind* so much?'

'I don't understand you,' the boy said stiffly, not looking at her.

'When you said that your father was the estate manager and not Madame Dupin's son, your face changed, as if you really minded very much about it.'

The boy reddened. 'You are too young to understand', he said curtly.

'I could try,' she offered, undeterred.

He struggled in silence for a moment, and then burst out, 'Oh – can't you see? There you are, with your fine clothes, and feathers in your hat, and a horse to ride, and a groom to follow you around, and I am just the steward's son. I'm nobody, and you are rich.'

'*I'm* not rich,' Héloïse said.

'Your father obviously is. It's the same thing.'

'But it doesn't make any difference,' she said.

'Of course it makes a difference. Don't be a fool,' he said angrily, and she forgave him his rudeness, for she could see he was right.

'Well, yes, it makes a difference,' she said, struggling with things she had no power to express, 'but the difference doesn't make any difference.'

He looked at her sharply, wondering if she was making fun of him, and saw she wasn't, and yielded a little. 'You don't understand – how could you?' he said. He tapped the cover of his book. 'It will all be changed soon, though, you mark my words. It's all in here – the ideal state, the way the country should be run. Justice, liberty, truth, equality. The end of feudal privilege and – and everything,' he finished a little lamely. 'Next year, when the Estates meet – ah, then we'll see!'

Héloïse didn't want to talk about those things. She was more interested in people. 'What's your name?' she asked.

'Henri Olivier Vendenoir,' he said with dignity. She smiled. 'Oh, Henri – I like that name. That's my father's name.'

'I am usually called Olivier, to distinguish me from my father,' he told her.

'Well, I shall call you Olivier, if you wish, but I shall think of you as Henri,' Héloïse said, prepared to forgive him anything for having the same name as Papa. He did not seem to be going to return the question, so she said, 'My name is Henriette-Louise, but I am usually called Héloïse. You may call me Héloïse if you like.'

The boy's interest was reawakened. 'Rousseau wrote a book called *La Nouvelle Héloïse*,' he said. 'Were you named after it? Did your father read Rousseau?'

'Oh no, I called myself Héloïse when I was little, because I could not pronounce my real name. Papa has read Rousseau's works, but I don't think he likes them very much. He and Tante Ismène argue dreadfully about it, because Tante Ismène thinks Rousseau is wonderful, as you do, but Papa says . . .' she recollected in time that nothing Papa had said about Rousseau was likely to recommend itself to the boy and said instead, cautiously, 'Papa is quite fond of Voltaire.'

The boy looked as though he was not to be deflected. 'Your father, I suppose, supports the old scheme of things, and won't hear of any change or reform.'

'It is hard to know what Papa thinks about anything,' Héloïse said. 'He makes a joke of everything. But do you think that change is possible?'

Now Vendenoir was all eagerness again. 'Oh, yes! We have only to get rid of the old ministers, and put some new men in power, men who aren't afraid of really radical changes, and we shall have a new society before you can turn around.'

Héloïse looked uncomfortable. 'Papa says,' she said cautiously, 'that when men who haven't got power decide to take it, they always give very good reasons, like getting rid of injustice and making people happy; but once they have it, they use it in just the same way as always, to make themselves rich and comfortable.'

Vendenoir shook his head. 'You don't understand,' he said kindly. 'You're too young.'

'I'm eleven,' she defended herself.

'Well I'm seventeen, and I'm studying law, and in three years I shall be qualified, and I shall go to Paris and one day I shall be a minister myself, so I know what I'm talking about.' He sighed. 'If only I were qualified now! I might be elected to be one of the deputies for the Estates-General. In three years' time, when I finally get to Paris, the revolution will be all over. It isn't fair.'

'I live in Paris,' Héloïse said, to deflect his encroaching gloom. 'Perhaps when you come to Paris I shall see you there.'

'I shouldn't think that would be very likely. You'll be married to some rich man with a title, and be living in the country in a vast château with ten children, and growing fat and lazy, and you won't remember that I exist.'

'Well, I don't think *that* is very likely,' Héloïse countered.

He looked a little ashamed. 'I'm sorry if I was rude.'

'You were,' she conceded. 'You must try not to hate me because Papa is rich. He is really very nice, and works hard, and is not at all proud or disagreeable, like some rich people. After all, he is working at this very minute, while you are only sitting on the grass reading a book.'

'Working? Your father?' the boy said in disbelief.

'Up at the château. That is why he came. Well, partly why,' Héloïse said.

'Who *is* your father?'

'Henri de Stuart, Comte de Strathord,' Héloïse said, cocking her head at him. 'Do you know him? You look as though you thought it was all right.'

'It is quite all right,' Vendenoir said. 'I know your father, of course I do. I saw him when he was here before, restoring the State rooms, and everyone has heard of the things he has done. He is *quite* all right, not at all like one of those proud, hard, stiff-necked nobles shored up with their manorial privileges, and--'

Héloïse thought she had better stop him before he got carried away again. 'I told you he was nice,' she said. 'Now do you think you can like me, too?'

'Yes, as long as you let me call you Héloïse. And you can call me Olivier,' he said, smiling, and she thought that really, he ought to smile more often, for it made him look quite different and *much* nicer.

'I suppose I ought to be going now,' she said with a sigh. 'I would not like Saultier to find me here.'

'By Jupiter, yes, I had forgotten about old Saultier!' He gave Héloïse what was almost an admiring look. 'I must say I think you did very well to give him the slip.' They both stood up, and walked towards Prestance, still peacefully grazing, and then he said suddenly, 'I say, have you been on the river yet?'

'On the river?'

'In a boat? You haven't? Because you really ought to see Chenonceau from the water – it is very beautiful, everyone says so. If you like, I could come up to the house tomorrow and take you out. I am a very good oarsman, you know.'

'Oh, I should like that above anything,' Héloïse said. 'But you would have to ask Papa if it would be all right.'

'Of course – I know that,' he said with some scorn. 'I'll come up to the house this afternoon and arrange it.'

'Oh yes, thank you. How very kind you are,' Héloïse said, smiling at him so radiantly that he almost blushed, and found that she was not such a plain little thing as he had first thought. He helped her up onto her pony, gave her the reins, and directed her the quickest way back to the path.

'I think you will not get lost,' he said.

'Oh, I am not at all afraid', she said. 'I am sure Prestance knows the way home.'

'He does,' said Olivier. 'I must say, you are a great deal more sensible than most girls I have met.'

Héloïse smiled. 'Until tomorrow, then?'

'Yes, until tomorrow, Goodbye, Héloïse.'

The boat was broad in the beam, and shallow, with a sharply pointed bow, and painted golden yellow, so that it floated on the water much like a slightly curling autumn leaf, fallen from one of the trees overhanging the river bank. Vendenoir had brought it up the river with strong strokes, but now it drifted, moving so little on the gentle current that he had only to dip the oars now and then to keep position, fifty yards down from the château.

Héloïse, not reclining on the cushions as a young lady should, but sitting bolt upright with her hands clasped about her knees, was perfectly happy. The sky above was a deep cornflower blue, and in the distance the river was blue too, though beneath the boat it was greenish and transparent to its green-gold bottom. Before her the château, pale gold as honeysuckle, hung above the tranquil water, resting upon its perfect reflection, so that with her eyes half-closed she could pretend that she did not know which was which: she might be lying in the sky, and looking down at a wide sky-blue river. Near by were a pair of swans, motionless on the water except for a slight turn of the head now and then as they watched the yellow boat suspiciously. By the banks of the river water fowl were busy, and when Olivier dipped the oars a ring of ripples ran across the water and bobbed them gently amongst the reeds.

A rich September-afternoon peace hung over everything. The sunlight was as thick and golden as honey, and the only sounds were the distant conversation of the ducks, the chuckle of the water on the boat's sides, and Olivier's voice. Héloïse sighed and smiled, and knew she was happy. It is a perfect day, she thought, and when I am an old, old lady, I shall remember it so, this last afternoon on the river. The days of her visit had sped by since she had met Olivier in the wood. His application to her father, supported by Madame Dupin, who told Henri that young Vendenoir was a perfectly suitable and trustworthy attendant for his daughter, had resulted in his being appointed in Saultier's place to ride out with her, a change welcomed by Saultier as much as by Héloïse. With Vendenoir by her side, Héloïse could ride as far and as fast as she liked; he had shewn her all his favourite places on the estate, had taken her on the river most afternoons, and had taught her to fish; and, she thought shrewdly, had surprised himself by finding that he even enjoyed her company, for his rather superior and patronizing attitude of the first few days had waned considerably as he got to know her.

But it was almost over. There was to be a grand ball tonight, and tomorrow Papa's carriage would come to the door to take them back to Paris. She sighed again, and Olivier stopped talking and looked at her sternly.

'Are you listening to me?' he asked.

'You have a very nice voice. I should think you would make a good lawyer,' she said. He was not deflected. 'What were you saying?' she asked meekly.

'I was talking about the Estates-General. The Third Estate of 1614 . . .'

'What is the Third Estate?'

He sighed impatiently. 'I'll tell you again, but please try to concentrate this time. The First Estate represents the nobility, the Second the Church, and the Third Estate everyone else. Now, attend – the Third Estate in 1614 had the same number of representatives as the other two, but since the first and second estates always vote together – to protect their privileges, you know – the Third Estate might just as well not have been there.'

'Yes, I see,' Héloïse said obediently.

'So this time we are saying that the Third Estate should have double the number of delegates – which is less than fair, still, since it represents a hundred times as many people as the other two put together – and that the three estates should debate and vote as one unit. That way we will have a chance of putting through some reforms.'

Héloïse smiled privately at the way he talked of 'we', but nodded intelligently and said, 'Yes, that sounds right. I am sure you will get what you want.'

'Well, some of the nobles are with us – Mirabeau, for example, and some of the more liberal clerics – but the die-hards are bound to press the King for the 1614 rules, and obviously the Queen and her faction . . .'

Héloïse stopped listening. She could not understand how he could go on being interested in such stuff on a beautiful afternoon like this, with the Château of Chenonceau before them, hanging like an enchantment above the mirrored river. The chapel windows were throwing back coins of sunlight to the dancing water. There was a gallery high up in the chapel from which the queens used to watch mass down below, and one of the maids had told her that her room was a sort of ante-room to the gallery where they could retire to refresh themselves during a long mass. She could see the window of her room from here; Manon would be waiting there when she went up, to bathe her and help her change. She was probably there now, watching out of the window to see that Olivier Vendenoir behaved himself properly.

Héloïse smiled at the thought, for while Papa had only worried whether Vendenoir's oarsmanship could be trusted, not

42

wanting to see Héloïse tumbled into the river, Manon had doubts of a different sort.

'If I had gone out in a boat alone with a young man,' she had said fiercely when dressing Héloïse for the first venture onto the water, 'my father would have whipped me until I could not stand. I cannot imagine what your papa can be about. That Vendenoir is up to no good, mark my words.'

'Papa says I am only a child,' Héloïse said soothingly.

'Eleven is old enough, and your father knows it. Princesses marry a good deal younger than that, and if your papa has not his mind on a match for you by now, he is not the man I think him.'

'Oh Manon, you are always talking about marriage,' Héloïse sighed. 'I don't want to marry until I'm quite old – eighteen, perhaps.'

'Never mind eighteen – the good matches get snapped up quickly, and if you are not betrothed within the year, you may call me a Dutchman. You will have a great fortune and a title one day, and don't tell me that Vendenoir doesn't know it, for why else would he be taking you on the river?'

'Would he be a good match, Manon?' Héloïse teased, her face innocent, and Manon tied the strings of the hat with a jerk that almost ricked Héloïse's neck.

'A good match is a young man with a fortune and a place in society, as well you know, mademoiselle – and don't dare to go out of sight of the château, where you can be seen from the windows.'

Olivier's voice had ceased, and Héloïse looked at him guiltily, but found he was smiling more kindly than he ever had.

'I'm sorry. I – my mind was wandering--' she began, but he stopped her.

'I was boring you. It is I who should apologize. What were you thinking about?'

'Oh – just that I am so happy here, and I cannot bear to think I must go home tomorrow, and leave the château and darling Prestance and you, and never see any of you again. I have been so *happy* here.'

'Well, there is still the ball tonight,' he offered her for comfort.

'Oh *yes*! And fireworks afterwards, on the river. And I am to be allowed to stay up for all of it.'

'And Madame Dupin has been so very kind in allowing me to attend,' Olivier said.

Héloïse heard the wry tone of his voice and wondered what there was in such an invitation to displease him. She sought for something to distract him, and as they had drifted closer to the long gallery, which Catherine de Medici had built upon the graceful five-arched bridge that Diane de Poitiers had added to the original castle, she said, 'It is so beautiful, don't you think? And imagine it lit with hundreds of candles, and how it would look from the water after dark.'

'Yes,' Olivier said thoughtfully, 'it is beautiful. Sometimes I wonder – I have thoughts which confuse me.'

'Yes?' Héloïse prompted. He looked at her doubtfully, as though wondering whether she would understand, but said at last:

'It was built by rich people, for rich people; it cost so much, a fortune beyond account – and if there had not been vast inequalities of wealth in our country, no one could ever have been rich enough to build it. And yet, if it did not exist, the world would be a poorer place, because it *is* so beautiful.'

Héloïse looked at him sympathetically. She could see he was genuinely upset by the problem, and offered him her own solution to life's complexities. 'You should talk to my Papa about it. He is so very clever. Tante Ismène always takes her problems to him, and he solves them for her. Dilemmas, he calls them. He laughs at her, but he always makes her comfortable again.'

'Does he?' Vendenoir asked, amused. 'Always?'

'Always,' she said firmly. The smile slipped from his face, and he looked at her, she thought, rather strangely, as if he were just seeing her for the first time. 'What is it?' she asked.

He shook his head, and after a moment smiled in a different way and said, 'I was meaning to ask you – will you dance with me tonight, Mademoiselle de Stuart? Or are all your dances taken already?'

Héloïse flushed with pleasure. 'Oh, thank you for asking me! I should love to dance just *once* in a real château, but I did not think anyone would ask me, for I am only a child.'

Vendenoir reached out a hand impulsively and touched hers

44

and, abandoning for a moment his dreams of a society where there was no great wealth and privilege and therefore no palaces, he said gently, 'I will dance as many dances as you like with you, and I am sure you will go to hundreds of balls in dozens of châteaux in your life.'

A hush was over the castle, which could only mean it was the hour of dressing, and that all the ladies and gentlemen had retired to their rooms with their servants, brushes, powder and paints. In the little tower room, Héloïse stood almost breathless as Manon fastened the new corset over her best chemise and pulled the strings tight. It was a little padded over the bosom, and with a horsehair-frilled false-rump tied on behind, it gave her a figure, and made her feel quite grown up, and very excited. Héloïse tied her pocket on herself, and would have put on her own stockings had Manon not stilled her with a glance and knelt before her to do it. The stockings were of cream silk with pretty openwork about the foot and ankle, and Héloïse gazed at them in bliss as Marie fastened the garters above her knees. I'm sorry, Héloïse said mentally to Olivier, but I'm glad Papa is rich enough for me to have real silk stockings, even if it is only this once.

'Now, mademoiselle, we are ready for your gown,' Manon said, and Héloïse ducked her head obediently as Manon lifted it over her head and pulled it down around her. It was beautiful. The petticoat was of cream silk, with a deep ruffle at the hem, trimmed with pink and green twilled silk braid; the robe was of brocaded silk, cream and shell pink striped, with the skirt looped and prettily draped over the false-rump, edged with serpentine bands of the same trimming. The sleeves were three-quarter length, ending in double embroidered muslin ruffles, and as it was a formal ball there was no muslin neckerchief to fill in the deep, square *décolletage*, which made Héloïse feel strangely exposed but very daring.

She stood for Manon to dress her hair.

'Everyone will be in powder tonight, won't they, Manon?' Héloïse asked hopefully, and Manon tapped her head with the back of the hairbrush in mild reproof.

'I'm not powdering you, mademoiselle, so don't think it.

Nor yet painting your face.' And relenting a little, she added, 'You will stand out from the others, without powder. I think it a great shame for those that have pretty hair to fill it with flour. Everyone will admire your dark curls.'

Manon was skilful with brush and pins, and arranged Héloïse's glossy hair in loose ringlets, drawn up and back a little from her face, the back hair taken up high and knotted and ornamented with a few white rosebuds. 'Better than feathers for a young lady,' she told Héloïse. The ensemble was completed by pink kid slippers, and Héloïse's best fan, of painted skin with wooden sticks and carved ivory guards, which Papa had bought for her birthday and which came from London and was very elegant.

'There, mademoiselle, you look very beautiful, though I say it myself,' Manon said at last, holding up the mirror for Héloïse and moving it about so that she could see herself in sections. 'Only a bit bare about the neck, I think – but your nice bit of pink ribbon will do, as you haven't any jewellery.'

'I suppose you think I'm too young for jewellery too,' Héloïse sighed.

'Well, I don't say that pearls would not be suitable, perhaps,' Manon said, rummaging in the box for the ribbon, but was interrupted by a tap on the door. She went to answer it, and returned after a muted conversation with someone out of sight of Héloïse, carrying a small package, and wearing a very satisfied smirk.

'Your papa's servant,' she said. 'This is with your papa's love, and his apologies that it didn't arrive sooner, but he had to consult with madame about what would be suitable.'

It was clear to Héloïse that Manon knew what was in the package, and she opened it with excitement and a strong suspicion of what was inside. It was a necklace of pink shells and coral, together with a matching bracelet, exactly the right colour to go with her gown.

'I expect there would have been earrings in the set, too,' Manon said, taking the necklace from her to fasten it about her neck, 'but earrings wouldn't do. There now, you look just right. Your Papa couldn't have chosen better.'

'It's the prettiest necklace in the world,' Héloïse said rapturously.

Manon laughed. 'Oh, you'll have diamonds and emeralds one day, I don't doubt!'

'I don't care. I shall always love this necklace best.'

Long before it was over, Héloïse had decided that the ball was perfect. She loved the look of the long gallery with its beamed ceiling and black-and-white chequered floor: it was lit with hundreds of candles in tall bronze candlestands, alternating down the sides of the gallery with orange trees in tubs and set pieces of flowers in great vases. At one end was the orchestra on a dais, and everywhere the guests stood and chatted, or strolled, or danced, dressed in their most elegant clothes, their hair powdered, their necks and bosoms and wrists and hands flashing with jewels.

Héloïse had expected to have only one pair of dances, those promised to Olivier, who came up to claim her hand as soon as the minuets were over. He bowed to her, and as he straightened up he looked her over very comprehensively, and said with the faintest, and not unflattering, surprise, 'Why, Héloïse, you look very fine indeed. Quite beautiful, in fact.'

'Not like a child?' she asked anxiously, in an undertone. He considered. Her cheek was flushed with excitement, her eyes brilliant with it. The arrangement of her hair, and the elegance of her gown, made her look very different from the merry child he had met in the wood: not precisely grown-up, but ageless, as if she were a creature from another world, whose time ran differently from our own.

'Not like a child', he said at last. She beamed and placed her hand in his, and as he led her to the set she whispered,

'I'm so happy I could *die*! Isn't the ballroom lovely? I love the way the candles reflect in the windows. Imagine, the river is flowing under our feet: we are to dance on the water!'

She chatted happily to him all through their dances, and he listened and responded with great good humour, and found himself more than once thinking he was happier in his partner, though she was only eleven, than the men he saw all around him leading languid or haughty beauties whose conversation was stilted and whose minds were fixed on their appearance and their marriage prospects. He was quite sorry when the

47

music ended, and Héloïse's hand was claimed from him by Charles Nordubois, who had needed little prompting from his wife's uncle before his good nature got the better of him.

'We all part tomorrow,' he said to her as they moved up the set. 'How sad it will be to break up this delightful party! But I am assured by your father that we shall have the honour of a visit from you in Paris. I must tell you how grateful I will be for your kindness in visiting my poor dear wife. Her condition confines her to a sofa for a great deal of the time, and she is so bored, poor girl, as you can imagine. She is used to ride, and shop, and take walks with her dogs, and she has never cared for embroidery. You will be as welcome as the sunshine to her.'

The two third and two fourth Héloïse danced with the languid young men, who had been driven to it by Madame Dupin, and whose reluctance to stand up with a mere child was greatly modified by her unexceptionable appearance, and by the information that she would have a considerable fortune. The two fifth she danced with a genial, white-haired duke, who told her she looked as fresh as spring flowers and that he deplored the powder habit; and at the end of these two dances it was time for supper, and Olivier hurried up to claim the right to lead her in to the supper rooms

After supper, her father strolled up to take her away from Vendenoir for a few moments and ask if she was enjoying herself.

'So much, Papa!' she said. 'I did not expect to have more than one dance, but everyone is so kind.'

'Nonsense! You are the prettiest young woman in the room, and I should be astonished if you did not dance every dance.'

'Oh, Papa,' she reproved him for his extravagance, and then added, 'I have not thanked you yet for your lovely present. It is just exactly right for my gown. How clever you are, and how kind.'

'You should have had your mother's pearls, if I had only thought of it,' Henri said ruefully. 'You shall wear them at your next ball, chick, I promise you.'

'That would be lovely,' Héloïse said a little wistfully, 'but I could not love them as much as this necklace.' And she stroked it with loving fingers, making Henri laugh.

'It is the merest trinket, Marmoset, not worth all that love!

48

And now I must give you back to your swain, I can hear the music beginning, and you will not want to miss your dance.'

After Olivier's second two dances with her, her hand was claimed with a bow by old M. Finsterwalde, who said, 'If you do not think me too old to be stood up with, mademoiselle, will you do me the honour to join me in the set?'

When they had taken their places, Finsterwalde smiled at her and said, 'Are you enjoying your first ball, *gnadiges Fraulein*? It is your first ball, I believe?' Héloïse assented, and he nodded. 'Yes, the bright eyes, the flushed cheek – I remember so well . . .' He sighed. 'You must know that I had a sister once – my dear Lotti is named after her. She died when she was sixteen, of the typhus, poor child, but I shall never forget her dressed for her first ball, at the Herrenhausen. She was all in white, with white flowers in her hair, like yours, and her eyes shone like twin stars, just as yours are doing this moment, my dear. I was only nine years old, but I watched her going downstairs to get into the carriage, and when she reached the hall, she turned, as she promised me she would, so that I should see her gown by the light from the chandelier in the hall. She held her cloak open for a moment, and she looked up – I was on the stairs, looking through the baluster rails – and she *laughed*, for sheer joy.'

He paused and Héloïse was silent, watching his face. Then he smiled sadly. 'She was dead within the year, poor dear girl. But I did not mean to give you sad memories, only to say that you look just as you should for your first ball. You remind me of a picture I have seen in the Herrenhausen, of the Duchess Sofia when she was a young girl – she who would have been Queen of England if she had lived long enough. You have a look of her: the eyes, I think, and the nose, perhaps.'

'Papa calls me 'marmoset',' Héloïse told him, 'because he says they have eyes like mine.'

Finsterwalde smiled more broadly. 'He also calls you the last Stuart princess,' he reminded her. 'And now we must save our breath for our exertions, for we will be next at the head of the set.'

The ball ended with fireworks, set off from rafts on the river itself, and watched from the windows of the gallery by the guests, and from the river bank by one or two of the young men, who had no fear of chills from night air. The candles in the ballroom were doused for the display, and the orchestra played quietly in the background as the brilliant coloured lights sparkled and fountained and shot up into the velvety sky, reflecting a million times in the rippling surface of the Cher. Then the candles were relit, and there was hot soup for all, before Héloïse trod footsore and weary to the point of speechlessness upstairs to her bed. Manon was waiting in her room to undress her, and seeing how tired her charge was, forbore to speak, even to ask if she had enjoyed her first ball. Within moments of lying down in her bed, Héloïse was asleep, twitching like a dog as her pink kid slippers danced in dream down endless sets between rainbow-coloured candles.

On the fourth of June 1789 the eight-year-old Dauphin died after long illness. The title passed to his younger brother, Louis Charles, Duc de Normandie, the Court went into mourning, and Henri Stuart returned to Paris to pay a visit to the Convent of the Visitation. He exchanged a cheerful word with the porter, who took his horse, and bestowed a bewildering smile on the diminutive maid who met him at the door and told him that his daughter was away visiting for a few days, her expression revealing that she thought he ought to have known that.

'Never mind – I will speak a word with mademoiselle, her friend. Is she in?'

'Mademoiselle Cotoy is in the garden, Monsieur le Comte. Shall I announce you?'

'No, no, do not trouble yourself. I know the way,' Henri said quickly, smiling again so charmingly that the maid, who ought to have known better, stepped aside and let him pass. A passage ran through the old house from the courtyard to the enclosed space at the back which they called the garden. It had always been Héloïse's favourite place, for there was a little square of grass, a tall tree, too big for its surroundings and full of birds, a tangle of roses growing over the walls, and a few geraniums in pots which the little girls tended. Against the wall which caught the most sunlight there was a stone bench, and beside it a large, chipped stone crock in which some long-ago inmate had planted a slip of white summer jasmine. The plant had flourished, and over the years patient hands had trained it over a framework of sticks to form what they now grandly called 'the arbour'. Here Héloïse liked to sit and talk to her friend; here, as arranged, Henri found Marie-France waiting for him.

She was a typical Norman in looks: tall, strong, well-formed, stately of figure, with a fair complexion, light-brown hair, light-blue eyes and an air of robust good health. She had been born sixteen years ago near Caen, in the apple-country of Calvados, and was brought up for the first six years of her life as an orphan on her grandfather's farm. Then the old man died, and the farm passed into the hands of a maternal aunt whom Marie-France had never seen, or even heard of, before, and the child was removed to a convent in Caen, to be brought up by the good sisters.

There she had lived for the next six years of her life; and though the maternal aunt lived on the family farm only a carriage ride away, Marie-France had received in those years no visit, no letter, and no news. Her fees had been paid, but otherwise she might have been entirely without family. Then suddenly one day the aunt had reappeared, with the news that she was to marry a rich Swiss banker and live in Geneva. Marie-France was therefore to be removed to a fashionable convent in Paris to learn society manners, and when she was fifteen she would be sent for, and go and live in Geneva, and take her place in society.

The very next day a hired chaise had called at the convent in Caen to collect Marie-France and take her to Paris, where she had been put down, with her baggage, at the doors of the Convent of the Visitation. The nuns were expecting her: they had received letters from the aunt, together with the payment of the first year's fees in advance, which circumstance had impressed them sufficiently favourably to put Marie-France into the best apartment. But that was the last they or anyone else heard of the maternal aunt. She had never come for Marie-France, nor sent for her, and at the end of the first year, when there was no more money forthcoming, Marie-France had been removed into a small attic room, where she remained at the charity of the good sisters, who after all had nowhere else to send her.

Marie-France had told Héloïse the story, and added that she thought her aunt must have been set upon by robbers on the road to Switzerland, robbed and murdered and buried secretly beside the road somewhere – for why else would she not have sent for her niece? When she was old enough Marie-France would take the veil, for there was nothing else she could do to provide for herself. Héloïse could never think of Marie-France's story without tears, and often wished aloud to her father that there was something to be done for her friend.

Henri had his own ideas, amongst which was the suspicion that the maternal aunt had borne a closer relationship than stated to the orphan of Caen – that she had in fact been her maternal mother. He knew Caen, often known as 'the Athens of the North', and how strait-laced and snobbish were its inhabitants, how they prided themselves on their elegant and cultured society. He could imagine that the young woman on the point, at last, of realizing an advantageous marriage, might have found the nearby presence of her youthful error a disadvantage and devised a scheme to get rid of her.

He had naturally not mentioned his suspicions to Héloïse, who believed implicitly in the robber band and the lonely, unmarked grave; but he had often caught a look in Marie-France's eye that suggested she had no real faith in her own story, but rather guessed in the same direction as him. He pitied her, and had been kind to her for Héloïse's sake, but he was none the less determined to find a way to detach her from his daughter, whose heart was as tenacious as a barnacle.

Marie-France looked up as he came through the door, and flushed not unbecomingly. Henri enjoying her confusion, bowed over her hand and touched it to his lips.

'Well, mademoiselle?'

'Well, Monsieur le Comte,' she countered as well as she could for the beating of her heart. 'Can Versailles spare you? How do the Estates-General go on?'

'They go on as they have gone on these five weeks – with endless wranglings about procedure. With luck they will never get to discussing reform – they will go on for ever debating on how they are to debate.'

'You are against reform, then?'

Henri smiled a little wolfishly. 'That depends, dear mademoiselle, on your definition of reform. The trouble is that everyone always thinks they can have just as much change as suits them, and then stop when they have got to the place where they want to be. But once you start a boulder running down a mountainside, you have no chance of stopping it. However,' he added more lightly, 'I don't suppose that is purely a French trait. I expect even the English thought that way, when they were having their revolution.'

'You talk in such a strange way, just as if you weren't French

53

yourself but a foreigner observing from outside,' Marie-France said curiously. Henri shrugged.

'As far as I know, I *am* a foreigner. Not one bit of me is French, though I was born and bred here in Paris.'

'Then, Héloïse is not true French?' she said musingly. Henri laughed.

'Oh, she is her mother's child: not only true French but true Parisian. And she looks it!'

Marie-France smiled. 'Sister Martin said yesterday that she was like a little dark monkey, *and* as much trouble.'

Henri groaned. 'Oh dear, what had she been doing to provoke such wrath?'

'She climbed on to a branch of the tree up there, out of the drawing-room window, to try to rescue the kitten. But then when she got half-way along the branch the kitten jumped over her back and got down on its own. Sister Martin punished her for being unseemly, and for not stopping when Sister Claire called her to stop.'

'What was the punishment?' Henri asked with interest.

'Ten aves and ten paternosters, and Sister Martin said she hoped it would teach her a lesson.'

'Yes, that in this imperfect world, good deeds must be their own reward; and that kittens never are really stuck in trees.'

Marie-France laughed at that, but her laughter stopped abruptly when Henri sat down beside her on the stone bench with an air of one coming to the point.

'Well, mademoiselle, have you thought about my offer?' he asked mildly. Her blush returned, but she met his eyes bravely.

'Yes, sir, I have. You say that you will take me from here and set me up in an *apartement*, and buy my clothes, and feed me, and provide me with a servant. But I wish to be quite clear, sir. Am I to be' – her colour deepened, but she forced herself to go on – 'to be your – your mistress?'

'Yes, mademoiselle, that was my intention,' Henri said unemphatically, amused by her embarrassment but impressed by her courage. 'Is it so terrible a prospect? Come, I am sure you would prefer it to taking the veil.'

She did not answer this directly. Her eyes were inward and thoughtful for a moment, and then she said, 'Why?'

'Why what?'

'Why are you asking me?' she said with difficulty. He hesitated, and she met his gaze again and said, 'Please be frank. I should prefer it.'

'Well, mademoiselle, if that is indeed the case, we should do very well together, for I like frankness above all things. I will tell you why – because I am attracted to you, because I think it will be a comfortable arrangement for us both, and because I feel I owe it to Héloïse.'

'Héloïse is very fond of me,' she said quietly. Henri smiled.

'Exactly so. Héloïse loves you, and if you were still here in this convent when she became mistress of her own establishment she would feel obliged to have you to live with her.'

'If that is so, why should I accept your offer?'

Henri's voice became ever more gentle. 'Because you love her.' Marie-France's eyes stung with tears, and she turned her head away from him. He spoke more briskly. 'Come, my dear, it is not so bad, is it? I am persuaded you will have a very good time of it – a dear little *apartement* in the rue Boudreau, a smart maid, a shopping account, a box at the Opera--'

She interrupted him, her voice a little harsh. 'She must not know.'

He raised an eyebrow. 'Héloïse? No, indeed, that would render the exercise useless. She shall not know. We will concoct a story between us – a distant cousin, perhaps, returned from distant parts to rescue you? – and you shall write to her at once with the good news.'

'Yes,' she said. 'Yes, thank you.' A handkerchief was pushed gently between her fingers, and she blew her nose and wiped her eyes and straightened her shoulders. The handkerchief was of silk, edged with lace, and faintly but expensively perfumed. She was sixteen and a penniless orphan, and had inherited some of the realism of her country forbears, and she knew that life could be a great deal worse than it was. She turned to Henri and met his eyes bravely and gave him a rather tremulous smile. 'Thank you, Monsieur le Comte,' she said more firmly. He took her hand and pressed it, and she felt the stirrings of curiosity and excitement about her new life.

'It is I who must thank you, mademoiselle,' Henri said politely.

The house on the rue Montmartre was large and old and rambling, and being inhabited by an architect and an engineer was in a constant state of being altered and modernized. There was always the smell of new paint and sawdust and the sounds of hammering and planing and whistling, and servants improvident enough to hurry round one of its numerous dark corners were more than likely to fall over someone in a workman's apron doing something inexplicable to the skirting boards.

Charlotte Augusta Nordubois, the mistress of the house, who had not yet managed to think of herself as anything but plain Lotti Finsterwalde, enjoyed it all enormously. She was a long-limbed, red-haired, merry romp of a girl, who was not more surprised than amused to find herself at sixteen wife, mother and châtelaine. Her father had died when she was two, and her mother had always been a distant figure, a pale, vapouring wisp of a woman who seemed in memory always ill and complaining. It was Uncle Johann who had brought her up, brought her to Paris, brought her to the altar, and brought her to this charming house where no one could ever scold her for being untidy.

Lotti adored her handsome husband, and thought marriage the most wonderful joke; and though she did not know it, she both disconcerted and delighted her husband by treating their marriage bed as a place for laughter and conversation. She even chatted to him while they were making love, for having been brought up largely by a man, and a bachelor at that, she had never received any instructions on how to behave in bed, and so carried on there exactly as she did everywhere else.

Her baby, Mathilde, was born in March 1789, and she adored her too, though she was not allowed to have much to do with her. The governess and nurse ruled over the nursery with an old-fashioned tyranny which regarded parental interference as unsuitable, and Lotti's habit of bouncing and tumbling the baby like a puppy as likely to damage her limbs and digestion. It was useless for Lotti to point out that the baby gurgled with pleasure under her mother's treatment: Lebrun had been governess to three families before, and Lotti was no match for her. She could only shrug and return to her other pleasures.

They were many and varied, and since Uncle Johann had had the kindness to provide her with a friend, they were no longer solitary. Héloïse might be four years her junior, but she was just the sort of unaffected, lively, affectionate girl that Lotti liked, and she was only sorry that Héloïse could not live with her permanently. Henri insisted that Héloïse remain at the convent and receive her formal education; but since Héloïse's principal friend, Marie-France, had left the convent to live with an elderly relative in Caen, she was happy to visit the rue Montmartre as often as she was allowed, especially since Henri had bought Prestance for her and had him stabled with Lotti's mare.

One day in June the two friends returned from a ride, and were glad to step out of the sultry heat into the coolness of the stone-flagged hall. Lotti dragged off her hat to the detriment of her coiffure, tugging impatiently as it caught on a pin so that when it came free her hair tumbled down, shedding pins like a metallic autumn.

'Oh, this heat!' she cried! 'If it weren't for the riots, I think I should take to riding at night, for the coolness. Oh, my wretched hair,' she added with a placating smile at her maid, who was stooping to retrieve the pins with a rigidity eloquent of disapproval. 'Really, Héloïse, I wish you could contrive to look a little more untidy after a ride. You are provokingly neat – I'm sure you do it to tease. Ah, Besser,' to a footman hovering near, trying to tell her something, 'bring some lemonade for us – lots of it! Bring it to the nursery. I must go and see my little Mathilde, and you must come with me, Héloïse, or that disagreeable Lebrun will refuse to let me hold her. You shall distract her for me while I play with my baby.'

'Perhaps you might be firm with her . . .' Héloïse suggested, but Lotti rolled her eyes.

'Oh, I dare not! Besides, she might leave, and then Charles would be cross.'

'Madame . . .' the footman interposed anxiously, but at the same moment Lotti noticed the hat and gloves on the marble hall-table.

'Oh, we have a visitor. Why did you not tell me, Besser? Who is it?'

Héloïse needed no telling. 'It is Papa's hat – he must have come back from Versailles,' she said excitedly.

'Monsieur le Comte is in the drawing-room, madame,'

Besser acknowledged, and Lotti instantly forgot her baby and shocked her maid by running up the stairs.

'Bring us refreshments, Besser – and tell my uncle if you can find him. Come *on*, Héloïse!'

Henri smiled with pleasure as he received his daughter's tiptoe kiss, and a hearty handshake from the mistress of the house, whose fiery, fox-coloured mane was hanging down her back, and whose cheerful face bore a fine coating of summer dust. 'You have been riding, I conclude,' he said mildly, and rolled an expressive eye at Héloïse, who was, as always, as neat as a sparrow.

'Oh Papa, don't tease her,' Héloïse said. 'Really, her hair is very hard to manage.'

'Like her horses,' he smiled, for Lotti had a predilection for horses too big and strong for her. 'And how is Prestance today?'

'Perfect. Oh Papa, I can't thank you enough for buying him for me. I should have hated anyone else to have him.'

'Oh dear – I foresee tears when you grow too big for him,' Henri said. Héloïse looked determined.

'I shall *not* grow too big for him. I shall not grow any more, if it means I must lose him. He is . . .'

'I know – the best horse in the world,' Henri teased. 'Ah, here are refreshments, if I don't mistake.' The door opened, to admit two footmen with trays. 'I confess to a great thirst. I have just ridden from Versailles, and the road is a wilderness of dust.'

Lotti remembered her duties as hostess, seated herself and waved Henri to a sofa. 'How do things go on at Versailles? We hear such rumours, though I dare say not half of them are true. About the Third Estate calling itself the National Assembly or some such thing, and finding itself shut out of its chamber, and setting up in a tennis court and refusing to move. It must be very diverting.'

Henri drank off a glass of wine, and received another from the footman. 'Diverting? Well, yes, I suppose it is, in a way. Refusing to move has become quite a feature of the Third Estate – you heard what happened at the *Séance Royale* on the twenty-third?'

'We heard rumours – were you there?'

'Of course – the whole court was. It was a great state occasion,

everyone in full robes and panoply, and the Third Estate looking very strange in their ordinary clothes, and quite determined
not to mind it. And the King looking quite determined to put
them in their place once and for all – after all, the Estates have
been in session since May the fifth, and they have done nothing
so far but wrangle about procedure.'

'We heard there was a great mob from Paris in the courtyard
outside,' Lotti said, spilling her wine on her skirt and rubbing
vaguely at the mark with her sleeve.

'There was, and four thousand of the royal guard under the
Prince de Conti to keep order, though as it turned out they
might as well not have been there.'

'What happened, then?' Lotti asked.

'The King's man, Barentin, read out the royal procla-
mations, firstly that all the resolutions made by the so-called
National Assembly were null and void, and secondly that there
were to be certain reforms, mainly to do with taxation, but that
the Third Estate was not to discuss anything to do with the
special privileges of the other two estates. Then he ordered
them all in the King's name to return, each Estate to its separate
chamber, to debate and vote separately.'

'But, Papa,' Héloïse said, 'that's what they have been arguing
about all along, isn't it?'

'Exactly, Marmoset. We had got back to the starting-point,'
Henri smiled darkly. 'The King and his attendants withdrew,
but I lingered in the gallery to see what would happen. There
was a great stirring and muttering, and some of the Third Estate
began gathering themselves to move, and then Bailly – the
president – jumped up and declared that the nation when
assembled could not be given orders, and Mirabeau shouted
out that they would not leave except at the point of a bayonet.
Some of the clergy and nobles declared with the Third Estate,
and all the worthy burgesses then folded their arms and sat
tightly in their seats, while the order was passed back to Conti
to bring in the guard to move them.'

Héloïse clasped her hands. 'Oh, it sounds so dangerous – not
amusing at all.'

Henri smiled at her consolingly. 'Don't worry, my love – the
crowd from Paris made it quite clear where their sympathies
lay, and Conti thought it imprudent to provoke a pitched battle,

and sent word to the King that the Third Estate would not leave the hall.'

'And what did the King say to that?' Lotti asked. Henri positively grinned.

'He said, I am told, "Oh well, Devil take it! Let them stay".' Héloïse's eyes grew very round at such tolerance of disobedience. Henri went on. 'Then yesterday he ordered the remains of the First and Second Estates to join the National Assembly, and for all to debate and vote together. So they have got their way at last.'

'The revolution is all over,' Héloïse said, remembering her friend Olivier Vendenoir and his prediction that he would miss it all.

'I'm afraid not. It rather looks as though it is just beginning.' It was Uncle Johann, appearing in the doorway in time to catch the last remark. He advanced into the room to greet Henri and receive the embraces of the young women, and then sat between them, his hands on his knees, shaking his head in disapproval as he went on, 'You may have been at Versailles, Henri, but I have been at the Palais Royal, and let me tell you that the temper of the people there is most alarming.'

'What have you been doing at the Palais Royal?' Henri asked. 'I hear that some very strange people haunt the gardens there these days.'

Finsterwalde smiled. 'I am advising on some alterations Orléans wants to the south façade – but you are quite right about the strange people. The arcades are filled with cafés which are hotbeds of gossip and revolutionary talk, and at night all the low life of Paris assembles there.'

Henri raised an eyebrow. 'Low life? In the Palais Royal?'

'Journalists and actors and students, members of political clubs, unemployed printers and lawyers – all the extreme revolutionary element, gathering there, my dear Count, to receive directives and slogans and – not to put too fine a point on it – money.'

Henri smiled, 'You believe that Orléans is financing a revolution against his own cousin?'

'Orléans is not like his father. He is quite capable of making a hole in the ship of state for his own purposes, and caring nothing if he sinks the ship in the process. He has orators and pamphleteers in his pay, and nightly they whip up the emotions of what I can only call the mob in the gardens. Everything that happens at Versailles is relayed straight there by messengers in his employ. Only today the discontents were being told that the King has no intention of allowing the National Assembly to have its way, and that he is secretly summoning troops to Versailles to repress the Assembly by force.'

'Quite true,' Henri said. 'The King has summoned regiments to come to Versailles, and after the events at the *Séance Royale*, who can blame him? But he will not use force. I know the King. He is stubborn, and will not be pushed, but he would never order soldiers to fire on his own people.'

'Then why the troops?'

'A show of force merely. Enough to sober the populace. After all, even if they are inflamed by oratory, they are not armed—'

'Not yet,' Finsterwalde interrupted with a bitter look. 'But they will be.'

'Oh, we have heard talk of a City Militia,' Lotti said. 'The Electors of Paris have set themselves up in the Hôtel de Ville, and claim to be ruling Paris in the name of the people. They are going to form a militia to keep order in the streets.'

'True, my love – but while their plans are all on paper, the Palais Royal has already sent out money and pamphlets enough to bring over the Paris garrison, and convince the soldiers of the Garde Français that they are now the troops of the Third Estate. I saw half a dozen of them today, drunk as lords, sporting red and blue cockades and chanting "We are the soldiers of the nation!" '

'But who will they fight?' Héloïse asked in a small voice. 'They will not march to Versailles and shoot at the King, will they, Papa?'

Henri and Finsterwalde exchanged a look over the heads of the women. Henri, though he did not admit it, knew already a great deal more than Finsterwalde of the antics of the extreme revolutionary element, for in his visits to Danton's house on the Left Bank he heard enough to worry him. The Cordeliers' Club might not yet influence opinion as did the more respectable Jacobin Club on the Right Bank, but it was so much more determined, and so much less scrupulous about what forces might be used, that he had no doubt one day it would. The mob was mighty, but had always so far been undirected, and the frequent bread riots in the *faubourgs* of Paris had in the past been subdued easily enough by armed forces under discipline. But let the hotheads, whether from the Cordeliers district or the Palais Royal gardens, give the mob leaders, slogans and a cause, and it would become a force that would prove difficult, perhaps impossible, to resist.

But whatever his fears, he saw in Héloïse's anxious look that enough had been said, and replied in a lighter tone, 'Of course not, little one. That would be unthinkable. But if things begin to look troublesome, I shall make arrangements for you to leave Paris, so do not be anxious. Everything will settle down eventually.'

'I should not like to leave Paris if you were staying here,' Héloïse said.

And Lotti added stoutly: 'It would be very poor-spirited to leave, just because of a little trouble. Besides missing all the fun, I don't think I should think of making any long journeys for some months to come.'

Finsterwalde caught her drift and said hopefully, 'Why, Lotti, *liebchen*, you don't mean . . .?'

Lotti laughed. 'Why yes, Uncle Johann, I *do* mean! How I have confounded you, have I not? You always wished I had been a boy.'

'Nonsense. If that were so, why did I make you my favourite, instead of your brother Ernst?'

'Because Ernst is so pious and dull, and because he has to stay in Leipzig to take care of the family business. I was free to wander round the world with you, though had I been a boy, you would have been able to wander a great deal further. As it is, we only got as far as Paris, and now I am tying you here with a litter of babies.'

Finsterwalde laughed. 'I always loved you best, *puperl*, because you reminded me of my grandmother, and if your babies resemble you, I shall be quite happy to be tied.'

Henri, glad to have the subject changed, said, 'You speak of your English grandmother, sir?'

'I said that I thought she was English,' Finsterwalde corrected. 'I never knew for sure, for though she spoke English she also spoke French and Italian, besides German. Have I ever shewn you her likeness, Héloïse?'

Héloïse's fears were quite ousted by her interest, as both men had hoped. 'No, sir, though you said you would. You promised to tell me her story, too.'

Finsterwalde rose and went to the drawer of a bureau in the corner, and returned with a miniature in a gold case, which he gave to Héloïse. 'There,' he said. 'Splendid, wasn't she? That is a lock of her hair, in the other half of the frame.'

'Hair just like mine,' Lotti said. 'Coarse and red and impossible.'

Héloïse looked at the likeness of a haughty young woman with bold features, a determined mouth and chin, and a mass of straight red hair, dressed in the style of a hundred years ago. 'She has a very interesting face,' she said tactfully, passing the picture to her father, who looked at it and smiled.

'You said she was not quite respectable, as I remember. Perhaps her story is not fit for Héloïse's ears,' he teased.

'Oh, please!' Héloïse begged, looking from her father to Finsterwalde pleadingly.

'I'll tell you what I know,' Finsterwalde said, 'though it isn't much. My grandfather met her in Prague, where she was supporting herself by selling horses to the local garrison. She was about twenty-five, and claimed to be a widow, running her late husband's business. Grandfather fell in love with her, and brought her home and married her. She bore him a son, my father Johannes, and then grandfather died, and she took control of the family business and ran it most efficiently.'

'An enterprising woman,' Henri said. 'Even for those enterprising days. But why did you think her not respectable?'

'There was some mystery over how she came to Prague, and no one seemed to have heard of her so-called previous husband. I used to hear my grandfather's relatives discussing her and shaking their heads. I was too young to understand what they were saying, but I knew they disapproved of her. However, there is no doubt she ruled the family most efficiently. In time my father married, and had five children: my sister of whom I have told you, Héloïse, and my three brothers and myself. My mother died giving birth to me, and my father followed her to the grave within the year, so it was Grandmother who brought us all up.'

'What happened to your brothers?' Héloïse asked.

'Well, Sebastien, the eldest, was a fine lad, tall and handsome and clever. He went to the University at Heidelberg, but he caught a fever there and died when he was only eighteen. Grandmother was heartbroken – I'm sure it was his death that hastened hers, for she was very strong and hearty until then. Georg, my second brother, took over the family business after that, and he married and became the father of my dear Lotti and her brother Ernst. He died just three years ago. Friedrich, the third son, went into the army and rose to be a colonel of cavalry, and died at the age of fifty, unwed.'

'And then there was you,' Héloïse said.

'Then there was me,' he agreed, smiling. 'I was my grandmother's pet, being the youngest, I suppose. She used to talk to me more than to any of the others – perhaps she thought I did not understand. And sometimes she used to talk about her girlhood in England, where she lived on an estate where they bred horses, somewhere in the north of England. The horses were famous all over England, she said, but there was not one she could not ride.'

'Is that not proof that she was English?' Henri said. Finsterwalde shrugged.

'It was never clear whether the estate belonged to her family, or whether she was simply staying there. She was vague about – or perhaps she was careful not to give – details. She told me the names of dozens of horses, but never of people and places, and when I went to England there was nothing on which to base any enquiries I might have wanted to make. So you see, I can never know for sure if she was English. But I like to think so. They are fine horsemen, the English, even if they are sadly irregular about their religious practices.'

There was a pause when he finished speaking, and Finsterwalde looked apologetically at Henri, who appeared deep in thought.

'I'm afraid I have bored you, my dear Count.'

'Eh? Oh – no, no, not at all. I was most interested. I wonder . . .' He looked from the miniature he still held in his hand to Héloïse, and thence to Finsterwalde, thinking hard. It would be, he thought, the most fantastic coincidence. And then he sighed and dismissed it. His longing to acquire family for his daughter was overcoming his reason. He stood up, handing the picture to Finsterwalde, and bowing to Lotti. 'I must thank you, dear Madame Nordubois, for your hospitality, and make my adieux.'

'You aren't leaving?' Lotti cried. 'Oh, I made sure you would stay for dinner. Charles will be so sorry to have missed you.'

'Unfortunately, I have an engagement. But I will call on you tomorrow morning, if I may, before I return to Versailles.'

'Are you going to see Tante Ismène, Papa?' Héloïse asked.

'Why – yes, my love,' Henri said. 'Shall I send her your love?'

Outside, his servant Duncan was waiting with the horses.

'To the rue Boudreau, Duncan,' Henri said. 'And then you can take yourself and the horses home, and come back for me in the morning. Not too early, however, I dare say mademoiselle and I shall be up late.'

'Very good, sir. You will not object if I go out on the town a little tonight?'

Henri grinned. 'How can I object, when you have the knowledge to ruin me?'

'You know I would never do that, sir,' Duncan said stolidly.

'Yes, I know. By all means, go and enjoy yourself – but I ought to warn you to stay clear of the Palais Royal gardens. They say the air there is becoming unhealthy.'

Duncan gave him an intelligent look. 'I understand, sir,' he said.

The heat of July bred troubles like flies, and Henri, moving from Versailles to Paris, from the Cordeliers district to the Palais Royal, found himself in receipt of more knowledge than was comfortable, and growing more and more out of patience with his former mistress, Madame de Murphy, and the *philosophes* of her circle whom he met at her salons. There were bread riots in the *faubourgs*; outside Paris, bands of peasants and starving vagrants roamed the countryside armed with pitchforks and scythes, protesting about the game laws and the repressive seigneurial practices, and attacking mills, granaries and food convoys; on the edges of the capital, shop-keepers and wine merchants joined together to attack and burn down the customs posts whose exactions they resented and whose officers they loathed with an almost personal hatred.

Yet Ismène and her friends refused to be alarmed. Thrilled with the success of the Third Estate in declaring itself to be the National Assembly, they thought that an ordered programme of reforms would now take place, and the perfect society would emerge, with their own cultured and educated friends at its head. There had been unrest in the countryside for the past two years, since the harvests had been so poor, and bread riots were almost an annual event, to be deplored but not regarded.

On the eleventh of July the King, having assembled loyal Swiss and German troops about him, dismissed Necker and appointed Breteuil in his place, with the intention of ousting the National Assembly and regaining control of the Estates-General. The news reached Paris the following day, and by the early afternoon the Palais Royal gardens were thronged with Parisians being harangued by orators who told them that the King was about to march on Paris with an army, that the National Assembly was about to be arrested, and that they must arm themselves if they were not to be shot down in the streets.

Within hours the streets were alive with bands of marchers, carrying busts of Necker and Orleans, and raiding religious houses, and the shops of gunsmiths and armourers in search of weapons. Rioting went on through the night, and on the following morning the Paris electors, under the guidance of Bailly, set themselves up as a permanent committee called the commune to rule Paris, and summoned all respectable house-holders to attend a meeting and help form a National Guard to put down the troubles in the streets. Lafayette, the hero of the American wars, was placed in charge of the National Guard, and guns and powder were given out from the Hôtel de Ville, but such were the crowds surging around its doors that it was imposs-ible to say whether the arms were being given to the right people.

Henri was no longer in any doubt that it was the Duc d'Orlé-ans who was directing the mobs. He knew some of the orators who were relaying orders, and knew that they were in Orléans' pay, and he had no faith in the ability of the well-meaning but timid householders of the National Guard to restore equilibrium. He hurried from the convent to the rue Montmartre, to the rue Boudreau, to the rue Saint-Anne, with the news that Besneval, in charge of the Paris garrison, had declined to fire on fellow Frenchmen and had withdrawn his troops to the Champs de Mars. Paris was in the hands of the mob, and he advised his various womenfolk, somewhat tersely, to pray for deliverance.

On the morning of the fourteenth the Palais Royal mob surged across the river and raided the Hôtel des Invalides, where a great cache of arms was discovered and taken, and waving these, the mob turned north and east, marching through the streets within earshot of the nervous household in the rue Sainte-Anne, chanting, 'To the Bastille!', where there was known to be a new consignment of gunpowder. Henri managed to get to the back entrance of the house, and was received in the salon by Ismène, alarmed at last, who clung to his arm and begged him not to go out again.

'I am sure it is not safe, Henri. You must stay. What is happening? I cannot bear it.'

Henri soothed her, though wondering whether she wanted him to stay for his safety or her own. 'There is a rumour abroad that the King has sent thirty thousand soldiers to reinforce the Bastille and slaughter the citizens of the Faubourg Saint-Antoine,' he said.

'But he would not! No one could believe such nonsense,' she cried. Henri smiled grimly.

'When will you learn that the mob will believe anything? But do not worry, it may still pass off peacefully. A deputation of the electors has gone at the head of the mob to parley with the governor of the Bastille, to let them have the powder, and to undertake not to fire on the mob. Let them do that, and let the mob have a few hours of chanting and fist waving outside the walls, and they may disperse peacefully.'

'And if they do not?' Ismène asked nervously.

'If not – then we must stay indoors like other good citizens and hope to sit out the riots in safety.'

It was not long before the sound of gunfire from the Faubourg Saint-Antoine put paid to any hope of a peaceful dispersal. Before nightfall the triumphant mob was surging back through the streets to the Hôtel de Ville, and waving the head of the prison's unfortunate governor, de Launay, on the end of a pike. Duncan slipped out for a while and brought back the news: that de Launay had received the deputation of electors and agreed to their requests – far from having thirty thousand men under his command, he had a bare hundred, and knew there was nothing he could do – but even while the parley was going on, the mob had managed to lower the drawbridge and surged into the inner courtyard. The terrified garrison lost its head and fired on the mob, the mob lost its temper, and force had prevailed. The Bastille, long supposed to be impregnable, had fallen, and de Launay, marched to the Hôtel de Ville as a prisoner, had been torn to pieces by the mob before he could mount its steps.

'What's happening now, Duncan?' Henri asked, for Ismène, white-faced, was incapable of comment.

'I think it's safe enough for the moment, sir,' Duncan said. 'There's a lot of chanting and drinking and marching up and down, but the mob seems to be happy enough with the victory, and they're giving the Hôtel de Ville the credit, so maybe things will quieten down now. The red-and-blue cockade is everywhere, and Bailly's name is the watchword. The mob's pleased with itself, so it's not out to harm anyone else for the time being.'

There was a silence. Ismène drew a long sigh of relief, and Henri turned to her with an ironic bow.

'I congratulate you, madame,' he said. 'It seems your National Assembly is safe.'

Ismène rallied herself. 'It was terrible, what they did to poor de Launay, of course,' she said. 'But if the revolution has been accomplished, I make no doubt it will be considered a small price to pay.'

Three days later the King travelled to Paris to be received by the Commune as the father of the French. Bailly gave him a red-and-blue cockade to add to his white Bourbon colours, and he put in on with an appearance of good humour. The restoration of Necker was confirmed, along with the status of the Commune and the National Assembly, and everything seemed to return to normal. But the King's brother, Artois, and the most unpopular of the Queen's circle had already begun to plan their escape abroad, along with those of the aristocracy who had most vehemently opposed the pretentions of the Third Estate. As July drew to a close, Héloïse wrote in her diary that the revolution had been accomplished, and that the National Assembly could now settle down to do its work; and Henri received a request from a prominent member of the Trianon set to use his contacts and experience to sell certain valuables on the courtier's behalf, and with the money so realized to arrange for his escape to England. Henri was at first a little disposed to be offended at this evidence that he was not, by the inner circle, considered to be above employment; but a moment's reflection convinced him that the future was so uncertain that a prudent man would take every opportunity to build up resources of his own. Such a commission would inevitably be lucrative to Henri, and he might one day need every penny he could lay hands upon to flee himself.

4

Allen Macallan Morland wandered into the steward's room at Morland Place in search of his wife, and found his eldest son, Edward, in process of having his neckcloth retied by his mother's skilful fingers. Allen regarded his son with a mixture of sadness and tolerant amusement. Edward was twenty-eight this year, 1790, and though not especially handsome, he had a pleasant, regular-featured face, wavy brown hair, and his father's pale blue eyes. His figure was good, muscled from years of hard riding and outdoor life, and yet for most of the year he paid no attention at all to his appearance, content to dress day after day in leather breeches, scuffed riding boots and the same shabby brown coat of coarse and serviceable wool, with his hair tied back more often than not with a piece of string.

Today, however, his hair was freshly washed and curled, his breeches were of well-cut fawn kerseymere, his cutaway coat was of a flattering sage-green colour, and his waistcoat and stockings (stockings! Allen marvelled) were of matching green-and-white striped silk.

'I conclude,' Allen said aloud, startling them both out of their deep concentration, 'that the Earl of Aylesbury is expected today. My dear Edward! Striped stockings! And can that be a fob? But your shoes do not have red heels – you are not yet quite a macaroni, I'm glad to see.'

Edward straightened, blushing a little, though his flush might have been attributable to stooping to his mother's fingers. Jemima, mistress of Morland Place, intervened on her son's behalf.

'Now don't tease him, my love,' she rebuked Allen sternly. 'It is only right that Edward should make an effort for his guest.'

'Chetwyn will be here for dinner,' Edward said, trying to sound casual.

'Ah, then I hope you have ordered something special, my dear?' Allen asked. Jemima frowned a little.

'Well, yes, I did give Barnard quite detailed instructions – the goose, you know, is ready, and I ordered the carp with the green gooseberry sauce that Chetwyn likes, and various other matters, but . . .'

'That all sounds most satisfactory,' Allen said. M. Barnard had been with them only three months, but already he had brought to the kitchens a revolution as complete as the one he had fled. He had arrived at Morland Place with a letter of recommendation from the second son William, a lieutenant in the navy, who had rescued the Frenchman from an open boat and, on learning of his profession, had sent him home with great satisfaction, knowing that old Abram, the cook, was growing daily more eccentric and deaf and ripe for retirement. 'I'm sure it will be delicious', Allen concluded.

'Yes,' Jemima said, still frowning, 'but I am not sure that he understood my orders. His French is so very bad, you know, not at all like the French I learned as a child, and the only English he speaks at all reliably is "God save the King" and "I must have more onions."' Are you quite sure he was cook to a great nobleman, my darling?'

Allen was laughing. 'Quite sure. I had a long conversation with him when he arrived, you know, and he speaks French like a native, but with a very strong Bordeaux accent.'

'Now you are teasing me,' Jemima said, unruffled. 'Well, I am sure there is no future in trying to interfere with him once he has started cooking, and Chetwyn is near enough one of the family not to mind if things are a little strange at first. There now, Ned, I have done with you. You look very nice, love. It's a pity we did not invite some young ladies over – the Fussell girls or Lizzy Anstey. You will be wasted on us.'

Edward kissed her cheek in thanks and hurried away without comment, and as soon as they were alone, Jemima came to her husband to be embraced, and standing comfortably in his arms she said, 'Did you want me for something?'

'Do you never lose hope over Edward, dearest?' Allen said. 'The Fussell girls or Lizzy Anstey, indeed! Even when we can persuade him to go to an assembly or ball, it's a labour of Hercules to get him to stand up with someone.'

'He may yet change,' Jemima said hopefully. 'He is not yet thirty – there's plenty of time.'

'That's what I wanted to talk to you about,' Allen said, sitting down in the chair beside the fire and drawing his wife on to his lap. She wore no hoops at home except upon special occasions, and the servants had grown accustomed to Sir Allen and Lady Morland's being discovered thus, locked in conversation, at all hours of the day, so that they hardly even thought it unseemly now. 'I can't agree that there is plenty of time. It wouldn't matter so much about Edward's indifference to the female sex if the others were married and bringing up families – but look at them! William in Gibraltar, on good terms with the governor and the admiral, but by his letters home he never enters a drawing-room, and spends all his time either on board or in the navy office.'

'William wants a ship, not a wife,' Jemima said wisely.

'Precisely. Then there's Mary, twenty-six, beautiful, the toast of society, going eveywhere with the Countess of Chelmsford, and no closer to being married than she ever was.'

'She has not yet met the right man,' Jemima said soothingly. 'I am sure that one day--'

'One day she may find she has left it too late,' Allen said. 'Dear Jemima, how is it we have six children and not one grandchild?'

'Oh dear, I don't know,' Jemima sighed. 'It worries me, too. Of course, Harry and Lucy may not follow the same pattern, but they are only thirteen and twelve, and I should not want them to marry before they were eighteen.'

'And so that leaves . . .'

'James.' There was a silence while they both considered James. At twenty-three be could hardly be considered beyond hope, and yet the symptoms were not encouraging. He had never favoured any one woman over another, though women had been favouring him since he was fourteen, and unlike Edward, he never had any objection to standing up for every dance at the Assembly Rooms. There had been several near-scandals consequent upon his Catholic taste in young women, and one real scandal, when the newly-married Mary Skelwith had proved with child, and not by her husband. James had been hastily packed off, first to court and then into the militia, and though his discretion seemed to increase, his desire to be respectably married had not.

'You know, I wonder sometimes if he were not more deeply affected by that business with Mary Skelwith than we realized at the time,' Jemima said. 'I think perhaps he really loved her.'

'Perhaps he did,' Allen consented to the proposition. 'I wonder sometimes, also, whether the militia is quite the right place for him. His attractions are so many that the additional lure of a scarlet coat and a great deal of spare time can hardly do him good. He graces every ball and review, and from what I hear he has a different beauty hanging on his arm every time. You know how young women are affected by a scarlet uniform.'

'Yes, it is very odd,' Jemima said solemnly, making Allen laugh. 'Well, my love, what do you propose?'

'I think we cannot expect Edward to marry within the foreseeable future, and William, being away at sea, is also out of the question. It must be James. We must find him a suitable wife and settle him down somewhere close at hand. I wonder if he might not consent to take orders? We have Shelmet already with a temporary incumbent, and old Rickard at St. Edward's will surely not last much longer.'

'You don't think James might have something to say to the matter?' Jemima asked drily.

'If he really has lost his heart to Mary Loveday – Skelwith, I should say – then it cannot matter to him who he marries,' Allen said firmly. 'He must do his duty to the family. The Church is a gentlemanly pursuit . . .'

'But not as exciting as the army,' Jemima pointed out. Allen looked thoughtful.

'True, but I think James would not want to stay in the army if we had a war, and I am much of the opinion that we will have war with this new revolutionary government in France, sooner or later.'

Jemima's eyes opened wide. 'But why? Everyone in London is full of praise for the – the National Assembly, is it not? They are doing excellent work: long-needed reforms, doing away with corruption and bribery and torture and–'

'And the Church. Don't forget that act they passed in July attacking the Church, confiscating Church lands and dissolving monasteries and forcing clergy to swear allegiance to the Assembly. At least half of them will refuse to swear, and the

T.T.T.—4

King will not permit the Church to be destroyed. He is too good a Catholic.'

'But . . .'

'Listen, my dear,' Allen said firmly, 'all men are greedy for power, and once they have a little of it, they will use it to take more and more. They have abolished all titles and ranks, they have control of the military forces. Look at history: think of King Charles the First.'

'Allen! Do not say they will murder the King! Surely they could not, would not? It would be too terrible?'

Allen looked weary. 'I do not believe any of them wish it, not now, nor planned it in the beginning. But think of their position. They will want to take more and more power; in the end the King will be no more than their puppet and their prisoner, just as King Charles was of Cromwell. King Louis will be forced to resist, and they will have no choice but to kill him. And long before that happens, we and all the other civilized countries of Europe will be forced to go to war with the new France in order to rescue the King and put him back on his throne. Men are such fools, and it is themselves they principally fool. It's all in history, my dear, all in history. "There is nothing new under the sun," as it says in Ecclesiastes,'

Jemima kissed him comfortingly. 'Ah, but Sophocles said, "There are many wonders, but nothing is more wonderful than man."'

Allen raised an eyebrow. 'How do you know that? You never learned Greek.'

'Lucy told me. Allen, that child is quite remarkable! Father Thomas says she keeps up with Harry and Jack in Greek, and she is far ahead of them in Latin and mathematics.'

'Praise indeed from Father Thomas,' said Allen. 'It was only six months ago that he was expressing strong disapproval of having to teach her those things at all. I remember he said something about education unfitting women for their proper place in life.'

Jemima gave a grim smile. 'I soon put a stop to that. I told him that that was how Methodists talked, and that I had been taught Latin and mathematics when I was a child, and since he

74

could hardly accuse me of being unfit for my place, there was no more to be said.'

'My dear Lady Morland, he was no match for you! An unfair contest, I'd say,' Allen laughed. 'But we have strayed a long way from the subject.'

'Of James?'

'Yes. Are you with me in this, that we should seek out a suitable match for him, and as soon as possible?'

'Oh yes, by all means. It would be nice to have him at home again. I miss his lively talk, and there is always more to do about the horses than Edward or I can oversee.'

The Morland stud and stables were at Twelvetrees, a mile or so from the house. In medieval times a house had stood on the spot, a manor house of the same name to which the family had repaired in summer when the main house was sweetened. Bit by bit it had fallen into disuse and disrepair, and as its fabric crumbled, pieces of it were born away to build up the stables, so that now there was no visible sign of the original structure in the rambling clutter of stables and outhouses and paddocks that bore its name.

Lucy, like all the Morlands, loved horses, and though she enjoyed her lessons too, the lure of the stables grew too strong to be resisted when a visit was due from Morgan Proom, the wandering horse-doctor; for if there was one thing that fascinated her more than horses, it was doctoring. When she was ten she had resolved to be a doctor when she grew up, only to discover that females were not admitted to any faculty of medicine, nor permitted to walk wards, nor to become pupil dressers. A bitter disappointment had followed her forced acceptance of these unpalatable facts but she was a cheerful, energetic soul, and not much given to sulks and glooms, and she had pretty soon recovered enough to decide that she would learn all about horse-doctoring, and when she was grown up, would marry Morgan Proom and travel the country with him, sharing his profession and his canvas-topped caravan.

The fact that Morgan Proom was already over fifty did not trouble her in the least. He had begun his career as a doctor of humans rather than horses, and had been a naval surgeon during the American wars, losing his commission through a combination of drink and fever on the West India station. Drink had always been a problem with him, and coming back to a society where respectability and wealth governed a doctor's popularity far more than did actual skill or knowledge, he had gradually drifted down into his present twilight world, travelling around Yorkshire and the Midlands with his horse and waggon, treating horses and cattle and sheep for those discerning customers who valued his skill and did not mind his disreputable appearance.

The Morlands were good customers of his, and there was always something for him to do when he came. He was made a little nervous at first by Lucy's haunting him, a rapt expression of attention and admiration on her face; but he soon recognised the quality of her enquiring mind, and despite the proposal of marriage she made him two years ago, he had almost forgotten that she was a girl, not a boy, and answered her questions fully and accepted her help gratefully.

It was a young carthorse foal with a hernia that occupied them on the day of Chetwyn's arrival. A groom held the colt's head and petted him soothingly, while the gaunt old horse-doctor and the round-faced child crouched beside its belly.

'Now, you see, it's just a loop of intestine slipped out through the muscles, where they're weak. Nothing serious, unless it gets damaged, and easy enough to push back in a young feller like this,' Morgan Proom explained. Lucy felt the protrusion with sensitive fingers, and nodded. 'Get a lot of hernias on shipboard, you know – in fact, I'd say it was the most common condition a ship's doctor has to treat.'

'Why is that?' Lucy asked.

'Oh, there's a lot of heavy work on a ship, hauling barrels around, dragging on ropes, pushing capstan bars. Not too many mechanical devices to help, either, and a man's body can only take so much. I reckon on the old *India* every third man had a belt or a truss of some sort. That was all we could do for them, poor creatures, strap them up.'

'Will you have to strap up the foal?' Lucy asked.

'No, he's young and his muscles are growing stronger each day. Unless he's unlucky, this won't happen again. But a full-grown man's a different proposition.'

'Tell again about Yorktown, and how you took off twenty legs in an hour while the battle was raging overhead.' Lucy said eagerly. The groom looked a little pale, and Morgan Proom laughed.

'You've heard that story enough times to know it wasn't twenty, if was fifteen.'

'Twenty sounds better,' Lucy confessed.

'Oh, amputations are easy, anyway. And speed is the essence – the quicker you work, the less the patient suffers, and shock can kill a man as easily as disease. Not but what tars are tougher than ship's pork – they'll take wounds that would kill a landman, and be running up the ratlines three days later. It's a hard life, and those that are soft are dead before you've cleared the harbour bar.'

'But the amputations . . .' Lucy prompted. 'Tell me again.'

Morgan shifted his weight more comfortably and told her again, good-naturedly, though he had told her ten times before. 'All you've got to remember is to leave a long flap of skin, because the skin shrinks back after you've cut, and to tie the ends of the arteries, and leave enough of a thread to bring out through the wound.'

'Is it hard to saw through the bone?' Lucy asked. The groom made a horrible sound and quit the stall hastily, and Lucy assumed his place at the foal's head without much noticing.

'No, not hard. It's a knack, really. But quick's the word. Give the jack a tot of rum, get your loblolly boys to take a firm grip on him – though mostly they don't struggle. They're good men, and as brave as lions, not like the Frogs. Cut quick and saw quick, and don't heed anything they say. Funny thing, though,' he added musingly, 'the one thing they dread is not so much being cut, but being cut with a cold knife.'

'What do you mean?' Lucy asked, intrigued.

'Well, when you clear for action, the last thing before the cook throws the fire overboard, you must get a bucket of hot water to put your instruments in, so that your knives are warm. I've heard the jacks say many and many a time, that if they're going to get wounded, they hope it's early in the battle, before the water gets cold, because they dread the thought of being cut with a cold knife.' He shook his head. 'Strange creatures – not like other men. There, now, this young feller will do all

77

right. Where's that groom gone? Oh, never mind, I dare say you know what's to be done next.'

'There's a mare with lampas, and a couple of cases of thrush, and a stitching job,' Lucy said. 'Can I do it? You said you'd let me try my hand at stitching.'

'Well . . .' Morgan Proom said doubtfully, and Lucy added with a wicked grin,

'I think I ought to warn you that it's Mansfield that needs stitching.'

'What, that big two-year-old with the teeth like chaff-cutters?'

'Yes, and the cut's on his belly, near the stifle, and you know how ticklish horses are.'

'Very well, Miss Minx, you can try stitching him,' Proom said with a laugh, and picked up his bag to follow her.

'Would it be the same, amputating an animal's leg?' she reverted, leading him across one of the yards. Proom shook his head.

'You can't amputate an animal's leg, nine times out of ten. They can't stand the shock, you see. Mostly you just have to put 'em away. Treating humans is simple compared with treating animals – you can explain things to a human, and get them to co-operate, and they'll put up with pain and discomfort where an animal won't, or can't. No, treating animals is by far the greater skill. I tell you, Miss Lucy, if you ever need a surgeon, go to the horse-doctor sooner than a human doctor you don't know.'

Together the ill-assorted pair lanced the lampas growth, sprinkling Lucy liberally with bright blood in the process, scraped out the thrush-feet and packed them with Stockholm tar, and repaired to the box of the racehorse colt, Mansfield, were Lucy crouched unconcernedly under his belly with a suture needle and prepared to make her first attempt at stitching.

'This is a job you need to be nimble for,' Proom remarked. A groom held Mansfield's head, and another held up one of his forelegs, on the principle that no horse can stand on two legs only and that he would not therefore be able to kick. 'You've got to keep one eye on what you're doing and another on his feet. I've been kicked more than once by a horse with his foreleg tied up to a hook in the ceiling, and the good Lord alone knows how he did it.'

'Oh, Manny won't hurt me,' Lucy said blithely. 'I helped foal him, and I've brought him salt every day of his life. Now, I start like this, don't I?'

Mansfield didn't like the pricking of his skin, but after an initial tendency to try to get his hind leg off the ground, he settled down with his ears back and his eye rolling apprehensively while Lucy worked. 'Let him turn his head, Josh,' she told the groom. 'I'm sure he'll mind less if he sees it's me, and sees what I'm doing.' Morgan Proom hovered near her and watched and advised, but he saw that there was little she needed telling. She had watched him to good effect, and her own sensitive fingers and common sense were all she needed more. He wished forcefully that she had been born of the male sex, and almost as forcefully that she had been his son. He could have gone back into practice with a son like that to follow him.

She had almost finished when her brother Edward and his friend Lord Aylesbury came in, having strolled up to look at the pair of carriage horses Edward was schooling. They were attracted by the crowd of idlers round the box, who melted away to their jobs as the young master and his friend arrived. James Chetwyn, the only son of the fifth earl, had succeeded to the title on his father's death a little more than a year ago. He had been Edward's fag-master at Eton, and their friendship had endured and grown after they both left school, until it was the most important thing in both their lives; and though his new duties and responsibilities on his accession to the title had meant that he and Edward saw less of each other, they still spent every moment they could together, and nothing diminished their affection for each other.

He was five years older than Edward, but like Edward looked much younger than his age. He was a remarkably handsome man, tall and athletically built, with a handsome, high-coloured face, lustrous green eyes and conker-coloured hair. He stood in the doorway of the loose box now with his arm draped over Edward's shoulder in their customary pose, and his good-natured smile broke into a grin at the sight of Lucy, blood-spattered, straw-bedecked and grubby, solemnly stitching up a colt's belly.

'Either the new horse-doctor is a midget, or I have the honour to be in the presence of Miss Lucy Morland,' he said, adding solemnly, 'I beg your pardon, I should say Miss Morland, since Mary is from home. Your servant, ma'am.'

Lucy glanced over her shoulder at him. She had always liked Edward best of her brothers, and took Edward's friend in her stride, like a part of him.

'Oh, it's you, Chetwyn. Edward said you were coming. Now don't disturb me, pray, I'm nearly done.'

'Very neatly done, too, Luce,' Edward said, glancing at Proom questioningly. 'Is it all your own work?'

'Of course it is,' Lucy said. 'Easy now, Manny, good feller. Don't fidget, Edward, you'll disturb him.'

'Yes, but should you really be doing this sort of thing?' Edward asked uneasily. 'I mean, what would mother and father say? It isn't really the thing for a young lady.'

'Oh stuff!' Lucy said stoutly, drawing the last corner of the torn skin together. 'I'm not a young lady. And it's a very useful thing to be able to do. And Father Thomas says all knowledge is good, and that nothing you learn is ever wasted.'

'The theory, though, rather than the practice,' Chetwyn said drily. 'You wouldn't find Father Thomas on his knees in a loose box.'

Lucy finished and stood up, stroking Mansfield's flank soothingly, and receiving a grateful nudge from his hard muzzle. 'Father Thomas couldn't do it,' she said calmly, 'Nor could you, I suspect. Doctoring takes skill, don't it, Morgan? You have to be born with the talent for it.'

'Well, it isn't everyone who has the patience, nor the touch, nor the spirit,' Morgan agreed with her cautiously, mindful of who it was paid the bills. Lucy looked at her brother triumphantly. She was standing with Mansfield's head under her arm while she pulled his ears, a process that reduced him to infantile dependence. Her riding habit, which she wore day in day out unless positively forced to change into some other garb, was decorated with various stains, bits of straw, and dried manure; her soft fair hair was so rough and tangled that it resembled hay in more than its colour, and her chubby face was liberally streaked and spotted with dried blood. Chetwyn smiled at her affectionately, thinking he would like to have her for his sister.

'Either you have developed enormous freckles,' he said, 'or you have become afflicted with rust.' Lucy caught his drift and rubbed vaguely at her face with the crook of her wrist.

'Oh, it's only blood,' she said nonchalantly. 'Are you going for a ride? Morgan and I have finished now, I could come with you – if you like,' she added hesitantly, remembering past snubs.

Chetwyn, his hand restrainingly on Edward's shoulder, answered, 'We should be honoured with your company later, but there is only just time for us to look at Edward's new pair before dinner. We'll probably ride out for an hour or two after that.'

Lucy, who had had her dinner at twelve in the nursery, thought the likelihood of her freedom continuing past dinner small, and settled for what she had.

'Oh well, perhaps I can ride with you tomorrow. Can I come with you now? I should like to see how the pair is going on. Edward thinks them vastly smart, but you know I cannot think them well matched. The gelding is a shirker, and never goes up to his harness like the mare.'

'He's young and spirited and a little shy,' Edward said, roused to defence. 'He's not a shirker – it's that the mare goes too strong for him, but I shall shape them up, and you shall eat your words, Luce, I promise you.'

'Pooh!' said Lucy, unabashed. 'You'd have done better to take the colt with the crooked race, but nothing would do but you must have a pair with four white socks apiece, and everyone knows looks don't make a horse.'

Wrangling cheerfully, Edward, Lucy and Chetwyn went off to look at the pair.

Chelmsford House in Pall Mall saw at the beginning of November, as it did every year, the return of Flora, Lady Chelmsford and her entourage from the country. The Countess's movements around the country were like those of the stars around the heavens, following a fixed course and season: London during October and November, some great country

81

house for Christmas, Bath in February, London in April for the Season, the sea in July, and the country for August and September. With Lady Chelmsford went her close circle, including more often than not her husband, which Society thought very droll. There was also her permanent companion, Miss Morland – Mary, eldest daughter of the Countess's cousin Jemima – and, latterly, the Countess's daughter from her previous marriage, Louisa, who, now that she was sixteen, was an object of interest to her mother. Until recently Louisa had lived, as her younger brother Jack still did, at Morland Place, where Jemima Morland had brought them up as her own children.

Lady Chelmsford was also from time to time called upon to escort her sister-in-law, Amelia, a bold-eyed maiden of fifteen, who threatened to be the most hardened flirt in London, and who had grown unmanageable since her older sister Sophy had made such a good match with Lord Carlton. A further, and not entirely welcome, addition to the circle was Amelia's older brother Horatio. He and his sisters were half-kin to Lord Chelmsford, the offspring of the previous earl's second marriage. Lady Chelmsford had no children of her present marriage, and if, as seemed likely, she had none in the future, Horatio would be the next earl. Though Horatio had perfectly polished manners, Flora could never feel at home in his presence, unable to rid herself of the feeling that he was watching her and gloating.

On the morning after their arrival, Lady Chelmsford and Miss Morland sat in the small saloon together going through the vast accumulation of letters, packages and invitations that always awaited them in Town. It was a close-run contest as to which lady had the greater pile, but as her ladyship's correspondence was sprinkled with such disagreeable matters as mantua-makers' bills, while Miss Morland's featured a number of messages and tokens from ardent admirers, there was no doubt as to which lady anticipated more pleasure from her correspondence.

The small saloon, which faced south-east, was filled with sunshine that morning, and an agreeable silence reigned, broken only by the ticking of the clock on the chimney-piece, the rustling of paper, and the occasional remark spoken in a low, well-bred voice. The two women presented an attractive sight. They were very similar in looks, both having the Morland cast of features, delicate-featured, high-cheekboned, blue-eyed, dark-haired; but while Flora had been accounted very pretty in her youth, Mary Morland was a beauty, with just that elegance and strength in feature and movement that turned prettiness into grace. Both were in fashionable morning gowns, Flora's of glazed cotton in lilac and white stripes, figured with small flowers, slightly hooped, with a fine lace fichu covering her neck and shoulders. She wore a cap of fine muslin, with long lace lappets and trimming of lilac twill, for now she was thirty-three she felt it incumbent upon her to behave a little more matronly.

Mary's gown was very simple, a robe of cambric of a subtle grey-blue, trimmed and frogged with navy-blue plaited braid, whose near-severity of cut was a perfect foil for her lovely face. Her glossy black hair was dressed wide, as was the fashion, drawn back from her face and falling in a profusion of curls over her shoulders and down her back. She shook the triple muslin flounces of her sleeve back from her wrist with a prac-tised movement as she selected another letter from the pile on the round table before her, just as Lady Chelmsford said: 'Dear me, here is Lady Tewkesbury sending back one of that pair of gloves I lost at Stratton Hall. How tiresome! I was very fond of them – you recall them, Mary dear, the olive kid. Where could the other be? Now I shall have to write to her again. I am sure one glove is no use to me – she may as well have saved herself the trouble of asking Tewkesbury to frank for her as send me *one* glove.'

'Hmm,' said Mary absently. 'Here is an invitation, ma'am, to the Dundrummonds' rout ball on the twenty-sixth. Isn't that the same date as the Fitzpatricks'?'

'Yes – and just like them, I declare! If it weren't that one knows how unlucky Mrs Dundrummond is, one would be ready to swear she did it to put Molly Fitzpatrick's nose out of joint. Do you remember when she had a ball for Horatia on the very day of Milo Fitzpatrick's wedding?'

'Yes – poor Horatia! We shall have to refuse both anyway, for this is the evening of the concert, with Mr Haydn's new work.'

Lady Chelmsford looked up in mild astonishment. 'Mary, you cannot mean you would refuse a ball – *two* balls – for the sake of a concert? How strange you are! You can hear music any time.'

'I can dance any time,' Mary said with a smile. 'Mr Haydn is to lead from the pianoforte, you know, and has agreed to attend Billy Tonbridge's supper-party afterwards.'

'Ah, yes, I had forgot, you are to go with Lord Tonbridge,' Flora said, her brow clearing. The Earl of Tonbridge was one of Mary's most eligible and persistent admirers.

'*And* his party,' Mary corrected mischievously. 'It will be a large party.'

'Well of course – Tonbridge would do nothing indelicate. He is a perfect gentleman, as well as an earl.'

Mary smiled privately at such nice distinction, but said nothing, continuing with her letters. Flora next broke the silence with,

'Oh dear, that tedious Mrs Markham, reminding me that I was rash enough to say I would dine with her.'

'You are too good-natured, ma'am,' Mary said. 'You should let Charles deal with her – he has a wonderful way of snubbing.'

'Oh, I should hate to hurt her feelings, she is a good creature, only so very dull.' Flora glanced across and saw Mary select a large envelope addressed in a strong masculine hand which was familiar to her. She hesitated, and then curiosity got the better of her, and she said, as casually as she could, 'Is that another letter from your Yorkshire correspondent? He is very faithful, I swear! Do tell me if he has any more news of anyone I know. Your mother has not written to me these six months.'

Mary put up a hand to her hair, which might or might not have been a gesture to hide a blush. John Anstey had been her admirer since she was a child of ten, and had made her an offer on several occasions. She had always refused him, but nothing deterred him from swearing he would wait for her, and though she had no intention of accepting the hand of a man who, though wealthy, was the son of a coal merchant, she had grown too used to him as her childhood friend to behave coldly towards him. She knew that Flora had a close and good-natured interest in her affairs, wanting for her the best and happiest match possible, and so she merely said mildly, 'John's letters are full of politics these days, ma'am, ever since he was chosen to stand for Parliament. And my mother never writes to you in the summer, because you are always from home.'

'True,' said Flora equably. At that moment the door opened, and Horatio Morland strolled in, resplendent in blue coat, yellow breeches and yellow-and-blue striped stockings, matching waistcoat with two fobs, and a herisson wig and queue. He had inherited his mother's vapid prettiness, a pale, rather weak-mouthed face, large, slightly protruberant blue eyes, whose blond lashes and brows gave him a look of bloodless surprise. He was much sought after in the marriage mart, by the mamas because of his connections and the near-certainty of his being seventh earl hereafter; but equally by their daughters for his looks and charm and fashionableness. He managed to steer a middle course between the excesses of the macaronis and the opposite extreme of the bucks, who sometimes did not bathe or pare their nails in protest against foppishness.

Flora looked at her brother-in-law with surprise, not at his appearance, but at his being there at all.

'Is it you, Horace? It cannot be!' She looked at the clock. 'Why, it is not yet eleven, and I know your valet never calls you before noon. Perhaps the clock has stopped.'

Horatio made his bow and sat down on a small sofa, lifting his tails out carefully from behind him. 'Now, Flora, don't tease,' he responded languidly. 'If you must know, I was early to bed last night.'

'But I understood you went to White's last night after Lady Packer's ball? You meant to meet Gilbey for piquet.'

'Gilbey didn't show, and there was no one else in the club worth playing with, so I came home. I was in bed by one o'clock. Strange sensation,' he mused, his eyes fixed on Mary, who was still perusing her letter. 'I say, Mary, you are looking dashed pretty this morning. I like that colour – what's it called?'

Mary looked up. 'It's called *brume matinale*,' she said briefly. Having achieved his object of making her look up, Horatio sought for a way to keep her attention.

'Well, it suits you. Unusual colour, ain't it? I don't recall seeing anyone else wear it.'

'Papa had it sent from Paris for me. It's supposed to be Marie-Antoinette's favourite colour,' she added with a wry face, 'but then I have heard *that* claimed of every colour from coquelicot to mustard, so I have no faith in it.'

'Must be useful to have a father in the cloth trade,' Horatio said. His choice of words was unfortunate, as he realised at once from Mary's slight blush of annoyance, and he hurried on. 'I wish you'd introduce me to your mantua-maker – she seems to have a better idea of cut than my tailor. Well, ma'am,' he said hastily, turning to his sister-in-law, 'what do you do today? Can I tempt you to a drive in the Park? Or can I convey you anywhere? Sure you must have some shopping to do.'

'Thank you, Horace, but we dine at Lady Tonbridge's at three, to meet her new Frenchman, the Marquis de Lannes I think his name is,' Flora said.

'Oh, is that what it's about?' Horatio said, stretching out his legs and lounging gracefully back on the sofa. 'She invited me too, but I thought it was another scheme to interest me in her fright of a daughter.'

'Isabel is not a fright,' Lady Chelmsford said crossly. 'I wish you wouldn't talk so. She's a very nice girl, and she'll make a good match.'

'As long as she makes it without me, I wish her nothing but good,' Horatio said with a calm that made Flora itch to slap him.

'I conclude you have refused, then,' she said, controlling herself.

'Oh, no, I have not said one way or the other, but if it is a dinner for her Frenchman, I may as well go. Every lady of good *ton* has to have her *émigré* this season – I wonder you have not acquired one, ma'am. Last year it was monkeys, as I recall, and the year before every lady had her Italian greyhound – but this year, nothing will do but some tame baron or marquis, complaining in fractured English about how the wicked revolutionaries robbed him, and how the ravening peasants burnt his château down.'

'I'm sure if you feel like that no-one wants you to go,' Flora said sharply.

'Oh, no, if you and Mary are going, it will be good entertainment. I suppose she'll have her son to act as host for her?'

'Yes, Billy Tonbridge will be there,' Flora said.

Horatio's mouth took on an unaccustomed firmness. 'Then

I shall certainly go. I'll take you both in my carriage.' He stood up, bowed, and strolled out, leaving Flora thoughtful, while Mary went back to her correspondence with an air of indifference. For some time Flora had wondered whether Horatio was shewing signs of jealousy of the young Earl of Tonbridge, and a certain proprietorial bent towards Mary. She looked across at her pretty cousin, and wondered also whether Mary might have more desire to be Countess of Chelmsford hereafter than any other kind of countess, for it was certainly true that in her girlhood Mary had shewn a tendency to languish after Horatio. She treated him now exactly as she treated all the other young men of her acquaintance, with a calm friendliness, but that would only inflame someone of Horace's conceit.

'Mary,' she said tentatively.

'Hmm?' Mary looked up as one returning from a long distance, and her blue eyes were soft. Flora thought again how very, very beautiful she was – far too good for Horatio, even if he did become Earl of Chelmsford.

'Mary, dear, I wondered – do you think Horace means to have you?'

Flora's bluntness was one of the things Mary had always liked about her. The glimmer of a smile lit the blue eyes that had been subject of many a sonnet.

'My dear ma'am, how could I possibly answer that? But even if he does, you may rest assured that *I* don't mean to have *him*.'

And with that she went back to her letter. Flora watched her even more thoughtfully, noted how avidly she perused the two pages, close-written and crossed (and this from a man!), how soft her expression was, how her lips curved in a tender smile; and she wondered if perhaps John Anstey of York might not at last make fools of all the great lords, and win his childhood sweetheart back through sheer persistence.

5

In February 1791 William came home to Morland Place to recover from the effects of a severe fever, much to his chagrin and Jemima's delight. His visit coincided with one of James's periods of leave, and since Lord Aylesbury was also visiting, Jemima said happily, 'I have my house full again, just as I like it.'

William, however, was deeply gloomy. 'I'm twenty-eight, and still a lieutenant,' he said.

'Flag-lieutenant,' Jemima corrected him. 'And your cousin Thomas was not made Post until he was thirty. There's plenty of time.'

William moved restively, but with the caution of a big man used to small confines. He was not only tall, but massive too, muscularly built with an air of restrained power about him. His face was very tanned, which made his pale-blue, long-sighted eyes the more vivid, and made a startling contrast with his fair, wind-bleached hair, which he wore in an old-fashioned pigtail almost a foot long. His strangeness and his power made the unmarried girls of York and its environs afraid of him, and Jemima could understand though she deplored it, for she was almost afraid of him herself. His clothes seemed to fit him ill, and threatened to rip under the bulging of his muscles; his sailor's roll did not desert him in such a short time on shore; his voice penetrated the social hush of a drawing-room like a bellow even when he spoke quietly. It was of no use to take him to assemblies and balls and card parties, Jemima thought with a sigh. If he was to marry at all, it would have to be a sailor's daughter: he had been at sea since he was twelve years old, and he was at home in no other place now.

James, on the other hand, she thought, turning her attention to her third son, who was sitting on the window-seat of the long drawing-room window, holding a sketch-book and taking William's likeness with quick movements of his pencil; James made himself at home everywhere he went. He was not, would never now be, a tall man, having the small, compact, wiry frame of his father; but he had his mother's dark-blue eyes, glossy reddish-dark hair which he never concealed under a wig except when he was on Parade, and a sensually beautiful face that might almost have been womanish, except that there was no weakness in it. He rode well, danced gracefully, made love prettily and with perfect propriety, and had, additionally, a surprising talent with the pen and pencil. His mother had looked through his sketch-book earlier that day, and found a series of closely observed, wittily executed drawings of scenes, each telling a story in miniature. There was the Colonel's inspection, for instance, where the strutting, pompous senior officer was scrutinising a soldier through his quizzing-glass, while himself, unnoticed, the object of serious interest from a small, sniffing mongrel dog; there was a scene in a drinking-house, of a handsome soldier, his uniform awry, with a buxom woman on each arm laughing raucously and calling for ale, while the expression on the soldier's face was one of great sadness. Jemima wondered uneasily if the sad soldier were meant to be James himself.

His present sketch of William, she noticed as she passed behind James's shoulder to look out of the window, was a brilliant depiction of his restless strength, making him look, though attempting to lounge, as if he might any moment burst out of his clothes. Yes, she thought, James had great talent, as well as charm, grace and good looks; but James took nothing seriously. If she praised his drawing, for instance, he would merely laugh in a strange way and probably tear the picture up into the bargain. He had always been difficult for her to understand. As a child he had led an absorbing inner life, keeping his counsel in a most unchildlike way, and now that he was twenty-four, she still had no more idea what motivated him, or what, at any time, he was thinking.

'Time there may be,' William was saying in response to her last remark, 'but ships there aren't.'

'I'm sure you will be given a ship soon,' Jemima said.

And James added, as if completing her sentence, 'After all, now you are flag-lieutenant, there is nowhere else for you to go but Post.'

'The admiral thinks well of you, and I'm sure he will give you the next ship that is available,' Jemima finished.

'Aye, but when will that be? You don't realise, mother, the navy is shrinking almost daily. The old *Thunderer* was laid up last week, and when *Squirrel* comes in from the Indies, she's to be broken up. At this rate we'll have a navy of six ships, with six hundred captains rotting on the beach.'

'What a very unpleasant simile,' James murmured, looking critically at his sketch, and then turning the page to a clean sheet to begin again. 'But Father thinks we shall have a war, soon, and that will be your chance, brother.'

William brightened. 'Yes, it would be famous to have another crack at the Frogs again,' he said, looking for a moment almost boyish in his enthusiasm. 'If we declared war they'd be fitting out ships as fast as they could, though God only knows how they'd man them . . .'

'But William, do *you* think there will be war?' Jemima asked anxiously. 'I hate to think of it.'

'Oh yes, we'll have to fight them sooner or later. The King of France, you see, is no friend of the revolutionaries.'

'But he signed their what-you-may-call, their "Rights of Man," doing away with all the titles and privileges,' James interposed.

'He had to, after the mob had marched to Versailles and taken him and the Queen back to Paris. The royal family is virtually imprisoned, you know, at the Tuileries, and the armed forces are under the control of the Assembly. The King won't stand for that,' William said. 'He's already sending letters to all his brother monarchs in Europe asking for support, and Condé's got an army of *émigrés* ready and waiting at the border. Sooner or later there'll be an attempt to regain his throne for him by force.'

'Well, that's not our business, is it?' Jemima asked.

'Do you think our King can sit back and allow a parcel of revolutionaries to strip a king of his powers?' William asked. 'If it could happen in France, it could happen here – or so he's bound to think.'

'Anyway,' James said teasingly, 'if there is a war it will be a matter for the army. There'll be nothing for the navy to do.'

William refused to be baited. 'War is war, and we've scores

enough to settle with the Frogs. Think of the West Indies, if nothing else.'

The door opened, and Lucy came in to lean against her mother's chair and stare in wonder at William, whose pigtail, above all, fascinated her.

'Well, for your sake, I hope there is a war,' James said easily, 'but for myself, I think I shall leave the militia the moment there is a serious danger of it. Abroad may be well enough, but the thought of marching and fighting and living in tents . . .!'

'Oh James, you are so poor-spirited,' Lucy cried, unable to stop herself, though she had not intended to draw attention to her presence, lest she be sent out again. 'Surely you would want to fight for your country, and win glory?'

'You forget, Luce, it would be fighting for someone else's country,' James said good-humouredly. 'And as for the glory — could it compensate one for the discomfort, and the poor food, and the uncomfortable beds?'

'I'm sure you don't really mean that, Jamie,' Jemima smiled.

James merely looked inscrutable. 'Don't mind it, mother,' he said. 'There would be plenty of hotheads ready to march off. They wouldn't need me.'

'It's trained seamen they'd need,' William persisted with his own concerns. 'The press is all very well, but experienced tars just melt away when they're needed, and landmen won't do.'

'Morgan says that landmen take three months to train, and that in time of war they usually die within a month, so they might as well be left on shore,' Lucy said.

'Who, pray, is Morgan?' William asked. 'And what does he know about the navy?'

'He's my friend,' Lucy said stoutly. 'And he used to be a ship's surgeon.'

'Did he indeed? Well, then, he's an even rarer bird than the trained seaman.'

'Morgan says if conditions were better on the ships, men would be more willing to go to sea. He says what with scurvy, and falls, and accidents with the tackle, a sailor's safer in the middle of an engagement with a seventy-four.'

'Your Morgan's got a lot to say for himself,' William said, and Jemima recollected her duty.

'And so have you, Lucy,' she reproved. 'You really are much

91

too bold. I shall have to stop you going to the stables if you don't mend your manners.'

Lucy looked so crestfallen that William felt sorry to have brought a rebuke on her, and said, 'Well, you tell your Morgan, Lucy, that if there is another war, he'd better get himself down to the recruiting ship as fast as he can. Ship's surgeons are rarer then hen's teeth. During the American war, practically one ship in three had no proper surgeon on board. They were so desperate, they'd take anyone with any medical knowledge at all. I've seen some very strange people wielding surgeons' instruments in my time – and of course as commissioned officers they share the lieutenants' mess, which can be a great nuisance.'

'Well, you wouldn't mind sharing your mess with Morgan,' Lucy began fervently, but Jemima interrupted her.

'That is quite enough about Morgan, Lucy. Why aren't you in the schoolroom?'

'I've finished my exercise, and got it right, and Father Thomas said it was enough for today. I came to see if Edward and Chetwyn were going to ride.'

'You're too late,' Jemima said. 'They went out half an hour ago.'

Lucy looked so disappointed that James, remembering his childhood when William and his twin Charlotte – long dead now – would never wait for him, put aside his sketch-book with the greatest good humour and said, 'Never mind, Luce, I have a desire for some fresh air myself, and my chestnuts need exercising. Should you like to come out in my curricle with me?'

'Oh, yes *please* – may I, mother? Will you let me drive them, Jamie? Your chestnuts are so much superior to Edward's pair, I wonder he can bear to think of them.'

'William, come with us – I'll shew you round the estate. I dare say there are lots of changes since you were last here.'

'No, thank you, brother,' William said quickly. 'I have no desire to be jounced about in your ricketty little trap, and overset into the bargain, I'll be bound. I've seen how you drive. I shall take a quiet stroll about the moat, and that will be enough exercise for me. Why don't you go with them, mother?'

'There isn't good room for three in James's curricle, even

when one is as small as Lucy,' Jemima said. 'No, thank you, I'll take a walk with you, William, if I may.'

William gave her one of his rare smiles. 'I should be honoured, Ma'am,' he said.

It would hardly have done for the neighbourhood if Lady Morland, with three sons at home *and* the Earl of Aylesbury, had not given a ball. The first full moon was chosen, the invitations sent out, and Jemima prepared to tackle her cook on the delicate subject of white soup and the obligatory oyster patties. She sought William out and asked him to come with her to interview M. Barnard, in the hope that his French would be better than hers.

'Come with you?' William said, raising his silvery eyebrows. 'Why do you not ring for him, mama, and have him come here to you?'

Jemima smiled indulgently. 'My dear, one might summon housemaids, or even the butler, but one does not summon the cook of a great household. He holds court in his kitchen.'

'How does he go on?' William asked. 'Is he satisfactory? I feel a responsibility, having sent him to you in the first place.'

'Oh, he is a genius at his art, and produces the most delicious dishes from the most unexpected ingredients. Your papa says it is a little like Scottish cooking, that it is as well not to ask what has gone into a dish, for they make use of the parts of animals we cannot at all fancy in the normal course of things. Imagine, he made the most delicious dish of – well, I suppose you'd call it brawn – out of a pig's cheek, and I know my mother would never have countenanced pig's cheek on *her* table'.

'A very paragon,' William remarked.

'Yes,' said Jemima, hesitating, 'only, his French is so very odd, you know, not at all like proper French, and he has not learned any English at all as far as I can see, which makes it difficult to give him instructions. And then again, he does so dislike being given orders, or being told to follow someone else's receipt, but really we must have white soup at the ball, or what will people think? and I can't see why I should not have it made from the Countess Annunciata's receipt, if I want it so,' she finished somewhat wistfully.

'Of course not, Mama. You are mistress of this house, after all,' William said. 'You must be firm with him. I shall come with you, of course, and we shall put this Frenchman firmly in his place.'

'Yes, dear, only you won't upset him, will you? Because he makes a perfectly disgusting Scottish dish that your father dotes on to perfection, and he doesn't drink as poor old Abram used to.'

'Don't worry, Mama, I can handle M. Barnard,' William said, and, offering her his arm, conducted her with ceremony across the great hall, through the green baize door, and down the passage into the kitchen. M. Barnard received them with massive dignity, though he was only five feet tall, wielding a huge ladle like a sceptre.

'Ah, M. Barnard,' Jemima said. The cook bowed to her, and then to William. '*Mon fils*, Monsieur William Morland,' she managed. Barnard bowed again, and waited. Jemima nudged William, and gave him the massive, leather-bound Household Book, with a marker in the page concerning white soup. Barnard's eyes narrowed at the sight of it, and William cleared his throat and tackled the matter manfully.

'*Bonjour*,' he began. It let loose a flood of French from the cook, so rapid and so impenetrably accented that Jemima recognised only the words '*cuisine*' and '*recette*' and '*mon Dieu!*', the latter spoken so emphatically as to bode ill for further negotiations.

When the flood ceased, there was a short silence. William cleared his throat again, placed the Household Book on the wide, scrubbed table, opened it at the book-mark, and said, '*La recette de la Comtesse pour le potage blanc traditionnel.*' Jemima could have applauded, for it was spoken not only in an accent so pure as to put, she hoped, the Frenchman to shame, but also with just the right degree of unemphatic firmness that must assure Barnard that he must do as he was told. The cook looked at the book, and spoke again, at length, rapidly, and with a number of manual gestures of determination. At the end of it he ceased abruptly, and bowed to William. William bowed back. He bowed to Jemima, and Jemima inclined her head graciously, and then the cook escorted them to the door of the kitchen, and bowed them ceremoniously but firmly out.

Out in the great hall, Jemima took William's arm and squeezed it, and said, 'Well, that was all very satisfactory, I'm sure. You certainly handled him firmly, my love. What was it he said to you?'

William inserted a finger into his cravat and eased it. 'Well, Mama, I'm not entirely sure. His French is certainly very peculiar, isn't it, and he spoke so rapidly I'm not sure I caught his drift exactly.'

Jemima halted and looked at him with consternation. 'But he did understand, didn't he? He did agree to make the soup?'

William considered for a moment, and then shook his head. 'I don't know. We shall just have to wait and see.'

The ball was a small one, numbering ten couples, just the right number, Jemima thought, for intimacy without insipidity. The dancing took place in the long gallery, supper was laid out in the dining-room, and the drawing-room was given over to cards for the chaperons and the one or two of Allen's friends who had been invited for whist. Remembering previous occasions, Jemima had given her four young men strict instructions that they were to dance every dance and pay proper attention to the young ladies.

In recent years York had returned to something of its old glory as capital of the north. Other towns like Leeds and Bradford might be thrusting ahead in trade and manufacture, but York was the scene of elegant society. New houses in the modern style were being built, and old ones rebuilt or refurbished. All the principal streets were now paved; street cleaning, begun piecemeal earlier in the century, had been extended to all streets since 1786. Street lighting was the rule now rather than the exception, and the corporation had a few years ago begun a scheme for fixing up street names on all the corners. New and elegant walks had been laid out, public gardens planted, and the more noisesome of businesses transferred outside the walls.

The shops in York were second to none, and it was a boast that anything could be got in York that could be got in London. York had its own newspaper, the *York Mercury*, its theatre, more than thirty coffee-houses and gentlemen's clubs, a very fine bowling green, medicinal baths (though not as fine as Harrogate's) and, of course, its crowning glory, the beautiful Palladian Assembly Rooms designed by Lord Burlington. In raceweek, the city was thronged with fashionable people from all over the country, but even outside of the season, it was the habitual residence of people of elegance and fashion, writers, artists, lawyers, doctors, and architects.

So on a moonlit night in February Lady Morland had no difficulty in assembling a number of suitable young ladies for her sons (amongst whom she had long included Chetwyn, whose mother had died when he was very young) to dance with. Miss Ingram and Miss Carr and Miss Grey and Miss Mary Drake had all been eager to attend, for they all had new gowns and had had no dancing for over a fortnight. The unmarried Miss Fussells, Valentina and Charlotte, had been high on the list of invitees, for the Fussell family used to rent Shawes, the nearby house belonging to the Chelmsfords, and had long been friendly with the Morlands. Shawes was empty at the moment, for the Fussells had moved to a new house in Fulford, near to where, according to James, the army was intending to build its new barracks, now that York Castle had grown too small and inconvenient.

Of the other family with whom the Morlands had long been friendly, the only unmarried female was the youngest daughter, Miss Elizabeth Anstey. James was exceedingly grateful that the eldest daughter, Celia, had finally married last year, for she had had a lifelong passion for James and had once or twice made things very unpleasant for him, and had it been necessary to invite her, he would have found it very difficult to make himself attend. But Lizzy Anstey was a pleasant girl with no nonsense about her, and her brother Benjamin, a year older than she and thus the same age as James, who was also invited, had always had a flattering admiration for him.

Edward was glad to welcome the eldest Anstey, John, not only because, of an age, they had been childhood friends, but because John was also still unwed, which gave Edward moral support.

'Does your mama plague the life out of you?' Edward asked him as they stood together in the interval between dances. 'I suppose she must, since you are the son and heir, as I am. This business of providing heirs for the family!'

'Oh, she used to,' John said, 'all the time. I was always having names pushed at me in the most embarrassing way, especially after poor Alfred died back in '89. But then Cissy got married, and Mama had practically given up hope of her, especially after that unfortunate business with your brother, and it took Mama's attention off me. Now I think she's pretty well given me up. It's poor Ben she talks at all the time. I heard her saying the other day that it was up to him to carry on the Anstey name, so she must think I am destined for single blessedness.'

'And are you?' Edward asked curiously. 'Don't you ever feel tempted?'

'Don't you?' John parried neatly. Edward grinned.

'*Touché*! But after all, you have seemed, from time to time, not indifferent to certain members of the fair sex. Mary Loveday, for instance, and my sister Mary.'

'The music is starting again – we must take our partners,' John said, nodding pleasantly and hurrying away. Ah, so the wind blew that way still, did it? thought Edward. He still hankered after Mary. It was too bad of her to keep him dangling.

Chetwyn wandered up to him at that moment and said, 'Ned, can you remember which of 'em I'm meant to be dancing with this time? I still can't tell one from another – they all giggle and languish so.'

'Easy enough to tell,' Edward said. 'All the hands have been claimed except those two, Miss Carr and Miss Ingram, so they must be ours.'

'Yes, but which is which? And which am *I* to dance with?'

Edward raised an eyebrow. 'My dear fellow, what *can* it signify?' And linking arms with his friend he strolled across to the two most eligible young ladies in York.

James took his place in the set with Miss Valentina Fussell. He liked her a little better than Miss Charlotte, who was too plump and giggled at anything that was said to her, and whose hand was always unpleasantly moist. Miss Valentina was twenty-two, and said to be the plain one of the family. Her elder sisters said she was insipid and colourless; her elder brother Arthur, a bold young man who was doing his best to ruin his father with gaming, and who was, in James's opinion, the worst rider in Yorkshire, said obligingly that all his sisters were ugly, but that 'Tina was far and away the ugliest'; and even Charlotte said she should try to be a little jollier, for she'd never catch a husband if she behaved as if she'd been struck on the head.

James stood opposite her in the set, and, since it would be too stupid to go all the way up in silence, he cleared his throat and asked, perhaps a little sternly, 'Tell me, Miss Fussell, how do you like your new house?'

'Very well indeed, sir,' was the reply, spoken in a light voice that hardly carried, though they were standing only two feet apart.

'Do you like it better than Shawes?' he persisted nobly.

'I do not know,' she said after due consideration. 'It is very different.'

A long silence followed. James looked at her, but she would not meet his eye, keeping hers downcast upon the floor, which in a maid of sixteen would have been becoming modesty – but in a woman of twenty-two! Why, his little sister Lucy was better company. He decided to try being bold.

'I saw you dancing with my brother William, Miss Fussell,' he said. 'Do you find him as strange as the other young ladies do? Miss Drake could not look at his pigtail for giggling.'

For a moment he could have sworn that her lips curled a little in a smile, but she said only, 'He seems a very agreeable young man, sir.'

Well, damn the woman, James thought, I'll not waste my effort again. They made a few places in silence, and then he looked up and found her eyes upon him, and a faint blush stole over her cheek.

'I saw you in town the day before yesterday, Mr Morland,' she said in her faint voice. 'I was in Mrs Skelwith's carriage, and we saw you turn down Stonegate.'

James met her eyes in surprise, for whatever he had thought about her, he had not thought she would be spiteful; but there was no spite in her expression, only sympathy and some veiled message. 'Indeed, ma'am,' he said neutrally.

'I visit Mrs Skelwith quite often,' Miss Fussell went on. 'I think she is lonely with her husband away. He is gone to New-castle for a month.'

'Indeed, ma'am,' James said again, astonishment, doubt and

gratitude struggling for precedence in his mind. They made two more places, and now they were at the head; it would be their turn to dance down next.

Miss Fussell placed her hands in his and said with great gentleness, 'Her little boy is wonderful company for her, however. He is five years old, you know, and so handsome and clever.'

It was well they had to dance, and no reply could be expected from him, for he would not have been capable of one. He went down the set mechanically, his mind filled as with a rushing wind. He saw nothing, heard nothing. My son, he cried inwardly with blind despair, my son!

The day after the ball, Jemima found herself faced with rebellion. 'We've done our duty now, Mama,' Edward said firmly, 'and Chetwyn is only here for another week, so pray do not arrange any other engagements for us.'

'You enjoyed it, didn't you, William?' she asked hopefully.

'Not really, Mother. I never cared much for dancing, and those girls seemed very dull to me. Quite pleasant, but very dull. I had sooner sit by the fire with a pipe and have a good chat with you.'

James was similarly resistant. 'I hope you will not be thrusting me at any more local females, Mother. It was embarrassingly like a cattle-market. I'm sure they all knew they were on approval, and really, it is too mortifying to be finding them all wanting. It makes one feel unreasonable.'

'But you *are* unreasonable! Really, I never knew such unnatural children! Ned and William I had not much hope of, but you, Jamie – you like women well enough, why can't you find one to marry?'

'I will, one day,' James said soothingly. 'In any case, I must go back to the regiment tomorrow, so you shan't have me on your hands much longer. Some dangerous beauty will spike my guns one day, and then you may laugh at my wedding and say you told me so.'

'I should do nothing so improper. Where do you go now?'

'I thought I'd drive the chestnuts over to Fulford, to take a look at the ground there,' he said

'Oh, then do, dear boy, take a note to Fulford House for me, and a basket – I promised Lady Fussell I would send her some cuttings.'

'Of course, Mama, to oblige you,' James said inscrutably. 'I shall be ready in half an hour.'

Luck was with James. Not only was Miss Valentina Fussell at home, but she was alone. Miss Charlotte, whose giggling, sweating presence would have been as disastrous as it was unpleasant, was shut up in her chamber with her mantua-maker, and thus safely incommunicado. Miss Valentina received Mr Morland calmly in the breakfast-parlour, bade him be seated, and folded her hands in her lap and regarded them in silence.

'I hope you had an agreeable ball last night, ma'am,' James began at last.

'Yes, thank you, sir,' she replied faintly.

'You do not find yourself too much fatigued this morning?'

'Indeed, no, thank you.'

'I am glad to hear it,' James said, and a desperate silence fell.

At length Miss Fussell said, 'In fact, I have been up since half past eight. I have many things to do about the house, and rarely lie long abed.'

It was the longest sentence he had ever heard her say, and gave him courage. It was a dangerous moment, for perhaps he might not have understood her the night before, or have read too much meaning into her words; on the other hand, the thing was too important not to take the risk.

'It is a fine day, ma'am, I wonder if I might persuade you to venture out a little? I have my curricle outside, and a drive would perhaps do you good, if you have been busy about the house all morning. Perhaps I might drive you into town? You will have some shopping to do there, I am sure . . .' – he hesitated and she looked up – 'or some calls you wish to make?'

There was what seemed like an endless silence to James, waiting as he was on tenter-hooks.

An expression of great sadness and kindness mingled seemed to come into Miss Fussell's eyes, before she lowered them again, and said, 'You are very kind, sir, I thank you. I should like to go into York, if it would not inconvenience you. I should like to visit Mrs Skelwith.'

Spring came early, and with William gone back, Edward visiting with Chetwyn at Wolvercote, and James in Scarborough, Jemima felt dull and restless. She was also worried about Allen, who seemed not quite well.

'I am sure you have been working too hard,' she scolded him. 'Really, what use can it be to give up your position as Justice of the Peace if you continue to do most of the work involved with it? And when John Anstey asked for your support for his candidature, I am sure he did not mean you to go addressing meetings for him. You really must rest more.'

'And what about you, Lady Morland?' he countered with laughter in his eyes. 'I don't think I have seen you sitting down for longer than ten minutes at a time. You have servants and housekeepers and stewards to oversee things for you, but you needs must go doing them yourself. And when will you learn to ring the bell, instead of jumping up and going in search of a servant? You know, I don't think Mrs Mappin likes you to go into the servants' hall – she thinks it an intrusion.'

'Intrusion?' Jemima said, outraged. 'I shall go where I like in my own house! The idea! And as for the bells – I try to remember, but old habits are hard to break, my love, and it is so much quicker to do a thing oneself.'

Allen's laughter told her that she had been successfully baited, and she went across to kiss him forgivingly, and said, 'All the same, I do think we both ought to have a little holiday from our cares. Do you know what I was thinking? I should love to go visiting one of the beautiful places one hears about. The Lake District – how should you like to go to the Lake District and explore in the carriage for a fortnight or three weeks? It is quite the thing to do – Flora and Charles took Mary there last autumn, you remember?'

'My love, the Lake District in October is quite another thing than the Lake District in March. It is a long way, and besides it will be very cold and wet there at this time of year.'

'Well, then, some other place? You do not object in principal to going away?'

Allen sighed. 'This fad for going away! Everybody travelling about, for no better purpose than to come home again. When I was young, people travelled when they had to, and then it was for the purpose of getting to some place they had to be.'

But Jemima knew he was teasing. 'That's settled then. We have only to choose the place.'

'Well, my love,' Allen said, 'if you have no preferences, I think we may as well do our travelling into Derbyshire. The Peak District is said to be as beautiful as the Lake District in its way, and I should not at all mind making a visit to Cromford.'

'Cromford? Where Mr Arkwright built his mill?' Jemima said.

'Yes, the mill and the mill-town are quite the wonders of the age, and I should be interested to see how a factory works in practice. One hears so much about them, and they are so reviled in these parts, but Cromford is said to be a perfect system.'

Jemima nodded. 'One cannot apply the systems that work with cotton to our woollen cloth production, but I own I should be interested myself to see how Mr Arkwright has contrived. Let it be Derbyshire then.'

Mr Richard Arkwright was one of the many men, as Jemima knew, to have claimed invention of the spinning-machine. Early spinning-machines had been attacked and smashed by irate spinners, who felt, quite rightly, that the machines would rob them of their livelihood, and for this, amongst other reasons, Mr Arkwright had chosen for his operation a place remote and rural and inhabited by no spinners who might object to it. Cromford was a tiny hamlet tucked away in an inaccessible part of the Derbyshire hills, and fed by a fast-running stream, and here he built his mill and the great water-wheel that powered the spinning-machines. To work in the mill he imported whole families of spinners and weavers, and since they came to him from outside, he had to provide them with housing. To serve the new 'town' came bakers and butchers and grocers, and very soon an entire, completely enclosed community had grown up around the mill.

'Which means,' Allen told his wife as the carriage jolted over the bumps in the road to Cromford, 'that Mr Arkwright is a great deal more than simply an employer. He is like a feudal lord, controlling the lives of his workers to a greater extent even than I do our estate workers. And Cromford is his manor and his castle. He is so afraid that rivals will steal his ideas, that everything is locked up like a fortress, and if anyone wants to have a closer look than can be got from the carriage-road, they have to apply in writing, as we did, for permission to visit.'

'I suppose we should be honoured, then?' Jemima said. 'What is he like, this Arkwright?'

'Energetic, ambitious, overbearing, tyrannical and bad-tempered,' Allen said. 'Not that I have ever met him, but talk about him is plentiful.'

'But is he a gentleman?' Jemima asked.

'He began life as a barber and wig-maker,' Allen said, and added, 'He comes from Lancashire, of course.'

'Oh,' said Jemima, not sure how to take this.

'His people seem to think well of him, however. And there's no doubt his factory is a wonder and provides work for a large number, and produces cotton stockings at a prodigious rate.'

'Well that must be to the good,' Jemima said sensibly. 'The more of them there are, the better.'

The Mill was more of a wonder even than they had imagined. It stood six storeys high, every floor filled with machinery, and the whole powered by the massive water-wheel which, except when the gear was thrown once a week to oil the machinery, never stopped turning, day or night, driving the rollers and spindles that carded, twisted and span the cotton. Mr Arkwright was away from home, and a very polite overseer named Leech shewed the Morlands round.

'We used to have looms in the mill at first, but they took up too much space, so we got rid of them. The weaving is done by the men at their homes; it's mainly the women and children who work in the mill, as you'll see.'

'And they work day and night?' Jemima asked.

'Not the same ones,' he smiled patiently. 'We have a day shift and a night shift. The night shift is paid a little more, of course. The shifts are called and ended with the factory bell, and on Sundays the machinery's shut down for oiling.'

The words spoke volumes to Jemima, who had grown up with the Morland employees' long-founded resistance to the idea of working in a manufactory. The spinners and weavers in her employ worked at home in their own time, and though they might be lazy and inefficient they at least had the freedom to organise their own time, which was worth more to them than the extra money they would have made by producing more. Here at Cromford the mill owned the men, demanding their services as long as the wheel turned, calling them in the morning with a bell, dismissing them in the evening with another. The machine was the master, and she could guess how people liked that.

'Do you have many latecomers?' she asked. 'I dare say there may be some who do not like to start work at the same time each day?'

'We have a few latecomers, but not many. We shut the gates after the bell has stopped, and all who come after that are fined. They soon learn to stir themselves,' Leech said cheerfully. 'We had some trouble when we employed hand-spinners – they couldn't get the idea into their heads that they had to be on time, every day. Used to take Mondays off, getting drunk. So we stopped using them, and took in untrained people – unemployed, mostly – who were grateful for the work and soon learned the job. We mostly use women and children, as I've said. They're quicker to learn, and nimbler with their fingers, and they take to the discipline better. And of course the machinery goes so low to the ground, we need the children to get underneath when the thread breaks or the bobbins want doffed.'

'Where do you get the people from?' Allen asked. 'Are they local families?'

'Most of 'em – plenty of destitute families round about if you look for 'em. And some from the new towns. And we get children sent in from the workhouses, orphans and foundlings.'

'What age would these children be?' Allen asked.

'We take 'em from seven to thirteen. They're 'prenticed to us, and we feed 'em and clothe 'em and teach 'em the spinning trade. They live in the 'prentice house over yonder, in the village, a very nice house it is too. Boys in one room, girls in the other, all very clean and airy and comfortable, I assure you, madam. You shall see it by and by. Now would you like to see inside the mill?'

The inside of the mill was bewildering, a wilderness of machinery, the metal frames grinding, the various parts jigging and bobbing up and down with an astonishing noise, clattering, screeching, thumping, and under it all the distant but omnipresent sound of the water-wheel, a regular, heavy thudding transmitted through the fabric of the building into, Jemima felt, her very bones. The smells were amazing, too, from the clean sneezy smell of the cotton, the burning smell of the overheated gears, the pungency of hot oil, to the smell of the work-force themselves. Women and children she saw; no others. The children were small and pale, from being confined indoors, she supposed, but their clothes seemed clean, and they certainly looked no worse cared-for than the cottage children she saw every day working for their living – except perhaps for their unnatural silence. However, conversation would have been difficult inside the mill, even had it been permitted. The children worked largely on all fours, crawling under the machines to repair threads and change bobbins. It seemed perilous work to Jemima.

'I hope there are not accidents – the children's fingers?' she bawled in Leech's ear.

'We do have accidents from time to time,' he admitted in a polite shout, 'but Mr Arkwright employs a very fine surgeon to be available at all times, and they have the best of treatment. We've never lost one yet.'

The women worked upright, tending the machines, and had the pale, gaunt, undersized look of pauper women everywhere, but their fingers worked nimbly, and they seemed to know what they were doing. Leech asked if they had seen enough, and they were glad to nod and make their way out into the peace and spring sunshine of the green valley.

'Now perhaps you'd like to look at the houses, and the 'prentice house?' Leech offered. 'Mr Arkwright is very proud of the houses. They are like palaces compared with what most of the workers were living in before he brought them here. You can imagine how grateful they are.'

They were strange-looking houses to Jemima, very sturdily built in stone and brick, with brick chimneys and good slate roofs, but very tall and narrow, being of three storeys, with a curious long window to the top storey.

'That's where the men have their looms,' Leech explained, and Jemima felt a fool for not guessing it. 'All the weaving is done in the cottages, as I mentioned, and most of the men we employ are weavers, apart from a few carpenters and labourers.'

They had a brief walking tour of the village, seeing the shops and the inn and the church and the school – 'The children go every night after work, and on Sundays, but I don't know that they learn much. Mostly they seem to sleep through it,' said Leech – and the 'prentice house, a large stone building next to the school, which seemed, to Jemima's relief, very clean inside, the walls whitewashed, the floors and windows scrubbed, the sheets on the beds not unduly grubby. And then their visit was over.

They had much to think about as their carriage pulled up the hill out of the valley.

'Good wages,' mused Allen. 'He pays his spinners around three and sixpence a week, and the rent of those houses is only two shillings a week. A man with a wife and children working must live quite comfortably.'

'Yes, but they must buy all their food – they have no bit of land to grow cabbages and keep a pig. And they must go to work every day when the bell rings, or be fined,' Jemima objected. Allen smiled at her and took her hand.

'You are too careful for them, my love. Remember, these people had no work at all; now they have the means to keep themselves respectably, and that's everything. I dare say a man with the choice might not like to serve the machines, but it is a great deal better than beggary, and I am sure they would tell you so.'

'Yes, I suppose so. And the children were better clad than some of our village ragamuffins,' Jemima sighed, 'and they don't go to work until they are seven.'

'They are being taught a trade, being given the means to support themselves when they become adults. Even we can hope for no more with our foundlings.'

The carriage reached the top of the slope and turned on to the track, and they had a view over the valley, of the stone buildings gleaming in the afternoon sunlight, the great wheel peacefully turning, the fine wooded countryside stretching away over the hilly horizon. The factory bell rang clearly across the valley, and a little while later they could see the day workers coming out of the factory to go home to their neat little grey houses. It was too far for Jemima to see their faces or judge how they felt at the day's end, except that the children seemed to walk very slowly, not running or playing or shouting with their release from discipline.

The carriage passed on, into a wooded section of the road that hid the view, and Jemima, settling back on the cushions, said in valediction: 'At least when the day is over, they have all that fresh air, and the lovely country to look at. That must be pleasant for them.'

6

'I understand that one must congratulate you, Monsieur le Comte,' said Finsterwalde, squinting up at Henri against the sunshine that filtered through the yellow-green chestnut leaves. It was a glorious day in early May 1791, and many a Parisian had been tempted out to the Bois de Boulogne to see the chestnut trees dressed in their fragrant pink and white candles, to smell the sweetness of the bruised grass under the horses' feet, and to look up at a sky incandescently clear and the colour, almost, of hyacinths.

Johann Finsterwalde was riding in the smart new barouche which Charles Nordubois had had built for his wife, who was in the last stages of her third pregnancy. Lotti, looking vast but comfortable in an all-enveloping blue pelisse and a huge, feather-covered hat to match, sat beside him, and opposite them, in the backward-facing seats, were Lotti's maid and the governess, holding the children. Mathilde was two now, and 'growing like a weed' as Uncle Johann proudly put it. She had her mother's unruly red hair and her father's sweet smile, and was, according to both parents, the most remarkable child that ever was.

That title Johann reserved for *his* favourite, her fifteen-month-old brother Charles-Louis, whom Johann had affectionately renamed Karellie.

'It's plain the boy is as German as can be,' he would say, bouncing the baby on his knee in a way that made the nurse-maids twitch and tut but which evidently delighted Karellie, for he cooed and gurgled under the treatment, and would bring up his wind for Uncle Johann as for no one else. Charles-Louis was sitting now on the governess's knee, a fat bundle of petticoats, frills and smiles, like a red-faced bolster with arms, watching Uncle Johann's face and bursting into chuckles whenever he caught his eye.

Charles Nordubois, with more sense than tact, had declined to ride in the new barouche with 'the menagerie', and had joined Henri and Héloïse on horseback for the outing. He intercepted Finsterwalde's remark to Henri with a frown and a shake of the head.

'Not "Monsieur le Comte", Uncle Johann. He is Citizen Stuart now, don't forget. We are all equal in the sight of the Assembly.'

'But the Assembly can't take away an *English* title, can it?' Lotti protested. 'It is Earl of Strathord really, is it not, Henri? And given by the King of England, so the Assembly cannot cancel it.'

'The point is, my heart, that he is a citizen of France,' Nordubois said, 'and as such—'

It was Héloïse who quelled the incipient argument. 'France cannot take away Papa's title, but it can stop him using it. But why, Herr Finsterwalde, do you wish to congratulate him?' she went on quickly to the point that interested her.

'Ah, he has not told you? That is like his modesty,' Finsterwalde said, and even Lotti could not have missed the irony in his voice. 'It is a public appointment of great honour—'

'It is one exactly suited, at least, to my accomplishments.' Henri interrupted with a smile.

'But what *is* it, papa?' Héloïse asked impatiently.

'I have been appointed, Marmoset, by the Assembly, to sell the stones of the Bastille.'

'*What?*' Héloïse laughed incredulously.

'You don't believe me? Assure yourself, love, that it is quite true! They are to pull down what is left of the Bastille at last, and lay out a pleasure-ground on the site. The Engineer, Paloy, is in charge of the business.'

'But *selling* the stones?'

'The Assembly is simply acknowledging a *fait accompli*. Every town in provincial France wants a stone from the Bastille as a memento of July the fourteenth and our glorious revolution, and Paloy has already built up a comfortable sum in his own coffers. The Assembly sees no reason why the public purse should not have the benefit rather than see it go on hats for Madame Paloy.'

'But why you, Papa?'

'Because I have so many contacts outside Paris – my former customers, I suppose,' Henri said indifferently. It was also, as he realised, a tribute to his ambivalent status in the *ancien régime*, half-nobleman, half-tradesman: they considered him to possess a perhaps unique combination of trustworthiness and efficiency. He hoped, with the faintest tremor of fear, that it did not signify a knowledge of his other activities over the past two years.

From the beginning, he had viewed the revolution with extreme caution, doing his best to remain outside it, trying, like a man in a circus riding with one foot on the back of each of two horses, to reconcile his personal friendship with the King and Queen and his undoubted attachment to the Court with his acquaintance with the *Philosophes* and, more recently, with the extraordinary and magnetic Danton. Having no political interests whatsoever, Henri had merely the desire to stay alive and, if possible, wealthy, and all his ambitions centred on Héloïse's future. He knew, at first hand, how revolutionaries argued amongst themselves, how little they agreed even on first principles; and he had seen, in the storming of the Bastille, and on other occasions since, how the ruthless were prepared to use the blind forces of the mob to achieve their own ends.

Danton, he knew, was one such, and much as he liked the man, he thought him dangerous. When the Assembly had reorganised the administration of Paris last year, the ancient district of the Cordeliers, where he had lived as Monsieur Écosse and where Danton still did live, in the Cour du Commerce, had been obliterated, merged into the district of the *Théâtre*. Danton had preserved the name by forming the Cordeliers' Club, welding together all the naturally dissident elements of the district with the heat of their fury at losing the ancient name. The Cordeliers' Club was becoming a force to be reckoned with, and would undoubtedly take the revolution further along the road than the comfortable bourgeois position it had reached. Already in inflammatory pamphlets and speeches it had championed the cause of the unemployed and of the 'passive citizens' – those who were disqualified through lack of income or property from voting – and Danton, Henri knew, would not hesitate to use the violence of the gutters, if necessary, to make his point.

There were many people in France who thought the revolution was over. The comparative quiet of the last year had encouraged the idea, but Henri was afraid that it was merely the quiet before the storm, and when the storm broke, he wanted to be in a position to raise shelter over his daughter. Cautiously, very cautiously, he must attach himself to the right people. Under the *ancien régime* he had used his title; in the modern *nation* he must use other gifts.

Abruptly he detached himself from the conversation around the barouche.

'My horse is restless,' he said. 'I must canter him a little. Héloïse, come with me – I see Prestance is longing for a gallop.'

Héloïse expressed her surprise with a raised eyebrow, for neither horse was shewing any sign of restlessness, but nodded her excuses to Lotti and followed her father obediently. He cantered ahead until they were sufficiently far from the carriage, and then slowed his mount to a walk and allowed Héloïse to come up alongside him. He looked down at her appreciatively. Though she had gained little in height in the last two years – so little that Prestance was still a perfectly adequate mount for her – she had grown up in every other way. In August she would be fourteen, and officially a woman, but already it was a little woman who looked up at him enquiringly, with nothing of the child about her except for her frankness and lack of artifice. Her figure had developed and her features had fined down, and she wore her dark blue habit and preposterous hat with an air. She would never be a beauty, his little monkey-princess, but her face had an arresting quality that made it hard to forget her.

'My darling,' he began, 'you know that the Assembly is to close the convent this summer?'

'Of course, Papa. The poor sisters talk of nothing else – though I must say that some of them seem to be very glad to be leaving. But there are others – poor Sister Luke, for instance – who will be very unhappy, and perhaps even suffer great hardship. I wonder, Papa, if we couldn't . . .'

But Henri had other things on his mind than the sufferings of the elderly nuns, and interrupted her attempted benevolence. 'You must have wondered what I propose to do with you.'

'Well, I thought I would go home, to Tante Ismène's house. Or perhaps I could come and live in your house, now I am more grown up, and look after it for you? I am sure it must need a woman's hand after all these years.'

Henri smiled in spite of himself. 'A woman's hand?'

'I shall be fourteen in August,' she reminded him with dignity.

'I know, little marmoset, I know, and I assure you that my house is a great deal beyond your ability to make it comfortable. That's why I spend as little time there as possible. No, you shall not be my housekeeper, love.'

'What, then, Papa?' she asked comfortably, her upturned face shewing no anxiety. She trusted him entirely. 'Shall I live with Lotti? I know she would like it.'

'No, my darling, you shall not. You are to be married.'

'Married?' Héloïse frowned, Henri nodded.

'Yes, of course. You must have known that I always planned a good match for you. In the old days, that meant a member of the nobility, a man with a title, and an old name, and, preferably, wealth. But those days are gone. We may no longer use our titles, and the time will come, dearest, when it will be dangerous to remember we ever had them.'

'Dangerous, Papa?'

Henri drew rein. 'Héloïse, you know that power has already passed into new hands, and I do not believe it will stop there. I must ally you with those who will have power, so that, when the bad days come, you will not suffer for having been my daughter. Do you understand?'

'I – I think so, Papa – but who? What sort of man--?'

Henri tried to smile. 'I do not know his name yet, Marmoset. Do not fear, he shall be young and handsome if I can manage it. A deputy, I think, not a minister – ministers smack too much of the Crown. I have to try to gauge which way the wind will blow, and then . . .'

Héloïse looked up at him mutely. His brow was drawn in a thoughtful frown, and she could see how he had changed over the past two years. There were lines in his face that had not been there before, and when he took off his wig, there was grey in his dark hair like frost. A shiver ran over her, like the little gust of wind that runs before the downpour, a shiver of foreboding, and suddenly the glorious May sunshine seemed less brilliant.

'Papa . . .' she began, not knowing quite what she wanted to say.

Henri came back from his abstraction, and smiled at her almost in his old way. 'Don't be afraid, Marmoset. I shall protect you. I must protect all my womenfolk. Come, let us canter back and join the party.'

It was on the following day that Henri received a visitor at his house in the rue de Saint-Rustique, an event in itself so surprising as to raise his suspicion.

'Who is it, Duncan?' he asked his servant, who shook his head.

'The gentleman is masked, my lord, and heavily cloaked, and evidently about some business of great secrecy and delicacy.'

'An assassin, Duncan?' Henri asked, raising an eyebrow.

Duncan looked pompous. 'I could not take it upon myself to say, my lord.'

Henri laughed. 'All right, Duncan, you are the perfect servant, fit to serve an English duke. Now, who is this heavily masked man? For you cannot fool me into thinking you have not recognised him, disguise or no disguise.'

Duncan lowered his voice. 'It would be hard not to recognise Monsieur le Comte de Fersen.'

'Axel de Fersen?' Henri murmured with surprise. 'Then I think we can both guess at his business. Shew him in, Duncan – and you had better go on pretending you don't know him.'

'Of course, my lord.'

Axel de Fersen, the Queen's intimate and faithful friend – some even said her lover! It was well that he had come so secretly, and to the rue de Saint-Rustique, which was so quiet and out of the way that he was unlikely to have been recognised. Henri had a good opinion of the Swedish count's intelligence, and trusted, for both their sakes, that he had made sure he was not followed. Duncan shewed him in, brought wine, and left them alone, upon which Fersen unmasked and Henri displayed just sufficient surprise at his identity.

'Well, sir, I can guess what your delicate matter is,' Henri said, 'and I applaud your secrecy. But what is it that I can do for you?'

'Monsieur de Stuart,' Fersen said, 'let us be frank with each other. I know that since the summer of '89 you have helped a number of nobles to escape from France.' Henri raised an eyebrow but said nothing, and Fersen smiled. 'Cautious! Yes, that is wise. We must all be cautious now – so admit nothing, I pray you. I shall do the talking, and by committing myself, prove that you can trust me. Your particular talents and connections, I know, have enabled you to raise money for certain of our nobility by selling their jewels and valuables for them; you have also arranged, through your knowledge of the provinces, for their journeys to the coast or to the border. We feel, therefore, that we can trust you, and we need your help.'

'We?' Henri murmured.

'The King and Queen must escape. You will perceive the necessity for it. I only pray they have not left it too late. The King's powers have been reduced to a shadow, the armed forces are out of his control, and he is more than nominally a prisoner in the Tuileries. You saw yourself, sir, what happened at Easter.'

Henri nodded. It had been a dreadful scene, though useful in clarifying the situation. The King had announced his intention of taking his family to Saint-Cloud for Easter, but when they had got into the carriage, the National Guard had refused to line the route, and a huge, silent crowd had gathered in the courtyard and prevented the carriage from moving. Lafayette had raised the red flag, to warn them to disperse, but they had ignored it, and the Guard had refused to use force to coerce them. For two and a half hours the royal family had sat in the coach, and were at last obliged to leave it and go back into the palace. It could not have been clearer that they were prisoners, and would never again be allowed to leave Paris.

'Well, sir, they must escape. What can I do to help?' Henri said.

Fersen smiled with relief. 'Bless you for that! I was sure we could count on you. The matter must be kept absolutely secret, of course, for there is no knowing who is watching and listening. I shall handle everything myself, for safety, and apart from you, no one will know the identity of the travellers.'

'Where will they make for?' Henri asked, and answered himself. 'Montmédy, and over the border into the Austrian Nether-lands, I imagine. That is the nearest point.'

'Yes, and I shall arrange for loyal troops to be ready at the frontier in case of trouble – but you may leave all that to me.'

'How can I help, then?'

'It is this: the Queen is terrified of being separated from her family. She is sure that if they travel separately they will never see each other again, and insists that they must all go together in one coach.'

'All? Who comprises this "all"?' Henri asked dourly.

'The King and Queen, the Dauphin and Madame Royale, Madame Élisabeth, the governess Madame de Tourzel, and two ladies-in-waiting.' Henri restrained from commenting, and Fersen added apologetically, 'I know, I know, and I did my best to persuade Her Majesty, but she is not accustomed to looking after herself, and she does not wish to arrive in a foreign country looking like a penniless fugitive.'

'Surely the important thing is to arrive,' Henri said. Fersen spread his hands.

'There is nothing more I can do to persuade her. And indeed, she has a point, Monsieur de Stuart: the royal family will need the help of foreign monarchs to regain the throne, and if they arrive without dignity, dressed in rags, they may fail to win support where it is needed. The Queen is having new clothes made, and a travelling case, so that she may arrive looking like a queen. You know how her beauty commands.'

It commands *you*, at any rate, poor fool, Henri thought, but he merely bowed his assent to the proposition, and asked again, 'How may I help?'

'The coach – a special coach will need to be built to carry them all. I hoped you would accept the commission, sell some of the Queen's valuables, and order and pay for it.'

'Two coaches – the ladies-in-waiting will have to travel behind with the luggage, of course,' Henri mused. 'That still means a coach big enough for four adults and two children. My God, Fersen, don't you see how big and cumbersome it will be? It will lumber along like a farm wagon, drawing every eye to it. You must persuade them to split up and travel separately, fast and light.'

Fersen shook his head in despair. 'Believe me, I have tried. I cannot. It must be this way. Will you help us?'

Henri was thinking. 'Wait,' he said, 'I have an idea.' He thought a moment longer and then snapped his fingers. 'I have it – listen, there is no possible way to disguise a coach like that. I think we must try to make it as conspicuous as possible.'

'What can you mean?' Fersen asked anxiously.

'Are you acquainted with the Baroness de Korff?'

'The Russian woman? Yes, I know of her. Why?'

'She often goes to Frankfurt, and part of her route lies on the road to Montmédy. She has a huge travelling-coach, well big enough for four adults and two children. It is so large it has to be drawn by six horses, and it is all the more conspicuous because it is painted bright yellow.'

'Bright yellow?' Fersen said, horrified.

'Her Majesty will have to take the part of the Baroness, and the others, members of her household. You must have the passports made out thus. The coach is so well known it will occasion little surprise, but I doubt whether many of the country people are well enough acquainted with the Baroness to recognise her face.'

Fersen clasped his hand in gratitude. 'Yes, I see it all. You are right, I am sure of it. Thank you, Monsieur de Stuart, thank you, on behalf of Their Majesties as well as myself. I will make sure you are suitably rewarded for your trouble.'

Henri raised an eyebrow at this unexpected piece of clumsiness, which he put down to emotion. 'Rewarded, Monsieur de Fersen? One is only doing one's duty.'

'I beg your pardon, sir,' Fersen began in confusion, but Henri cut him short.

'One other thing occurs to me, sir: Provence and his wife must not remain behind. When the revolutionaries discover that the King has fled, they will not hesitate to seize and punish the King's brother.'

'Of course, you are right. I had intended calling at the Luxembourg Palace tomorrow.'

Henri bowed. 'You have so much to do already – permit me to perform that task for you. I will make all the arrangements for the Duc.'

Fersen smiled. 'No doubt they will be simpler than the arrangements at the Tuileries.'

The arrangements were made as decided, except that Madame de Tourzel persuaded the Queen to let her play the part of the Baroness, with whom she was acquainted. It would be much better, she said, if the Queen was not placed in a position where she might have to speak. The two children would be the Baroness's children; the Queen could play the part of their governess; the King and Madame Élisabeth could be her steward and personal maid.

Henri did his part, organising the building of the coach by a coachmaker in Clichy who had a large barn in which it could be done without attracting attention. Fersen brought him jewels and trinkets to sell to finance the business. Henri had, over the last two years, built up a network of trustworthy people in the provinces and abroad for disposing of such things; but one or two things, this time, he purchased himself, for he was fond of the Queen and thought it would be nice, one day, for Héloïse to have something that had once belonged to the Queen of France. He kept a little gold cachou box with diamonds round the rim and an enamelled lid with the Queen's initials, MA, inscribed in gold on dark blue, and a necklace of rubies which he had seen the Queen wear to the Opéra, long ago in her careless youth. Rubies, he thought, would suit Héloïse's dark looks.

In comparison with the escape from the Tuileries, the escape from the Luxembourg Palace was simplicity itself. The Duc and Duchesse de Provence were not in the least difficult to persuade that speed and secrecy were of the essence, and Henri arranged matters for them along the same lines that he had used for his previous clients: a fast chaise-and-four and the minimum of luggage. They did not make the mistake of offering Henri their gratitude for his endeavours on their behalf, preferring to suppose that he did it for love of their rank, or that the King and Queen would reward him; but that was only what he expected – he knew Provence of old.

The Convent of the Visitation was closed in the middle of June, and Héloïse took a tearful farewell of the nuns who had cared for her for four years, and returned in the carriage which had been sent for her to her childhood home in the Rue Saint-Anne. She went up at once to Madame de Murphy's private drawing-room, and found her, to her surprise, lying on a *chaise-longue* with the drapes drawn against the sunshine.

'Tante Ismène! Why are you lying down? Are you ill?' Héloïse asked anxiously, stooping automatically to caress Bluette, the spaniel, who had run to meet her.

Ismène opened her eyes and smiled. 'Dear Héloïse, have you never heard of a lady lying down in the afternoon? Must I be ill to wish to rest a little?'

'I have never heard of *you* lying down – and especially when Marie tells me you have a salon this evening. Why are you not bustling about making preparations?'

'It is because of the salon that I am lying down – I wish to be fresh for my guests,' Ismène said, and sought to distract Héloïse's attention. 'Well, my love, so you are home again! You must be sorry to leave, I know, but exciting things lie ahead for you.'

Héloïse picked up Bluette and came to sit on the end of the sofa with the little dog on her lap. 'Now I am home', she said, refusing to be distracted, 'you must let me take charge of things for you. You are looking tired, Tante Ismène, no matter what you say.'

Ismène sighed. 'Well, to tell the truth, my dear, I am feeling a little tired, but it is probably no more than the heat. Meurice says that I should go into the country for a few weeks. He talks of hiring a house in Saint-Germain for me, by the river. Would you like to come with me? We could take Prestance, and you could ride in the woods in the afternoon while I rest. Dr Houlet says--'

'You have seen Dr Houlet?' Héloïse asked, alarmed. Ismène smiled.

'Do not be anxious, dearest. It was only Meurice fussing, that's all. I must rest in the heat of the day, and go into the country for a few weeks, and I shall be quite well again, that is what the good doctor says.' She met Héloïse's eye steadily, and after a moment the girl relaxed and smiled.

'If that is all – but do take care, won't you, Tante Ismène?'

'Of course I will – I want to be perfectly well for your wedding, whenever that is.'

Héloïse made a face. 'Oh, my wedding! Has Papa told you yet who I am to marry?'

'No, he has not – and I am sure he will tell you before he tells me, so don't look like that, my love,' Ismène laughed. 'Are you going to grace my salon with your presence today?'

'Who is coming?' Héloïse asked. 'Will it be amusing?'

'Oh, vastly, I assure you. Barnave and Duport and the de Lameths are coming, and the usual friends, and Condorcet said he would drop in later, and Fabre d'Églantine is coming to read his new poem, which I'm afraid will be very dull, but I knew his mother, and feel I ought to encourage him. And I have a little coup planned for this evening – this journalist Jacques Brissot whose pamphlets Meurice so disapproves of has agreed to honour us with a visit.'

'But he is a republican, is he not, Tante Ismène?'

'That is what will be amusing. He and Barnave are bound to disagree, and we shall see which side Condorcet will come down on. Oh, I am looking forward to in enormously,' she cried, sitting up with a sudden burst of energy. 'Ring the bell, will you, dearest, for my maid? It is time I went to get dressed. You will come, won't you, and wear your new gown? I haven't seen you in it yet.'

'Wear a new gown for all those old men?' Héloïse teased. 'I wonder you should suggest it, madame.'

'Fabre d'Églantine is not an old man – though of course he is a poet, which doesn't count. But Brissot said he would bring one of his young disciples with him, so if my pleasure isn't enough for you, you may say you are wearing it for the protégé of Brissot.'

Héloïse put down Bluette and kissed Ismène's cheek. 'I will wear it for you,' she said. She went over to the fireplace and rang the bell, and said, 'Now I will go to my room, if you will excuse me. Would you ask Marie to let me know when Uncle Meurice comes in? I want to see him the very moment he gets back.'

Meurice de Murphy, who had been a colonel in the Royal Écossais and who was now in charge of a section of the Bodyguard, greeted Héloïse affectionately, but his face betrayed his anxiety all too clearly.

'She has not been well for some weeks. She tires easily, and has pains in her head and *here*.' He put his hand to his side. 'But you know her – she will not be persuaded. It has taken Houlet weeks to convince her that she should go into the country even for a few weeks. This is to be the last salon, Héloïse. I will tell you, because I know you can be trusted. I want to get her away from Paris altogether. When she is in the country I will find a way to persuade her to stay. Will you go with her to Saint-Germain?'

'I have already said to her that I will,' Héloïse answered.

'Good. All the arrangements are made. You will pack tomorrow, and leave the day after.'

'So soon?'

'I must have you both safe out of Paris. I cannot – I must not tell you more, but believe me that it will not be safe here.'

'Uncle Meurice . . .' Héloïse said, startled, and stopped herself abruptly. He met her eyes and she read in them the answer to the question she must not ask. 'I understand. I had better go and change now, hadn't I?'

Meurice kissed her forehead. 'Bless you, Héloïse. Take care of her for me.'

The new gown was of white figured muslin over a pink underdress. It was tight in the bodice, and full in the skirt, over a false-rump, and had a very deep waistband which had the effect of pushing up the bosom. The sleeves were long and tight, and ended in a chiffon frill at the wrist, and the *décolletage* was filled with a lace fichu. Héloïse wore her front hair frizzed out and the back hair in long sleek ringlets, and when she took a look at herself in the mirror she decided that she looked every bit sixteen, and absolutely *à la mode*. A brief doubt about the sin of vanity crossed her mind, but then she decided that it was not sinful to wish to appear to the best advantage, and that she was not conceited, knowing she had no great beauty. I will go to confession tomorrow, she promised her conscience, only let me enjoy my new gown tonight.

Tante Ismène, looking beautiful but somehow frail in Trianon grey, was very complimentary about the new gown. 'Ah, the high waistband – the Rose Bertin style – how very modish of you, Héloïse! You look lovely, my dear, quite lovely,' she whispered as she brought her forward to introduce her to the guests. Many of them were known to Héloïse, who had been meeting them since her childhood in Madame de Murphy's drawing-room. Some of the older gentlemen greeted her affectionately and complimented her on growing into an attractive young woman, some asked after her father, others still asked what she would do now that the convent had been closed. The elder de Lameth even chucked her chin and said he was sure she'd be married soon, and that he'd a mind to speak to her father himself, to which Héloïse replied with just the right wide-eyed look that she hoped she would make a suitable companion to his wife.

Finally, Tante Ismène led her over to the group in the corner, saying, 'And now I must present to you the guest of honour this evening, Monsieur Brissot, who is going to explain to us all about his new ideas for government.' Brissot, a good-looking man in his thirties, with dark curly hair which he neither disguised with a wig nor with powder, smiled and bowed to Héloïse. 'And his young protégé,' Ismène went on, and then stopped, flustered. 'Oh dear, I do beg your pardon, but I'm afraid I have forgotten your name. How stupid of me – my wretched memory!'

The tall young man, whose attention had been perfectly absorbed by Brissot's conversation, turned and looked gravely down at Héloïse. His green-brown eyes surveyed her with interest and seemed to assess the changes in her with approval, while Héloïse, a most becoming blush warming her cheeks, curtsied and said, 'No need for introduction, Tante Ismène. We have met before.'

'Indeed we have,' said Vendenoir, 'and the honour then, as now, was all mine.'

During the interval for refreshments later in the evening, Héloïse had the opportunity to talk with her former friend. He seemed to her very much grown up, taller, more heavily built so that his height did not make him seem gawky, and with an air of assurance that made it hard to remember his awkwardness on their first meeting.

'So you have left the convent,' he said, standing by her side as they helped themselves from the buffet to cold meats and delicacies.

'Yes. It has been closed, and so I have left for good. I shall live here until--'

'Until?'

Héloïse blushed a little. 'Until I am married.'

'Ah, yes, of course,' Vendenoir said thoughtfully, gazing at her again. 'Yes, you have grown up, I can see that. You were just a little girl when we met. I do not think,' he added with the sudden smile Héloïse remembered had always transformed his face, 'that your Papa would allow me to take you out on the river in a boat now.'

'And you,' Héloïse said hastily, to change the subject, 'you got to Paris at last.'

'Yes, I am a lawyer, and hope one day soon to be a deputy. I have great hopes of being elected to the new Assembly, when it is at last convened, for you know no-one on the present Assembly may be re-elected, and Brissot says . . .' He checked himself, and Héloïse smiled privately to see his old enthusiasm had not died, but was simply masked a little by his newly grown-up air.

'I remember you were afraid the revolution would be over before you managed to get to Paris,' Héloïse said, to fill the awkwardness.

'Was I? Oh, I was young then. I hadn't met any of the real thinkers – I had everything out of books. But now I meet them all, you know, on equal terms: Brissot, Desmoulins, Danton, even Robespierre . . .'

'Danton?' Héloïse said. 'You know him?'

'Yes. Why do you ask?'

But she was not supposed to know of her father's acquaintance in the Cordeliers district, and shook her head. 'I had heard he was – a rough diamond. Well, I am sorry for your sake that you did miss the revolution, but--'

'Miss it? It is only just beginning!' he exclaimed. 'There is so much more to be done, and I assure you that what has passed so far will be seen in time to be just the preliminary steps towards a *truly* perfect state.'

Héloïse smiled up at him mischievously. 'Now I can see that you are indeed the same Olivier Vendenoir that I once knew! You still hope to educate me in politics.'

It was his turn to blush, but he smiled at her all the same, and said, 'Mademoiselle, I should be honoured if you would allow me to call upon you one morning, and present you with a reading list.'

Héloïse laughed. 'As to that, sir, I am sure my Tante Ismène has all the books which may be on your list, but by all means ask her permission to call. But,' she remembered suddenly, 'it will have to be tomorrow morning, for on the day after I am to accompany her into the country.'

'For how long, mademoiselle?'

'For several weeks, at least. She has been unwell, and has been advised by the doctor to leave the city during the heat of the summer.'

'Then I shall endeavour to call tomorrow, and hope that I may be allowed to continue our acquaintance when you return to Paris.'

To which proposition Héloïse consented with a curtsy and a private, satisfied smile.

On the morning of the twentieth of June, Madame de Murphy set out in her travelling-chariot for Saint-Germain. They started very early, to avoid the heat of the day, and to arrive in good time for dinner. It was a stately cavalcade, the chariot pulled by four horses, guided by two postilions, in which rode Madame de Murphy, Bluette, Mademoiselle de Stuart, and their two personal maids, followed by a second carriage containing the luggage and two footmen, and finally a groom riding his own horse and leading Prestance.

Meurice de Murphy had said goodbye to them while they were still taking their early morning chocolate, for his duty was at the Tuileries that day, and he had to leave before the hour of their departure. Henri had said goodbye the day before, promising to visit them at Saint-Germain as soon as he could, so there were only the servants to wave goodbye as the carriage drew away from the house and rattled through the almost-deserted streets in the faint early-morning haze.

The journey was performed without difficulty, so easily in fact that Héloïse could not quite account for Madame de Murphy's seeming so tired when they reached the house which had been rented for them. The servants who had been sent on ahead were there ready to receive them, and dinner had been prepared for them. Héloïse tried to persuade Tante Ismène to go up to her room at once, and take her dinner there, on a tray, but she roused herself from her languor and said, nonsense, she would simply wash the dust of the journey from her hands and face and dine properly with Héloïse.

After dinner, however, she consented to lie on a sofa, while Héloïse explored the house and garden, and reported back to Ismène that it all seemed very pleasant, and that though the wallpaper was somewhat marked and the paint needed renewing, the furnishings were quite adequate and the garden was a mass of roses.

'I shall go out as soon as it is cooler and pick some for your room, dear Tante Ismène,' Héloïse said. 'And there is a lovely walk along the river bank, under the willow trees, that I am persuaded will be perfect for your walk tomorrow.'

'I hope you won't be bored, dearest,' Ismène said anxiously when Héloïse persuaded her to go straight to bed after they had drunk tea. 'How will you amuse yourself this evening?'

'I shall play a game of patience, and play to myself on that harpsichord if it is not too out of tune – though I have small hopes of that! – and then I shall read *Candide* and go to bed early. I must somehow work my way through the list of books Vendenoir thinks essential reading if I am to be a proper companion to you.'

Ismène managed a smile at that, though Héloïse could see she was exhausted. She stood up to kiss her goodnight, and said, 'I shall tell your maid not to disturb you in the morning. Sleep long and well tonight, dear aunt.' And if you do not look a great deal refreshed, she added to herself, I shall send for the doctor, whatever you say.

Héloïse was awake early the next day, and having had her chocolate and bread, dressed herself in a simple linen dress that reminded her of convent days, and went out into the garden to pick roses. There were so many, and they were so lovely and so fragrant that she was rather carried away, and by the time she had arranged several bowls full and placed them at vantage-points around the house, it was almost eleven o'clock and she was beginning to wonder if Tante Ismène would be stirring, and whether it would be wise to wake her.

A commotion in the kitchen regions attracted her attention, and resolved itself after some minutes in the somewhat abrupt entrance of Ismène's maid, Marie, breathless, red in the face, and bursting with news.

'Mademoiselle, word has just arrived from the city – the King and Queen have left Paris! They escaped in the night, mademoiselle – the King's valet found him gone this morning when he went to wake him. And Madame Elisabeth and the children too – there is such a commotion, mademoiselle, and the guard sent after them.'

Héloïse paled, thinking first of Uncle Meurice, remembering his veiled warning to her. If he were involved – he must be involved! That was why he had been so anxious to have them leave Paris. She could not imagine what the consequences might be to such an involvement, but one thing was clear.

'Madame must be told at once,' she said. 'But tactfully. I shall go and wake her myself, and break the news gently. Bring her tray up, Marie, and tell the other servants to stop making so much noise.'

'Yes, mademoiselle,' Marie said and dashed away without even curtsying, sign of her enormous excitement. Héloïse went upstairs, tapped softly on the bedroom door, and went in. The curtains were drawn, of course, but the sunlight was so strong that even through the closed curtains it filled the room with a twilight. Tante Ismène was lying in bed, propped up on her pillows, her hands folded over her chest. She did not stir as Héloïse came in, and she thought she was still asleep.

'Tante Ismène, wake up. It is past eleven, and there is some news you ought to hear.'

She went over to the window and drew the curtains just a little, and, turning, saw that Ismène's eyes were open. She smiled.

'I thought you were asleep. Dear aunt, there is some-thing--'

She stopped, approaching the bed in puzzled silence. Ismène still had not moved, nor blinked, nor acknowledged her presence in any way.

'Tante Ismène?'

The maid Marie came in through the open door behind her, and Héloïse heard almost simultaneously the crash as she dropped the tray of bread and chocolate and the scream as, quicker-witted than Héloïse, she realised that there would be no need to break the news gently. Ismène de Murphy was dead.

7

Because of the heat, Madame de Murphy's obsequies could not be delayed. The doctor and the *curé* who were summoned from Saint-Germain were both adamant on that point; but Paris was in such an uproar over the escape of the King and Queen that it seemed impossible for anyone to be consulted about the arrangements. Héloïse, at the age of fourteen, found herself in charge of an entire household, and appealed to on every side for orders, instructions, advice, comfort. She looked from face to face, bewildered, still so stricken with her own grief – for Madame de Murphy had been as a mother to her – that she could not gather her wits about her. It was the *curé* who came to her rescue, sending everyone abruptly from the room, and drawing Héloïse over to a sofa to sit beside him.

He took her hands and chafed them – such cold little hands! – and when he had her attention, he said, 'My dear, it is very hard for you, I know. But the funeral must take place tomorrow at the latest, and you must give the orders for it.'

'But Uncle Meurice – Papa – I don't know what to do. I have never had to order a – a – funeral before.' She controlled her voice with an effort.

'It had better take place here, at Saint-Germain. I will arrange for the funeral mass, and I will send the undertaker later today, and the women to lay out the body – there, there, don't cry. Remember, it is only an empty shell now. Your aunt is in paradise, with Our Lady and all the blessed saints.'

'Yes,' Héloïse said, wiping her tears away with her fingers ineffectually.

'What you must do, child, is to write to anyone who ought to know about it, and send one of the servants off on horseback at once. If the letters arrive in time, this Uncle Meurice will come straight away and take the arrangements out of your hands. But if they do not – you will have done all you can.'

'Yes, Father,' Héloïse said waveringly.

'Now, can I leave you to write the letters? I must go at once and speak to the undertaker.'

'Yes, Father. Thank you.'

He left her in the parlour, closing the door behind him and restraining the red-eyed Marie from going in at once. 'Let her alone for a while. She will want to have her weep.'

Inside, Héloïse had buried her face in the sofa cushion and was sobbing with abandon. She was aroused some time later by Bluette, whining miserably and pawing at her knee. She sat up, fumbling in her sleeve for a handkerchief and not finding it, and the dog at once jumped up on to her lap, waving its clamped-down tail apprehensively and thrusting its muzzle up into her face to lick her tears, which was such a disagreeable sensation that it made her snort and then almost laugh.

'Oh stop! Poor Bluette, you don't understand what's happening, do you? Poor, poor dog. She's gone, Bluette. You'll have to make do with me.'

The last words almost made her lose control again, and she bit her lip and hugged the little dog tightly while she looked around for her handkerchief. Marie, having heard her voice, poked her head tentatively round the door at that moment, and Héloïse was able to say with moderate control. 'Oh, Marie, will you bring writing-paper, ink and a pen? I must write letters at once. And tell Pierre to be ready with one of the horses to take them into the city.'

'Yes, mademoiselle,' Marie said, and giving her an admiring look, hurried away to do her bidding. The admiring look helped Héloïse enormously. She found her handkerchief, blew her nose, and straightened her back. She was head of the household, for the time being at least; everyone depended on her. She must not let them down.

It was Sunday when Henri finally arrived in Saint-Germain, and was ushered out into the tangled garden where his daughter was sitting in the sunshine, Bluette on her lap, contemplating the bees working amongst the roses. She was in black – a dress hastily and rather clumsily run up for the funeral – with her hair drawn back smoothly and modestly into bands, and her face looked rather pale, and thinner. She looked, in her tranquility, like a young nun. Henri's heart turned over in him with love and pity. She looked suddenly older, and her resemblance to her mother at that moment was marked. It was a moment before he could control his voice.

'My dear child', he said. She turned, her face lit, she jumped up, tumbling the startled spaniel, who had been asleep, onto the grass, and a moment later she was in his arms, her face pressed to his jacket. 'Héloïse, my love.'

'Oh Papa, I am so glad to see you!' she cried, somewhat muffled.

'You have been left alone to do everything – I am so sorry – but there was no help for it. You shall not be alone again, I promise. There, there, dear love. Come and sit down.'

He sat down with her on the stone bench, his arm around her shoulders, and the dog jumped up between them and tried to force its way on to her lap again by the simple method of putting its head under her arm and shoving. Héloïse laughed shakily.

'Poor Bluette, she won't leave me for a moment. She sleeps on my bed, and if I get up in the night she trots after me anxiously. She thinks I shall disappear if she lets me out of her sight.'

She lifted her arm and the little dog clambered with a sigh of relief on to her lap. Héloïse looked at her father with mild reproach. 'Didn't you get my letters, Papa?'

'Yes, my love, I did, though not until Thursday,' he said gently, 'and I would have come if I could, but it was not possible. There has been trouble. Paris has been in uproar. I have been – covering tracks.'

Héloïse's eyes widened. 'Th.n you were . . .' She stopped herself, glanced around to see if anyone was in earshot, and continued in a low voice. 'What happened, Papa? Can you tell me?'

'The King got as far as Varennes, but he was recognised, and the town council ordered his arrest.'

'Yes, we heard that much. It must have been frightful for Their Majesties.'

Henri shook his head in anger and frustration. 'A few more miles, a few more, and they would have been safe. There were loyal troops just across the river. But the whole affair was bungled, from start to finish. The delays! The carelessness! If they had only done as I suggested, travelled light, in fast, small carriages, in separate parties, they would have been safe in a few hours. Provence was safe in Brussels before the King had even reached Châlons. And then they stopped for this and that – picnicking on the grass! – and the King would lean out of the window to look at the view. No wonder they were recognised. The wonder is they got as far as they did.'

'And they are back in Paris now?'

'They were brought in yesterday. The National Guard lined the road, muskets reversed like a funeral. Lafayette was afraid they might be attacked by the mob, but though there was a huge crowd, they were absolutely silent. It was – awesome.'

'They were taken to the Tuileries?'

'Yes – though no doubt they will be moved to some more secure prison now. The sentries are doubled on every door, and patrol the corridors. They will never escape again.'

Héloïse shivered. 'But, Papa,' she remembered suddenly, 'what has happened to Uncle Meurice? He was on guard duty at the Tuileries that day, and he has not written or visited. Pierre left messages for him everywhere. Is he all right?'

Henri took her hand. 'Uncle Meurice has fled, child. His life was in danger, as you must see, for he was in charge of the bodyguard. The Queen saved those who went with the royal family – her first words on leaving the carriage in the palace yard were to Lafayette. "General, save the bodyguard before everything. They have done nothing but obey orders," she said. Lafayette got them away, and they will be posted out of Paris. But nothing could have saved Meurice. He has fled into exile – Fersen too, for it was he who organised everything.'

'I guessed that, Papa,' Héloïse said, an anxious frown between her brows. 'Did he know before he left, about Tante Ismène?'

'Meurice? Yes, I told him.' Henri frowned too as he remembered his friend's anguish. 'There is nothing you can do,' he had told him fiercely, 'nothing. Don't sacrifice your life too. Think of Héloïse, if of no-one else.'

'And what about you, Papa?' Héloïse asked, very low, her eyes cast down on her lap. She was afraid to hear the truth, but she must know.

'The night of the escape I spent with Danton in the cour du Commerce,' he told her. 'I got so drunk I could not go home and stayed there all night, sleeping on cushions on the floor of their parlour. When I heard of the arrest, I rejoiced publicly that the perfidious King and Queen had been foiled in their attempt to overthrow the Nation's elected government.'

'Papa!'

'Hush, listen. I have spent every night since then at the Cordeliers' Club, talking with the republican party. I am beginning to be well thought-of there. That man Brissot – Desmoulins – Robespierre – Danton.'

'Papa, how could you? They wish to depose the King – you have been his friend.' Héloïse looked immeasurably shocked. Henri pressed her hand, speaking rapidly and low.

'My darling, try to think. They will never escape again. You cannot imagine the outcry there has been in Paris. Before he left, the King wrote a letter to the Assembly condemning it for reducing the Crown to a cipher, and repudiating any support he ever gave to it, as having been forced on him. The mob is clamouring for the abolition of the monarchy; the King and Queen will be more and more straitly imprisoned; in the end, the mob will demand their execution--'

'No, oh no!'

' . . . and the Assembly will have to agree,' Henri went on inexorably, 'because if they do not, others more ruthless will execute *them*. Understand, my love, that there is nothing, *nothing*, that I can do to help the King and Queen again. I must concentrate my efforts on making us safe. There must be many who know I have helped various nobles to escape, and who will suspect I helped the King and Queen. I must give them no reason to make their suspicions public.'

'And Uncle Meurice,' Héloïse asked after a moment. 'Did you help him escape?'

He touched her cheek. 'Better you know nothing, dearest. I would have you innocent of all this business.'

Héloïse straightened her shoulders. 'I can never be innocent again, Papa. I am a grown woman now, not a child.'

Henri looked at her sadly. 'Yes, I see you are. You managed everything on your own, did you not?'

'The curé helped me,' Héloïse said. 'It was not so very bad, after the first shock of it. She must have died as soon as she lay down to sleep, the doctor said. Her heart failed, probably after the strain of the journey. It would have been very quick and painless, he said. The undertaker was very kind, agreeing to wait for his money, for of course I could not pay his bill. Papa, who will pay the bills? Uncle Meurice cannot, now he is gone into exile.'

'The whole of Meurice's estate has been confiscated, child. He is a proscribed person,' Henri told her gravely.

'The house? The furniture and everything?'

'Yes, all confiscated. They will be sold and the money will go to the public purse. But Ismène had a fortune of her own, and she left it all to you, along with her personal possessions. Her marriage settlement gave her possession of those. It means the estate is in a very complicated condition, and the Assembly had to appoint someone to sort out the matter on its behalf.'

Héloïse found herself smiling for almost the first time. 'You, Papa?'

Henri shrugged modestly. 'Who better? The man who has sold the Bastille for the National Assembly should find a mere private estate simplicity itself. I should not be surprised if you found yourself a rich woman. But I shall have need of a lawyer, of course.' He eyed her thoughtfully. 'I have been renewing my acquaintance with your friend Vendenoir this past week. Did you know Madame Dupin bought him a practice in Paris, and the office of *Avocat és Conseils*? I met him several times at the Cordeliers' Club, and I must say he grows on me. He is rather earnest, to be sure, but I expect he will grow out of that. But he is certainly turned into a handsome young man, don't you think?'

'Oh yes, I think so,' Héloïse said easily. 'But Papa, if the house in the rue Saint-Anne is to be sold, where shall I live?'

'You can stay with Lotti for a while, if you wish, but in the long term – would you like to go back to the rue Saint-Anne?'

'Of course – it is my home. But how could I?'

'I told you it was to be sold for the Assembly. I think it should not be beyond my powers to see that it is bought by an agent acting for the heirs of the unfortunate Madame de Murphy, heroine of the revolution, who was betrayed even at the moment of her death by her perfidious husband, who hustled her out of Paris so that she could not prevent his wickedness.'

'Oh Papa,' Héloïse said reproachfully. 'How can you say such things about Uncle Meurice?'

'My dear, he is in exile; he cannot come back to Paris, and his reputation cannot matter to him. Why should we not utilise it to our advantage? I am sure he would not begrudge it. Those who will think badly of him will be just the sort of people he would not *want* to think well of him.'

'That is true, I suppose, but it seems to me, Papa, that you are becoming very unscrupulous . . .' She stopped abruptly as the thought struck her. 'But *I* am Tante Ismène's heir, you said. Do you mean--?'

'Yes, dear Marmoset, I do. The house in the Rue Saint-Anne shall be yours.'

Henri had hoped that Héloïse would remain at Saint-Germain for the summer, out of the city's heat and out of danger, too; but she was lonely there, and when she learned that Henri would be returning to Paris straight away, she begged to be allowed to go to stay with Lotti.

'It is lovely here, but it will always have sad memories for me,' she said. 'Besides Lotti must be very near her time, and I am sure she would like to have me by her side at her time of trial.'

Henri laughed at that. 'You are perfectly well aware, Marmoset, that Lotti drops her young like a hill-goat, without the least trial in the world, and that she will be clamouring to be allowed out of bed the next day. But if you want to go back to Paris, of course you shall.'

Henri remained two days with Héloïse, to help her with the arrangements that had to be made. The servants who had been part of Ismène's household had to be paid off, the various bills in the town covered, and Ismène's boxes packed. On Henri's advice, Héloïse retained Ismène's servant Marie to be her personal maid, and the footman Pierre to be her footman. 'It is time you had your own retinue, child, now you are, as you assure me, a woman.'

Finally in the morning of Wednesday the twenty-ninth the

carriage started for Paris, with Henri riding alongside and the groom leading Prestance behind. Héloïse arrived at the rue Montmartre at noon, suddenly wondering whether she would be as welcome with a maid, footman, groom and dog to accommodate as she was as an unaccompanied child; but when the door was opened to her all such worries were driven out of her head, for she was greeted with relief by Besser, who exclaimed,

'Oh mademoiselle, you have come so timely! Madame has gone into labour this hour past, and has been asking for you. We were just going to send a man off to Saint-Germain to see if you could be persuaded to come.'

'Is she all right, Besser?' Héloïse asked anxiously, stripping off her gloves.

'The midwife says she thinks the child may be laid wrongly, mademoiselle. That was why madame was so anxious you should be brought.'

Héloïse wasted no time, but ran upstairs, pausing only to command Marie to keep Bluette from following her. She found poor Lotti in bed, white and strained with pain, but still cheerful.

'Oh Héloïse, you can't imagine how glad I am to see you,' she said. 'They must have ridden fast to bring you so soon,' she added vaguely, worrying Héloïse more by her loss of sense of time than anything the midwife might have said. 'I wanted you here in case anything should happen.'

'What should happen, Lotti?' Héloïse said soothingly. 'You have had two children already, as easily as – '. She could not quite echo her father's choice of words, and altered it to 'as easily as a ewe lambs.'

Lotti grimaced with pain, and Héloïse gave her her hand. Lotti gripped it hard, and said, 'The midwife says the child is laid wrongly, and you know what that means. Or perhaps you don't – why should you? But if I should die, I want you to take care of my children.'

'You're not going to die, don't be silly,' Héloïse said, but Lotti only gripped her hand harder, hurting her.

'Promise me, Héloïse, promise me. If I die, you will take care of my poor children, be a mother to them: promise me!'

'Yes, all right, dear Lotti, I promise. But you are not going to die, I assure you. I never saw a stronger person than you.'

Lotti was calmed by the promise, and the midwife pushed Héloïse gently out of the way. 'You'd better leave now, mademoiselle,' she said, but Lotti said at once,

'No, no, I want her to stay. Please stay with me, Héloïse. I'm--' she swallowed, and said with difficulty, as though admitting a shameful thing, 'I'm afraid.'

'Of course I'll stay,' Héloïse said, trying to sound matter-of-fact; though inside she was quaking. This was growing up with a vengeance, she thought, Tante Ismène dying and now Lotti having her baby. Don't let her die, please, Holy Mother, she prayed inwardly. Not Lotti!

The labour was long and hard, not at all like dropping a lamb on a hillside. Héloïse felt that her initiation into the secrets of womanhood had been a baptism of fire, for poor Lotti suffered terribly, and Héloïse suffered with her, cry for cry. Lotti would not be easy if she was not holding her hand, so Héloïse stayed there by the bedside, all through the afternoon, all through the evening, and into the night, until at last, at four in the morning of the thirteenth the baby was born, buttocks first: a pathetic, croaking, purple scrap, almost suffocated by the birth-cord's being wrapped around its neck.

'A girl,' said the midwife. 'Lucky she was no bigger, as well, or we'd have lost both of you. Now, madame, you'll do well enough by and by.' And, turning to her assistant: 'Issy, take the baby from me, girl. Do you think the good Lord gave me four hands?'

'No, let me – yes, it's all right,' Héloïse said as the midwife hesitated.

'Mind your dress, then, mademoiselle – and take care, she's slippery as a wet eel,' said the woman, passing the baby over and returning to the more pressing problem of the mother. Héloïse received the minute thing, and looked at it with wonder and pity. Its legs were drawn up as if the bloody stump of the cord hurt, its face was screwed up, and it had as yet no strength to cry, being occupied with drawing air into its starved lungs with a little croaking noise. It was covered, moreover, with smears of blood and some kind of slimy substance, and despite the intense heat of the room, where a fire had been burning all day, in defiance of the climate, it seemed to be shivering.

'I'll wash you, poor thing,' Héloïse said, and as she said it, it seemed a good idea. To wash the baby, and wrap it in clean linen – that was the thing.

The midwife's assistant, Issy, said, 'There's hot water here, mademoiselle, and towels, and clothes. Shall I do it, mademoiselle? You'll get yourself all in a mess.'

'No, please, I'd like to,' Héloïse said, and the girl was silent, embarrassed at a lady saying 'please' to her. Learning as she went along, Héloïse washed the infant, dried it carefully, and then with the girl's help dressed it in its belly-bands, a fine linen shirt and a warm woollen shawl.

'There now, you are comfortable, aren't you?' she murmured, cradling the child and rocking her a little in her arms. The baby was breathing more easily now, and seemed to be asleep. Héloïse took her over to the bedside, where the midwife was washing Lotti, and offered her the baby to hold.

'No, you keep her,' Lotti said, her voice faint with exhaustion. 'I just want to sleep. Thank you for staying with me.'

'Did you decide on a name for her?' Héloïse asked.

Lotti's eyes were closed, but she nodded, and murmured: 'If – it was a boy – Claude. If – a girl – Clothilde.'

Lotti did not die, though she did sleep for almost thirty hours after giving birth, and was in bed, feeling weak and exhausted and sore, for a whole week, before she began to talk about getting up. During that time Héloïse looked after Clothilde, interviewing suitable wet-nurses, choosing her christening gown, superintending her changing and actually bathing her with her own hands. When she cried, which she did often once she had got over the shock of her birth, it was Héloïse who rushed to pick her up and comfort her. Uncle Johann thought it vastly amusing, and began to call her 'the little mother'; and Charles said drily that she didn't need to take her promise to Lotti so seriously. Héloïse only smiled at them, and continued to be enchanted with the new baby, pointing out every change in her as proudly as if she had been the mother in truth.

Only two people, however, seriously objected to Héloïse's obsession: Mathilde, who thought the new baby ugly and disliked having attention taken away from herself, and Bluette, who, having been soundly smacked for disputing possession of

Héloïse's lap with Clothilde, sulked and pined, and took to lying in prominent positions looking mournful, in the hope that her cruel mistress might take pity on her and reinstate her.

Henri leaned up on one elbow and looked down at the long-boned, fair body of Marie-France with appreciation. They were both naked in the heat of the summer; her delicately nacreous skin was flushed from their exertions, and a little sweat had gathered under her eyes, which were slumbrous with sated passion. The orphan *bourgeoise* from respectable, stiff-rumped Caen had proved an eminently satisfactory mistress, taking to her physical duties with the delight and vigour of a duck to water. Henri, in his mid-forties, even found her occasionally enough for him.

He pushed her tangled honey-brown hair back from her brow and smiled at her, and she smiled back langorously, like a sunbathing cat. Reaching with one hand he found without looking the bowl of black Corsican grapes beside the bed and detached a sprig, and leaning over her fed one into her part-open mouth.

'And are you happy, in your new life?' he asked her. Her eyes registered the question but she did not answer. She was always rather silent after lovemaking. 'Is there anything that you want? Anything that you miss?'

'I miss . . .' she said and stopped, consideringly. Henri prompted her with a 'Hmm?'

'I miss Héloïse,' she said at last, unemphatically. Henri slid another grape into her mouth and rolled over on his back, away from her, and ate the rest of the sprig himself. Marie-France sat up and spat the pips delicately into her palm. Henri glanced at her out of the corner of his eye, thinking how magnificent she looked: tall and shaped for love, with her creamy skin and full, rose-tipped breasts like a Grecian goddess, nobly formed but disconcertingly human. She looked at him and he slid his eyes away.

Then she said, 'You are angry with me for speaking of Héloïse.'

'No, not angry. I have sometimes thought you may be a little lonely. You have little company except for me.'

She was surprised at his concern, and shewed it, and he smiled ruefully and went on, 'I know what loneliness is. Ismène, my dear friend of half a lifetime, is dead, and I have no one to talk to, no one to tease.'

'You have so many friends,' Marie-France protested.

'I have many acquaintances, but no friends. Ismène was the one friend I could talk to without reserve, about anything. About everything.'

'You could talk to me,' Marie-France suggested tentatively.

'Could I?' Henri said, amused. 'What should I talk to you about?'

'Anything. About the Court, and your friends in the Cordeliers' Club, and the Assembly. Those were the things you discussed with Madame de Murphy, were they not?'

'You would be so bored,' Henri laughed.

'I would not. Tell me,' she said, settling herself back against the pillows with some more grapes.

'Shall I? Shall I tell you of the ludicrous attempt of the Assembly to convince the people that the King's escape was not an escape, but that he was kidnapped by "enemies of the revolution", as they put it? That was Ismène's old friends, Barnave and de Lameth, trying to reinstate the King. Barnave is afraid that the revolution may go too far and put the power and wealth of the land in the wrong hands. He made such an eloquent speech in the Assembly, begging for an end of the revolution before it degenerated into a general attack upon property; and property, as you may have gathered, is the principal concern of the Assembly. They and one or two others have left the Jacobin Club because too many of its members are now advocating the King's abdication. They've formed a new club – the *Feuillants* – who are dedicated to forming a government on the lines of the English government, a monarchy by the grace not of God but of Parliament. Well, there are worse forms of government I wonder what their chances may be of achieving it. They still do not seem to realise that once you have loosed the tiger from its cage, you are not in a position to request it to return behind bars. The tiger decides from then on – the tiger in this case being the mob – and I doubt whether it will decide to accept a chain round its neck and a very meagre share of the meat. What do you think, my love?'

'What do I think about what?' Marie-France asked a little indistinctly, being preoccupied with detaching a rather sticky grape-pip from her lower lip. Henri began to laugh. 'I was listening,' she protested.

'I know you were. My question was – what do you think you would like to do tomorrow? I feel I should spend more time with you, to stop you feeling lonely.'

She turned on him an expression of tender gratitude, and said, 'Oh Henri – well, tomorrow – I don't know. Oh, perhaps you might take me to the celebrations on the Champs de Mars. I expect there may be dancing and coloured lights like there were at the Bastille on the fourteenth. I should like that.'

Henri shook his head and groaned. 'My dear Marie-France, you are deplorably ignorant about the things going on in your own city.'

'It is not my city,' Marie-France protested, sticking out her lip. 'I am from Calvados.'

'You are a Parisian now. And the affair on the Champs de Mars tomorrow is not a celebration of the fall of the Bastille, it is to be a protest against the monarchy. They have set up what they call "the Altar of the Nation" – one of the deplorable things about these revolutionaries is the way they manage to make their greedy concerns sound like religious crusades – and on the Altar will be a petition demanding the abdication of the King, which they will invite the assembled masses to step up and sign.'

'Oh,' said Marie-France blankly.

'Yes, very much "Oh"! My new friend Brissot and my old friend Danton are behind it. They are the coming men, I think,' he added thoughtfully, and fell into a silence, from which Marie-France roused him at length.

'Then I think perhaps I should like to go for a drive, Henri, if you would not mind it.' He grunted assent, and rolled over towards her to draw her down again, but now she was thoughtful, and though she did not precisely resist, he was provoked to ask her after a moment what was wrong. She hesitated, and said, 'Have you not noticed anything, Henri? Have you not noticed that something which should have been with us has not arrived?'

He caught her drift, and frowned, trying to calculate. 'In all the excitement of the King's escape, I must have lost count. How long ago should our friend have begun the visit?'

'It is three weeks now, Henri,' she said. 'It may yet be nothing, but I thought at least you should know as soon as possible.'

There was no missing the anxiety in her voice, though she tried to speak matter-of-factly.

'It's early days yet,' Henri said, and then thought: *a child? a son?* His only son had died in infancy many years ago, a few days before his wife. He would have been thirteen now. The old, obsessive loneliness rose up in him like the empty pangs of hunger, hunger of a man who had always devoured money and position and the amusements of fashionable society, and found they left him unsatisfied. If Marie-France were to prove pregnant, he did not think he would be angry. He might even find himself looking forward to it. 'Don't worry,' he said aloud. 'I shall always take care of you.'

The Parisians, who liked to give titles to things, were soon talking about the Massacre of the Champs de Mars. Huge crowds had gathered to walk up to the Altar of the Nation and sign the petition, and six thousand signatures had already been added when the National Guard, ten thousand strong, under the command of Lafayette, arrived with the orders of the Paris Commune to disperse the meeting. In the ensuing struggle, the Guard opened fire, and sixty people were killed or wounded, and a further two hundred were arrested, and the leaders of the republican group were forced to go into hiding. For a time things settled down, and the National Assembly hastened to complete the drawing up of the Constitution which, when the King had signed his assent to it, would mark the end of the Assembly's span. It would dissolve, and elections would then be held for a new Legislative Assembly which would put into operation the schemes the National Assembly had devised.

One of the rules that had been formulated about the new Assembly was that no-one who had served on the first Assembly would be eligible to be elected. All the deputies would be new men; ambitions and hopes ran high. Brissot, popular in his own *département* as well as in Paris for his oratory and his revolutionary journalism, was sure to be elected, which meant, in turn, that his friends and protégés would be the people to know that autumn.

On the sixteenth of September the King signed the royal assent to the Constitution at a formal ceremony in the Manège, where the Assembly had taken to meeting because there was a little more room there than in the council chamber. He was then formally reinstated as head of government, and the National Assembly dissolved, its work done. There was a mood of optimism in Paris that the worst excesses of the revolution were over, and that everything would return to normal under the new Legislative Assembly, which could settle down in peace to do its work of bringing about the Golden Age in France.

In this atmosphere of hope, there was to be a royal performance at the Opéra, which Queen Marie-Antoinette was to attend, on the eighteenth of September, and Charles Nordubois, by the use of a little influence, managed to obtain a box for the performance for his wife and himself. The other two seats he offered to his wife's intimate friend, Henriette-Louise de Stuart, and the young lawyer who was always haunting his house, Henri Olivier Vendenoir.

Héloïse dressed in great excitement for the first public engagement of her majority – for she had celebrated her fourteenth birthday in August. Her gown was a triumph of her own devising, inspired by Henri's acquiring, in his mysterious way, some lengths of very fine, thin, burgundy-coloured velvet, a material not much in fashion in recent years but which, Héloïse felt when she handled it, could not be matched for its tactile splendour. The finished gown was low-necked and high-waisted, with a long, full skirt worn over a false-rump of moderate size. It was opened at the front to reveal a petticoat of burgundy-and-gold striped silk, and the long, tight sleeves were decorated at the wrist with a cuff of the same material. Héloïse's luxuriant hair hung in ringlets to her waist at the back, the front hair being curled up and puffed out, and the ensemble was topped off by a ridiculous small hat of silk and muslin with three plumes dyed to match the gown.

But the glory of it, as far as she was concerned, and the

inspiration for the whole thing, was the necklace of rubies which Papa had given her the week before.

'It is your birthday present, Marmoset,' he had said, kissing her tenderly as he gave her the little box. 'I am sorry it is so late, but I had to send it a long way from Paris to have it reset.'

Héloïse opened the box and drew out, to her breathless delight, a necklace of gold set with rubies so rich that they glowed in her hands like drops of blood, lit from within with a life of their own.

'They belonged to the Queen,' Henri told her, taking advantage of her speechlessness. 'Never mind how I obtained them – quite above-board, I assure you, only it is better you don't know. But I thought I ought to have them reset, just in case anyone recognised them and wanted to know how you came by them. They are very fine stones.'

The rubies were strung on fine gold chains to hang in gracefully drooping curves, and they glowed against Héloïse's tender flesh as revealed by the *décolletage* of her new gown. On the evening of the opera she took her place in the box aware that more eyes were upon her than simply those of her own party, though Lotti stared at her with open admiration, Charles with a certain amusement, and young Vendenoir like a man lightly stunned. There was not another gown like hers in the house, nor rubies so fine about any neck; but as much as anything it was the arresting quality of her face, and her enormous, lustrous, magnetic eyes that drew smiling attention to her, and made her escort suffer some of that same confusion engendered by the beauty of Chenonceau.

There was a long delay, filled with rustling and chattering sounds, as if a flock of exotic birds had roosted in the tiers of the opera house, which ceased abruptly as the Queen appeared at last in the royal box. Héloïse heard Lotti exclaim in surprise to her husband, 'Why, she has powdered her hair!' and Charles reply, amused, 'No, dearest, no powder. Her hair has gone quite white since Varennes.'

And then someone in the pit cried out '*Vive la Reine!*' The cry was taken up, and soon the opera house rang with cries of '*Vive la Reine!*' and '*Vive le Roi!*' just as it had for centuries, and the Queen raised an elegant white hand to the crowds, and bowed her white head and smiled graciously. It was a wonderful moment. Héloïse found her eyes full of tears, and feeling Olivier's hand close beside her own was seized with the desire to squeeze if comfortingly, because after all, the revolution had taken place without him; it was all over, and he had missed it. The back of her fingers touched his for an electric moment, before they were withdrawn by the necessity of lifting her back skirts out of the way as she sat down.

The opera was by Mozart, and Héloïse enjoyed it enormously. Afterwards, Charles took them all to a fashionable restaurant nearby and they had a very elegant supper, featuring the first oysters since the summer, and roast pheasant, and goose-liver patties, and a delectable baked ham from Germany, and Héloïse drank her first champagne and liked it, and glowed across the table at her companions like an illuminated Madonna.

The next morning she was sitting alone in the breakfast parlour – for Lotti had not yet risen, and Charles had long since gone to his work – eating her morning bread and chocolate, and petting Bluette, who had successfully stormed her lap, when much to her surprise her father was announced.

'Papa, I did not think you were ever up so early,' she said. 'Will you have some breakfast?'

'I breakfasted long ago, chick,' Henri said, amused, 'but you may order some coffee for me.'

Héloïse did so, and when they were alone, Henri stretched out his legs and said with a smile, 'I understand you enjoyed your evening.'

'Who told you so? Yes, I did, very much.'

'I have spoken this morning with your escort of last night. He was lavish, my child, in his praise of you. I think you quite surprised him with your velvet gown.'

'No one had anything like it, Papa, and the rubies looked so--'

'Yes, no doubt,' Henri stemmed the flood of enthusiasm, 'but I rather think young Vendenoir's admiration was for you, not for your dressmaker. He had not thought you so grown up.'

Héloïse made no answer, and her blush, as she lowered her eyes away from her father's smiling ones, was not all pleasurable.

'You know, don't you, that I have been looking for a suitable husband for you, child?'

'Yes, Papa,' she said, subdued. He cocked his head.

'You do not sound very interested. Come, child, you knew you would have to be married, and sooner rather than later.'

'Yes, Papa. Only – I hoped you would not find anyone until – for a long time.'

He took her hand. 'Listen to me, little cold-hand. You think the troubles are over? Don't think it! Papa knows better. Things are going to get more difficult, and you must have someone to protect you.' Her eyes were raised to his, but he anticipated her objection. 'Not me, dearest – someone young and vigorous! I promised you I would find you someone young and handsome if I could, and I think I have found you someone for whom you have already a certain affection – am I right? You have seen a great deal of Vendenoir this summer, while he has been winding up Ismène's estate. Would he not be more agreeable to you, as an acquaintance of your childhood, than a complete stranger?'

'I am to marry Olivier Vendenoir?' Héloïse tried to analyse her feelings, but a hot embarrassment was all she seemed capable of. One thing to chatter to a man, to go riding with him, or sit beside him in the box at the opera; quite another to enter with him into the intimacies of marriage. No, she was not sure it would be easier thus; she was not sure it would not be easier to do such things with a compete stranger than with someone she had known for several years. 'Does he want to marry me?' she asked suddenly, meeting her father's eyes. His expression was veiled, thoughtful – she thought, even, a little sad.

'Any man would want to marry you, Princess,' he replied, and though Héloïse did not press him further, she was aware that the answer had been – and was meant to be – evasive.

8

The fact of the matter was, that though Vendenoir had not been difficult to persuade, his reasons for marrying Héloïse were financial rather than personal. He began his interview with Henri by stating firmly that he had no intention of marrying yet, and ended by accepting a large dowry and naming a date early in October. It had not been necessary for Henri to press too vulgarly, for Vendenoir not only had his debt to Madame Dupin to repay but was also, despite his republican principles, an expensive young man, with political ambitions which also came expensive. His reluctance stemmed only from a desire to impress upon Henri that in the new society of equals, a rising young lawyer who would one day be a deputy or a minister was easily a match for an ex-count's daughter.

Henri went away from the interview with his emotions held well down. There was no harm in the boy, and he would of a certainty go far. He would not be elected to the Legislative Assembly this October, for there was an age qualification which disbarred him; but as a protégé of Brissot, he would be given some official position, and go in as a deputy next time. Yet if things had been otherwise, Henri would have been angling for a far more glittering fish for his adored child, and would not have noticed the existence of an estate-manager's son from the provinces.

He was determined at least that the wedding should be a splendid occasion, even if it did have to be conducted by a Juring priest. During those peaceful days in September and the beginning of October he went about his preparations cheerfully and with an open purse, rousing enthusiasm in everyone at the rue Montmartre. Since Héloïse had no maiden home, she was to be married from there, and Lotti and Johann Finsterwalde flung themselves into the preparations with a will, the former helping Héloïse with her wedding-clothes, and the latter helping Henri to prepare the house in the rue Saint-Anne to receive the happy couple afterwards. Charles Nordubois watched from a safe distance, but even he was inspired to offer to conduct the two ladies around the cloth warehouses in his carriage.

One afternoon Héloïse and Lotti were returning in the carriage with their maids, Charles having been called away on business, from a warehouse in Clichy. As they were passing the Opéra, they were held up for a moment by a fiacre in front of them turning right into the narrow rue Boudreau, affording Héloïse, who happened to be looking out of the window, a view of the occupant, a handsome young woman in a sea-green pelisse and a jaunty hat decorated with cock's feathers.

'What a love of a hat,' she was commenting, when suddenly she froze, and beat with the end of her parasol on the roof of the carriage, crying, 'Turn right, turn right, after that fiacre!'

'Héloïse, what is it?' Lotti asked in alarm. The carriage stopped, and Héloïse let down the window and leaned out to call to the coachman,

'Turn down that street – please hurry!'

The coachman said something unintelligible, and behind them the driver of a cart shouted something quite intelligible and comprehensively insulting, but Héloïse had now seen that the fiacre had stopped, and calling a hurried excuse over her shoulder to Lotti, she opened the carriage door, jumped down, stumbling a little but recovering herself, and actually *ran* down the narrow side-street, holding her skirts clear of her ankles and hearing a confusion of voices behind her, some concerned, some jeering. Lotti, sure that her friend had suddenly gone mad, poked her head out of her side of the carriage and ordered the coachman to follow her. The coachman assured her that this would be a dangerous and all-but-impossible manoeuvre, and a crowd of idlers began to gather about the promising scene.

But Héloïse had sped along the side-street to reach the house just as the fiacre was drawing away. The front door was in course of being closed by a young and rather grubby footman, and catching a glimpse beyond him of a sea-green pelisse mounting the stairs within, Héloïse arrested the door with an upraised hand, gasped, 'Pray excuse – friend – haven't seen her for years . . .' and pushed past him, running up the stairs, and reaching the top as the green pelisse was about to open the door of one of the rooms that let off the landing.

'Marie-France! Oh, I am so *glad* to see you!' Héloïse cried, as the woman in the green pelisse turned in surprise, and paled a little at the sight of her former friend. For a moment Marie-France could think of nothing to say, and Héloïse, thinking perhaps her more grown-up friend disliked her manners, apologised, while holding out both her hands in delighted welcome.

'I'm sorry to burst in so, but I saw you in the fiacre, and was afraid I would lose you. I jumped out of my carriage and ran after you – the footman was just closing the door – I ran past him – not his fault. Oh Marie-France, I have missed you since you went away! What are you doing in Paris? When did you arrive? Why did you not let me know you were coming?'

Marie-France found her hands taken, and almost despite herself she smiled down at her eager little friend, though the barrage of questions were all unanswerable. Fortunately for her, Héloïse answered some of them herself.

'You cannot have been here long, or you would have called on me. Is your guardian here? I wonder you should ride in a fiacre – has he no carriage? I do not think you should, Marie-France. But I love your hat! It was that which attracted my attention.'

'I meant to call on you,' Marie-France said, since at last an answer of some sort was required by Héloïse's running out of breath. She stepped back to the length of her arms and looked her friend up and down approvingly. 'But you have grown up, Héloïse. Not a little girl any longer, but a smart young woman. It suits you, dearest.'

'I am to be married next month,' Héloïse said shyly. Marie-France raised an eyebrow. 'Oh, do come to the wedding – won't you? You know my poor aunt died, and I have so few people of my own to ask, only Lotti. Say you'll come.'

'My dear,' Marie-France frowned, and when Héloïse's face fell, she said gently, 'I don't think your father would like you to invite me.'

'But why not? He knows you were my very *best* friend. Why should he not like it?' Marie-France shook her head, and Héloïse, looking around her for the first time, realised that none of her questions had been answered. 'Is it your guardian? Did he bring you here? Do you think Papa will not like him?'

'I have not come with my guardian,' Marie-France said in a low voice, wondering desperately what to say.

Héloïse was looking puzzled when several things happened. From within the room which Marie-France had been about to enter came the sound of a distinctly masculine cough. Marie-France, realising that the door was not quite shut, reached across to the handle to pull it to, releasing into the air a little puff of cigar-smoke from within the room, and revealing, as her pelisse fell open, the outline of her swollen figure under her high-waisted gown. Hot blood rushed to Héloïse's face as her rapid thoughts sorted the information, but she was quick-witted enough to say in a natural voice as Marie-France completed the movement and turned back to her:

'But you have a visitor . . . I am so sorry, it must be inconvenient to have me bursting in on you like this. I will go at once – but please, dear friend, may I call on you again?' Marie-France hesitated, looking down at Héloïse with a mixture of doubt and regret and longing, and Héloïse took her hand and pressed it and smiled reassuringly. 'A morning visit – a formal call? Tomorrow morning? I do not know why you think Papa will not approve of your husband – for it is with your husband you have come to Paris, is it not? – but if I do not tell Papa, and you do not tell your husband, we may surely meet again?'

Marie-France returned the pressure, and nodded, but before she could say anything further, Héloïse gave her a farewell smile and nod and ran back down the stairs and let herself out into the street.

The episode had been so brief that as she walked back towards the main road, the Nordubois carriage was still trying to manoeuvre itself round the corner. The coachman, seeing her, gratefully abandoned the problem, and the footman jumped down to let down the step for her, and Héloïse had time to press back the tears that wanted to spring, and compose herself to say cheerfully, as she climbed in beside Lotti: 'How mortifying! I thought it was someone I knew, and rushed after her to claim her acquaintance, and then found myself facing a complete stranger. I'm sorry, Lotti, I must have shocked you. Please forgive me.

'I thought you had gone mad,' Lotti said frankly. 'Do drive on, Merlot, before these carters die of rage.'

As soon as they were back at the house, Héloïse excused herself and ran upstairs to her room, dismissing the maid with a distracted wave of the hand, waiting only to be alone before pulling off her bonnet and pelisse and flinging them and herself down upon the bed. Face down, her head in her arms, she sought darkness and solitude to come to terms with the unwelcome new knowledge.

In that one moment of illumination, when she had recognised the cough and the smell of cigar-smoke as her father's, a dark country had been revealed in harsh and unrelenting detail; things half-seen, un-guessed-at, were made plain. They had lied to her; *he* had lied to her, her father, her beloved, revered, trusted, godlike Papa. Marie-France was his mistress, and pregnant, and the whole story of her guardian sending for her had been concocted – by whom? – simply to deceive Héloïse and keep her from the truth. All this had been plain in that lightning-flash moment, and only her lifelong training in restraint and courtesy and consideration for others had kept her from crying out, had enabled her to ease her friend's embarrassment and allow her to make a dignified exit.

And now, what did she feel? She tried to push the shocked numbness aside to determine what grieved her. The frailty of her friend? But no, it was not that – she had inherited enough of her mother's practicality to know that for Marie-France the choices would always have been limited, and there was nothing in her that could blame the other girl for choosing the life of the *apartement meublé* rather than that of the cloister, though it would not have been *her* choice in the same situation. Besides, loving Papa as she did, how could she blame Marie-France for loving him too?

Tears burned her eyes as she thought of him. Yes, here was the heart of it. She felt betrayed. He had betrayed her by lying, deceiving, plotting – not simply to take a mistress, but to take away her best friend, and to keep her from her. There had been a part of her which wanted her father to be perfect, and now she had discovered him in error, that part of her was wounded and struggling. Deceived, betrayed! it cried. Oh Papa, how could you? She shed hot and bitter tears, and wondered how she would ever be able to meet his eye again. She thought of the reproaches she would utter, tried to imagine his response.

'You have grown up, Héloïse. Not a little girl any longer – '

The voice her memory offered her was not Papa's, and with it came the remembered image of her friend's face, the mixture of regret and longing with which Marie-France had regarded her. It must have been a hard choice for her, Héloïse thought with quick sympathy. And Papa – ? Ah, that was harder. He was, as she knew, as she had always known somewhere deep inside her, an imperfect man, a sinner, one who liked things to be easy sooner than right, one who would sacrifice principle for comfort. You have *known* this, she addressed herself sternly; how then are you wounded?

A child no longer. She turned her searching eyes further inward. Part of her inner world, which she had created for her own comfort, had been changed; and her self-esteem, ah yes, that had been bruised! *Know thyself*, her training bid her. Yes, it hurts, to discover that two whom you love have been deceiving you – it hurts your pride!

She struggled for a long moment more, and the images that flickered through her mind were of her peaceful childhood in the convent, the little garden-court, the silent corridors where nothing disturbed the drifting dust-motes, the dark and peaceful parlour where she had read her devotional works, hearing through the half-open window the drowsy drone of bees amongst the gillyflowers. She thought of vespers in the tiny chapel, the small stars of candle-flame and the mingled smell of incense and lilies from the altar. Childhood was over, and an unknowable adult future stretched ahead of her. Marie-France was her friend, Henri her father, and nothing about them was changed. It was she who must change, mould her love to fit them as they were, not try to make them fit the shapes she wished for them. She sat up, dried her eyes, straightened her shoulders like a small soldier, and found that everything was all right after all. She had made much of little, she told herself, as she jumped up and went about tidying herself for her reappearance downstairs. She would love Papa just as before, and go on seeing Marie-France, and somehow it would all be all right.

All the same, as she turned the handle of the door, she hesitated, and glanced back over her shoulder with an unbidden pang of sadness, as if she might see behind her the golden world of her childhood receding into the darkness of the past, like something seen from the window of a speeding carriage.

Marie and Lotti and Lotti's maid Cécile had finished dressing her, and had left her alone for a few moments' private reflection while they went to complete Lotti's toilette; but she had had no time to begin before a tap at the door roused her, and her father came cautiously into the room.

'May I speak to you for a few moments, dearest?' he said.

'Of course, Papa,' she said turning to face him, and for a long moment he could only stare at her.

Her gown was of embroidered cream satin, opened at the front over a petticoat of gold brocade; the broad waistband was of gold brocade, and the bodice of cream satin was softly gathered and ruched about the neckline, drawn up by pale golden rosebuds. Her hair was completely covered by a long veil of delicate gauze, held on to her head by a coronet of the same pale-gold-coloured roses. Within its frame her face looked suddenly fragile and ageless, like that of a mediaeval angel-carving, and the expression of her great dark eyes was too much to bear. Oblivious of her dress, Henri suddenly strained her to his breast, cradling her veiled head amd murmuring. 'You look like a princess – too good for him! Oh, my child! You should have been a duchess at least.' After a moment he controlled himself and set her back from him, straightened her crown of roses, and forced himself to smile. 'You *will* be a countess one day, whatever revolutionary government rules us, and don't you forget it. And if he does not make you happy, he will have me to answer to.'

'Yes, Papa,' Héloïse said calmly. 'I'm sure you have done what's best.' He looked at her for a long moment, but there was no fathoming what might be going on in her mind. He gave himself a mental shake, and drew out from his pocket a box which he opened for her.

'Your mother's pearls,' he said. 'A bride should wear pearls. I meant to give them to you before, but somehow I kept forgetting. Let me fasten them on for you.'

'Oh, Papa, they are beautiful,' Héloïse exclaimed, examining them in the mirror. 'Did you give them to her for her wedding?'

Henri was too old to blush, but not too old for the question to be unwelcome. 'Yes, my love,' he answered, and to change the subject went on to the other matter he had come to broach. 'Perhaps your wedding-morning is rather late to be asking this, Marmoset, but I wonder whether Lotti has spoken to you at all?'

'Spoken to me, Papa?' Héloïse was puzzled. Henri coughed.

'I wanted to be sure, love, that you understand what marriage means.'

'I don't perfectly understand the question,' Héloïse said after a moment.

'Being married, dearest, involves – well, certain physical intimacies,' Henri said with difficulty. 'As you were brought up in a convent, naturally you – I should have asked Lotti to – has she spoken to you about it?' Héloïse continued to look puzzled. 'Explained what will take place – afterwards.'

Héloïse shook her head. 'I think I know what you mean,' she said shyly. 'Lotti sometimes looks sly and laughs about – about – sharing a bed with Charles. Is that what you mean, Papa?'

Damn the woman, Henri thought. Why didn't I think to ask her to – 'Yes, love, that is what I mean. It's something you should have been told about, only you have no mother, and I – well, it isn't something a father can discuss. I don't want you to worry, however. I'll have a word with Vendenoir – yes, that's the best thing. Don't be anxious about it, will you, Marmoset? It will be perfectly all right.'

Héloïse looked through the tangle with her clear, straightforward gaze, and said, 'I'm not afraid, Papa. After all, every human being in the world except Our Lord was brought about that way, so it must be all right, mustn't it?'

Henri kissed her forehead in gratitude. 'Yes, love. Of course.' He turned to leave her, pausing in the doorway only to say, 'You are very beautiful, child. It will be a lovely wedding.'

Héloïse had privately wondered whether the cathedral would seem terribly empty, but as she walked in on her father's arm out of the sunshine and into the candle-pricked, incense-smelling darkness, she saw to her relief and delight that there was enough of a crowd to satisfy even a proud person. All her father's friends, both the old ones from the Court circle, and the new ones from the Jacobin and Cordeliers' Clubs, had come; there was a wide circle of acquaintances of Finsterwalde and Charles Nordubois; and Olivier's own friends and some of his relatives from the Cher valley.

Olivier waited for her at the altar, looking tall and well built and even handsome in his wedding clothes, an embroidered peacock-blue coat and white satin breeches. Héloïse's eyes were too dazzled from the sunlight to recognise the guests as she walked past them, but coming to rest beside her husband-to-be she was able to see in the front row on the bride's side the familiar, comforting faces of Lotti and Charles and Uncle Johann, and on the groom's side the grotesque, battered visage of Danton beside his pretty wife Gabrielle, and fair handsome Camille Desmoulins with his delicate wife Lucile.

It seemed to take only a few moments to change her into Madame Vendenoir; then they took the Blessed Sacrament and then they were walking out to the sound of bells to the waiting ribbon-bedecked carriage which was to take them to the house on the rue Saint-Anne where the wedding breakfast was prepared, and where they were to live together, man and wife. Héloïse risked a sideways glance at her husband as the carriage clattered and swayed over the bridge, for he had not spoken to her yet, except in the formal language of the wedding service; but he was looking straight ahead, not exactly forbiddingly but not encouragingly, so she held her peace.

At last the carriage drew up in front of the familiar facade, and Héloïse, looking out of the window, could not help exclaiming in delight:

'Oh, it has all been repainted! It looks so smart! And there is dear old Jacques – and Abby – and all the servants! Oh, how wonderful – Papa has got all Tante Ismène's servants back! It will be like going home.'

'It is home – your home,' Vendenoir said, breaking his silence at last. Héloïse looked at him shyly

'Yours too,' she said. He gave a tight smile.

'By *your* courtesy. It is in the marriage settlement – didn't your father tell you? He insisted – the house and furnishings are to remain your absolute property.'

'Oh,' said Héloïse.

'Oh indeed,' Vendenoir said. 'It seems your father does not trust me.'

'I didn't know of it,' Héloïse faltered. 'But I am sure it is not that he does not trust you. Oh, Olivier – please don't be cross. We must be happy on our wedding day.'

It would have taken a hard man to resist the large pleading eyes and the small outstretched hand, weighted by the new gold-and-diamond wedding ring. He swallowed his bruised pride, took her hand, and kissed it.

'I'm not cross,' he said. 'It's just that it is an unusual arrangement.'

'Yes – but we shan't mind it, shall we? I expect Papa wanted me to have something of my own, but we shall think of it as *our* house, shan't we?' Vendenoir was not required to reply, for as the carriage door was opened and the step let down by the footman, a violent outburst of barking and a brown-and-white flurry of movement distracted his bride. 'Oh, there's darling Bluette! Yes, yes, I love you too. Get down, you bad dog, or you'll mark my gown. Oh how pleased she will be to be living here again, Olivier! I can't wait to see what Papa has done inside – he has been so secretive, and Uncle Johann would not tell me anything either, except that it is all new and splendid.'

The wedding breakfast was laid out in the dining room, and those guests who had not been invited, through lack of space, to dine, joined them afterwards in the large drawing-room on the first floor. Between rising from the table and joining the party in the drawing-room, Héloïse found time to make a quick tour of the house in her father's company to see what he had done.

It had all been redecorated and refurnished, though there were one or two pieces that Héloïse recognised, those items of furniture that had belonged to Tante Ismène in her own right. The rest of the furniture had been chosen and arranged by Henri with his own genius for creating interiors, which before had always been used in the service of other people, for profit. Now he had created a house for Héloïse, and she gazed and marvelled and asked again and again, 'Oh, where did you get *this?*' – a question which Henri declined to answer other than by a smile. Some of the furniture was new; others were fine pieces he had acquired in the process of helping the fleeing nobles to escape to safety abroad.

'We must not stay away from your guests any longer,' he said after a while, 'But I do want just to shew you one more place: your own private boudoir and sitting-room.'

It was the small drawing-room that Tante Ismène had used for her salons, but it presented a very different appearance. The green silk which had covered the walls had gone, and three of them were now papered with a very elegant, modern, Chinese paper. The fourth wall was covered with a sixteenth-century Flemish tapestry, whose green background over the years had taken on a blue tint which went very well with the Chinese paper. The oak parquet floor had been polished to mirror brilliance, and the centre portion was covered with a thick Chinese carpet of white decorated with blue. There was a sofa and several chairs, newly covered with a smart blue-and-gold striped silk; two japan-lacquered commodes with bow fronts, and an ormolu-inlaid ebony side-table; Delft and blue Chinese vases and bowls everywhere; and on the chimney-piece, where Tante Ismène had had a bust of Voltaire, there was a charming biscuit group of Cupid Disarmed offering a basket of flowers to a naked nymph.

In the boudoir next door was a boat-bed with gauze hangings, two gilded rose-pink armchairs, and under the window, a charming *bonheur-du-jour* with Sèvres inlay in circular medallions depicting different flowers. Henri guided her to this and pointed out the largest, central one, on which was a painting of a marigold. Around the edge was the motto in Latin: *Quae non mortalia cogis*.

'The marigold is you – and your motto. It says, "What human heart can you not conquer?" Héloïse turned glowing eyes on him. 'It belonged to the Duc de Vesle. He had it made for the Queen, when she was expected to visit, just after her wedding, but the visit never took place. It has a secret compartment. I will shew you the trick of it. You may one day need a secret place to keep things.'

Héloïse looked at her father with some doubt. 'It is lovely,

Papa. Everything' – she waved a hand to comprehend the boudoir and the drawing-room – 'Everything is lovely, but . . .'

'These two rooms will be above all your place, your own place to be private in.'

'Papa,' she went on firmly, 'was it quite right to insist that the house and furnishings should be my property? It seemed to me that Olivier was upset by the idea.'

Henri took both her hands and looked down into her face seriously.

'Listen to me, child. Above all, you must be safe. I have done the best for you I can. You know why I chose Vendenoir for your husband. But things may change again. No-one knows what the future may hold. I am trying to cover any eventuality. That is why you must have things which are yours, and yours alone.'

'I don't understand,' Héloïse sighed after a moment, 'But I'm sure you must be right. I love my house, Papa, and everything in it. Thank you, with all my heart.'

He kissed her, and led her away. 'We must go back to your guests, and dance, and be merry. I wanted these last few moments alone with you; but from now on you belong to your husband.'

Héloïse assented to the notion by her silence, but inwardly she laughed at the very idea of Papa's giving her up to anyone.

Much, much later she lay propped on the pillows in bed, waiting for her husband to join her. Not the boat-bed, this, with the rose silk counterpane and gauze drapes, but the huge canopied bed hung with red sarsenet of the main bedchamber, which she and Olivier would share at least for the first month. He climbed in beside her in his bed-gown and cap, and she was suddenly cold with fright at the unaccustomed proximity of an almost naked male body. Olivier, his ears still ringing with the 'talk' he had had with Henri, in which his assertions of Héloïse's youth and innocence had contained barely-veiled threats of what he would do should Olivier shock, hurt or frighten her, looked at her for a moment doubtfully. She seemed, in the unrelieved white of her bed-gown, so very young, and small even for her age, with her thin little body and the large melancholy eyes too big for her face. What must be done must be done – but how to approach the matter? He was not inexperienced, but all his adventures so far had taken place with older and extremely willing partners. How to broach a convent-bred virgin of fourteen he could not in the least imagine; he had no idea, even, how much it was likely to hurt her; and if she cried, what would he do then?

It was Héloïse who took control of the situation. Despite her apprehension, she had a streak of her mother's down-to-earth Parisian practicality. She slipped a small cold hand into Vendenoir's somewhat sweaty one, and said:

'I think I should like it better, husband, if you were to put out the light. Just this once, if you wouldn't mind it?'

'Of course,' Vendenoir said gratefully, and snuffed the candles, plunging them into all-embracing, safe darkness. In the dark it was so much easier to gather her into his arms, to caress her, to kiss her shy mouth and whisper that he would be careful to try not to hurt her. She did her very best to co-operate, though it seemed a clumsy, gross and painful business. In the dark it was easier to bear the extraordinary and outrageous intrusion of what seemed like a very large portion of his anatomy into a very small and delicate part of hers. He did hurt her, and though she tried not to flinch she could not help drawing her breath sharply; and as the burning pain got worse, she had to hold back her tears. It seemed monstrous to be being hurt like this, and it was difficult to dissociate in her mind the infliction of pain from anger and disapproval: she felt as though he were punishing her, and had to make herself remember Lotti's sly-eyed laughter, and tell herself that she would probably get to like it, though she simply could not imagine how.

At last it seemed to be over. Olivier eased himself from her, hurting her again in the process, and whispered something kind, and settled himself to sleep. She waited until his breathing had grown regular before she found her handkerchief to blow her nose and dry her eyes, for she did not want him to know she had been crying, and then she lay sleepless in the dark for some time, wondering and doubting and trying to rearrange her thoughts to accept this extraordinary new aspect to her life. After a long time her tears finally stopped, and she began to feel drowsy, and as she settled herself cautiously into a more comfortable position to sleep, Olivier put his arm across her and his face to hers to whisper,

'I'm sorry, Héloïse. It won't hurt so much next time, I promise.'

The kindness warmed her, and the arm and the warmth of his breath were comforting. At once things seemed better. She whispered, 'It's all right – really,' and, relaxing against him, went to sleep.

One day in March 1792 Henri called at the house in the rue Saint-Anne, and was shewn up to 'madame's sitting-room', where he found his daughter enjoying a band of sunshine that fell across the room, tranquilly sewing a baby's shirt, with Bluette asleep in her lap. She put her work aside with a smile as Henri came in, and would have risen, but he said:

'Don't disturb yourself, my love. And above all, do not disturb Her Majesty!' Bluette, as if recognising her title, raised her head and beat her fringed tail softly in greeting, but declined further to exert herself.

'I must disturb her if I am to ring for refreshments for you,' Héloïse smiled.

'I do not require anything,' Henri said.

'But I do, Papa, so pray ring the bell for me.'

Henri did as he was bid, and then seated himself where he could look at her. He was not entirely satisfied with what he saw: she did not seem blooming to him. To be sure, it had been a hard winter – the number and ferocity of the bread-riots had been testimony to that – but Héloïse looked pale and peaked to his fatherly eye, too thin in the face, and with something in the expression of her eyes he could not like. A faint anxiety, or restlessness, was it?

'You do not look well, child,' he said abruptly. Héloïse laughed, and folded her hands in her lap, like a proper little matron. She was wearing a high-necked, closed gown of slate-blue wool, unrelieved except for a scrap of lace at neck and wrist; her richly coloured, long-fringed Persian shawl had fallen from her shoulders on to the back of the sofa; and her hair was plaited at the sides and fastened up under a starched linen cap whose three layers of lace did not manage to make it look frivolous.

'I am perfectly well, Papa,' Héloïse said calmly. He frowned.

'And I do not like to see you wearing caps. What is it has got into you, Marmoset? You are behaving like a matron of thirty. I thought to find you out riding or shopping or making assignations with your lovers, not sitting there sewing . . .'

His eye took in what it was she had been sewing, but at that moment the footman entered in answer to the bell. Héloïse ordered coffee to be brought for herself, and wine for her father, and a selection of cakes and sweetmeats suitable to the time of day, and Henri, thinking that if he nibbled something, much as he detested sweet things, she might eat too, which would be an advantage, forbore to protest. When the servant had withdrawn, he said,

'I see you are making a baby-shirt. Is that why you are looking pale? Can it be that you are with child, my love?'

She heard the suppressed eagerness in his voice, and a flicker of sadness crossed her face. 'No, Papa,' she said. 'Do you think I would not have told you if I were?' She looked down at the linen to hide her eyes. 'Baby-shirts are always needed – by someone, somewhere. I like to sew them because they are quickly finished, and one has something to shew for one's labour.'

Henri was not unaware that this was so much subterfuge, but mistook the cause.

'Has Vendenoir . . . is Vendenoir doing his duty by you?' he asked darkly.

'Oh yes – of course, Papa,' Héloïse said expressionlessly. The nights together in the red-hung bed were her dread. Sometimes he came in so late that she could pretend to be asleep, but otherwise he did his duty by her with a regularity she could well have forgiven him, especially as she was now sure he did not derive much more pleasure from it than she. Though she did not tell him, he still hurt her – not as severely as at first, but still burningly, bruisingly, so that afterwards she must lie very still or wake the pain. She hated the messy, clumsy business; it made her cry as much with humiliation as with physical distress, and from what she had gathered from the servants and other matrons, it would not be likely to cease until she was with child. Then she might sleep apart from him until the child was old enough for her husband to want another.

But there was no sign of a pregnancy. Her monthly flux arrived with a regularity which was both disappointment and relief – for at least during the five days of its course she was spared Olivier's attentions. If only she could conceive, she would be quite happy, for everything else about married life she enjoyed. She liked governing her small household, and ordering what she liked to eat; she liked driving out with her maid beside her, with the greater freedom accorded to a married woman; she liked shopping and taking tea with other matrons; she liked dining at the foot of her own table, with her husband at the head and his friends to either side. But the anticipation of the nights cast a shadow over the days, which Papa, who loved her, could evidently see in her face.

'Don't worry about me, Papa,' she said firmly. 'I have been a little too confined to the house, that is all. I shall be well enough when I have had some fresh air. I shall take Prestance out tomorrow, when Lotti comes back.'

'Oh yes, she has been visiting her brother, hasn't she?'

'Yes, with the children, too. I shall be glad to see them again. I miss my little Clothilde.' She saw her father about to comment, and realised that the topic of children was best avoided, and said hastily, 'But tell me all the news! I am sure there must be something exciting. You always hear everything before I do.'

Henri got up and walked about the room. 'Let me see – I suppose you know that the Queen's brother, Leopold of Austria, is dead?'

Héloïse laughed. 'Oh yes, and the Romans have sacked Carthage! Really, Papa, I am not so isolated as that! His son Francis succeeds him, but I know nothing about *him*. Will it make a difference to us?'

'I think it will, Marmoset,' Henri said grimly. 'He is a young man, and no grey-bearded diplomat like his father. He is hot-headed, and aggressive, and will not hesitate, I feel sure, to give his support to Artois and the *émigrés*.'

'Well, that should please Olivier, at least,' Héloïse said calmly. 'He would like a war.'

'Aye, don't I know it,' Henri said, turning on her. 'What the

Devil are these madmen after – your husband and all Brissot's little clan? War with Austria? It is unthinkable! Our armies are all to pieces – the officers have deserted – no veterans to salt the ranks. And the national debt no smaller than it was when the Third Estate used it to lever the nobles out of power.'

'Oh, you don't understand, Papa – this is not to be the old-fashioned sort of war. This is to be a crusade of the most elevated character.' Héloïse said. 'Monsieur Brissot has explained it all . . .'

'Yes, I heard him in debate, addressing the Assembly,' Henri said bitterly. 'Quoting Plutarch and Horace. *Dulce et decorum est, pro patria mori.* The sacrifice of life – the spilling of blood – so noble, so thrilling, as long as it is someone else's.'

'Papa, you are so cynical,' Héloïse said. 'Brissot believes that a war will consolidate the people as nothing else, make us one country, purge away impurities and vice that had grown up during the ten—'

'Ten centuries of slavery,' Henri finished for her. She smiled at him.

'I forgot you had been there. You remember it word for word, just as Olivier does – but then he hears it all so often. They talk about nothing else, you know. A war to purify the people, so that they will drive out the enemies of the revolution who corrupt them. A war to carry the gift of freedom to the other enslaved races of Europe. A war fought without any desire of conquest—'

'Spare me,' Henri said, putting his hands over his ears. 'I know all the arguments. But tell me, love,' he went on anxiously, 'do you believe all this rhetoric?'

'Believe it? I don't see that it is for me to believe or not believe. I am Madame Vendenoir. I receive his friends, and applaud their speeches. Where does belief come into the matter?'

'Thank God,' Henri said. 'Listen to me, child: this talk of war and the people is all nonsense. The disciples of your Brissot want war because it will give them power, and if Austria paves the way for them, all the better.'

'If it gives power to Brissot, it will be good for the friends of Brissot, won't it?' Héloïse asked, meeting his eyes levelly. 'Friends like Vendenoir – and you, Papa?'

Henri sat down again, and said quietly, 'In the short term, perhaps. But in the long term – if you put a sword into the wrong hands, it may prove impossible to take it away again.'

Shortly after her father had left, Héloïse was interrupted by more visitors, whom she received in the drawing-room proper, amid much hugging and kissing and a great deal of noise.

'Oh, it seems forever since I saw you!' Lotti cried, knocking her hat askew with the violence of the embrace she bestowed on Héloïse. 'Paris is such heaven after Leipzig, you can't imagine! Everyone is so dull, and my brother needs must marry the dullest of them all: Anna Strelitz, one of our cousins on my mother's side, limp and white and fat, like a maggot, and already she is fancying herself ill, so what Ernst will do for company I can't imagine. Oh, and the fashions! Ten years out of date! Such wigs, such panniers – twenty different colours to every toilette, stripes and spots and ribbons and frills every-where. They look like Bartholomew tents, blowing about in the wind. I am so glad to be back! I shall never, never leave France again, I promise you!'

Three-year-old Mathilde was noisily claiming Héloïse's attention, wishing to display her new dress and tell her adven-tures, and Uncle Johann was eager to bring to her notice how well Karellie had learned to walk during the winter, and how much he had grown, as witnessed by the fact that his skirts were now a good inch above the ground, and Héloïse was longing to hold 'her baby', and had to exclaim to anyone who was listening that Clothilde was as heavy as lead and was certainly going to be the beautiful one of the family.

More refreshments were brought, and the level of noise low-ered as Lotti explained that they had been back two days but hadn't had a moment even to send word, because of the unpack-ing and the fact that the roof had leaked during the winter and quite ruined two of the bedchambers.

'I thought you were not to return until tomorrow,' said Héloïse, passing Clothilde back to the nurse in order to accom-modate Karellie, who wanted to climb on to her lap. 'Mathilde, please don't tease poor Bluette. I'm sure it would be your own fault if she bit you.'

'We travelled much faster than I expected,' Lotti said. 'There were such comings and goings at the border, I never saw so many soldiers, and Uncle Johann didn't like the look of it, so we didn't stop as we intended, but changed horses and did another stage before nightfall. Then the next day there seemed no point in not pressing on all the way to Paris, so we did. The children were so tired, they cried all the way, but it was worth it to get home.'

'I didn't cry,' Mathilde said stoutly, kicking the sofa leg rhythmically with her booted foot. 'Only the babies cried.'

'You were the worst of all,' Lotti said unsympathetically. 'You were sick. I dare say,' she added more kindly, 'it was the swaying of the carriage. But we reached home at last well after dark, only to find no beds ready for us, because of the leaking roof. But what is going on, Héloïse? Are we to have a war, as everyone says? I depend upon you to tell me everything. Uncle Johann is odious, he tells me nothing. For my own sake, he says. He was at the palace all day yesterday, and what is the use of that if he brings home no gossip?'

'It seems there will be a war,' Héloïse began cautiously, and Lotti cried in triumph:

'There, I knew it! I said it could be nothing less, with soldiers and horses and I don't know what, all marching up and down the border and filling every inn so that there was nowhere respectable to stay. But what a fool I am – I quite forgot! I have brought you a present, Héloïse.'

Lotti's interest in the war was so fleeting that the subject did not arise again during the visit. When the children grew too noisy and restless, she stood up to take her leave, and Héloïse begged her to sup with them the following evening, when some of Olivier's friends would be present. Lotti accepted the invitation, kissed her heartily, and ushered her brood out of the room.

Uncle Johann lingered behind, and when they were alone, he stepped close to Héloïse and took her hands and said in a low voice, 'My dear girl, there is something I must tell you, but I beg you will keep it the strictest secret. Tell no-one.'

'Very well, if you wish,' Héloïse said, surprised. 'What is it?'

'I was at the palace yesterday, as Lotti told you. I spoke privately with the Queen. You will not know – and no-one must know – that Fersen was there last week.'

'What!'

'Yes, he came in disguise, as an envoy from Sweden. He was with the Queen almost two days. He came to try to arrange another escape, but the King refused.'

'Refused? Oh, why?'

'Because he had given his word to the Assembly not to try to escape again,' Johann said sadly. 'He will not break his word – it is a point of honour with him. And the Queen will never leave without him.'

There was a silence as Héloïse absorbed the knowledge. On such a point, to insist on keeping his word! The last chance, then, was gone. 'But why did you tell me, Uncle Johann, if it is – as I see it must be – the most deadly secret?'

'Fersen brought a message, which he asked the Queen to pass on to you, by whatever means she might. I am the means.'

'A message for me? But – oh, can it be? It must be from--'

'Your Uncle Meurice, yes,' Finsterwalde said, smiling faintly at the joy he had awakened in her face. 'I am to tell you that he got safe away, and came at last to Sweden, where he was kindly received by the King, for Fersen's sake. He has been given a commission in the Swedish army – soldiering is all he knows, you see. He begs you to take care of yourself, and to forget him, until the day comes when France is free again and he can come home to embrace you in the flesh, as he does daily in his thoughts.'

He is safe, she thought gratefully. It was a small comfort, and since she had no great hope that the day when they might meet again would ever come, she had to be content with it. She smiled her thanks at the man who had brought her the news, whom she called Uncle Johann and who, she knew, would be glad to stand in the place that Uncle Meurice had occupied. Ironic, she thought, that neither of them was any relation to her: she was almost as much an orphan as poor Marie-France.

9

Héloïse dined alone that day, for shortly before the hour, Olivier came in with an air of suppressed excitement, and cried,

'Well, madame, do you know what day it is today?'

Héloïse had had many things to brood upon that afternoon, and amongst other things, her flux had begun, and she answered without thinking: 'It has come, Olivier – it began just after noon.'

He stared at her in surprise, and then frowned as he realised what she meant. 'Oh – yes, I see. But I was not meaning that, madame. I was referring to matters of mere national interest.'

Héloïse flushed. 'I beg your pardon. What is it that has happened?'

'The King has appointed Dumouriez as Minister for War, and has asked him to advise upon the appointment of the other ministers. Our moment has come, Héloïse!'

'Oh, yes, of course,' Héloïse said, trying to sound as excited as he would expect her to be. 'Dumouriez will advise the King to appoint his friends, of course.'

'It will mean a Brissotin ministry, and Brissot has already said that he wants the plum of the appointments, Minister of the Interior, to go to his old friend George-Jacques Danton! What do you think of that, madame?'

'Danton will not forget his friends, to be sure,' Héloïse said.

'There will be many a little plum coming our way now, Madame Vendenoir. Your husband and your father will be in the forefront.'

Héloïse was not sure that Papa would want to be in the forefront, but forbore to say so, murmuring only, 'I am so pleased for you, Olivier.'

'I must change my clothes and go back to the Cordeliers,' Olivier said, heading for the door. 'This is not the time for my face to be absent from sight.'

'You will not dine here, then?' she asked, faintly dismayed at the thought of an evening entirely alone.

'No, no, I shall stay at the club all evening. You will sleep in your own bed tonight, of course,' he added thoughtfully, pausing at the door. Héloïse nodded, trying not to look relieved, and he went on carefully, not quite meeting her eyes, 'This new development will mean I shall be very busy for some time to come. I expect I shall be home very late most evenings. Perhaps it might be as well if you were to sleep in your own bed all the time – for the time being, that is. So that I will not disturb you,' he added as a happy afterthought.

'As you please, husband,' Héloïse said, lowering her eyes. It was absurd in her to feel a ridiculous and paradoxical hurt. She had suspected that he disliked the business almost as much as she; why then should she not be glad that the one shadow over her life was to be lifted?

'Yes,' Olivier said hesitantly, looking at her bowed head. He felt oddly like a man who had struck a child. 'Well, then – so it shall be. Just for a little while.'

She did not look up, and he coughed slightly and made his exit, fleeing the complicated world of emotions for the more congenial one of politics.

Héloïse woke the next morning in her rose-pink boat-bed, and knew by the angle of the sun against the curtains that it was late. She rang, and Marie came in at once with her tray, and with Bluette bouncing at her heels.

'I let you sleep late, madame. I thought you were looking tired. Your chocolate and bread, madame.' She placed the tray, and went to open the curtains. Héloïse picked up her cup and sipped.

'Is monsieur up?' she asked drowsily. Marie's hand paused at the curtain for a second, but she answered in a matter-of-fact voice.

'Monsieur did not come home last night, madame. His man came in this morning for clean linen, and to say that he is going directly to the palace.'

'Oh,' said Héloïse. She put the tray aside, the bread untasted. 'I had better get up, I suppose.'

'Yes, madame. What dress shall I put out for you?'

Héloïse looked past her at the window, absently stroking Bluette's ears.

'What does it matter?' she said.

There was much to be done in connection with the supper that evening, for Olivier liked a good table to be spread for his friends, and today he would certainly be more eager than ever to impress. There must be two courses, with removes, and a dessert, even though they would all be placed at once, as it was supper and not dinner; and as March was not a lavish month for supplies, it would take ingenuity to choose the dishes.

The dessert would be easy enough, built up in a pyramid in the centre of the table, for there were always meringues and ratafias in the store, and a pupton of apples and a ratafia cream, or perhaps a cheesecake would suffice. A ham and a raised pie – Olivier favoured chicken-liver pie – would do for the removes; but the main dishes were more difficult to decide. She turned the pages of the receipt-book and pondered. Well, there were always pigeons – pigeons fricando with morilles and walnut pickles; or veal with an anchovy sauce would look well; and salt cod was a good standby, elegant enough done in a cream sauce with plenty of sorrel. Would there be enough eggs to do sweet rolls stuffed with eggs and bitter oranges, she wondered? Perhaps she should send out for a lamb or a sucking kid . . .

The precipitous entry of Marie interrupted her musings.

'That girl has come, madame,' she confided, her eyes very wide. 'The daughter of the concierge in the rue Boudreau, that you gave money to, to send word,' she added, seeing that her mistress had not yet caught up with her. Héloïse started up, dropping the book and narrowly missing Bluette, who was sitting at her feet.

'It has begun?'

'This morning.'

'I must go at once, then. You had better come with me. Go and order the carriage while I gather what I need.'

'Yes, madame. But madame – the cook and the housekeeper have not received their orders yet for tonight, and the cook is already very cross, saying that no-one can make a supper fit to be eat unless there is time enough, and he says--'

'Yes, I can imagine what he said. You had better call him

up. No, wait, he will only argue with me. I will write down a list of the dishes, and you can give it to him.'

'I, madame? But he will not care for that.'

'Oh, then give it to Jacques to give to the cook,' Héloïse said, writing frantically. 'Don't make so many objections, Marie, there is not time to argue.'

'Very well, madame,' Marie said, offended, and took the paper with an offended sniff, and flounced out.

Marie-France was still on her feet when Héloïse arrived at the Rue Boudreau, but was pale and sweating, more with fright than pain.

Héloïse came in briskly, a basket on her arm, and flung off her cloak in a businesslike way saying, 'Have you sent for the midwife? How long have the pains been going on?'

'Héloïse! What are you doing here? You should not, indeed you should not! Oh, pray, go at once.'

'You cannot think I have come all this way to be sent away again so easily,' Héloïse smiled. 'I shall stay with you until the child is born. Marie and I will prepare things while your servant goes for the midwife.' She directed a severe look at the untidy girl who was hovering near the door with her mouth open, and the untidy girl shrank back from the look, sidled out and bolted.

'Héloïse, you cannot stay. I am very glad to see you,' Marie-France said with an effort, 'but you must see it cannot be – oh!' She was seized by another pain, which prevented her from arguing further, and Héloïse took the opportunity to say:

'Please don't distress yourself, dear Marie-France. I must take care of you, at least until Papa comes. Have you sent word to him?'

'Your father? What can you mean?' Marie-France made a gallant effort, despite her inward preoccupation. Héloïse smiled.

'There is no need for that. Come, do you think I did not know? I heard him cough that day I first came here – and your *apartement* is always scented with his particular brand of cigars.'

'You have known all along?'

'All along.' She put on a capacious white apron and rolled up her sleeves. 'Now we must get busy. You are quite right to walk up and down, and you shall continue to do so while Marie and I make the bed. I brought a clean suit of linen in case you were unprepared, and all sorts of other things we may need, and all the baby-clothes I have been making for you these months past. Come, Marie.'

Marie-France stared in a mixture of amusement and gratitude at the little matron in her apron and cap, who looked almost like a child dressed up for fun, and yet who inspired her with a ridiculous confidence. Héloïse, stripping the bed, caught the look and smiled reassuringly. 'I was with Lotti all through her last delivery, and know just how things are done, so you need not be afraid to trust me.'

Marie-France laughed, and if it was a touch strained, it was at least laughter.

'Oh Héloïse, you are such a comfort,' she said.

At a little after five, Héloïse left Marie-France sore and exhausted, but otherwise clean and comfortable, tucked up in her bed and growing drowsy, and beside her in a wooden crib her new, red-faced baby, a boy. Héloïse herself, now that the effort and excitement was over, felt very tired, and hungry too, for she had taken nothing to eat that day. She left the room quietly, and was about to pass down the stairs when the door of the drawing-room was flung open and she was confronted by her father, looking dishevelled and very angry. He opened his mouth to say something that was clearly going to be explosive, and Héloïse forestalled him with a finger to her lips and a beseeching glance at the closed bedchamber door. Henri seized her arm and pulled her roughly into the drawing-room, leaving Marie standing outside apprehensively, shut the door, and shook his daughter, saying in a hiss:

'What the devil are you doing here, you minx? What do you mean by it? Don't you know that the rue Boudreau is not a respectable place? How did you find out about Marie-France? Don't you know what she is?'

'She is my friend,' Héloïse said firmly.

'Everyone is *your friend*!' he flared at her. 'You should learn some discrimination!'

'Don't shout – you'll wake her,' Héloïse said. His face grew ominously darker.

'I'll shout if I please – and wake whom I please! You little fool, don't you realise what you're doing? You are a respectable married woman, and respectable married women don't go visiting whores in their rented apartements.'

Héloïse went white. 'How dare you say that! Who was it made her a whore?'

For the first time in his life, Henri raised a hand to strike her, but the sight of her white, tense face prevented him from completing the gesture. He controlled himself with a vast effort, led her to a sofa and made her sit beside him, unaware that he was gripping her upper arm so hard it was hurting her.

'Don't let your soft heart betray you, Héloïse,' he said, trying to speak reasonably. 'Marie-France is not like you. She is not of your station in life, and she knows it, even if you do not. Don't tell me she did not try to stop you coming here?' Héloïse's silence was his answer. 'If she had been a lady, I should never have made her the offer I did, and she would not have accepted it. Your worlds are apart, and you must not try to cross them, or you will make nothing but trouble for everyone.'

Héloïse raised stubborn, rebellious eyes to his. 'We were brought up together, as friends,' she said.

'It is different now. You are respectably married--'

'But she will be respectable if you marry her,' Héloïse burst in. Henri gave a short, humourless laugh.

'Marry her? Are you out of your mind, child? I am not going to marry her.'

'But Papa, you must marry her, now there is the child.'

'The child makes no difference.'

'But . . .'

'Don't be ridiculous, Héloïse. I shall take care of them both, but marriage is out of the question. It was never *in* question.'

'The child,' she said desperately, gripping her hands together in her effort to make him understand, 'is my brother.'

The word let loose a flood of emotions in both of them, some at least of which were similar, and for a moment as their eyes met in silence it seemed as though there might be accord; but Henri's memories were not as Héloïse's. His life had been dark, and with many secrets and some shame. He remembered, unwillingly, how he had treated Héloïse's mother, how his darling child had been born a bastard and largely ignored by him for the first years of her life. Guilt made him angry, and he pushed her away from him, standing up abruptly and turning from her.

'You mind your knitting, my girl. You are getting a great deal too managing. I shall take care of my own in my own way, and you are not to visit again. I utterly forbid it. Now you had better go home – your carriage is waiting for you downstairs.'

Héloïse reached home in scant time to dress before the supper-party, and was spared all but a brief conversation with her husband. She had expected him to question her sharply on her day-long absence, but he had other things on his mind.

'The folly of it!' he exclaimed as they came together in the drawing-room just before the first guests arrived. 'I can't believe they can have been so foolish. It will be the very thing to drive him into Robespierre's arms.'

Perceiving in time that it was not her folly which was under discussion, Héloïse was able to ask, 'Who?'

'Danton, of course. It will drive a wedge between the two halves of the party. I have never seen him so furious, and you know what he is like when he is in a rage.'

'But what has happened to him?'

'Nothing has happened to him, that is what is wrong! He was to have the Ministry of the Interior – everyone said so. Now the news has come that they have given it to the milksop Roland.'

'Who is Roland?'

'Oh, *you know*. The fellow on the correspondence committee of the Jacobin Club. Lives at the Hôtel Brittanique, holds those salons – or rather his wife does. Mark my words, it's she who's behind this. She's as ambitious as the very Devil, and she loaths Danton – thinks he's a rough, vulgar man.'

'Well, so he is,' Héloïse said reasonably.

'Maybe, but he's worth ten of Roland – or Madame Roland,' Olivier snorted, as the butler entered to announce the first arrivals.

The supper party went as well as could be expected, given that Héloïse was very subdued, and awkward with her father, and that Danton and his wife, understandably, were absent.

Camille Desmoulins and Lucile had come, and spent the evening mourning over their friend's misfortune, when Lucile was not discussing domestic matters with Lotti. Olivier and Charles Nordubois had a vigorous three-cornered conversation with Olivier's lawyer friend, Antoine Saint-Just, about the war they were now sure of bringing about, to which Charles contributed an unexpected knowledge of war-machinery and military engineering. Héloïse, unable to speak to her father, since the only subject that came to mind was one they both wanted to avoid, listened to this conversation with half her attention. She decided very quickly that though Saint-Just was an exceptionally handsome young man, she did not like him: there was an unpleasant arrogance about him, and when some social necessity made him turn to smile at her, it made her shiver, for there was something inhuman about his eyes.

The talk of war presently engulfed them all, and Héloïse was surprised to hear with what detached enthusiasm Charles spoke about it, as if, she thought, it were a game played on paper, how many men could one kill in a given time with the least expenditure of ammunition. She saw at once how well he and Saint-Just were getting on, and how, while Olivier's passion for war was hot, theirs was steely-cold: Saint-Just's a cold desire to further his cause without regard to the means, and Charles's a cold desire to extend his knowledge and experience to the arts of war, and to invent the perfect gun.

It was not a party that Héloïse was to look back on with any pleasure; and when the guests were gone, she had to face the postponed trouble with her husband, which she had hoped she had entirely avoided.

'Where were you all day?' he demanded of her angrily. Héloïse's mouth was dry, and she was trying to pick the rights words when he went on, 'And you need not trouble to lie to me – my coachman at least is loyal to me.'

'I was not going to lie,' Héloïse flared up, her pride touched. 'Why should I lie about visiting my friend?'

'She is not your friend,' Olivier said scornfully, 'she is your father's mistress. A nice sort of wife I have got myself, who has no more sense of propriety than to go visiting her father's whore! What would people say if they knew where you had been? And what would become of my career? I don't suppose you thought of that, did you? But then, you always felt yourself too good for me, didn't you?'

Her eyes stinging with tears at this unjust attack, Héloïse could only stammer. 'I did not – I have never thought . . .'

'I gave you the protection of my name,' Olivier went on, ignoring her protests, 'and, by God, you seem to need it! I don't know how you thought you were going to behave if you married one of your own sort, but as my wife you'll behave decently, and not make my name a butt of gossip. You will not visit that woman again, ever, nor write to her, nor receive her, nor speak of her. Do you understand?'

'Even if my father marries her?' Héloïse cried.

'Don't be a fool, madame. Men don't marry their mistresses. And if you had any sense you wouldn't even speak of it. If he married her, the child would disinherit you – or are you too stupid to see that?'

'I don't care about that,' Héloïse cried passionately.

'Not care if you lose all your father's property?' Vendenoir snapped. 'You should care! Why do you think I married you?' There was a stricken silence, and Héloïse stared up at him, her pale cheeks bearing one flaming spot of colour. 'I'm sorry,' he said quietly. 'I shouldn't have said that.'

'Why not? It's true,' Héloïse said, turning away. He caught her by the arm to turn her back, but when her chin went up and her flashing eyes met his, he let his hand drop quickly.

'I meant what I said,' he said evenly. 'You are not to visit her.'

She met his gaze burningly. 'I thought everyone was supposed to be equal in this new nation of yours.'

'Not as equal as that comes to,' he said grimly.

War was declared with Austria in April 1792; the French soldiers marched over the border into the Netherlands; and Charles Nordubois was given a position in the Ministry of War at a handsome salary. The Brissotins were triumphant, but not for long. The deficiencies in the French army were soon displayed: at the first meeting with the joint Austrian and German forces, it was horribly routed by the veteran general the Duke of Brunswick, and by the end of the month Lafayette was suing for peace. Anti-Austrian and anti-German feeling led to demonstrations in Paris. The Queen was reviled in every pamphlet and news-sheet, and even Charles's new appointment did not prevent his wife's uncle from being attacked in the street, and hostile slogans from being daubed on the walls of his house.

Héloïse hurried over to stay with Lotti for a few days, for she was almost hysterical with fear that her favourite uncle would be murdered if he stepped out of the house; and Henri took advantage of her preoccupation to remove Marie-France and the baby from the rue Boudreau, for he had no faith in Héloïse's obedience, or in his mistress's ability to discourage her. On a hot day in April a hired chaise drew up outside a small, plain house in the rue Papillon, in the Poissonnières district, an area which Henri knew from his youth but which he was fairly sure Héloïse would never pass through. The house was three storeys high, the ground floor being occupied by the concierge, Madame Buffon, and her family, and there were attic rooms for the servants up in the leads.

Madame Buffon, stout in rusty black, with a white cap and the apron and huge bunch of keys of her trade, came hurrying out as the chaise stopped and a group of urchins gathered round it. Behind her came her idiot son, over six feet tall and strong as a tree, but with the brain of a six-year-old, and as Henri opened the door and jumped out to let down the step, he could hear madame's tongue running full spate.

'Welcome, welcome, M. Morland! No, no, you must not let yourself out – it is not seemly. Jean, don't stand there like an ox, let the step down for monsieur! There now, he has been obliged to do it himself! What a hen-witted statue you are! And you children, be off at once, staring like that! Jean, hold the door and help madame out. Ah, monsieur, this is your poor niece, is it? Poor, sweet lady, how tragic for her. Those wicked Austrians! At Lille was it, monsieur? Ah, a soldier's widow will always be welcome, when her husband has given his life for his country. Come in, come in, madame . . .'

'Cotoy,' Henri supplied, handing down Marie-France, and glad that her habit of deep mourning included a thick and completely enveloping veil, for even through her black kid gloves he could feel her shaking with laughter. 'Thank you, Jean, I will help madame. You see to the boxes.'

'That's right, Jean, do as the gentleman bids you. Not that you need to fear him, madame, for he is as gentle as a kitten, though God saw fit to give him so much strength of body and so little in his attic. This way, if you please. I've had all the rooms aired, though with this hot weather there wasn't a trace of damp in any of them. Very pleasant rooms, I'm sure you'll find them, and newly painted only two years ago.' She led the way up the stairs, clanking and panting, to the first floor, which had its own front door opening off the stone-staired close. 'Here you are, directly in the dining-room, and the drawing-room is through there. And upstairs of course the two bedrooms, and in the attics there are three servants' rooms, ample I should think, until madame is ready to think about entertaining again, but of course, that won't be for some time yet.'

'It is very nice, madame, I'm sure,' Marie-France said in a low voice, which hinted of suffering bravely born. Jean loomed massively in with two of the boxes dwarfed by his huge hands, and behind him, looking apprehensively at his back, came the nursemaid with the baby in her arms.

'And this is the dear little baby!' Madame Buffon cried, darting at the maid who took an instinctive step backwards into the wall. 'Oh, the moppet! What a little pigeon! What a little cabbage! What is he called, madame? After his father, I dare say.'

'His name is Morland,' Marie-France said, suppressing her mirth. Madame Buffon looked enquiringly at Henri.

'After me, madame, as his nearest surviving relative, and his godfather.'

'I'm sure,' Marie-France added, 'that is what his father would have wanted.'

'Of course, madame,' Madame Buffon said warmly. 'Well, little Monsieur Morland Cotoy, you must grow up big and strong so you can look after your mama, and be a soldier like your papa.' Her eyes filled with tears as large and shiny as her buttons. 'A posthumous child, I understand, madame! How tragic. How very affecting! I vow it makes me feel quite overcome!' She put a hand to her huge bosom and sighed, only to snap back to normal like a whiplash as her son put down a box clumsily and marked the wallpaper. 'To be sure, Jean, you grow more imbecile by the moment. Go downstairs at once and

175

bring up the other boxes. Is this your maid, madame? Upstairs, girl, don't stand mooning about. I believe in being strict with maids, madame,' she added confidingly as the lady's maid, another new girl, scuttled towards the stairs with a bandbox, 'otherwise they are nothing but trouble. And never let them out at night, if I may be so bold as to advise, madame, or they'll bring you back more than they went out with.'

She left them in peace at last, and when the maids had gone upstairs, taking the baby with them, Marie-France was finally able to throw back her veil and fall, laughing, into Henri's arms.

'I thought I should die when she warned about the maids!' she gasped.

Henri wiped his eyes. 'I never knew you were such an actress, my love. Those affecting sighs! The tremulous voice!'

'I have missed my vocation,' she said, releasing herself and straightening her hair. He took her hand and kissed it.

'I don't think so,' he said, smilingly. 'I must leave you now, but you are in safe hands.' He met her eyes gravely for a moment. 'You know it had to be this way, don't you?'

'I know,' she replied. 'I always agreed upon the necessity.' But when he had left her, she stood where she was in deep thought for a long moment, and when roused by the sound of the baby's voice raised in protest, it was with a long sigh.

Downstairs Henri had not far to seek Madame Buffon before returning to his coach, for she was lurking in the doorway like a large black spider, and it took the minimum of movement for the coins in Henri's hand to find their way into her palm.

'You take care of her for me, won't you, madame?' Henri said, and though the old eyes of the concierge were sharp, she nevertheless gave him a sentimental smile and a cock of the head that was almost winsome.

'You hardly need to ask me, M. Morland, indeed you don't. She's a sweet young thing, just the sort of young woman I would have liked for a daughter, had God not sent me nothing but sons, and if I can't take care of a widow of one of the heroes of the revolution, then you may hang me from the nearest lamp-post, for I'm a patriot through and through, poor sweet pretty thing. You don't have to pay me to keep an eye on her.'

'Thank you, Madame Buffon. That was exactly what I

thought,' Henri said, and bowed a farewell to her as the coins passed from her hand to her pocket and out of sight for ever.

On the fourteenth of July there was a public celebration in the Champs de Mars, which the King and Queen attended, and afterwards the Nordubois gave a grand dinner and ball for all their friends at the house on the rue Montmartre. The heat of the summer was oppressive, and they decided for comfort's sake not to dine until seven, by which time they hoped it might be cool enough for their guests to enjoy the splendid dinner they had planned. In spite of the shortages and soaring prices caused by the war and the long run of bad harvests, the table was spread with a superb array of meats and fishes, delicacies and made-dishes, and afterwards meringues and creams and custards and fruit-tarts by way of dessert, the whole washed down with quantities of iced champagne.

'See Madame Roland asking for lemonade,' Uncle Johann murmured to Héloïse, who was next to him at the table. 'She used to serve nothing but sugar-water at her salons before Roland went to the Ministry. Now I believe they have graduated to weak tea. "Taste without profusion, amusement without frivolity," she used to say. How Madame Dupin would have loathed her!'

'How un-Parisian, at least,' Héloïse murmured in return. 'Frivolity is the one thing we Parisians do well.'

'Not the only thing,' Uncle Johann smiled at her. 'Your toilette, for instance, is delightful: taste *with* frivolity, I should call it. This high-waisted business is the latest mode, is it not? Where did you get the material?'

'Papa got it for me – but he would not say where,' Héloïse said. 'There is never any profit in asking Papa where he gets things. But it *is* lovely, isn't it?' She smoothed the stiff folds of pale-apricot-coloured taffeta lovingly. The dress was high-waisted with a full skirt over a false-rump, and had long, close-fitting sleeves with four tiny buttons apiece. The low-cut, tight bodice was visible through an overjacket to the waist of almost transparent chiffon. 'Though I would not precisely say it was frivolous. I hope Olivier does not think so – he would not like that.'

'He is a fool if he does not think you the prettiest woman in the room – and your bonnet is *definitely* frivolous, say what you will,' Uncle Johann said, intercepting the glazed duck as it passed him and cutting himself some slices.

'It isn't a bonnet,' Héloïse laughed, 'it's a turban.' It was of yellow satin and decorated with three long, curled ostrich feathers and a bunch of artificial cherries that bobbed over her right eye when she nodded her head. 'I am rather pleased with it, though. I contrived it myself, Lotti and I have found a wonderful stall in the Champs Élysées where they sell all sorts of cunning trimmings for hats for almost *nothing*, and you know with the right trim you can make over a hat ten times without anyone's ever noticing.'

'Well, I hope it is not wasted on your husband, that's all,' Uncle Johann said severely. 'I have been watching him across the table, and you know he has been talking to Charles on one side and Saint-Just on the other, right across the ladies actually next to him. I wonder if he even knows they are there.'

'I doubt it,' Héloïse said lightly, though Uncle Johann's quick ear detected a note of sadness. 'He is so very busy at the Ministry of Justice, he never thinks about anything but the government and the state of the country and the war and – that sort of thing.'

'It must be lonely for you when he is away at his office all day, and at the club all evening,' Finsterwalde said gently.

'Lonely for Lotti, too, now that Charles has his appointment in the Ministry of War,' Héloïse countered.

'But she at least has the children.'

'Yes,' she said flatly.

'And me.'

Her lips curled upwards in a smile. 'Yes, and how lucky she is! I'm sure that you, at least, tell her what is going on. Olivier only ever tells me bits of things, and when I can't make sense of them, because he hasn't told me enough, he gets impatient and says women can't understand such matters. Papa used to explain things properly, and I never had any difficulty in understanding, but I see so little of him nowadays,' she sighed.

'Have some of these rolls stuffed with asparagus before they all disappear' he said, helping her from the dish that had come their way, and looking at her with quick sympathy. 'You know that your father isn't deserting you, don't you?' he said quietly. Her dark eyes met his questioningly.

'It is very bad?' she asked.

'I think so,' he replied. 'You remember in June, when the mob broke into the Tuileries?'

Héloïse shuddered. 'Of course I do. It was horrible. I could hear the shouting from my house. It must have been a miracle that the King and Queen weren't hurt.'

'It was,' he said grimly. 'But do you know why the mob broke in?'

'Because the King dismissed Monsieur Brissot and his friends, and they wanted them restored to power. And it worked,' she added thoughtfully, 'because he did.'

He untangled her grammar without difficulty. 'In a nutshell that is true, but it is not the whole story. The original disagreement arose because of Madame Roland's pet scheme for raising an army in the provinces and bringing it to keep order in Paris.'

'Yes, the *fédérés*,' Héloïse nodded. 'I can't understand why the mob should have wanted them.'

'I doubt, dear one, if they did. The invasion of the Tuileries was not a spontaneous uprising, you know. It was organised to achieve that end it did achieve.'

Héloïse's eyes grew round, and she dropped her voice instinctively. 'No, Uncle Johann – surely not?'

'Smile, *hertzlich*, and look light for a while – we are being observed,' he warned, as Olivier frowned across the table at them. Héloïse stitched a broad smile across her face, and turned to exchange a few light words with the gentleman on her other side about the excellence of the dinner. When a safe interval had passed she returned her attention to Johann, who continued with the story.

'Yes, I'm afraid it is true – but what is worse is that others can and will use the same weapons to achieve their ends. You have heard of Marat?'

'Everyone has heard of Marat, though Olivier will not permit me to read any of his news-sheets . . .'

'They are not news-sheets, they are rantings of the most violent and horrible sort, and your husband is quite right to prevent your reading them,' Johann said sternly. 'But the fact is that he and his sort control the men of the gutters, and power

179

is passing out of the hands not only of the Assembly, but of the Commune too. Did you know that forty-seven of the forty-eight sections have voted for the King's abdication? And that many of them have sent deputations to the Assembly saying that if *it* won't take action, they will?'

'Action?' Héloïse asked faintly.

'They have seen that the Tuileries can be invaded,' he said.

Héloïse was silent a long while, and then said, 'Papa once said that if you loose the tiger from its cage, you are in no case to ask it to return behind bars. Oh Uncle Johann, does papa know this? And Olivier? Can nothing be done?'

'Your papa knows it; and there is worse. I tell you because you are a sensible girl, and you ought to be warned, so that you can take steps to make yourself safe – yes, and Lotti too. There's no point in my telling her – a dear girl, but feathers between her ears.' He smiled, and Héloïse felt herself smile too, though she knew not how. 'The Brissotins know that power is slipping into the hands of the wild men, the *enragés*, and they are in the process of loosing a tiger of their own, in the hopes that the one will kill the other. They are calling up this army of *fédérés*, to summon it to Paris. God knows who they will recruit – I doubt that it will be sober citizens. When it arrives . . .' He shrugged, and Héloïse caught herself thinking, irrelevantly, that he had grown a little French of late. Then he patted her hand. 'You are very young, little one, to be burdened with all this, and perhaps it will pass over, this storm. But be ready, that is all I ask. If the time should come, I will do everything I can to get you and Lotti and the children away. Be ready.'

She nodded. 'I'm not afraid,' she said. 'I know Papa will keep me safe; and I have you, too.' It was not until some time afterwards that she realised she had not included her husband in her list of protectors.

BOOK TWO

The Garb

On her cheek an autumn flush
Deeply ripened; – such a blush
In the midst of brown was born,
Like red poppies grown with corn.

Sure, I said, Heav'n did not mean
Where I reap thou shouldst but glean.
Lay thy sheaf adown and come,
Share my harvest and my home.

Thomas Hood: *Ruth*

10

William Morland first went to sea at the age of twelve, in 1775, and for the next twelve years he served continuously in His Majesty's Navy, hardly setting foot on shore until the end of the American war saw him, like so many, paid off. The sea was his chosen career, and he never ceased to solicit Their Lordships for a commission; but in time of peace, with nine out of ten ships laid up in ordinary, it needed more than long service and professional ability for a half-pay lieutenant to feel a deck under his feet again: it needed luck, and that intangible force, interest.

He was never averse to making a trip to London, where he might badger the Lords of the Admiralty more effectively in person than by letter; and in March 1792, his father having business in London but being unwell, William offered to undertake it for him, and posted down to London in good spirits. Learning that Lady Chelmsford and his sister Mary were at Chelmsford House, he called in at Pall Mall at the first opportunity to pay his respects.

'I did not think to find you here so soon,' William said when the flurry of greetings was over. 'It is before your time, is it not? I thought you would still be in Bath.'

'Oh, Bath was monstrously dull!' Flora said. 'No-one there that one knew, and the rain made it intolerable, mud everywhere – so depressing. So we came up early, and I must say I am glad we did, for it seems everyone else had the same idea, and Town is full of friends.'

'How is everyone at home?' Mary asked.

'Papa is unwell,' William said. 'That is why I have come to harangue the Customs House on his behalf. Ned offered, of course, but he does not really like to leave everything at this time of year, with lambing so late this year, and the mares coming into season.'

'And James?' Mary asked. William shrugged.

'James avoids Morland Place as much as possible, because

every time he appears Mother talks about marriage. I wonder she doesn't just arrange something for him – I dare say he would not actually defy her. But then she is worried about Papa, of course.'

'Is it serious – Papa's illness?'

'He's seventy-seven, Mary – everything's serious at that age,' William said with a shrug. Mary frowned.

'You are the most abominable cold fish! What is wrong with him?'

'The old trouble: he won't leave things to other people, but must do everything himself. He overtaxes his strength. But if you are contemplating posting home, there is no need. I don't think he is in immediate danger. So tell me, how do you amuse yourselves in London? Is Charles here? Have you seen John Anstey?'

'John Anstey? Has he come up, then?' Mary asked.

'To take up his seat in Parliament,' William said. 'Mother said she had written to you to tell you he had been elected.'

'Yes, I know that, but we haven't seen him yet. I dare say he will call some time,' Mary said with studied indifference. William grinned to himself, and Flora said hastily:

'Charles is being perfectly odious, talking nothing but politics all day long, and spending his time at the House of Lords and the Palace, and going to White's every night, though he hates gambling. Fortunately one of my old flirts is in Town – Hannibal Harvey – so I am doing my best to make Charles jealous.' She sighed. 'Not that it will work – Charles will never notice. He is too sure of me.'

'Hannibal Harvey – *Captain* Hannibal Harvey?' William asked eagerly.

'Yes – do you know him, then?' Flora said. 'He was a friend of my poor Thomas.'

'I have met him many times. He was in Gibralter in '90 when I was there,' William said, pleased. 'He is an excellent fellow. I should be glad to shake his hand again.'

'Well then, you shall,' Flora said good-naturedly. 'Come to dinner tomorrow. Mary and I were to have a flirting dinner, with Captain Harvey and Lord Tonbridge, but now I have a better idea. We shall have a naval dinner instead. It is a long time since I entertained all my old friends, and I know that

Charles has a social debt to repay to Sir Henry Martin – the new Comptroller, you know, William, just taken over from Middleton. That will make sure Charles dines at home, and actually *sees* me flirting with Captain Harvey, because otherwise I cannot think how I shall ever get him to notice me.'

'Well, ma'am, but are your naval friends respectable?' Mary asked solemnly. 'I am afraid Hawkins will give his notice if he is obliged to open the door to a crowd of threadbare, leather-faced old tars.'

'Really, Mary!' Flora cried. 'How can you speak of our nation's heroes like that? But you are quite right about Hawkins. I shall invite some admirals to keep him sweet. Lord Hood will come for sure, and I'll ask Black Dick. He is staying at the Golden Lion, and I know for a fact that they haven't a drop of claret fit to drink in their cellars.'

'Who, pray, is Black Dick?' Mary asked, and both her companions turned shocked eyes on her.

'Why, Lord Howe, of course,' Flora said, and William added,

'Admiral Lord Howe, to be sure.'

'Ah,' said Mary, 'I see I shall be a fish out of water at thi dinner. I shall just have to shrink into a corner with Lor Tonbridge and talk of fashions.'

'I shouldn't count on that, Polly,' William said with a grin. 'Didn't you know that he is godson to Cuthbert Collingwood, who is Hannibal Harvey's particular friend?'

'I wonder should I invite Captain Collingwood as well?' Flora mused.

'As he lives in Northumberland, ma'am,' William smiled, 'I think it would prove too expensive a dinner for a captain on half-pay.'

'On half-pay, is he?' Flora said. 'In that case, I should not want him. It would not do to have two of you competing for attention.'

Flora, Lady Chelmsford's first marriage had been to her cousin Thomas Morland, a sea-captain. His father had been in the navy too, and had risen to flag rank before his untimely death, and Thomas had been killed at the battle of Chesapeake Bay in the American war while commanding the *Daring*. Flora had helped him to obtain his commission, for she had a large acquaintance amongst admirals and naval lords. She hoped now to be able to use her influence to advance her brother William's career.

Despite the shortness of the notice, she had no difficulty in assembling her chosen guests: she was a popular hostess, with an excellent cook, and Charles's cellar was second to few. Around the dinner table the talk naturally revolved around the American War: Lord Howe had been commander-in-chief for part of the campaign: Hannibal Harvey had been a young captain on the West India station; Admiral Hammond had been Captain Hammond of the *Achilles* during the battle of Chesapeake Bay; and William had been a midshipman on the *Daring* when Thomas Morland fell. Everyone had something to contribute; familiar names were tossed back and forth – Rodney, de Grasse, Parker – and the ships which were as much characters as their officers to these sailors – the *Hinchinbroke* and the *Shannon* and the dear old *Bellerophon*, which they called 'Billy Ruffian'.

Later in the drawing-room, when the tea had been brought and Lord Tonbridge had hastened to be the one to hand Mary her cup, she leaned towards him with a faint, conspiratorial smile, and said, 'You know, these hardened old tarpaulins are as sentimental as girls when it comes to ships. They speak of their former commands as if they were childhood sweethearts, with a sigh and a moist eye, thus.' She demonstrated, and Lord Tonbridge choked over his tea. 'It makes me realise,' she went on, 'how tedious hunting talk must be to people who do not hunt.'

'Are there such people?' Tonbridge said, raising an eyebrow with an air of mild shock. 'I must say, I am glad I don't know them.'

'*I* am glad Lady Chelmsford does not make a habit of holding naval dinners,' Mary said.

'But she did it for the best of reasons.'

'Yes, to help William, and I hope it may do him some good, for otherwise he will never be made post, unless there is another war.'

'He and Lord Howe seem to have a great deal to say to each

other,' Tonbridge said, nodding towards the fireplace where Black Dick and tall, blond William were blocking the heat from everyone else.

'Doesn't Lady Chelmsford's china look absurdly delicate in William's huge hands?' Mary murmured. 'The more I see my brother, the more sure I am God meant him for the quarter-deck.'

'You have an acerbic tongue, Miss Morland,' Lord Tonbridge reproved. 'I hope it will never be turned upon me.'

Mary was not obliged to answer, for Captain Harvey came up to them at that moment.

'I come to take refuge with you, Miss Morland, from my wounded feelings. I have not spoken one word with our hostess since we left the table, and now look at her, flirting with Admiral Lord Hood so outrageously that he looks ten years younger! I could almost believe she invited me here tonight expressly to make me jealous.'

'Quite wrong, captain,' Mary replied. 'She invited you here to make Lord Chelmsford jealous.'

'Ah, was it so indeed? then she is rightly served, for he has not looked her way once! Lord Tonbridge, I believe my friend Collingwood is your godfather? I have not seen him in an age. I trust you can give me a comfortable report of him?'

'As comfortable as any captain without a ship can be,' Tonbridge replied. 'I hear you have been fortunate enough to be continuously employed since the war ended?'

'Fortunate is the word,' Harvey said with a bow, 'though things will be better for all of us as soon as the government decides on a war with France. This new revolutionary government . . .'

'Oh, if you are going to talk of war, I shall excuse myself at once,' Mary said. 'My father has been predicting it these two years past, and nothing ever comes of it. And William speaks of it as though it were to be arranged for his own personal benefit.'

'Quite right too! But it is a shocking thing to bore a lady,' Harvey said. 'What shall we talk of instead? Let me see . . . were you at the play on Saturday, Miss Morland?'

'No, sir, I was not at the play. I was in Bath, as you very

well know, since we had not been arrived an hour before you presented yourself on the doorstep,' Mary said severely.

'Well then,' he went on unabashed, 'shall you be at the play tomorrow? Do let me offer myself as your escort, *dear* Miss Morland. I believe it is to be the *dullest* play in the world, and that the farce will be quite *odious*, and that *everyone* will be there.' He put on the languishing air and affected voice of a society lady, and pretended to fan himself rapidly like the most obvious sort of flirt. Mary could not help laughing, though she saw that Lord Tonbridge was a little put out by it.

'Go away at once, you odious creature,' she said, 'and stop making fun of me, or I shall tell Lady Chelmsford all your dark secrets, and you'll never be invited to dinner again.'

Harvey lifted his hands in surrender. 'What, pay for my own dinner every night? You could not be so cruel to one of England's sailor heroes! Besides, my bill at Fladong's has got so large I dare not shew my face there, and a naval officer cannot be seen dining alone anywhere else.'

'Oh, you are breaking my heart! Go and persuade Lord Chelmsford to take you to White's. I believe the First Lord dines there on Tuesdays,' Mary retorted.

Harvey laughed, and bowed, saying:

'I see my hostess has torn herself away from Lord Hood, so I shall go and ingratiate myself with her. By the by, when I passed Lord Howe just now, he was asking William if he could make it convenient to call upon him at the Admiralty tomorrow, so it looks as though the purpose of the dinner has been served, and you may now be as rude about the navy as you please.'

Lord Tonbridge watched him walk away with a frown, and then said to Mary,

'Do you find Captain Harvey's manner rather too free, Miss Morland? I hope he did not offend you by being too familiar?'

Mary heard the jealousy under the controlled question, and smiled to herself, but said evenly, 'His manners are very open, but I do not think there is the least intention to offend. He is an intimate acquaintance of Lord and Lady Chelmsford, and since he calls here every day, I see a great deal of him. I think he regards me rather in the light of a favourite niece.'

Lord Tonbridge considered the dashing air and dark, gypsyish good looks of Captain Harvey, and the fact that he could not be more than ten years her senior, and decided to accept the comfort as it was meant. 'The weather is so mild for the time of year,' he said. 'I wonder if I could tempt you to a drive in the park tomorrow morning? I should value your opinion on my new bays.'

Mary inclined her head and smiled. 'And I,' she said, 'should value your opinion of my new walking-dress.' And the troubled look left Lord Tonbridge's face.

The next morning dawned fair, and at eleven o'clock Miss Morland was ready in the morning room, looking extremely elegant in her new dress of strawberry-coloured kersey, very full-skirted with a double-breasted jacket piped with black, black velvet revers to the collar, and a very dashing small tricorne hat with a half-veil of black net and a black ostrich feather curling over the brim. Lord Tonbridge arrived promptly to collect her, driving his new curricle, to which was harnessed a pair of very large, glossy bay horses, gleaming with health and rippling with solid muscle packed over their shoulders and haunches. Miss Morland mounted nimbly with his lordship's help into the carriage, noticing with a slight sinking of the heart that the groom, instead of riding in the seat behind, was mounted and was to follow the equipage at a discreet distance. This could only mean, she told herself, that his lordship wished to have conversation of a private nature with her.

Lord Tonbridge drove as far as the tan along the side of Green Park, and then handed the reins to Mary. She handled them with all the assurance of a Morland, for though she had never been as passionately fond of horses as the rest of her siblings, she could not well have grown up at Morland Place without knowing plenty about them.

'They seem a very well-matched pair, my lord,' she said as she brought them round a second time. 'Light-mouthed, and they go well up to their bits.'

'Thank you,' he said absently. 'Miss Morland, I suppose you may have guessed that it was not principally to shew you my bays that I asked you to drive this morning. In fact, I wished to have private conversation with you, of a particular sort.'

It was a moment Mary had hoped to put off indefinitely. Lord Tonbridge had been the most constant of her admirers, and it was not to be expected that he would pay court to her for ever without coming to the question; but Mary most definitely did not want to answer the question, for it would mean that she would have to make a decision, and whatever her answer, it would be the end of their comfortable relationship. If she accepted him, she would be pitched into a flurry of wedding plans and interviews with his family; and if she rejected him, he would go away and court some other woman, and she would lose a pleasant companion. It was with great relief, therefore, that she heard a hail, and saw two young men coming towards them along the footpath.

'I beg your pardon, my lord,' she said apologetically, 'but here is an interruption.' Tonbridge, looking most put out, halted his pair, and Horatio Morland and John Anstey came up to the curricle to greet them.

'Well, Miss Morland, here you are! I am dashed glad you had not gone as far as the Serpentine, for Anstey would have forced me to go with him, and though his legs would have carried him, mine are Town legs, and won't go more than a mile without a bait. He called this morning at Chelmsford House, but Flora wasn't up, and you had gone out, so I offered to bring him to you, and here we are. What a splendid hat that is!'

John Anstey's eyes had been fixed on Mary's face all along, and he made his bow and murmured his greetings to her, while Horatio talked on without pause.

'Your servant, Tonbridge. Is this your new pair? Famous! I heard you was pretty pleased to get them, for St. Auban wanted them but couldn't raise the wind. Flora wants you all to come back and take a nuncheon with her, by the by. She was dressing when we left, so if we go back slowly she'll be down by the time we get there. How do your bays go, Tonbridge? Are you pleased with 'em? They look sweet goers. Mary, why don't you jump down and let me take your place? You could walk back with Anstey while Tonbridge takes me a turn round the park. I dare say you've a thousand questions you want to ask about home.'

It was all arranged within moments, though three of the four could hardly tell how. Mary was helped down from the curricle, and walked away towards Pall Mall on her old friend's arm, and Horatio jumped up beside the bemused Lord Tonbridge and, blithely assuming he had been offered the reins, took them and turned the team the other way, and drove off down the tan with a broad smile and an inward satisfaction. Tonbridge, he was persuaded, was by far the more dangerous rival; he was sure Mary would never take Anstey, Member of Parliament or not, so he could use Anstey with perfect safety to block the progress of any other pretenders to her hand.

When they arrived back at Chelmsford House, Mary and John Anstey found that Lady Chelmsford was not only up and dressed, but already entertaining a visitor in the small dining parlour. Mary stopped short in the doorway and put her hands on her hips in pretended exasperation.

'You again!' she cried. 'I swear one would think you had no other home. Dear ma'am, do not let him impose upon you!'

Captain Harvey stood up with an engaging grin and said, 'Do not scold me, Miss Morland. Indeed, Chelmsford House is such a convenient distance from the Admiralty, one can hardly step out of the latter without finding oneself here, almost unknowing – and then, you know, it would not be the thing to go away without paying one's compliments, now would it?'

'I see Horace must have found you,' Flora said, ignoring all this with accustomed blandness. 'Mr Anstey, you have met Captain Harvey? Is Lord Tonbridge coming back, Mary? I hope Horace gave the invitation properly. Louisa and Amelia will be down at once, so we shall have a nice little party of it.'

A collation of cold meats, fruit and cakes was spread, and Horatio and Lord Tonbridge arrived simultaneously with the entrance of Amelia and Louisa, the latter pale, quiet and shy in lilac cambric, and the former almost elbowing her out of the way to shew herself in billowing white muslin and a broad blue sash, and smiling simultaneously at Lord Tonbridge and John Anstey, for Captain Harvey she thought ugly and dark, besides being a sailor, which was not fashionable. The party disposed itself about the room, and since John Anstey kindly engaged

Louisa, who he had known from her birth, in conversation, Captain Harvey remained seated beside Flora, and Horatio claimed Mary's attention too firmly to be moved except by outright rudeness, Lord Tonbridge fell an easy prey to Amelia, who chattered to him and flirted with him so determinedly that he was made silent by an agony of embarrassment and pinned resistlessly in the corner she had chosen. Even Mary felt sorry for him, and itched to slap Amelia hard; but Flora, her dark head bent close to Hannibal Harvey's, did not seem to notice; and when Horatio noticed his sister's conduct, his inner complacency led him only to apostrophise her as a 'horrid bold chit' and then to ignore the situation entirely. Mary, therefore, could do nothing but feel uncomfortable; she found, too, that she disliked the proximity of the two dark heads on the sofa, and the bursts of laughter that punctuated their low-voiced conversation, and when Charles arrived she told herself that she had been anxious on his behalf.

His arrival, however, tempered Amelia's behaviour, and broke up the private conversations, bringing everyone into a general discussion of the King's health, the Prince of Wales's latest antics at Carlton House, and the newest little Fitzclarence to arrive at Bushy Park. The more comfortable atmosphere was then interrupted by the arrival of William, who burst precipitously upon the company and cried, 'It has happened! It has happened at last! Mary – Flora – I am made Post!'

'Oh William, I am so glad,' Mary cried, hugging her brother, while Flora exchanged a look of satisfaction with her husband.

'Congratulations,' said Captain Harvey. 'Tell us how it came about, Captain Morland.'

'Oh, – how strange that sounds,' William said, looking a little confused.

'I think it sounds lovely,' Flora said firmly, and Harvey gave her a look of sympathy. 'Tell us, William – it was Lord Howe, I suppose?'

'Yes, he asked me to call on him this morning, as you know, and when I got there he said that there was to be a summer cruise, beginning next month, to the West Indies, and that he needed West India station officers, because the Yellow Jack is very bad out there at the moment, and they don't want to lose half the fleet before they have been there a month. Then he asked me if I would like to serve, and when I said yes, of course, he said I would be made Post into the *Thames*, thirty-two.'

'Oh William, how lovely!' said Mary, and Harvey said,

'The *Thames*? I know her – she's a good ship. Belton had her at Martinique back in '85. As good a frigate as you could wish, Morland.'

'I know she is,' William said, his eyes bright. 'Does everyone feel like that about their first command? I know I shall never like another ship better than her. Captain Morland of the *Thames*. I can hardly believe it!'

'William, it occurs to me,' Flora said slowly, 'that it might be a very good thing if you were to take Jack with you to sea. I am sure you could find some place for him in your ship.'

'Why, of course, ma'am, if you wish it,' William said promptly. 'He could go in the books as my servant. I'm allowed four servants for every hundred of the ship's company, though of course they're not really servants – more like apprentices really. Has he a mind to go to sea? He has never mentioned it to me – though to be sure, he asks me questions all the time when I am at Morland Place, and asks for sea stories. But then all boys do, don't they?'

'I always expected him to follow in his father's footsteps,' Flora said, 'though I should not have insisted on it if he had not the mind to do so. But he has mentioned it several times in his letters to me, and if you would take him with you, it would be a good start for him, I am sure.'

William nodded. 'He's . . . how old? Thirteen?'

'Thirteen and a half.'

'That's good. He can qualify for midshipman at fifteen, and as lieutenant at nineteen; just as it should be. And I hope he does not have to wait as long as I have after that to be made Post.'

'Well, it is come at last, William, and I am so pleased for you,' Flora said. 'Will you write to your mother and father?'

'Write? Good heavens, no! I must go there and pack my dunnage and be back as soon as possible. I have to fit out my ship and man her, and there will be a thousand things to do before we sail. I cannot spare a moment. I must leave today, ma'am, and travel post. The utmost speed is necessary.'

'Oh, but surely,' Flora began, but Captain Harvey laid a hand on hers and said with a smile,

'As well stop a lover flying to his mistress as a captain to his first ship.'

William grinned. 'Don't worry, I'll give mother full instructions on what to pack for Jack, and he can follow and meet me at the ship later. Will you excuse me now? I had better go and pack my bag and be on my way.'

The excitement at Morland Place on William's arrival was no less intense, and certainly more vocal, and while William was flying about packing his sea-chest and looking out his uniforms, Jemima was downstairs dealing with protests and tears from her youngest son. In a little while she came up to William's bedchamber and said apologetically, 'William, dearest, may I trouble you?'

'Of course, mother. What is all the bellowing about? It sounds like a bull-calf with the colic.'

'It's Harry – his voice is beginning to break. William, he is very upset about Jack going away. You know that the boys are inseparable here at home, and it seems they have both talked endlessly about going to sea together, and though Jack is too pleased and excited to give up the idea on Harry's behalf . . .'

'Not the least need in the world for him to do so,' William said, turning to her with a smile. 'I can take both of them as easily as one.'

'Oh, William, can you? I didn't like to ask, but . . .'

'If you can get them both ready, I can put them both in the books. But you had better warn them that discipline on board a ship is very strict, and there will be no special treatment for them on account of their being my relatives. They must obey orders and keep their mouths shut, or they'll be bent over a gun by the master-at-arms.'

Jemima smiled. 'I think *you* had better say those things to them, William. It will carry far more weight.'

His excitement suddenly welled up in him, and he put his arms round her and hugged her hard, a thing he had not done in years. '*I* shall carry weight wherever I go now, Mother. I am made Post! I have only to go on living long enough, and I shall be an admiral – Admiral of the Fleet, even.'

'You deserve it, my son,' Jemima said, her eyes bright with pleasure for him. 'I had better go, then, and tell Harry he need cry no longer. Then I shall have to comfort Lucy, because she wants to go more than either of them.'

On a hot day that August, James Morland came riding up the track to Morland Place on his big chestnut, on his way home for race-week. All the family, other than those at sea, were going to assemble this year, and he was looking forward to it, despite his doubts as to his reception from his mother. All around him spread the lush greenness of his family's land; it was still early enough for the skylarks to be up, shrieking in the dizzy crystal heights of the flawless sky; and Nez Carré's gay, dancing hooves struck up spurts of white dust from the track as if he were glad to be back. James contemplated the dust and wondered if the going would be too hard for good racing, and thought of the colt he had been interesting himself in. He and Edward had a side-bet on the book at the Maccabees' Club, for of the two most promising colts that were to be raced, Edward favoured one and James the other. It gave a little extra interest to race-week.

The thoughts were dissipated as Nez Carré shied violently, and then halted, his forelegs stiff, his whole body quivering on the edge of flight. James's consummate horsemanship had kept him in the saddle though his mind had been elsewhere; now, soothing his trembling horse, he looked about for what had startled him, and saw something moving in the bushes by the path. He stared, and then began to smile.

'It's all right, Lucy, you can come out,' he said. Reluctantly the dishevelled figure shewed itself, rising from a gorse bush and making Nez Carré snort and back, his eyes goggling in amazement. 'What do you mean by skulking there and frightening my horse? You nearly unseated me,' James said, trying to sound stern. Lucy raised a grubby face to him and looked Nez Carré over with the frank eye of a hardened old horse-coper.

'No I didn't,' she said. 'You weren't in the least shaken. I didn't mean to startle you, though. I was just afraid you might make me go back.'

'Oh, are you running away again?' he asked.

'It's so dull doing lessons on my own,' she said, 'and Father Thomas hates me. Why do I have to be a girl? Boys have all the fun. Harry and Jack have gone to sea, and it's what I've always, always wanted, and I can't just because I'm a girl.'

James sympathised, thinking how very dull it must be for her without her playmates, and with no-one of her own age to associate with. 'I thought you wanted to be a horse doctor?' he said. She made a sound of exasperation which made Nez Carré jerk his head back.

'No, I wanted to be a real doctor, a ship's surgeon, like Morgan was before he took to drink.' James's lips quivered but he controlled himself. 'I only decided to be a horse doctor,' she went on seriously, 'because nobody can stop me being that, but they won't let me be a real doctor because of being a *girl*.' She invested the word with so much scorn that James couldn't help smiling.

'There might be good things about being a girl, you know,' he said.

'Well I can't think of any, and I am one, and I should know,' Lucy said frankly. 'Are you going up to the house? Where's Durban? I thought you never travelled anywhere without him?'

'He's following behind, driving my curricle with the luggage. Here, child, I must move on, or Nez Carré will start digging.'

'Oh take me up, just to the drawbridge, James, do!' she cried persuasively, catching the saddle-flap and putting her small dusty foot onto the toe of James's immaculate boot. James thought of Durban's annoyance at his handiwork's being sullied by a mere child, and reached down for Lucy's hand.

'Come then, jump!' She flew up through the air like a bird to settle in front of him, and at once seized the reins from his hands, though Nez Carré was sidling and snorting like an outraged dragon.

'Send him on, James, I have him. Let's gallop!'

A short and hair-raising ride brought them to the draw-bridge, where Lucy managed to pull up the big horse and jump down all in one movement. 'By God, you're a good little rider,

Luce! I'll wager if you rode cross-saddle, you could handle anything on four legs,' James said breathlessly.

'Of course I could,' Lucy said stoutly. 'I *should* have been a boy. I wish and *wish* God hadn't got it wrong.'

James grinned. 'One day you may find out why He did what He did. In the meantime, I must see if I can't arrange a little fun for you.'

Lucy clasped his boot adoringly. 'Oh *please*! Dear Jamie, I always liked you best of my brothers. Don't tell Father Thomas you've seen me.'

'Where are you going?' he called after her as she darted away.

'Twelvetrees,' she called back. 'I'll be back for dinner.'

'I'll bet you will,' he murmured to himself with a smile, and turned Nez Carré and rode over the drawbridge.

He met his mother crossing the staircase hall, and her face lit when she saw him, and she came to him with a light tread to be embraced.

'Dearest James! How lovely to have you home again.'

'Mother, darling, your eyes have gone the colour of corn-flowers! Papa always said it was a sure sign you were happy. How is he?'

'Just the same,' she said, leaning against his broad chest as if it comforted her. 'He's still in bed – I have managed to persuade him not to get up until midday these days, though I suppose there'll be no keeping him in bed during race-week. The doctor says he must be very quiet and not exert himself, but – you know your father.'

James kissed her brow in acknowledgement, and she slipped her arm through his and led him into the drawing room. 'Tell me all the news,' she said. 'Where have you been?'

'Oh, here and there, you know,' he said airily, and then, to distract attention, 'I met Lucy on my way up from the road. I think she was waiting for me.'

'That naughty child,' Jemima sighed. 'She leads Father Thomas such a dance, but in truth I think he does not understand how to handle her.'

'She says he hates her.'

'It is almost as bad as that. He can't beat her, you see, because she's a female, and he doesn't know how else to make her attend. Where has she gone now? To the stables I suppose?'

'Yes – but she says she'll be back at dinner time,' James grinned.

'Poor child,' Jemima sighed again. 'It is hard for her, now the boys have gone. She is too much on her own, and with no friends or companions of her own age. I did think of asking Flora if she would have her – at least Louisa and Amelia are nearer her age – but Lucy was horrified at the idea, and grew quite passionate, and said she wouldn't go and live with a lot of silly women if she died for it. You may laugh, dearest, but she meant it, indeed she did! Nothing we can do, short of actual cruelty, will stop her hanging around the stables.'

'With that red-nosed horse doctor I suppose,' James laughed.

'When he is here. I don't object to Morgan Proom – he behaves very properly when she is around him, and does not swear – well, not very much. And she has a real skill with sick animals, you know. Humby can't actually encourage her, but when there's a difficult labour, or a sick mare, Lucy turns up by magic, and he can't bring himself to turn her away, for, really, you know, animals get better for her that would die for other people. And it isn't only the horses,' she added musingly. 'I've discovered recently that people with ailments come to her. If anyone in the stable has a cut or a splinter or a broken bone, it's Lucy they ask for, not the doctor. And people from the village bring their troubles to her too.'

'Not really!'

'Yes, indeed! Only yesterday there was something going on out in the yard, and when I asked Oxhey what it was, he said it was Mrs Mabberley – you know, the weaver's wife – who had brought her baby up for Miss Lucy to look at. The poor little thing can't breathe properly – it goes purple and croaks. Oxhey says a lot of villagers swear by Miss Lucy. I daren't think what will happen if the doctor finds out. He'll probably refuse to come any more.'

'Perhaps you'd be better off if he didn't. Maybe Lucy could cure Papa,' James said. Jemima smiled in a distracted way.

'I just don't know what to do about her, Jamie, really I don't.'

'Oh, she's young yet, mother. I shouldn't worry. She'll settle down in the end. She's a sensible girl after all, and one day she'll fall in love and get married, and be glad she's a female.'

As soon as he said it, he realised his mistake, for Jemima's face took on the familiar lines of anxious disapproval. 'If she is like my other children, she will never get married. Why God saw fit to send me a brood of spinsters and bachelors I shall never know. What is to become of Morland Place if none of you will marry and get children? Now here's Mary refusing Lord Tonbridge – Flora wrote to me last week – and it isn't because there's anyone she prefers to him. She just won't marry. I can't understand it – such an eligible man, and Flora says they're thick as thieves, or were until she refused his offer. And you, James – when you were here last you were seeing a lot of Valentina Fussell, and though it wasn't the match I wanted for you, I'd have been glad enough to have her for a daughter-in-law, rather than no-one. And now Ned tells me that she's engaged to Crosby Shawe from Heslington.'

'I'm glad,' James said thoughtfully. 'He will suit her very well, and be kind to her.'

'Ned tells me that it is partly your doing that she is married,' Jemima said, looking closely at him. 'He says that your paying her attention made the other young men think they were missing out.' James shrugged. 'Well there's no use in that for you, is there, James?'

'I never meant to marry her, mother,' he said. She looked angry.

'No, nor any of the others, either. Miss Ingram's married now, you know, and Miss Carr's engaged. Who will there be left for you, if you go on in this way?'

He smiled. 'The world is full of women.'

'What if it is, when you won't wed any of them? I suppose you won't take Lizzie Anstey, and God forbid you should think of Charlotte Fussell. Oh Jamie, what's to become of us?' she cried.

He took her hands and chafed them, hating her to be upset. 'Don't, Mother, please. It isn't so bad as that comes to.'

She pulled her hand away to brush a tear from her face with an angry gesture. 'You are wasting your life, James,' she said seriously. 'What were you doing in Scarborough?'

'Scarborough?' he repeated, his face white and grim. She looked into his eyes.

'Things get about,' she said. 'Did you think no-one would

know you had been there, at the same time as Mary Skelwith? Oh Jamie, don't do it! Don't ruin her again, and yourself with her. Leave her alone, please, before it's too late. Your father would die of shame if he knew what you were about.'

'Father doesn't know, does he?' James said quickly.

'No, I've kept it from him so far – but if you go on seeing her, everyone will know. What is it that makes you do these terrible things, James?'

'I love her,' he said quietly, and she saw the bleakness in his handsome face, and was stricken. He looked up, meeting her eyes with a look of such pain that she put her hands out to him instinctively. 'And there is the child, Mother. Had you forgotten?'

'No, dearest, I had not forgotten. But *you* must. It is madness to dwell on that. Put it behind you, and make a new life for yourself.'

'I can't.'

'You must.' She held his gaze, and her face in its turn became grim. 'If you are hoping that Skelwith will die one day, and that you can have her then, you are digging a pit for yourself, my son. I beg you, James, marry someone, some good girl, and have some children, and forget all that.'

He pulled his hands away and stood up, turning from her, and saying in a muffled voice, 'I had better go up and see Father, and unpack my travelling-bag. When Durban arrives, have him take my valise up and unpack my blue suit, will you, Mother?' And he strode out of the room, leaving her to sit with her hands in her lap, staring out of the window with unseeing eyes.

Flora and Charles, with Mary, Louisa and Amelia, arrived at Shawes a week before race-week, and proceeded to be very gay. Horatio had followed the Prince of Wales down to Brighton, where he was hoping to astonish the *ton* with a suit of lilac silk so covered in spangles that in some lights it was necessary for spectators to shield their eyes from it, and Flora felt eased by his absence. They had planned a series of dinners, routs and balls, including a masquerade, which she was sure the society people of York would think very daring. In the event it was even more daring than she intended, for the Earl of Aylesbury, aided and abetted by Edward, came dressed as Queen Cleopatra, and even after the unmasking no-one realised the deception until, rather drunk and helpless with laughter, Edward snatched off the black wig to reveal Chetwyn's conker-coloured hair. There was a shocked silence, and it might have spoiled the evening, had Flora not had the wit to applaud loudly, while James stepped forward and made a deep bow and insisted on having the next dance with the Queen; and after a moment others joined in the applause and there were indulgent smiles and talk of 'the pranks of those wild Morland boys'.

For the families at Morland Place and Shawes, the climax of the week would be the race for the St. Edward's Plate, in which the chief protagonists would be the two Morland Place colts, Goldenrod and Firecrest. Betting on the colts was intense and very close, for there was little to choose between them. Goldenrod, the colt favoured by James, was a little lighter in the bone, a golden chestnut with a white star and one white foot; Firecrest, a little bigger and more heavily built, but known to be a great stayer, was a reddish chestnut with a blond-streaked tail, and was the favourite of Edward Morland.

The rivalry between the brothers, though friendly, was intense, so much so that in the week before the race, they kept their training secret from each other, James even removing Goldenrod from the stable and keeping him at the establishment of a friend, Lord Ashley of Naburn, who entered into the contest with amusement. Goldenrod had his exercise and training on Naburn Moor, while Firecrest was run on Acomb Moor, and there were a few spectators every morning to see how the two colts compared. The steadier part of the betting world reckoned to trust Maister Morland's judgement, aye, and that o' th'Earl of Aylesbury, as was by his side naight an' day, an' was knawn to be a sharp 'un when it came to 'osses. The younger set, and the wild striplings that gathered in the Maccabees' Club and similar haunts of ill-repute, generally thought it would be worth their while to risk a pony or two on Captain James's fancy, even if only for the fun of it.

And there was a third element, rather a strange one to the keepers of books: many a humble villager came sidling up at quiet moments clutching a battered purse with a shilling or even a guinea to put on Goldenrod, because it was well known that where the Young Master had his friend the Earl to help him, Captain James had Miss Lucy permanently at his side, and Miss Lucy was a wonder with animals, and had so kindly stitched up little Billy's leg the time he gashed it open climbing the old dyke.

The race itself was probably the best attended in the history of the racecourse. Sir Allen, with Lady Morland on his arm, had a fine view from the grandstand, where many attentive neighbours asked him how he did, and which colt he favoured, to which he replied, his eyes bright and a closed smile on his lips, that he left all of that to her ladyship, who was the expert. Her ladyship, when pressed, admitted to having bet on both colts, rather than favour one of her sons over the other.

Lady Chelmsford and Miss Morland attended the race in a vastly smart barouche, drawn by two enormous, glossy Cleveland Bays, in which they could properly display their race-meet finery: Lady Chelmsford in coquelicot silk with a draped skirt and hoops, a cape over her shoulders of delicate Brussels lace, and a turban of red and gold with a stiff white cockade; Miss Morland looking ravishing in harebell blue with a gauzy white overskirt and ruched fichu, and a small hat perched on her luxuriant black curls that appeared to be made entirely of real roses, white and faint pink. They were attended on horseback and on foot by Lord Chelmsford and Mr John Anstey MP, who took their bets for them and fanned them when it grew too hot under their parasols.

Miss Louisa Morland and Lady Amelia Morland were in a large party of young people gathered in the lower part of the grandstand, which included from time to time, to Amelia's intense delight, the Earl of Aylesbury and Mr Edward Morland. Louisa was rescued from obscurity and from missing the race altogether, owing to her having been elbowed away from the railing by Lady Amelia, by the kindness of Mr Benjamin Anstey, who advised her to put her bet on Goldenrod, and procured a glass of lemonade for her in the most obliging way.

Mr James Morland remained the whole time in and around the owner's enclosure and the collecting-ring. Nobody knew where Miss Lucy Morland was, but everyone was sure she was with someone else.

'An excellent race, Lady Morland,' Allen said, smiling at his wife as the cheers rang out all round them. 'You've won.'

'I could hardly lose,' Jemima said, squeezing his hand. 'Ah, here's Edward and Chetwyn. Well done, Edward. It was a close-run thing.'

'Yes, you came a good second,' Allen said. 'Firecrest shewed very well; it could have gone either way.'

'I don't mind,' Edward said genially. 'I collect the Plate either way, as the owner of both colts. But I'd like to know who that jockey of James's was. It was he that won the race, you know. Firecrest had it sewn up, until that jockey pushed 'Rod through the gap on the rails. Up on his neck like a monkey – damned lucky he didn't break his leg on the railings, too! Which of us did you bet on, mother?'

'Both of you,' she admitted, shamefaced.

'Like mother like son,' said Sir Allen, smiling. 'We'll have a case of champagne back at the house, to celebrate your mother's decisiveness. Ah, and here's James beckoning to us. I think he wants us to go down.'

'Yes, to the enclosure. Come and see the horses, sir, and congratulate the riders,' Edward said. The party rose and moved down the steps, and Jemima looked round and said vaguely, 'Where is Lucy, by the way? I suppose she has been with James all the while. She'll be as pleased as any of us that her help has made the difference to the race.'

In the enclosure, the sweating horses were being walked about, and the interested parties were crowding around James, who was protecting his diminutive groom with an arm across his shoulder. Way was made for the Morland party, and Allen shook his son's hand and then looked down at the jockey with a thoughtful air. Jemima rushed up to embrace James, and said, 'And now do introduce us to your jockey, Jamie. He did so well for you. Where did you find him?' She too looked down, and the smile froze on her face.

James, grinning broadly, his arm still round the jockey's shoulders, said, 'I couldn't have done it without him, ma'am. Allow me to introduce the Fearless Flyer, as they are calling him in the collecting ring . . .' And with his other hand he whipped off the silk cap, revealing Lucy's hay-coloured hair crowning her mud-speckled and scarlet face. 'Luce Morland!'

Lucy looked from face to face with scared eyes, and said in a very small voice, 'It was only a bit of fun.' And then Allen began to laugh, and others joined in, and finally even Jemima admitted it was a good joke, and so it was all right after all; though Jemima took the opportunity under cover of the general exclaiming to say crossly to James that it was most irresponsible of him to encourage Lucy, who might have been hurt or even killed.

And James accepted the rebuke, but patted his mother's arm, saying, 'She was never in the slightest danger, mama. She rides like the very d--, like a centaur in fact.'

The celebratory dinner was held at Morland Place that evening, and Lucy allowed herself to be clad in voluminous pink muslin and ribbons, for once with a good grace, and enjoyed her moment enormously, as heroine of the hour. Lady Amelia might look down her nose and try to persuade Lord Aylesbury to agree that it was a shocking thing to have done and that Miss Lucy Morland was no better than a hoyden, but everyone else regarded the prank with indulgent amusement and, in Louisa's case, frank admiration simply for her daring. James kept Lucy on his right hand all evening, and raised so many toasts to her that in the end she told him, quite brusquely, to shut up.

The case of champagne was duly broached, and M. Barnard excelled himself with a mixture of French and English dishes, the centrepiece being a glazed saddle of lamb dressed with apricots on a huge square ashet, and on its four sides a raised oyster pie, baked salmon with lobster sauce, six roast pigeons stuffed with pâté on a bed of green peas, and a ham mousse dressed with prawns and truffles. The removes were a cod's head with sage and parsley sauce, fricassee of rabbits and Yorkshire curd tarts, which M. Barnard had now learned to make so well that many people thought his the best in the West Riding. Besides this there were the usual salads, cold chickens, glazed eels, custards and cheesecakes, and on the sideboard venison pasty, a baked ham and a French galantine; and after the cloth was removed, as well as fruit and pistachios there were sorbets, and white port to drink as well as red.

After dinner some more guests arrived, amongst them enough young people to make it worth while for Father Thomas to get out his fiddle and accompany Jemima on the harpsichord in the long saloon, playing music for them to dance to. Lucy, who usually thought dancing a poor sport, took her place in the set and danced with such enthusiasm that James was provoked to murmur to her as they passed that she had found out at last the joys of being female, to which she replied with most unladylike grimace. When Jemima's fingers grew tired, Flora took her place at the keyboard, and Jemima was able to go back to her husband's side, and sit holding his hand and watching their children enjoying themselves with their friends.

'They are a handsome brood,' she mused aloud.

'And doing well,' Allen replied contentedly. She looked sideways at him, and saw that though he was obviously tired, he seemed to be very happy.

'Shall I make up a table of whist for you?' she asked. He pressed her hand and shook his head.

'No, I just want to watch the young people.' After a moment he turned his head to look at her, his eyes bright with love. 'We are very lucky, Lady Morland, don't you think? So many happy years we have had together, and such a brood of handsome children.'

She carried his hand to her lips by way of answer, and forbore to add that the only thing they lacked was an equally handsome brood of grandchildren.

After his parents had retired for the night, James slipped away to keep an appointment at the Maccabees' Club, where those of his acquaintances who had bet on his winning the race were anxious to shew their gratitude by buying him a series of drinks that threatened to keep him from his bed until morning. It was nearing three of the clock when a club servant came to his elbow to tell him that his valet was downstairs and asking for him. James, reeling only slightly, followed the man out, to where Durban waited for him in the vestibule, his face grave, his master's cloak over his arm.

'What's this?' James asked cheerfully. 'Come to fetch me away? You're astray there, Durban! I don't mean to leave until I'm thoroughly foxed, and I'm still a deal too sober.'

'That's as well, sir,' Durban said, holding out the cloak. 'You wouldn't want it otherwise. It's your father, sir. They sent me to fetch you home.'

II

Paris was gay that summer, and a stranger would have thought she had not a care in the world. Each day dawned clear and hot under a sparkling sky, and by eleven it was hazy with heat, and every café had its awnings spread to shade the idlers who sat sipping coffee and cognac and watching the world go by. The theatres played to full houses every performance; the boxes at the opera were thronged with bare arms and jewelled bosoms; by night the restaurants were full, and music sounded from every open door.

Héloïse, with the resilience of her fifteen years, enjoyed it all, despite what she knew. There were gay supper parties to go to, plays to see, dances to be danced. An English milord was staying at the Hôtel Mandar, and many were the balls and routs given in his honour. Every day had its engagements. She visited Lotti and played with the children, rode in the Bois, strolled in the Champs Élysées where there were booths and jugglers and music and fortune tellers; she shopped in the rue Saint-Honoré and exclaimed over the new fashions, which were abandoning hoops and stays and favouring lighter materials and simpler lines; by night the public places were lit with coloured lanterns, and she joined the crowds there to see the puppet plays and pantomimes and listen to the concerts.

There were differences. Héloïse was no longer called upon to entertain Olivier's friends. In fact, he was hardly ever home, working long hours at the Palais de Justice and spending his evenings at the club or the cour du Commerce, preferring a friend's sofa to his own bed. When they did meet, he treated her with a vague politeness, as if he were not entirely sure who she was.

'He is up to something,' Henri said on one occasion when Héloïse mentioned her husband's abstraction. 'But God knows what it is. I have seen him keeping company with Marat and Billaud-Varennes, and that is company I would sooner he did without.'

And despite the gaiety of the main streets, Héloïse could not but be aware of the squalor that existed in the side streets. Once as a child she had given away her shoes to a beggar-child; now, returning home in her carriage, she saw from its safety the dirt and poverty and hunger that was the other face of Paris – and something new, a suppressed violence. The back streets seemed more than usually thronged, and there were some strange, dark faces whose expressions, momentarily glimpsed, made her shudder.

One day at the beginning of August, Héloïse and Lotti were sitting in the morning room of the house in the rue Saint-Anne, engaged in the perennially amusing task of refurbishing bonnets. Uncle Johann was sitting on a sofa nearby reading a book and joining in their desultory argument over the rival merits of artificial flowers and wax fruit as trimmings, while the nursemaids were playing a game of spillikins with Mathilde and Karellie.

A sound, of which they had been half aware, gradually became loud enough to demand their attention. Héloïse lifted a finger to hush Lotti, and cocked her head to listen.

'What is that in the street? It sounds like singing,' she said. 'Yes, it is a marching song.'

It drifted in through the open windows, growing nearer, and though they could not yet distinguish the words, the tune came to them, a gay, stirring tune with a wonderful marching beat which made Lotti's feet tap beneath her frilled hem.

'What a splendid tune!' she said. 'It's like something from an opera by Gluck.'

'Oh, better than that,' Héloïse said. The children had already scrambled across to the window, and the grown-ups joined them there, leaning out to look down the street towards the junction of the rue des Petits Champs. And then suddenly the marching band came into view, heading, Héloïse supposed, for the gardens of the Palais Royal: a band of drunken cutthroats, dressed in a strange and motley array of ragged clothes, their arms bare, their heads sporting the red cap, some with a cockade of red, white and blue. Some carried bottles from which they refreshed themselves as they marched; many sported weapons, or wore knives in their belts. Around them, in support, the dregs of the poor suburbs tagged along. Their faces were dark and strange, their expressions ugly, and all sang as they marched along:

Allons enfants de la Patrie!
Le jour de gloire est arrivé!

The children, knowing no better and stirred by the song, began to cheer, and Mathilde jumped down from the window-seat and marched about the room, stamping her small boots and singing gibberish words to the stirring tune.

'Who *are* they?' Lotti asked in a dazed whisper. 'They look like murderers, or madmen.'

'They are the *fédérés*,' Johann said grimly. 'The men from Marseilles.'

'The *fédérés*?' Héloïse said, bemused. 'But--'

'Yes, the loyal patriots, summoned to assist the government and keep down the unruly element from the suburbs,' Johann said bitterly. 'They are the pick of the scum that hang around the seaports. Blanc-Grilli, the deputy from Marseilles, says that most of them aren't even French, but Corsicans, Greeks, Genoese – even their leaders are a Pole and a man from the Indies. Some of them have been released from gaol for the occasion, and most of them ought to be inside one. And the government is well served for its folly, for you see they have joined with those very gutter-elements they were meant to combat.'

There was a silence as they watched them pass the end of the street, like an endless flood of rats disturbed from a sewer.

'Hundreds of them,' Héloïse whispered in horror. 'There are hundreds of them.' Behind her she heard one of the maids shake Mathilde into silence. She turned her head slowly and met Lotti's eyes, and her friend gave her a death's-head smile.

'It *is* a marvellous song,' she said.

The night of the ninth of August was stifling hot, unnaturally quiet. The palace of the Tuileries was under guard by the Swiss regiment, commanded by the Marquis de Mandat, and all was still, though no-one was sleeping. At the Hôtel de Ville the officers of the Commune sat in tense silence, waiting for whatever was to come. In the distance there could be heard the rattle of side-drums, as the *faubourgs* called their citizens to rallying points.

209

Héloïse, lying sleepless in her rose-pink bed, heard the drums. The clock in the hall downstairs struck twelve, then the half. She heard the church bell, and for a moment thought it was striking the time, until she realised that the next strike should have been one. She sat up, and heard other bells, near and distant. There was a movement in her room, and a shape loomed against her gauze hangings.

'It's all right, Marie. I'm awake,' she said. The curtains were drawn back, and Marie looked down at her anxiously. 'I could not sleep. What are the bells for?'

'It's the tocsin, madame. Listen – that is the bell of Saint-Eustache beginning now. What can it mean, madame?'

'I don't know,' Héloïse said, but she had her fears. She got up, and Marie helped her into her robe, and they went to the window to listen. The night hung thick and dark and still, but it was not at peace: it was a listening stillness behind the tolling bells. To keep Marie's mind occupied, Héloïse set her to telling which bell was which. Bluette came shivering about her ankles, and she picked up the little dog absently.

Then they heard the sound of marching feet, and Marie stiffened and looked at her mistress in fright. Héloïse motioned her to stay still, and in a moment they came into view: a platoon of National Guard, sober and under discipline. A young subaltern rode beside them, and Héloïse leaned out of the window and called him softly: 'Officer! Officer!'

He reined his horse and looked up at her, his white face striped by a black moustache.

'Where are you going? What is happening?'

'I don't know, madame,' he called back, keeping his voice low. 'We were guarding the Pont Neuf with cannon, and we had orders from the Commune to withdraw, so we withdrew.' He shrugged, a man washing his hands of the situation, and rode on after his men. So the Pont Neuf was no longer guarded, Héloïse thought as she drew in from the window. That meant there was nothing to stop the mobs from the south bank crossing to join with those from the faubourgs of Saint-Antoine and Saint-Marceau. But who could have given such an order? The Commune was pledged to protect the King.

'Is monsieur in his room?' she asked.

'No, madame,' Marie answered. 'He did not come home last

night.' She searched her mistress's face for reassurance. 'Pray God he is safe, madame.'

It was necessary to keep Marie occupied, Héloïse thought. Caring for one's servants was a way to avoid thinking of one's own fears. 'Marie, will you make me some tea? I am very thirsty. But try not to wake anyone.'

'Yes, madame. But no-one is sleeping. Shall I bring it here?'

'No, I will go downstairs to the morning room.'

The night seemed endless. Again and again she went to the windows to look for some sign of approaching dawn, to listen for some sound that would tell her what was happening, but though Paris seemed to stir stealthily, there was nothing distinct enough to recognise. The clock on the chimney-pièce struck a silvery chime of four, and Héloïse realised that the sky outside was beginning to flood with red. She went to the window, and saw that it was the sunrise at last, and thanked God for it, though she hardly knew why, except that it seemed less frightening that whatever was to happen would now happen in daylight.

A little later Bluette whined, and there were sounds below. She thought it was Olivier returning, but a moment later the door opened and her father came in.

'Oh, Papa,' she said. He embraced her absently and put her back from him. His face was lined, his expression grave, his brows drawn down in thought.

'I came to tell you what is happening,' he said abruptly.

'Has it begun?' she asked timidly.

'Yes. The Commune has been taken over. There is a new, revolutionary commune, with Danton at the head.'

'Danton – oh, but that is good,' she said gladly. 'He will not harm us – and he is loyal to his friends.'

'Mandat is dead,' Henri said, as if she had not spoken.

'Mandat? How?'

'He was ordered to present himself to the Commune. He left the Tuileries for the Hôtel de Ville early this morning. He found the new Revolutionary Commune in charge. They dismissed him from his post, but as he left – someone – someone shot him in the back of the head.'

'Dear God!' Héloïse shuddered.

'No-one knows who did it. I think – it was not intended. They dragged his body away and tumbled it into the river.'

'Then – is the palace unguarded?'

He made a strange grimace. 'Lachesnaye is second-in-command. He is a good man, and the Swiss Guard will never desert their posts. But, child, there is a crowd of thousands gathered before the gates already, the men from Marseilles and the scum of every gutter in Paris, and a mob – almost an army – is marching from Cordeliers this very moment with field pieces. It is the end, Héloïse. They cannot hold the Tuileries against so many; and if they did, more would gather every day until it was taken.'

'What is to be done?' she whispered. 'Will they . . .?'

'I am going there now, to try to persuade the King and Queen to go to the Assembly for protection. It is their only chance for survival. If they are in the palace when it is taken they will be butchered. It's my belief Brissot and his friends knew this was to happen tonight. I can see no alternative but that the King will be deposed.'

'But then – what will they do with him?' she asked, her mouth dry. His eyes met hers.

'You are so young,' he mused. 'But I have never hidden the truth from you, however grim. Child, what can one do with a deposed king?' They looked at each other in silence for a moment; then he said, 'I must go now. Stay within doors. I think you will be safe enough. I will come again when I can, to tell you what is happening.'

He was almost out of the door when she remembered.

'Papa, what of Olivier? Do you know where he is?'

'He was at the Hôtel de Ville earlier,' he said expressionlessly. 'I think he went back to the cour du Commerce with Camille and Fabre d'Églantine. Don't worry about him – he is safe enough. I don't think he will go anywhere near the Tuileries today.'

It took Henri time to get inside the Palace. The mob in the place du Carrousel was in an ugly mood: the King had shewn himself at the railings that divided them from the palace courtyard, and they had booed and bellowed insults at him. Within the palace, most of the National Guard had deserted, but the Swiss Guard were loyal, even in the face of three antiquated cannon drawn up in the place du Carrousel.

When he finally managed to slip in through one of the side doors, he found the royal family up and dressed, sitting together in one of the drawing rooms, attended by some of the ministers of the Crown, and Roederer, the *Procureur Général*. Henri told them about Mandat, and the approach of the army from the Cordeliers, and Roederer quickly saw the necessity of evacuation.

'Their Majesties must seek refuge with the Assembly,' Henri said to him urgently. 'The deputies are sworn to protect them. Look, it is past six – they will be assembling in the Manège now.'

'Yes, I agree, it is the only way,' Roederer said, and he and Henri looked doubtfully at the King and Queen. The King's wig was askew, and he sat with his hands on his knees looking dazed, almost beyond making any decision. The Queen's eyes were red with weeping, and her hands moved continuously, wringing themselves together as if of their own accord; but she looked alert, a wife and mother with a family to protect, rather than a queen facing a revolution. It took time to persuade them.

'I did not see many people in the place du Carrousel when I went out there,' the King said.

'We have troops, Monsieur le Comte,' the Queen argued. Roederer and Henri exchanged a look.

'Madame, Mandat is dead, murdered by the Commune,' Henri said.

'All of Paris is marching. We cannot fight them all,' Roederer added.

'Are we alone? Can no-one help us?' the Queen cried.

'There are vast crowds coming in from the suburbs,' Roederer said. 'Monsieur le Comte has seen them with his own eyes. They have a dozen pieces of artillery. There is no time to lose.'

At last the King rose to his feet and turned to the Queen. 'Let us go,' he said simply.

It was a little after seven in the morning when the royal family left the palace and tramped through the early-fallen leaves the few yards to the Manège. The last few loyal National Guard escorted them; Henri and Roederer walked in front, in case of snipers; then came the King and Queen, Madame Royale and the Dauphin, the Princesse de Lamballe and the governess, Madame de Tourzel; and lastly the ministers, hurrying in their wake. The Assembly had already begun its scheduled debate on the abolition of slavery, and the crowds around the doors were in a state of high excitement, but the guards fixed bayonets and forced a way through, and a few minutes later the President of the Assembly, Vergniaud, was welcoming the King, and promising protection.

'We have pledged to give even our lives to maintain the rights of the people, and the constituted authority,' he said. The King sat down beside him, and at once one of the deputies jumped to his feet to object.

'Under the rules of the Constitution, *Monsieur le Président*, no debate can take place in the presence of the sovereign. Do I need to remind you, sir, that the Assembly is at this moment officially in session?'

These little men, Henri thought, mentally rolling his eyes. One would hardly think there was a raging mob of murderers outside, baying for the King's blood.

'The press box,' he murmured to Roederer. Roederer considered the small room behind the President's desk, divided from the chamber by a grille: it was barely large enough to hold the royal family, but on the other hand it was in full view, and close by.

'We should have to rip out the grille,' he said. 'But it will be poor quarters for them. The children will have to sit on their laps.'

'Better than being dead,' Henri returned.

'Yes. I will attend to it. Do you, monsieur, try to procure some other quarters for them in the convent next door. And some fresh clothes?'

'I'll do what I can,' said Henri, and bowing, made his exit. The sound of firing outside arrested him, and instead of leaving the Manège, he went upstairs to the gallery where a window gave him a view over the palace gardens. It was too late. The mob had broken through into the palace courtyard and was preparing to storm the palace, into which the Swiss Guard had retreated. Someone fired from an upper window, and immediately was answered from the courtyard below. Henri cursed under his breath, realising that the Swiss guard had not been ordered to stand down, and were loyally defending their posts. The firing was almost continuous now, and already there were bodies sprawled in the courtyard. The sun was brazen, though it was not yet eight o'clock. It was Friday, August the tenth, he remembered irrelevantly: Héloïse's fifteenth birthday.

It was three hours before a hastily scribbled note from the King could be carried the few yards from the Manège to the palace, ordering the Swiss Guard to stand down. After that, the blood-crazed mob hunted them down, cornering them in the corridors of the palace, clubbing them to death in the gardens. Some escaped as far as the place Louis Quinze before being cut down. The women of the mob mutilated their bodies and decorated their caps with bits of them. The streets all around were filled all day with milling crowds, drinking and singing and displaying heads on pikes, and it was impossible for Henri to get away from the immediate area of the Manège.

He managed to arrange quarters for the royal family in the deserted cells of the Convent des Feuillants next door, and later in the afternoon, when the fighting had died down, he slipped into the palace to look for food and clothes. It had been thoroughly looted, and he managed to find only some clean underclothes, and a shirt for the Dauphin. There was no food or wine: only cold water to drink.

All day the debate went on in the Manège, no longer about slavery, but about the future of the monarchy; while the King and Queen sat and sweated in the tiny press box, and the children slept fitfully, worn out by their sleepless night. Henri slipped in to the chamber from time to time during the day, and heard the royal powers gradually being whittled away, until at last at ten in the evening the debate ended, with a formal declaration that the Assembly was the sole and supreme authority, and by that authority it suspended the King from his functions. The Assembly rose, and Henri went forward to escort the royal family to their temporary quarters.

No-one slept that night. The mob surged around the convent, howling for blood and trying to batter their way in. Lachesnaye came in, a long cut down his face, to tell them the extent of the previous day's massacre: almost six hundred of the Swiss Guard had been killed, and seven hundred of the mob. The numbers horrified everyone, though they were dazed with the heat and lack of sleep. Towards dawn the King's valet Thieri managed to get in, bringing some bread, and at seven, after the sparse breakfast, the royal family was escorted back to the Manège for another stifling day in the press box; while Henri was able at last to get away, and headed for the rue Saint-Anne through streets littered with the evidence of the rioting, but – for the moment – quiet.

The gates of the house were locked, and the porter who came out at last to open them carried a heavy brass poker in his hand.

'Have you no firearms?' Henri asked. The porter shut and locked the gate behind him before answering.

'Madame's orders, monsieur, not to shew any firearms at the gate, in case the mob tries to break in for the sake of them. The butler's armed, though.'

'Very wise,' Henri said. The old man's hand came out involuntarily to him.

'Is it – is it very bad out there, sir? Are they – is his Majesty . . .?'

'I think the worst is over for the present,' Henri said. 'The King and Queen are alive and well.'

'Thank God, thank God,' he muttered as he shuffled away to his room. The butler opened the door to him, but had no time to speak a word before Héloïse rushed past him into her father's arms. He held her tightly in silence until she released herself.

'Are you hurt?' she asked.

'No,' he said. She was fully dressed, and as neat as a pin, as always, though she had hidden her hair in a large cap to save dressing it. A thick shawl was round her shoulders. Her eyes looked too big for her face; she did not look fifteen, he thought, with the responsibility of the household on her shoulders. 'I did not wish you happy birthday,' he said foolishly.

'Oh Papa,' she said. She surveyed his face, saw how exhausted he was. 'Breakfast, I think. And hot coffee – lots of it. Jacques . . .'

'At once, madame. I have drawn back the curtains in the morning room.'

Héloïse led her father upstairs, and when they were alone,

turned to him with her face full of questions she hardly dared ask. He shook his head.

'Not yet. When I have eaten.'

'Very well. But the King and Queen? Are they--?'

'Safe, for the moment,' he said. She let him be, until the doors opened and footmen came in with trays laden with bread, and coffee, and buttered eggs, and hot mutton steaks, and cold Westphalia ham. 'Lord, I'm hungry!' Henri said. 'I haven't eaten for thirty hours.'

Héloïse helped him, and he sat down to eat wolfishly, sparing a thought for the royal family, who had had nothing but bread and water. Héloïse filled and refilled his cup, and at last he sat back and said, 'Well then, Marmoset, I should tell you, if you don't know already, that France is no longer a monarchy.' Then he told her of the events of the previous day, while she sat silently, her hands folded in her lap, her eyes never leaving his face.

'What happens now?' she asked at last.

'The Assembly will dissolve, and a National Convention will be formed to rule the country.'

'And the King and Queen?'

'For the moment, they are to be taken to the Luxembourg Palace,' he said, 'but as to--' He broke off as the door opened again, and Vendenoir stood on the threshold, looking tired but triumphant. Héloïse jumped up with a glad cry, and he held her off with a gesture of the hand.

'No fuss, madame, please – I could not bear it. No, no, I am not hurt, only devilish hungry. I see you have breakfasted pretty well. Is there anything left for me?'

Héloïse shrank back into herself. 'Of course,' she said evenly. 'I will ring for clean covers.' She pulled the rope by the chimney, and then could not help saying a little reproachfully, 'I was worried about you, husband. You might have sent word where you were.'

'I had not time for that,' he said shortly, sitting down and fixing his father-in-law with a sardonic eye. 'What was it you were saying as I came in, sir?'

'Only that the King and Queen are to be housed in the Luxembourg for the time being,' Henri said.

'Ah – you are not quite up to date with the news, then. The

Luxembourg is too difficult to guard, it had been decided. The Commune favours the Temple as a lodging for their former majesties.'

'Where, in the Temple?' Henri asked coldly. 'The Royal Residence – or the castle keep?'

Vendenoir gave a mirthless grin. 'I think you can guess the answer to that.'

'Olivier, you cannot mean--' Héloïse began anxiously, but he interrupted her firmly.

'Well, my wife, this is a great day for us. France is a republic at last! Do you remember how I used to talk of it long ago, at Chenonceau? Little did I know then how close I would be to the heart of events; but our friend Danton is the man of the hour. He is to be Minister of Justice and head of the new Executive Council, and he does not forget his friends: Camille is made private secretary, and Fabre is to be Secretary of the Seals, and I – I am to be a deputy, when the new National Convention is formed. A deputy at last!'

'Oh, I am so glad for you,' Héloïse said, and then, hesitantly, 'But what will happen to the King and Queen?'

Olivier was looking at her, but his gaze was not seeing her; he had a strange, visionary sort of smile on his lips as he said, 'That is a matter that will have to be dealt with. A new age is dawning, a new society is in the making, a society based on reason and justice and brotherhood. France – the Republic of France – will rise to greatness; but there are one or two matters which will have to be dealt with first.'

There was a brief silence, during which Henri surveyed his son-in-law's face with some misgiving, and wondered what mischief was afoot: whatever it was, he thought, it boded ill, and not only for the King.

'Do you think the Commune will manage to persuade the Assembly on the matter of the royal lodgings?' he asked.

'The Assembly knows who is ruling France,' Vendenoir said easily. The door opened. 'Ah, here are my covers. Madame, may I trouble you to help me to some of those eggs?'

On the thirteenth of August the King and Queen and the royal children were taken to the Temple and imprisoned in the mediaeval keep. Their servants and attendants were removed, and they were left there alone in the charge of guards selected by the Commune. The houses around the keep were pulled down and a high encircling wall built to make their prison impregnable.

Outside, life settled down once more. Lotti announced herself pregnant again, and as Charles was away from home, having been sent to Dumouriez to advise the French army on fortification along the border, where it was suffering serious reverses, Lotti spent much of her time with Héloïse. Héloïse began teaching Clothilde to walk, and had to placate the jealous Mathilde by promising to teach her to play the harpsichord.

Olivier was as busy as ever, and was often away, though when he was at home, he treated Héloïse more affectionately, and even slept with her, which she decided was the result of high spirits, and perhaps a certain jealousy of Charles's increasing family. Héloïse found she still disliked the process, but Olivier seemed pleased with her, and she hoped that she might conceive. A child, she thought, would make all the difference to her life. Her flux, due on the twenty-sixth of August, was late, and with each passing day she carried herself more carefully, almost breathless with anticipation.

Then early in the morning of the thirtieth the sleeping house was roused by the unexpected and violent arrival of Lotti. She beat on the door demanding admittance, and fled up to the drawing-room, followed by her maid, governess, children, footman and two nursemaids, demanding that the mistress should be summoned at once, and then sitting down in a chair and burying her face in her hands. When Héloïse and Olivier appeared at the door, both in their dressing-gowns, Lotti cast herself into her friend's arms crying: 'Oh we are undone! What will become of me? Oh, my poor babies! Héloïse, you must save us! Tell Vendenoir he must go to them – get him released. Oh that Charles were here! Don't let them take me too, I beg of you! I know they will come for me next!'

'Lotti, what is it? What has happened?'

'They have taken Uncle Johann away, and locked him up, and they will come for me, too, and what will become of my babies?'

'Lotti, calm yourself. Sit down, do, and tell me what has

happened. Nothing will harm you, I promise,' Héloïse said, gently pressing Lotti into a chair, and detaching from her skirts the older children, who looked very frightened, alarmed, she guessed, by their mother's fear. Olivier stood just inside the door eyeing the scene with misgiving, but held there by curiosity. One of the maids produced a smelling-bottle, and after a few moments Lotti was calm enough to speak.

'They came this morning, Héloïse, four of them. They knocked upon the door as if they would break it down, and arrested Uncle Johann and took him away to prison.'

'But what for? What has he done?' Héloïse cried. She glanced at her husband, whose face was blank.

'I don't know. Nothing, of course nothing. They were from the committee of something or other – I cannot remember. No, it was the committee of the Section, with orders from the Committee of Surveillance, I remember now. They had a paper with Uncle Johann's name on it, and signed by that man Marat. They bade him pack a small bag and come at once.'

'But they must have said *something*,' Héloïse said, bewildered. 'They could not just take him for no reason.'

'They said he was a suspect person, because he was German. I told them Charles would vouch for him, but they would not listen. And, Héloïse, I am German too, though I am married to Charles, and my children are half-German, and I am so afraid. So I came to you. You must help me. Vendenoir must tell them we are not suspects.'

'Be calm, Lotti dear, no-one shall harm you. Olivier will help, of course he will.' She looked across at her husband, who with a sharp gesture ordered the servants and children from the room, bidding the butler to see them fed.

When the door was closed and they were alone, he said grimly, 'This was not meant to happen. It is a mistake, I am sure. If Charles had been here – but it must have been the local Section committee that did it.'

'But, Olivier, what does it all mean?' Héloïse asked, shocked that he seemed to understand the business.

'I will tell you, but on no account must you allow it to go any further. It is a matter of the greatest secrecy. Now, listen – it is not generally known, but the Duke of Brunswick has invaded France. Oh yes, he is over the border, and he has already taken

Verdun, and is marching on Paris. The news will be made public in a few days' time, and we have to organise our defences and send out an army to meet him. But before we strip Paris of her able-bodied men, we must make sure we cannot be stabbed in the back by enemies of the revolution. That is why suspect people are being arrested and taken into custody until the emergency is over.'

'But Uncle Johann is not an enemy of the revolution!' Lotti cried. 'How can he be a suspect?'

'I know, I know,' Olivier said. 'His name should not have been on the list. But there is nothing to worry about – he will be released when the emergency is over. If I had known this was going to happen, I might have prevented it; but the arrangements had to be made in strict secrecy – you can see why.'

'Yes, of course,' Héloïse said, automatically soothing Lotti's wild hair. 'But you will go to the Commune and get him released, won't you, husband? And make sure that Lotti is safe?'

'Very well,' he said, with some reluctance. 'I'll see Marat – he is in charge of public safety. It was a stupid mistake, that's all. I'm going to get dressed now. For God's sake, keep quiet about all this – not a word to anyone, you understand?'

It was late before Olivier returned to the house, and hearing that Lotti was resting in Héloïse's boudoir, he sought his wife in the drawing-room. She looked up from her sewing as he came in, and saw at once from his expression that all was not well.

'It's no use,' he said shortly. 'They won't release him until the emergency is over. I told them who he is, but they said they can't make exceptions. Now don't begin arguing,' he raised a hand to stop Héloïse's protests. 'I've done everything I can. He's safe enough – safer perhaps than he would be at home, once the news gets out that Brunswick is marching on Paris. You remember what happened in April.'

'Where did they take him?' Héloïse asked quietly. 'Did you see him?'

'He is in the Conciergerie. Yes, I saw him. He is comfortable enough, though a little cramped for space. He is sharing a – a room with two other gentlemen.'

Héloïse guessed he had changed the word from 'cell' to 'room' at the last moment.

'Oh, Olivier!'

'Don't,' he said irritably. 'I told you he is all right. He has all he needs, except for some books. I said I would take him some in tomorrow.'

'I'll make up a basket for you to take, with extra clothes, and food, because I don't suppose they have very nice things to eat in prison. Oh Olivier, to think of his being in prison! Uncle Johann, who is so kind, and gentle, and good!'

She raised tragic eyes to him, and he met them for a moment with an expression of anger that she did not understand, before turning abruptly and leaving her.

In the early hours of the third of September, Héloïse again waited sleepless in the drawing room for news, this time not of the King and Queen, but of one almost as close to her as her father. The events that had begun the previous afternoon were so shocking they were beyond comprehension; her mind had thrust them aside, and seized on the one thing it could tackle at a human level – fear for Johann Finsterwalde.

It had begun at the Abbey of Saint-Germain, in whose prison cells three hundred priests had been incarcerated for refusing the oath of loyalty to the Assembly. Some carriages bearing a new consignment of monks and priests for imprisonment had arrived to be met by a crowd of strange-looking men who claimed to be a Tribunal of the People sent to try the priests. The prisoners were dragged from the carriages and butchered on the steps of the Abbey. The Tribunal then went to the nearby Convent of Carmes, where a further hundred and fifty priests were similarly despatched, before returning to the Abbey to deal with the three hundred inmates of its prison.

It was Henri who had brought the news. He had been away for some days in Touraine, and had come riding back in the evening along the rue Saint-Germain, heading for the Pont Neuf. When he reached the junction of the rue de Seine he had heard the disturbance and seen lights in the distance, and had ridden a little way up the street to see what was happening. A group of women were gathered at the corner of the street and he called to them to ask what was happening. One turned and favoured him with a ghastly grin.

'Why, monsieur, you must have been out of town not to know. They are taking care of the rubbish in the prisons. Look, don't you see, there in the gutter?'

Looking down, Henri saw a trickle of red running down the gutter from the direction of the Abbey, and as a gust of wind arose, he heard the horrible sounds more clearly, and smelled the indescribable smell of butchery. His horse smelled it too, and reared and snorted, pulling backwards.

The women laughed, and one of them shouted, 'Your horse is too delicate, monsieur! Vermin must be taken care of!'

At the rue Saint-Anne, he had burst in on Olivier, having a rare night at home with his wife, and told the story, looking like a man in a nightmare.

Héloïse had cried out at once to her husband, 'Olivier, if they are going round all the prisons, what will happen to Uncle Johann?'

'Calm yourself, madame,' Olivier had said, though he looked pale. 'You see they are priests that are being attacked. The people do not like traitor priests, and the news of the Duke's approach with his army must have driven them into a panic. They will not dare to attack the Conciergerie, I assure you.'

Henri shook his head. 'She did not say, that hideous woman, that they were taking care of priests, but of everyone in prison. We had better go and make sure that it does not happen.'

'They will not attack the Conciergerie, I tell you,' Olivier said irritably. 'Besides, what could you and I do against a panicking mob from the suburbs? We should be mad to go outside tonight.'

'Oh, please, Olivier, I beg you,' Héloïse had said. 'I know you have influence with the Commune. I do not wish you to risk your life, but if you can get to the Conciergerie, you may be able to persuade them to let Uncle Johann out, and bring him back here.'

Reluctantly he had agreed, and gone with Henri. That had been hours ago, and Héloïse, sitting alone with her dog and listening to the strange noises-under-silence of the streets outside, wished more than once that she had not begged them to go, for as they had not come back, she feared something might have happened to them. It was near dawn when Olivier came back, alone, and came up to the drawing-room, his face a white mask, his movements automatic, like a man at the far end of weariness. Héloïse jumped up as he came in, and stood unable to speak, her hands clasped, as he walked to a chair and sat down. She thought he would never speak; when he did at last, it was without raising his eyes to her.

'It was no good,' he said. 'There was nothing we could do.'

'What – what do you mean?' she whispered. 'Is he – did they--?'

'They executed everyone in the prison,' he said. His voice was dull, as though it meant nothing to him any more. 'Three hundred and twenty at the Conciergerie. Two hundred and twenty at the Châtelet. They set up a sort of – trial, but none was allowed to speak.'

'Where is Papa?' she managed to say at last.

'He went on elsewhere. He's all right. I had no stomach for it, but he thought he might do some good – God knows how. I came home.' Now he raised his eyes to her, but unseeingly. 'They are beyond controlling, the mob.'

Héloïse thought of the bare-armed men from Marseilles, and shuddered. Uncle Johann, she thought, gentle Uncle Johann, would have been no match for such subhuman creatures. Her mouth dry, she had to ask one other thing. 'Olivier, did they – how did they--?'

He looked at her now, and made one effort on her behalf. 'No,' he said, 'they did not butcher them. It was quite quick – with a sword.' The words seemed to release something in her, and she sat down and began to weep. He looked at her for a moment, and then went away, to his own bed, without a word.

It went on for a week, and Paris, smelling of blood, seemed a place out of the world. The normal life of the city went on, and people moved around as if dazed, avoiding each others' eyes, as the gangs of murderers visited one prison after another and butchered the inmates with indescribable ferocity. Fifteen hundred people were massacred, amongst them many who had been imprisoned for no other crime than being homeless, including a large number of beggar-children in Bicêtre and Salpêtrière.

And when it was all over, the knowledge of it was so terrible that the citizens of Paris could not speak of it or think of it, could do nothing but shut their minds to it and try to forget. Héloïse mourned Uncle Johann, but alone and in silence, for she could not speak of him to Olivier, and Lotti shut herself away from her friend, did not visit, and was not at home to Héloïse's visits. Héloïse felt she blamed Olivier for not somehow rescuing her uncle, and she could understand the feeling, though she knew her husband had done all he could. She was not surprised that her father did not call for a long time afterwards, either; the memory of those events were like a raw wound between people.

The National Convention met for the first time on the twentieth, and Vendenoir, as he had been promised, was elected as a deputy, and took his place in the Manège alongside Vergniaud, Brissot, Gensonnet and their friends, who were now called the Girondins because so many of them came from the Gironde. His friend Saint-Just was also elected, and admiring the cold aesthetic beauty of Saint-Just, Olivier began to copy his style, had his hair cut à la Brutus, wore a flowing scarf instead of a cravat and a gold earring in one ear.

He was at home a great deal more now that he was a deputy, and began to entertain again, and in some style, and Héloïse, pleased with his pleasure, was once more hostess. At the end of the first week of the Convention they gave a dinner, to which Héloïse was anxious to invite Lotti; but her invitation was refused, with a note to the effect that Lotti had miscarried her child and was not well enough to go out in public. Héloïse was deeply afflicted by the news, and, still denied access, sent round a basket of fruit. Her own hoped-for pregnancy had come to nothing, and Olivier had not slept with her again since then.

On the evening of their dinner, she and Olivier were waiting in the drawing-room for their guests to arrive. Olivier was in a good mood, and had complimented Héloïse on her appearance so warmly that she blushed with pleasure. She was wearing a gown in the new style, of voluminous, multi-layered muslin, with no hoops or stiffening, and a wide sash around the high

225

waistline which made the most of her small bust. Her long ringlets had been wound up in and out of a gay turban with a long drooping feather down the back, and she was wearing her ruby necklace, whose stones glowed like drops of blood against her neck and made her colouring look more vivid.

'The new style suits you well, my wife,' Olivier said. 'It makes you look taller. Tonight you look . . . almost beautiful.'

'Thank you, husband,' Héloïse said, her eyes bright. 'And you, if I may say so--'

But she had no time to finish, for the doors opened, and a flustered footman made a botch of announcing her father, and was almost pushed out of the way by him. Héloïse came forward in surprise, for Henri had not been invited to what was intended as a dinner for young people, and stopped before she reached him at the sight of his drawn brows and grim expression.

'Papa, what is it? You look distressed. Has something happened?'

'Has something happened? Oh yes, Marmoset, it most certainly has. But not tonight. You are entertaining?' he seemed to see belatedly that they were dressed up.

'We are awaiting our guests every moment,' Olivier said drily. 'Our *invited* guests.'

'You can so calmly think of entertaining? Have you forgotten the events of three weeks ago? Have you forgotten fifteen hundred murdered prisoners?' Henri said harshly. Héloïse made a gesture towards him, but could not quite touch him, for he seemed to bristle like an angry cat.

'Papa, it was terrible, too terrible to remember. Life must go on.'

'Life must go on,' he repeated strangely. 'And Vendenoir is a deputy. How proud he is of it, too! That was your price, was it, boy?'

'Papa!'

'Price? I don't know what you mean, sir, but I don't like being called boy in my own house,' Vendenoir snapped back.

'To think I gave my daughter to you,' Henri said, as if he had not spoken. 'I thought you a suitable husband for her, fool that I was. I wanted to protect you, Marmoset, and instead I have tied you to this – this . . .'

'Papa, don't!' Héloïse cried in distress.

'Is it too much to ask why you are so bent on insulting me?' Olivier asked coldly.

Henri eyed him strangely, and said, with some force: 'I should not have thought you would want it spoken aloud. But I mean my daughter to know what sort of creature you are, before I take her away. The September massacres, child, which have been blamed on the panic of the faubourgs at the approach of the Duke of Brunswick, were carefully planned, weeks before they happened, by the Committee of Surveillance, under the genial leadership of Marat.'

'What do you say?'

'The arrests in the few days before the massacres began were part of the plan. It was discussed in open committee how to execute them. Marat favoured setting fire to the prisons, but that was thought too dangerous. So Billaud-Varennes suggested simply butchering them.'

'No, Papa, no!'

'Someone said it would be hard to find killers enough, but Billaud-Varennes said they could always be found, if you paid.'

'Even if the – this fairy-tale were true, what has it to do with me?' Olivier said angrily.

'It's true all right. Danton was at the meetings. Danton may be a friend of yours, Vendenoir, but he is an even older friend of mine, and when I asked him for the truth, he told me. He is a very truthful man, you know – it is one of his virtues. It would be better for him if he were not.'

'Papa, please, you cannot mean it,' Héloïse cried, dragging at his hands. '*Please* don't say such things. I think you must be mad or – or ill--'

'My darling, your husband helped Marat and Billaud-Varennes draw up the lists of people to be arrested. I told you I had seen him in their company, did I not? Oh, Finsterwalde was not on the list – I acquit him of that. It was the local committee, a man called Durand, who hates all Germans, who added his name later. Vendenoir went to Marat when he knew and asked for the name to be taken off, but Marat said there could be no exceptions, or the whole plan would be in jeopardy.'

Héloïse looked at her husband at that point. His face was

227

livid, his lips working soundlessly, and her heart went cold inside her. 'Olivier--' she cried despairingly.

'He promised he would be all right. I did not know he was to be killed – Héloïse, I *swear* it! Marat said he would be released later. You must believe me! I did all I could.'

'Swear all you like, it makes no difference now,' Henri said. 'Héloïse, send your maid to pack your bags. You are coming with me. I told you once that a time might come when he would no longer be useful to us, and that time has come. I shall see to it that you are safe. You need no longer depend on this murderer's henchman for protection.'

Héloïse looked from one to the other, from her father's face suffused with anger, to her husband's livid with emotions she could not guess at. She remembered the day he had come back from trying to have Uncle Johann released; she remembered how upset – and guilty? – he had been. *Did* he know about the proposed massacres? She shook her head, trying to clear it.

Olivier saw the gesture, and said to her quickly in a low voice, 'Héloïse, if you want to go, I cannot prevent you – but I beg you not to. I beg you!'

'Afraid your reputation will be damaged?' Henri said nastily. 'A deputy must be above reproach.'

'A new world is beginning, a wonderful new world,' Olivier said, ignoring him, his eyes fixed on Héloïse. 'We talked of it in the woods at Chenonceau, remember? We are to be privileged to help form it. I have not been a very attentive husband to you, I know, but that will change. The good times are coming for us, Héloïse, I promise you. We must go forwards, not cling to the past.'

What was done was done, she thought. Nothing could help those poor murdered people, or bring Uncle Johann back. Did Olivier know more about it than he had told her? She would perhaps never know; but he was right in one thing – they must go forwards. She moved the few steps to his side, and turned to face her father, flinching inwardly at the look of betrayal in his eyes as she said: 'Olivier is my husband, Papa, and my place is here. I will not go with you, and I must beg you never say such things to him again.'

For a moment the scene was frozen, and then Olivier put his arm round her shoulder, drawing her against him, and she straightened proudly. She saw the expression in her father's face become veiled; and just then there was the sound of knocking at the front door below. The first guests were arriving. Without a word, Henri turned and left them, and Héloïse began to tremble.

'Thank you,' Olivier said quietly. 'I shall never forget that. I will make you happy, I promise.'

But Héloïse could not speak, and her legs trembled so much that she had to sit down to try to compose herself to receive the guests for her husband's triumphal dinner.

12

The fine summer weather lasted on through September, and only improved as the month progressed, losing August's harshness, gaining a softness and a gentle, refreshing breeze. The trees did not turn, but lifted green faces to the blue sky, and all the roses in Yorkshire seemed to burst into new life and fragrance.

James brought his mother a white rose from the garden on Michaelmas Eve, to pin to her corsage.

'You can tell it's an autumn rose,' she said, lifting it to her face to breathe its delicate scent. 'They bud and bloom and die so quickly, as if they can't be sure the sun will last them, that they always have a fainting look.'

'Mother, are you sure you want the picnic to take place?' James asked her for what must be the fourth time.

'Of course, my dear. I'm not an invalid, you know,' she said. The Michaelmas Eve picnic had been planned so long ago, that Jemima had expressed surprise when Edward first supposed it should be cancelled, and gently persuaded him that it would not be improper, especially as it was a family outing, on Morland land. She even persuaded them to leave off their mourning: 'Your papa loved beautiful things, and pretty clothes around him. He would not like to see you all in crow black.' She herself had put off her black mourning, and was arrayed in grey silk that was so becoming it hardly seemed like mourning at all. Edward had insisted that everyone must at least wear bands, and Jemima had given up at that point. She touched the black band around James's arm now with a wry smile. 'Your brother is becoming a high stickler, Jamie. Who would have thought it?'

'Old age and spinsterhood,' James said, and Jemima rapped his hand reprovingly.

'You have not so much yourself to be proud of,' she said.

The smart barouche from Shawes, complete with enormous bay horses, coachman and two liveried footmen, arrived in good time carrying Lady Chelmsford and Mary, and took up Jemima and the principal picnic basket. Mary gave up her place and took the drop-seat facing backwards with good-natured promptness, which made Jemima remark as they drew away from the house, 'Age has only improved you, Mary, my love. There was a time when you would have refused the drop-seat with horror, as impairing your dignity.'

'Was I ever so intolerable?' Mary said, smiling. 'Well, yes, I suppose I was. Pray don't remind me of my youthful folly, Mother. It is not kind in you.'

'None of us is entirely free from things we would rather not remember we did,' Flora said.

'Very true,' Jemima said. 'Thank heaven all my children have grown up so satisfactorily. You may assure yourself, Mary dear, that you are now quite perfect!'

Mary laughed. 'Except in one respect, I think you are about to add.'

'Ah yes, there is that,' Jemima sighed, but her eyes were still laughing. 'It might content me just to *understand* why you refused Lord Tonbridge.'

'Is my marriage so important to you, Mother?' Mary said. 'After all, my children would not be vital to the family, and I cannot conceive any other reason you should want me to marry.'

'You wrong me, dearest,' Jemima said. 'Not but what your children would be important, if none of the others marries either, for the property is not entailed, you know, and I must have someone to leave it to. But more than that, I want you to be happy.'

'I am happy,' Mary said promptly.

'But I think it is in the nature of all creatures to want a mate,' Jemima said.

Mary reached across and pressed her hand. 'That may be so, but I would be a great fool, would I not, Mother, to exchange my happy condition for one which did not offer me *more* happiness? I am very happy as I am, you know. I have everything I want – fine clothes, a lovely home, the friendship of dear Flora and Charles, and a great many amusing people around me with whom to do a great variety of amusing things. Now what could marriage offer me more? I should lose by the exchange, I believe.'

'Did you not love Lord Tonbridge, then?'

Mary laughed. 'Oh, mother – love! I like him very much, and I considered carefully, I assure you, before I refused him. But I saw at once that marriage with Billy Tonbridge would not give me *more* of him than I already had. And you see, I have not lost him, for though he has given up pretending for my hand, he is still our good friend – is he not, Flora?'

'I think you could have lived very happily with him,' said Flora, firmly placing herself on Jemima's side. Mary only dimpled engagingly at them, making Jemima think for the thousandth time that there could not be a young woman in England more truly lovely than Mary, though she was eight-and-twenty.

'Very true, ma'am, but I do not believe that is enough to tempt me to marry. I am very sure I shall not say yes until I find a man I can't live without, not one of many I could live with.'

The others were assembled at Watermill Field, and had chosen the best spot for laying out the picnic by the time the barouche arrived. Charles had escorted Louisa and Amelia on horseback; James had brought Lucy in his curricle, and had let her drive his chestnuts part of the way; and Edward had brought Chetwyn and *his* curricle behind his blacks, whom Lucy insisted were not a good pair, despite their perfectly-matched appearance. The estate brake was also there, with the plates and rugs and other paraphernalia of picnicking, and sufficient servants to make all comfortable.

'But they can't start without us,' Jemima said cheerfully, 'for we have the basket with the food in it.' To her slight surprise, John Anstey was also there, having ridden over from York at Edward's invitation.

'Because I was thinking James and I might race our teams later, and settle the business once and for all, and then I should need an unbiased referee,' said Edward.

John looked a little awkward, seeing it was so much a family party, and Jemima hastened to make him welcome, saying, 'I think of you as much one of the family as my dear son Chetwyn.

After all, John, you spent almost as much time at Morland Place as at home when you were a boy.'

John Anstey bowed gratefully over her hand and said, 'Dear Lady Morland, you could not think me more a son than I should like to be.'

'Prettily said!' Mary laughed. 'Come and sit by me and tell me all the gossip. How *comfortable* it is to be with old friends!' Which, Jemima thought, was just Mary's way. There wasn't an ounce of romance in her.

It was a thoroughly pleasant party. The sun shone like liquid gold from a deep blue heaven, and the tree-shadows crept slowly across the grass, cooling them in the middle heat of the day. Monsieur Barnard was equally a master of cold food as hot, and the array of pies and pasties, galantines and brawns, pickles and salads, cakes and creams and jellies, was as impressive in its way as any banquet. There were plums and pears and the finest English apricots from the orchard, and sweet, scented little muscat grapes from the succession-house; and there was Morland cider to drink, and champagne kept chilled by a box of ice from the Shawes ice-house, willingly donated by Charles.

They ate at their leisure, and chatted, and groups were formed and re-formed, conversational alliances made and broken; until, when the sun was at its greatest power, a pleasant languor fell over them, talk grew desultory, and often it was only the sound of the sweet autumn breeze rustling the leaves, or the champing of the horses grazing which broke the silence. Edward and Chetwyn had gone down to the river bank and were sitting together against a tree trunk, leaning against each other, their heads touching, absorbed in one of their long, muted conversations. Near by, Lucy sat on the bank, her shoes and stockings off, dabbling her feet in the fast-running water, and occasionally adding something to their talk.

There was something disarming in the way they accepted Lucy's company, Jemima thought. No, there was no vice in them, or in their strangely intense relationship. It was simply, she thought, that Edward had never grown up, in his heart. Forced into an early maturity by his being the heir, isolated from the company of his peers, he had developed such a hunger for friendship that it could never be appeased. As far as his heart went, he was still the lonely boy Chetwyn had befriended and championed; and that innocent love they shared was Ned's refuge from the responsibilities of his adult life. Chetwyn's too, she thought, though Chetwyn's hunger was more lazy than chronic: it was easier to love Edward than to risk loving a woman and a stranger.

A group consisting of Mary and Charles, John Anstey and Louisa had broken up, and John had taken Louisa a little aside, and was teaching her, with the aid of a piece of fern and two flat stones, how coal was made, and how it could be extracted. Jemima observed that alliance indulgently. Louisa, who had always loved Allen best of all creatures in the world, was stricken and lost without him, and it was like John's thoughtfulness to pay her attention now, when she most needed it. It crossed her mind, vaguely, that it might be a good idea . . .

'Matchmaking again, Mama,' James said in her ear, making her start. He leaned on her shoulder from behind, and rested his cheek against hers, looking in the same direction as she. How sweet he smelled, she thought. His father had always had that same sweetness to his skin, the result of something natural in him, not of any artificial perfume.

'I should not do anything so improper,' she said. 'I was just thinking how poor Louisa misses him.'

'We all do,' James said quietly. 'You must miss him most of all.'

'In a way,' she said. 'But in another way, he seems to me still here. He's all around, for we had all our lives together here. When I was a little girl, he was the one who cared for me, and stood up for me, and educated me.' She thought of the time she had fallen off the orchard wall, and he had bathed her cut hand, and given her cakes and gooseberries, and talked to her kindly. In her lonely, unregarded childhood, he had been her place of refuge; and when, after ten years of miserable marriage, she had been widowed and homeless and penniless, he had come, like a knight on a white horse, to rescue her. 'He gave me a home, when I was homeless. He bought Morland Place back for me, and then . . .' She could not speak for a moment, and James pressed his cheek against hers in understanding. She went on after a moment, 'Just after – he died – you remember, Jamie, how I cried terribly, and I said . . .'

'You seemed almost angry', he remembered.

'Yes. I said, "You promised you would never leave me." But I was wrong, you see. He didn't.' The breeze brought for a moment the reedy smell of the river, ruffled their hair about their brows, and died down again, leaving the sound of a chaffinch somewhere near by chipping away at the silence. 'He is always here with me. It's wrong to want to die. I am glad to be living still in this beautiful world of God's, and when He calls me home at last, I shall be glad to go, too, and be with your father again. God knows best. He always knows best.'

James swallowed against a pain in his throat, and said, 'That is true serenity, Mother. I wish I had it.'

They sat in silence for a while, watching the others, and the slow shadows lengthening, and then Jemima said in a renewed voice: 'It will come to you. I know a mother should not have favourites, but you always seemed to me the one of my children most like him. You have that inner strength of his. You'll find your place one day. Only . . .'

'Only,' he asked, smiling a little, knowing what was coming.

'Only I wish you could let go of the past. I know – I think – you really loved her, and none of us realised it at the time. If we had, we might have tried to arrange things differently; but it's too late now.'

'Is it?' he said in a hard voice. She turned herself enough to see his face, and put her hand up to his cheek.

'Yes,' she said. 'Make a new life, my darling. Find someone to love you and marry you, and have children. You owe that much to your father, at least.'

'Oh, Mother,' he said in exasperation, and then jumped up, crying, 'Come on, Ned, stir up! Everyone's fallen asleep. What say we start a game of something? Or what about that race? We could do it here as well as anywhere, round and round the field like Roman chariots.'

'Oh, Oxhey, where's Miss Lucy?' Jemima asked one day in October as she came out of the steward's room.

'I believe she's in the long saloon, madam, reading,' the butler said. I should have guessed, Jemima thought with a smile, heading for the stairs. Had they been a fashionable family, they would have renamed the long saloon and called it the book room or even the library, for Jemima's great-grandfather, Martin Morland, had been quite a collector of books and had removed the Jacobean beaufets from the long wall opposite the windows and had had the estate carpenter cover the whole wall with bookshelves. One day soon, she thought, they would have to see about making extra shelves on the short walls, for the number of books was beginning to exceed their accomodation. Then she laughed, remembering how often she and Allen had said the same thing to each other over the past thirty years.

Lucy was there all right, sitting in one of the window-seats, her head so buried in her book that she did not at first notice her mother's entrance. The window looked over the inner court of the original, fifteenth-century house, called the herb garden, or sometimes Eleanor's garden; though since they had built on the servants' rooms in the attic it got too little sunshine for the herbs to do well. I must see about making a new herb garden somewhere else, she thought, and remembered that she had thought that before, too. Between the windows along that wall were some of the family portraits: Nanette Morland by Holbein, in a blue velvet coif; India Morland, with dogs, by Kneller; Mary Moubray, rather stiff with heraldic shield, by Lely; Mary Esther Morland, very dainty, by Van Dyck. How well she knew them all. Above Lucy's bent head was the wedding portrait of Arabella Morland, her great-grandmother, by Wissing, looking positively rebellious: she had been one of the stormy characters in the Morland family's history, daughter of the Countess Annunciata, always happier on horseback than in the drawing-room, and crowning her uneasy career by abandoning her four-year-old child and running away, never to be seen again. Why is it we seem to breed them, Jemima thought with a sigh, these women who would sooner be men? It was appropriate that Lucy should have chosen to sit beneath that pagan goddess.

'What is it you are reading, love?' she asked. Lucy's head shot up, and her immediate frown was replaced by a glad look.

'Oh, Mother! It's a book on anatomy that Charles lent me, from Shawes' library. Did you want me for something?'

'I brought you this letter, from Harry, dearest, sent under cover with William's letter to me. He writes it to you, personally, you know,' she added, temptingly. It would normally have been a matter of great excitement to Lucy to get a letter of her own, but her mind was on other things today. She received it from her mother's hand, looked at it absently, and then put it down on the seat beside her.

'I'm glad you came up, Mother – there's something I wanted to talk to you about,' she said.

'What on earth was Charles doing with a book on anatomy?' Jemima asked, sitting beside her daughter and picking up the book in amazement. 'This is quite a new book, too. It must have cost a great deal.'

'Of course it's new, Mother – there'd be no point in a book that was out of date. Charles is very good about it – he gets all the latest works in London, and sends them up to Shawes, and he said I can borrow anything I want from there, for as long as I like.'

'That's very kind of him,' Jemima said doubtfully. 'But I expect he knows you'll take good care of them.'

'But the point is, it isn't enough. I can learn so much out of books, but after that – I need someone to explain things, and then I need the practice they have, too.'

'Who have?'

'And there's dissection, too – how can one possibly get on without dissection demonstrations? And surgery, and ward-walking. So you see, Mother, it's essential that I go to the university.'

'Lucy what are you talking about?' Jemima said, bemused.

'It came to me, you see, when Jamie and I had that bit of sport at the races, and I dressed as a boy. Women can't go to medical school. Edinburgh would be the best: they have the best teachers there, and there's no lower age limit. I'm positive I could pass the matriculation examination, and my Latin and mathematics are better than I'd need, but I'd have to have your help, because you see there are the fees, and the lodgings and tuition to pay for.'

'Lucy, please tell me what you are talking about!'

'I mean to dress up as a boy and go to Edinburgh University to read medicine, so that I can become a doctor,' Lucy said patiently, as one talking to an idiot.

'What? You're dreaming, child! It is impossible, and even if it weren't, it would be most improper,' Jemima gasped.

'But you must help me, Mother,' Lucy wailed.

'I shall do no such thing! Besides, it would never work.'

'It would! I was just like a boy in those jockey clothes.'

'Listen to me, Lucy,' Jemima said firmly. 'It is one thing to dress up as a boy for a joke, for one race, but quite another to try to keep up the deception day after day, week after week. The course is something like four years, I believe – how could you hope to deceive people for that long? And even if you did, what good would it do? You couldn't pretend to be a man all your life.'

'But, Mother--'

'No. You must forget this nonsense. Women can't be doctors, and there's an end to it. I should have forbidden you to read these books, if I had known what silly nonsense they were putting into your head. Now don't argue with me any more, Lucy. It puts me out of all patience with you. I think you had better put that book away and go out into the fresh air, take a walk around the gardens until dinner time. And I shall speak to Father Thomas about directing your interest into more fruitful channels.'

She stood up, and looked down at her daughter, and a strange sympathy for her frustration made her say more gently, 'I am sorry, Lucy, but it's the way the world is. There's nothing we can do about it.'

Lucy looked at her for a long time before answering, and when she did speak it was absently, as though she were thinking about other, more important things.

'Yes, Mother,' she said.

Scarborough in October was at the end of its season, though the weather was still mild enough and the sea warm enough to tempt a few hardy souls, and the last of the bathing-machines was still being drawn up and down by its stolid, hairy horse. The familiar seaside smell of seaweed and horse-dung was overlaid with the misty smell of autumn, and every rooftop sported a row of birds, like a strange architectural detail, refugees from less clement, more northerly climes. The sun rose veiled and hazy in the mornings, and the evenings were cool enough to make one glad to hurry home to a bright fire from the grey, darkling seascape.

238

But eleven in the morning was still the hour of promenade, when the professional invalids made their way to and from the medicinal wells, and the other visitors strolled up and down the railed walk along the sea-shore or sat on the benches provided by the civic council in sheltered places. There was the circulating library to visit, too, and the elegant tearooms to patronise, and for an hour or two, the town had a populated air, all be it with a faint overtone of melancholy that was inevitable to the time and the place.

The last two artists were also in evidence on the promenade, survivors of a fashionable army of sketchers put to rout by the advance of autumn. One was a young lady in a handsome brown pelisse, her hat secured by a long scarf of gauze, making yet another careful copy of the view from the seat nearest the tearooms of the promenade, cliffs, sea and sky. The other was a slightly built but extremely handsome young man, who lounged at different points of the promenade with his back to the sea and executed a series of rapid and revealing sketches of the people passing by. A close observer might have noticed that he seemed particularly interested in a young woman who had come to sit on a bench nearby but who had not, as yet, looked at him. He edged nearer, lifted his hat to her in an absent sort of way, and proceeded to draw the piece of wall and two straggling butterfly-bushes behind her right shoulder.

'How is he today?' James asked after a moment. They spoke in low voices, without looking at each other. This end of the walk was not popular, but if anyone approached, he moved a little away and tried out a piece of perspective, while she dipped again into the book of essays on her lap which she had got from the library, her excuse for being out.

'Better. A little better, I think. It suits him here. But I think we will leave soon. Haven't you noticed how cold the nights are getting?'

'All my nights are cold. All my life is cold without you, Mary.'

'Oh Jamie, don't. Please don't.'

'I can't help it.' He looked at her for a moment, a burning blue gaze that she could not meet. 'How long can we go on with this – this *farce*?'

'As long as we have to. For ever,' she said evenly.

'No!' His voice was no less passionate for being kept low. 'I won't do it, Mary. I want you, I want you entirely, properly, for my wife.'

'I am someone else's wife,' she said.

'What kind of a marriage is it, to an old man, an invalid, whom you have never loved, whom you never will love? Oh Mary, leave him, I beg you, and let me make a life for you.'

'How can I leave him? He is old and ill, as you say yourself. What kind of a woman would I be to leave him now? What would people say of me?'

'I don't care what people say.'

'Well, I do. I don't want to live in shame, with people whispering behind my back.'

'They could whisper all they liked, if we couldn't hear them. We'd go abroad, where no one knows us.'

'I don't want to live abroad. I want to live in my own country, in my own town, and bring up my child as an English gentleman.'

'*My* child,' James said savagely. 'Don't forget that. Mine!'

'No!' She looked at him for the first time, holding his gaze with her dark steady one. 'He is John Skelwith, son of John Skelwith. Understand that, Jamie: he is John's son, and I will never allow anyone to say differently, not even you. I don't want him branded with my sins, and that's what he would be. You are never to tell him, never! I want him to have a normal life. That's why I must stop seeing you. I have lived in the shadow all these years, skulking and plotting, seeing you secretly, snatching a little forbidden joy here and there. But it's got to stop. He is getting to the age where he will notice things. I don't want him to be ashamed of me.'

James had paled. His hands stopped drawing, and gripped upon his pencil until the knuckles whitened. She looked at him steadily, though her heart was breaking, for his lean, handsome face was so familiar to her, dear beyond any other, and his blue eyes were filled with such pain that she hated herself for inflicting it upon him. But there was nothing she could do. His strange preference for her, when he was scarcely more than a boy, had endured against all expectation, but it was destroying both of them, and she, as the elder and wiser, had to be the one to end it, for she knew he never could.

'It has to be, dearest,' she said gently. 'There is nothing else we can do. It has gone on too long already, and it brings no happiness to either of us. I have no right to risk my husband and my child, and I won't do it, for something that is so little use to us.'

'But one day – perhaps soon – when you are free again . . .' James stammered, but she shook her head.

'I won't wish death on him. He has been good to me, James, though you won't believe it. And I don't think I'd marry you even if I were free. There's little John to consider, you see. Do you think you could live with him as his stepfather, and never tell him? No, of course you couldn't. When that day comes, that John dies, I will go away from York and set up in some other town – Harrogate perhaps, or here – and bring him up in peace.'

'But if I am never to see you again, what will become of me?' James said.

'You will be better off by far – yes, yes you will, believe me! You have wasted so much of your life loving me. You must find someone else, and marry, and have children and be happy.'

'How can I be happy without you? How can I have a wife who is not you? You are my soul, Mary, my very soul!' he cried.

She looked more stern now than sad. 'It's wrong, Jamie, and you know it. I can't go on sinning all my life. I am so *tired* of sin: I want a little peace. Can't you see that?'

The pencil snapped, and he cast the two halves away from him in a gesture of anger and despair. 'I can see that you are tired of *me*!' he said, and he sounded, even to himself, petulant, which made him angrier. 'If you don't love me any more, why don't you just say so, instead of making fine speeches?'

'Very well,' she said, her voice wavering a little. 'I don't love you any more.'

He met her eyes; there was a silence, in which a gull roaming the air above them cried achingly, and Jamie thought he felt something inside him break, something that could not be put together again. Then he dropped his sketch-book and sat beside her on the bench, taking her hands and kissing them, one after the other.

'No, no,' he said, 'not like that, my love. Don't let us part on a lie. If you really want me to, I'll go away, but say you love me.'

She closed her eyes, for otherwise he would have seen her tears, and she did not want to do that to him. She bit her lip, and nodded.

'Say it,' he urged softly.

'I love you,' she whispered. There was someone approaching, an elderly man with a stout dog on a leash. James stood up hurriedly and picked up his sketch-book, and cast about him for the working end of his pencil. The elderly gentleman passed, his eyes decently averted. Mary recovered herself, and searched her pockets for a handkerchief, which presently James supplied.

'You never have one about you, my love,' he teased her gently. 'What you will do--' He had meant to make a joke, to ease things, but his throat closed on the words.

Mary blew her nose and straightened herself, and said in a matter-of-fact voice, 'I had better go. I have been away too long really.' She stood up. Is that all, he thought? Is that the end of our lives, just like that?

'You needn't go – I mean, you needn't leave York,' he said abruptly. 'I shan't make things difficult for you. I don't think you are right, but I shall respect your decision.'

'What will you do?' she asked him. He turned his head away from her, looked at the grey, slowly-lifting sea.

'War is coming,' he said. 'I shall take a commission in a line regiment, perhaps.' They both had the same vision, of his dying bravely in battle, her name on his lips. She shook the idea away, and almost smiled.

'You would hate it, my dear,' she said lightly. 'Such discomfort, and no hot water for weeks on end.'

He laughed aloud, his face lighting, making her heart turn over in her. 'How well you know me! Oh, Mary . . .' Suddenly serious again. 'Can't you . . . ?'

'Goodbye, Jamie,' she said hastily. 'God bless you.' She turned and was gone, walking lightly, a thin woman in a well-cut, grey wool pelisse, seeming what she was, a well-to-do, middle-aged housewife; but concealing, James thought, so much more. The gull swooped past him, crying, and he turned away to look at the sea again. What to do now? He felt numb inside. Marry someone else, he supposed. It didn't much matter whom. Let his mother choose a bride for him, and he would do his duty.

A sunny day early in November, after almost a week of rain, was so tempting that despite the lack of companion, Mary Morland could not resist going for a walk in St. James's Park. She considered taking a maid or a footman with her, for propriety, and then dismissed the idea. She was old enough for society not to misjudge her, and servants did so dislike walking, that they made one feel obliged to curtail the outing. She put on her new sage green pelisse with the sable trim, and a jaunty hat – for one never knew whom one might meet – and set off.

She was not half-way to the pond when a voice interrupted her reverie.

'Why, Miss Morland! What pure delight, to meet you thus unexpectedly.'

Mary turned, smiled, and curtsied. 'Why, Captain Harvey. What are you doing here?'

He made a vague gesture over his shoulder. 'The Admiralty, ma'am, combined with this unseasonal sunshine, and the proximity of the Park. But you, ma'am – all alone? This will not do.'

'Now I beg you will not be absurd, Captain Harvey,' she said firmly. 'I am far beyond the age of needing to be chaperoned everywhere, especially since I am virtually on my own doorstep here.'

'But I was not thinking of propriety, Miss Morland,' Captain Harvey said, fixing her with a look which would have made a lesser woman blush to her shoes, 'only of the terrible waste! London's most fascinating woman, walking alone? What can men have come to, since I was last here?'

'You cannot soften me by such gross flattery,' she said sternly, 'for now I come to think of it, you are not in my good books.'

'How can I have offended? Tell me, and I will make amends,' he said, with grovelling gestures. Mary bit her lip to stop herself laughing.

'You have been in London a whole week, sir, and not called

upon us. What can you have been doing, to make you so remiss?'

'A sea-officer, especially a captain, has so many things to do when he arrives in port, ma'am, that I have had not a moment to spare,' he said, but his eye was so merry, she distrusted him.

'Aye, but *what* things?' she asked suspiciously.

'Oh Miss Morland, I would so *very* much rather not answer that question,' he laughed.

'Just as I thought! Flora says you are *not* respectable. I shall probably do more harm to my reputation by being seen talking to you, than by walking in the Park alone.'

'In that case,' he smiled, offering his arm, 'may I have the honour to escort you?'

She laughed, tucked her hand under his arm and walked on with him.

'That's better,' he said. 'I feel strange without a woman on my arm. Where were you going, particularly? Was it the cows, or the pelicans?'

'I was going to feed the ducks,' she said, a little defiantly, for she knew it was not a tonnish thing to do. 'And you?'

'Why, as a matter of fact, I was upon that same errand myself.'

She stopped, withdrew her arm, and looked at him severely. 'None of your sea stories, Captain,' she said sternly. 'I warn you I am very hard to placate.'

He spread his hands in innocence. 'But indeed, you wrong me, ma'am. I was going to feed the ducks, truly. Look, I have a bag of crumbs in my pocket, if that is proof enough.' He pulled open a pocket and she peered in, and then cocked her head at him doubtfully. 'They do enjoy the sunshine so much, poor things, I love to watch them,' he said sentimentally, and then began to laugh. 'Oh dear Miss Morland, you look just like a very wild bird eyeing a gamekeeper's trap when you tilt your head like that! Indeed, I can't bamboozle you. I called at Chelmsford House, and they told me where you had gone, so I begged a bag of crumbs and hurried after you.'

'That's better,' Mary said with a satisfied air, giving him back her hand. 'That sounds more like the truth. But tell me, you did not ask Hawkins for crumbs?'

'No, indeed! I can face a French man o'war with three decks

of guns blazing, but it would take more than mere courage to do that! I asked the second footman, the one with the face like a flounder.'

'Walter,' Mary said. 'Yes, now I come to think of it, he does look somewhat like a flounder. And talking of French men o'war, how was your cruise? From William's letters I understand that it was composed of a great deal of pleasure and no action. Did you come across him at all, and my young brother, and Jack?'

'Oh, we had a fair amount of diplomatic business on shore,' Harvey said airily. 'Governors' dinners and balls and private house parties. Most important, you know, to keep the people on our side.'

'I imagine so,' Mary said drily. 'Dancing with the pretty daughters of local government officials must be the most tiresome part of a captain's duty – and dangerous, too! I wonder you have not come back wounded in the heart.'

'Pretty girls are more in William's line than mine,' he said. 'I saw him at a number of dances, flirting quite dreadfully.' He shook his head, making Mary laugh.

'William never flirts – he's too serious. Did you see the boys?'

'No, I was not likely to. Only officers get invited on shore, you know. And I hardly danced above a dozen times, I must tell you, being past the age when young ladies consider me an eligible dancing-partner. I spent all my time in the card-room, playing chicken-whist with the powdered old dowagers.'

'Doing it very much too brown, Captain Harvey!' Mary laughed. 'You, too old to dance? Another of your sea-stories.'

'As much a story as your being too old to need a chaperone,' he said, pressing her hand against his side. 'Besides,' he went on in a different voice, 'pretty girls bore me. When I am wounded in the heart, it will be by someone with conversation and character, not by a mere canvas, however well executed.'

It might have been a deliberate and very handsome compliment; but Mary restrained her gratitude, remembering both Flora's and William's comments about Captain Harvey. Flora, telling Mary that he was not respectable, had enumerated a very young widow in Deptford, two ladies of mature charms in Bath, a renowned courtesan in Wimpole Street and a number of naval lights o'love from Torbay to Spithead; while William

245

had innocently let drop the existence of wealthy ladies in Jamaica, Santa Lucia and Antigua with whom Captain Harvey was evidently on more than friendly terms. Glancing sidelong at her companion under her lashes, she thought what a very dangerous-looking man he was. His skin was naturally dark, even without the addition of his sea-tan, and his eyes were dark too, and though often lit with laughter, it was as often as not a sardonic and mocking laughter, which did nothing to lighten his unfashionable darkness for those who like fair skins and blue eyes. His hair was black, vigorously curling, rather coarse, as though with the sheer force of his vitality. He wore it long, not plaited like William's, but in loose lovelocks like a gypsy or a Corsair. But looking past all that, Mary observed that his features were well cut and fine, his lips beautiful and his chin decorated by a perfectly frivolous dimple. She imagined for a wild second running her finger down that dimple, and shivered suddenly; he looked down at her, and smiled faintly, so much as if he knew what she was thinking that for the first time in years she felt herself blushing. It was very necessary to introduce a neutral topic of conversation, so she said, 'William says we shall certainly have a war next year. Do you agree with him?'

'Oh, yes,' he said promptly. 'Events in France have gone too far now, after the terrible massacres in Paris, and the king being deposed. And the French armies have been doing altogether too well. Did you know their General Dumouriez is in Brussels? The Flemings, I think, rather welcomed the change of master, and were glad enough to see the Austrians driven back. But after that comes Holland, and if they manage to annexe all the low countries, they will seriously interrupt our trade.' He glanced at her. 'Are you really interested in world politics, Miss Morland? Or should I tell you what a very fetching hat you are wearing?'

'No, no, politics, I pray you,' Mary said hastily. 'Is it true that the navy is already being expanded?'

'Well, not entirely. The government will leave it to the last minute, as governments always do, to fit out the ships and man them; but those of us who were commissioned for the summer cruise will not be paid off, so in that sense it is true.'

'You are lucky, I think.'

'Yes, it will put us a step ahead of all the good officers on the beach. It's an unfair world, Miss Morland.'

'Fairer than the army – at least naval captains have to be able to sail their ships.'

'There are some who – but I will not stoop to slander. There's a seventy-four for me, I know, and perhaps for William, too. Lady Chelmsford is a good friend, and well liked by the old admirals.' There was something in his tone as he said it which Mary could not quite understand – something almost like disapproval; but he went on lightly: 'And shall you worry for me, Miss Morland, as well as for William, when war begins and we go out to face the French guns? Shall you be a *little* bit sorry, even, when my cannon-shot gets me?'

'Please don't talk so,' Mary said quickly.

He pressed her hand again, and said with mocking eyes, 'It distresses you?'

'It is most improper,' she said repressively. He gave a shout of laughter.

'Holed and sunk! I should know better than provoke you into firing, Miss Morland! And here we are, at the pond, and the ducks are eyeing us already like pickpockets at a country fair. Let us produce our bags, and shew ourselves to society engaged in this most innocent of pastimes. Who could think ill of a man who feeds ducks in St. James's Park?'

'King Charles the Second used to feed them every day,' Mary said severely. 'I think you had better not rely on it for your rehabilitation.'

13

A January afternoon in 1793 was so dim and grey that a lamp had been lit in the big foaling-box at Twelvetrees. By its warm light, the mare Lyonesse sweated and strained, encouraged by a groom and the horse-doctor, but far more by the very small freckled assistant who stood by her head and murmured to her between pains, and strained when she strained.

'Next time should do it,' Morgan Proom said, trying to sound cheerful, though his head ached and his limbs seemed filled with lead. Having been paid yesterday for some work he had done at a stud farm in Wensleydale, he had embarked on a drinking-bout which had been intended to go on for several days, but which had been interrupted by an urgent message from Twelvetrees. Lyonesse was a very valuable and successful brood-mare, and so he had obeyed the summons, but he doubted if the golden-chestnut mare could feel worse than he did at this moment. 'Now, you lad, take this rope, and keep a steady pull on it when I say so. Ready, Lucy?'

'We're ready,' Lucy said, rubbing the mare's cold ears.

'Pull,' said Morgan, as the mare's flanks braced for another pain; the lad took up on the rope, and after a moment or two the foal came slithering out in a wet and leggy bundle to land in the straw, and the mare gave a strange, low whickering cry. Morgan was bent over the foal at once, wiping away the remains of the enclosing caul with a whisp of hay, and removing the foaling-rope from the slim pasterns. 'It's a filly,' he said. 'Big 'un, too. Who was the sire, Lucy? Yes, let her turn, now, she wants to lick her over. Good girl. Off you run, lad, and see about that warm mash.' The mare nosed at the new foal, knuckering constantly, and the foal sneezed and flapped its ears, and under the stimulus of her mother's rough tongue began trying to get her legs under her. 'That's the girl. Good mare, good mare.'

'Shouldn't we help her?' Lucy asked, aching to do something.

'No, let her struggle. It'll make her strong. She'll be up in a minute, and then all will be right. See, there she goes – straight for the udder. Marvellous how they know.'

Lucy looked at him sideways. 'You sound as though you feel a little better.'

He grimaced. 'Not at all. I feel terrible. But I love to see mother and child like that, when the little one gets his nose into the udder for the first time.'

'I'm glad its a filly – that will mean we'll keep her here always. And I hate it when they're gelded.'

'You shouldn't be sentimental, not if you want to be a horse-doctor,' Morgan teased her, and she looked indignant.

'I'm not sentimental. And I know they have to be gelded, if they're going to be hacks or carriage horses. I just don't like – nature to be tampered with,' she said consideringly. 'Anyway, it is a filly, and Edward said I could name her. She's by Mansfield, you know, so she'll probably be quite light. I shall call her Mimosa. If she'd been a colt, I'd have called her Maréchale.'

'Well, a good name's never wasted. You can use it another time,' Morgan said. 'She's a fine little filly all right. Now what do you say to coming back to my caravan when we've settled the mare, and wetting the baby's head with a drop of lemonade?'

Lucy snorted derisively. 'Lemonade be damned!' she said. 'You're desperate to get back to your caravan because you were interrupted in your drinking. If you haven't got half a dozen bottles of smuggled French brandy under your bunk, I'm a Dutchman. You'll be drunk as a brewer's pony by supper time.'

Morgan Proom drew on his dignity. 'Lucy Morland, I'm ashamed to hear such language on your lips! And the brandy isn't smuggled, it's free-traded. I'm a firm supporter of free trade, you know.'

'Well, I'll come with you anyway,' Lucy said, unperturbed, 'because I doubt if you'll find your way alone. You're cross-eyed with the headache as it is. And I've always wanted to try brandy. Edward won't let me.'

'I should think not, indeed,' Morgan said, genuinely shocked. 'And nor will I. I've beer or cider or lemonade, take your pick.'

'I can't understand why you have lemonade to hand,' Lucy

said later, when she was settled on the only stool the caravan boasted, watching Morgan draw her a piggin of cider. 'It seems so unlike you.'

'Old habit,' he said, handing her the wooden piggin and offering griddle-cakes on a wooden plate. 'I got used to my tot of lemon juice in the navy, and it keeps me healthy. A man that drinks a lot, has need of help. Ruinous to the health, drink is, but what is a man to do?'

Years ago Lucy would have argued with him, but she knew him too well now, and understood, in a dim and wordless sort of way, the pain in his soul that made him drink.

'Well, here's to Lyonesse, and Mimosa,' she said, raising her cup. Morgan lifted his brandy in return.

'Here's to them! We did a good job today, Lucy Morland. By God, what a doctor you'd have made! I'd give an arm to have you for my son, if the good Lord hadn't seen fit to make you a female.'

Lucy frowned. 'It's hateful. Everything nice happens to boys. I hate being a girl! I can't go to university, or join the navy like the boys, or be a doctor.'

'Some females serve in the navy,' Proom said, chuckling. Lucy's face brightened.

'A story!' she said, tucking her left foot under her and settling herself for it. 'I know the signs. Come on, Morgan, tell me a story. Females in the navy — you don't mean officers' wives or anything like that, do you?'

'No, no, there are always a few of those on a ship. It's not permitted, but it's winked at, provided there's no trouble. We always had a few women on board, and they came in handy from time to time. In battles they'd work in the magazine, handing out powder charges, or in the cockpit, helping with the wounded. Not officers' wives, of course,' he added hastily, 'but ratings' or petty-officers' women. No, this is something quite different I'm thinking of. This was a woman who served in His Majesty's Navy as a rating — ah, and a damn' good one, too.'

'Begin at the beginning,' Lucy demanded, taking a thoroughly naval swig at her cider and selecting a griddle-cake to munch.

'Well, it was during the American wars, on board the *Vener-*

able – not the present one, you understand. She's a seventy-four. No, the *Venerable* I mean was a fifty, but she was only carrying forty-four guns, because she was so old and rotten she couldn't carry the weight. She went down off Martinique back in – well, I can't exactly remember the date, seventy-eight or nine, I think -- in a moderate sea.'

'But the woman, Morgan, get to the bit about the woman sailor.'

'Well, we had this sailor – damned good one, too, rated foretopman – called Lazra Bowman. A negro, you know. Don't get many of them in the navy, but they can be good seamen. Everyone thought Lazra was short for Lazarus – it wasn't. It was Elizabeth. Served five years and never got found out.'

'Did no-one know?' Lucy asked, breathless.

'Well, her mess-mates did, but they kept her secret. I suppose she made it worth their while – sharing her rum-ration and so on. And sometimes messes get very tight together – vows of loyalty and brotherhood and so on. Anyway, they never gave her away.'

'It must have been dangerous for her,' Lucy mused. Morgan took a swig at his brandy.

'Oh, they wouldn't have touched her,' he said. 'She wore a marlinspike in her belt day and night, and she'd have put it through the throat of any man who touched her. Besides, she was as ugly as the Devil – not that *that* would stop a sailor after three months at sea – but still.'

Lucy had not been thinking of that particular danger, and blushed to hear such talk, even from Morgan, but he was not looking at her, and the moment passed. Many a question was seething in her brain, but most of them were not the sort of thing she could ask. Instead she said. 'I'm astonished *no-one* else realised. I mean, after five years . . .'

'I expect her being a negro helped,' Morgan said easily. 'And actually, one other person *did* know. She took a splinter wound during an action one day, and had to be taken down to the surgeon. It was in a place that couldn't help revealing her gender. But he kept her secret too.'

Lucy smiled slyly. 'And why did you keep her secret, Morgan? Did she make it worth your while too?'

'Lucy Morland, I've told you she was as ugly as a Spanish

guardacostas,' he said hotly, 'and I don't like to hear such talk from you. If you persist in being so vulgar, I shall have to forbid you to visit me.'

'Oh, don't worry, I only say things like that when I'm with you, never at home. I have a little sense, you know. But why did you keep her secret, Morgan?'

He shrugged. 'She liked being a sailor, and she was a good one. Why should I peach on her? Who would it have served?'

'I should think if she had ever been found out, it would have reflected badly on you that you didn't report it. They'd have thought you didn't notice the difference.'

'Now that is the outside of enough, madam. You had better go home, and this instant before you shock me,' Morgan said, rousing himself. Lucy finished her cider and stood up.

'I know, you want to get properly drunk, and you can't do it with me here. Well, I'll go. Goodbye, Morgan. I'll come and see you when you're sober again – next week.'

But the following week, Proom, though sober, was ill, for the long bout of drinking combined with the cold weather had given him a chill which rapidly developed into a fever. When she heard about it, Lucy went at once to visit him, and found him in a poor state, crouched shivering in his cot, with a blanket round his shoulders and a shawl over his head.

'Now, Lucy, don't look so upset,' he said, his teeth chattering. 'There's nothing to this – just a touch of tropical fever from a long time back. It recurs from time to time. I'll have it out of me in a day or two.'

'I've come to nurse you, Morgan,' she said, but he drove her determinedly away.

'You'll do nothing of the sort,' he said. 'I don't like to have women fussing round me. That's why I never married.'

'You need someone to take care of you,' she said stubbornly; but it wasn't for another three days that she was able to persuade him that he needed attention, and by then the fever had developed alarmingly. Lucy persuaded her mother to have the physician from York visit Morgan's caravan, much to Morgan's disgust.

'I know more than any lily-handed pill-roller from the city,'

252

he gasped as well as he could, trying to raise himself from the pillow and failing. The physician examined him with distaste, which he overcame only through his loyalty to Jemima and the extra-large fee he had been offered, and pronounced that he had fever of the lungs.

'Will he recover?' Lucy asked anxiously.

'If he is kept warm, and fed nourishing broths, and above all, if he abstains from alcohol, I believe he may,' the physician said graciously. 'He has a strong constitution.'

Jemima appointed one of the women from the house to nurse the horse-doctor, telling Lucy firmly that it was not a child's business; and indeed, Morgan did begin to recover, growing strong enough to complain bitterly that his nurse was worse than a gaoler and would not let him stir without hovering about him. Jemima's orders had been specific, and old Margaret was determined not to allow him to get to his bottles of brandy. But in spite of everything he did manage it, and on the tenth day he suffered a severe relapse after drinking the best part of a bottle of smuggled cognac under his bedclothes. Lucy, on her daily visit, was shocked to see how weak he was, and turned frightened eyes to Margaret, who pursed her lips and shook her head.

'Morgan, what have you done?' she asked, leaning over him and almost shaking him in her anxiety. His open eyes fixed on hers, but he had no breath for speaking. 'Finished,' he managed to say.

Lucy's emotions rose up in her in the form of anger. 'Why did you drink the brandy, you fool? You know it was bad for you. Now see what you've done!' she cried.

Margaret touched her shoulder warningly, and Morgan's hand came up from the bed and grabbed her collar, pulling her down so that he could whisper. His breathing was like a roaring in his chest; he dragged the air in, and whispered soundlessly on the out-breath.

'Finished,' he said again. 'Not – anyone's – fault.' He tugged at her again peremptorily. 'You – you.'

'What, Morgan? I'm listening,' Lucy said.

'Want – you – have – my box. Cupboard. Fetch.'

He released her, rolling his eyes sideways to the cupboard under the caravan window. She went and opened it, and amidst the clutter inside saw what he must have meant, a flat box covered in black leather with his initials tooled in gold on the lid. She had seen it many times: he was inordinately proud of it. She took it back to the bed, and held it so that he could see. 'This, Morgan? But it's your instruments.'

'You – have,' he gasped, and nodded, and then lay very still for a long time, recruiting his strength. Lucy opened the box and looked at the shining array of knives and suture needles and scissors, all kept in perfect condition. When she looked at him again, there were tears in her eyes.

'You'll get better,' she said. 'You'll need them. I'll – I'll just look after them for you.' Their eyes met, and they both knew the truth. Morgan managed to smile, and she slid the ends of her fingers into his hand, and his hand closed about them, and he closed his eyes, satisfied.

'You – should – have – been--' The next word was so long coming she thought he would not manage it; it came at last, a faint and sighing sound, like the wind under the eaves: 'my son.'

The long-awaited war with France was declared on the first of February 1793, following the shocking news that the revolutionaries had executed King Louis XVI on the twenty-first of January. Charles brought the news home to Chelmsford House when the king's signature was still wet upon the paper. The Chelmsford household had come up to Town because of the impending crisis immediately after Christmas, which they had spent at Wolvercote, Aylesbury's seat.

'So it looks as though there will be no visit to Bath for you this year, my love,' he said to Flora. 'Unless you care to go without me.'

'Of course not,' Flora said, shocked. 'I would not leave now, just when things are happening.'

'I don't know that they will be very exciting for you,' Charles said apologetically. 'I shall be at the House a good deal, and at the palace too, I should think. And your friend Captain Harvey will be leaving at once, I hear. He has been ordered off to the Mediterranean as soon as the wind will serve, so you won't even have your second-best cavalier to amuse you.'

254

'I think it is a good thing that he is going,' Flora said decidedly. 'He has been paying too much attention to Mary lately. My love,' she added to Mary, who was seated nearby listening quietly, 'I have tried to give you the hint about Captain Harvey, but you seemed not to heed it.'

'I know, ma'am – he is not at all respectable. But I am not a young girl in her first season, you know. And I find him amusing.'

'So do I,' Flora said, 'but he is not a suitable person for you. He is all to pieces, you know: bills everywhere unpaid, tradesmen forever dunning him, and he lives so expensively that his pay must be spoken for for months to come.'

'In fact, pockets to let, and quite in the basket,' Charles finished for her with a grin.

Mary responded with a smile. 'Thank you for the warning, but I am very sure I should never be tempted to lend him any money, even if he were so indelicate as to ask.'

Flora looked shocked. 'You know that is not what I meant.'

Mary laughed, and patted her hand. 'Yes, I know, but be assured I don't mean to marry him either, so there is nothing to worry about.'

'I should think Mary's fortune is not enough to tempt Harvey, my love. He would need an heiress at least. Besides, he has gone so long without marrying, I don't know what would change his mind now.'

'War changes many things,' Flora said darkly, 'and Mary is quite rich enough to need warning, with what her father left her, as well as her allowance, and anything her mother might agree to settle on her.'

'One good thing about having money left me by my father,' Mary said soothingly, 'is that I don't have to think about getting married. I am rich in my own right now, and can do as I please. And what I please is to stay with you, dear Flora, as long as you'll have me.'

It was a day for visitors, and the knocker on the great door was never still, as friends and acquaintances dropped by to discuss the news and speculate on what it would mean to them. No few of the visitors were pleased and excited rather than dismayed by the thought of war: the young saw it as a chance for adventure and perhaps glory, the old declared with satisfaction that at last they would teach those damned revolutionaries a lesson.

John Anstey walked up during the morning with the news that his father was to be raised to the peerage for his services to the government by means of the City.

'He's to be made a baron, so you'll have a Lord Anstey beside you in the House, Charles,' John said. 'It's Pitt's doing, of course, and he'll expect father's loyalty. Pitt's the man for us now, you know. We need someone steady, someone who won't be bullied by these revolutionary clubs all over the country, and the rabble clamouring for reform every moment.'

'Don't you believe reform is needed?' Mary asked, more to provoke him than because she had any views on the subject. John pursed his lips.

'Of course there are abuses – no human-devised system is perfect. But reform has to be taken slowly, and has to be instituted by the proper authorities. If changes can be forced on the country by violence you soon get – well, France shews you what you get. Pitt's not against reform: look how many times he's spoken up for the abolition of the slave trade.'

'I can see he's chosen his man well, at any rate,' Charles said drily, and Flora intervened with a warm clasp of John's hand.

'I'm sure your father is to be congratulated, John dear, and you too, of course: you'll be a lord one day now.'

John turned his eyes to Mary, as if expecting her congratulations, but when she smiled and began to speak, he interrupted her, not rudely, but distractedly.

'Mary, I wonder if I might have a word with you in private? Ma'am, would you permit me to take Mary aside for a few moments?'

'Of course,' Flora said, with a significant glance at her husband. 'Why not go into the blue saloon? It's warm and quiet in there.'

Mary followed John with a look of resignation, and braced herself to refuse yet again the offer of his hand. But when they were alone, he turned to face her with a gentle, serious look, and said:

'It's all right, Mary, I'm not going to torment you. It's just that I want to be quite sure I understand your mind. A long time ago, now, I told you I would wait for you, and that I believed one day you would come back to me.'

'So you did,' Mary said lightly, sitting down and settling her skirts about her. 'I remember being *told* that, and very firmly too.'

John looked uncomfortable. 'I realize now that my language was perhaps improper, but I hope you will make allowance for the ardour of my feelings. I still love you, Mary, as much as ever . . .'

'Please--' Mary began, lifting her hand, but he took her hand and pressed it and continued.

'As much as ever, I say. But the time has come when I must marry. War changes things, you know. Benjamin wants to join the army, and I must provide an heir, in case anything happens to him, especially now there is the title to consider. So I want to ask you once more, for the last time, whether you will do me the great honour of becoming my wife, Mary? I promise you, I shall never trouble you on this score again, if you refuse me.'

It sounded, Mary thought, almost like a threat, and yet she could not help feeling a pang as she said, 'I am very sensible of the honour you do me, and I am very fond of you, dear John, but I do not wish to marry you.'

'The title does not make any difference?' he asked. His expression was inscrutable.

'No.' She looked up at him, her dark blue eyes serious. 'I admit that once it might have. When we were very young, and you first offered for me, I refused you because, though I loved you, I was ambitious. But now' – she shrugged – 'I don't think I shall ever marry. I love you, John, but as a brother, and since there is no-one I love more than that, I am not tempted to change my state.'

'I hoped, when you refused Lord Tonbridge . . .'

'I'm sorry, really I am.'

'It's all right. I only hoped for a very little while. I soon saw it made no difference. I did not expect you to say yes, but I had to be sure. I'm sorry too, Mary. We can still remain friends, I hope?'

She stood up and offered him her hand. 'Of course! I should be more sorry than I can say to lose your friendship. I have known you all my life.'

'Yes,' he said, and lifted her hand to his lips, and then without another word, left her. Mary went over to the window and stood looking out towards the bare treetops of the park, feeling strangely cold and alone, and wondering whether she had made a great mistake. Dear John, her childhood knight: she was in no doubt that his emphasis on the words 'the last time' meant that he would look about him for another bride, for family reasons. How would she feel when he found one? she wondered. Would she dance with light heart at his wedding? She could not imagine it, and she sighed, and drew her shawl closer round her shoulders, and at that moment the door was flung open and Horatio burst in, looking excited and a little dishevelled.

'Oh, there you are, Mary!' he cried, and for a ludicrous moment she thought that he was going to propose to her as well, but he went on, 'Where are Charles and Flora? Hawkins said they were in the library, but they are not. I have something to ask Charles that simply can't wait.'

'I left them there only a few moments ago,' she said, but he hardly seemed to hear her. He paced a few steps up and down the room, and then standing still, he thrust his hands under his tails, threw out his chest, and said,

'It is the most exciting thing! I must tell you, Mary – the King has made the Prince of Wales Colonel Commandant of the 10th Light Dragoons, and the Prince has offered *me* a commission! He says he is going to make it the most fashionable regiment in the army – because everyone says that York's Coldstreamers are so fine, you know, and he will outshine his brother somehow. It is famous, is it not? Oh, this war is a fine thing! How do you think I shall look in regimentals, Mary? As soon as I have 'em fitted, I shall get Beechey to paint m'portrait. Captain the Honourable Horatio Morland, 10th Light Dragoons. Sounds well, don't you think? Schweizer must make up my uniform coats – I've seen officers before now looking like rag-bags, and that won't do for me. Excuse me, won't you, ma'am – I must go and find Charles at once, for he must put up the money for the commission, and then I must go to White's and ask Donney where one goes for military wigs. He's bound to know. Excuse me, ma'am.'

He whirled out, leaving Mary bemused. Her rout was completed an hour later when, having composed herself, she returned to the library to rejoin Flora, who looked up with a faintly anxious frown and said:

'Ah, Mary, dear, there you are. There is something I want to ask you – or rather, tell you – or – well, my dear, it is the oddest thing. Charles and I have been closeted with John Anstey this hour past, and, not to mince up the meat too finely, he has made an offer for Louisa.'

Mary sat down, and said, in a voice so calm it was almost expressionless, 'For Louisa, ma'am? And have you accepted it?'

'He spoke very properly,' Flora said, watching her closely. 'He said he must marry, to get an heir, and that he has formed a very good opinion of Louisa, and holds her in affection, having known her since her childhood. And it is quite a good match for her. He is already very wealthy, as well as being a member of Parliament, and now he will have his father's title one day too. And Louisa – well, she's a good girl, but in spite of everything I can do, she has never really *taken* in society. She is not particularly pretty, nor brilliant, and she is too shy to attract suitors, and I'm afraid she would be unhappy if she were made to marry a complete stranger, because of her timidity. So all in all, I tend to think this offer is the best thing that could have happened for her. If only, that is, it does not upset you, Mary dear.'

'Upset me?' Mary said, raising her eyebrows. He did not waste much time, she thought resentfully; but a second thought told her that he had been thinking of this for some time, and that his interview with her in the blue saloon had been what he said it was, a desire to be sure he knew her mind. 'Why should it upset me? I have been refusing John Anstey since I was fifteen. I should be guilty of stark unreason if I were to feel slighted now that he has offered for someone else.'

'Yet when he took you apart this morning,' Flora said hesitantly, 'I thought perhaps--'

'No, ma'am. If you like this match for Louisa, you may accept it without any fear that I shall do other than rejoice for her, in having an offer from so unexceptionable a source.'

Flora's brow cleared. 'Oh, Mary, I am *so* glad! For we did accept, you know, only I told John it could not be if you were

259

to be mortally wounded, and he assured me that you did not want to marry him, and Louisa would have been hard to place, and John Anstey will be the very person for her, for he will be kind to her, and she will be able to live only a mile or two from Morland Place, which will be a comfort for her, and she will be Lady Anstey one day, which is as much as I could have hoped for. And I think it is what Thomas would have wanted for her, too,' she added in a different tone. Mary looked at her curiously, for she hardly ever mentioned her former husband, and never with such feeling.

War changes things indeed, Mary thought with an inward sigh. All her principal suitors were deserting her – Lord Tonbridge, John Anstey, Horatio, Captain Harvey – not that Captain Harvey was really a suitor, but it would be dull without him. But there were always others, she assured herself, squaring her shoulders. She had chosen her state of her own free will, and it would be foolish to repine, especially when most women – like Louisa – had no such freedom.

Lucy's plans were carefully laid, for both nature and education had made her methodical. Clothes were no problem, for there were trunks full of things outgrown or discarded by Harry and Jack in the nursery, and her masquerade with James had taught her how to put them on. Money was rather harder, for she rarely had any, and she would need at least her stagecoach fare. She had saved the guinea that Edward had given her on her birthday last October, and the rest she contrived by selling at a pawnshop in York a few trinkets she had been given over the years, telling her conscience sternly that it was for the very best of causes.

She had discovered the information she needed gradually by dint of asking apparently casual questions, learning that the stagecoach from Leeds to Portsmouth took thirty-six hours, leaving at six in the evening and arriving at six in the morning the second day after. She would have to walk to Leeds. Much as she would have liked to take one of the horses from the stables, she could not do so, nor could she hope to ride there in any sort of conveyance without attracting attention to herself. In Leeds, in boy's clothing, she hoped no-one would know her; closer to home, she was likely to be recognised. Well, it was near ten miles to Wetherby, over the fields, and she could do that in something over three hours. She could escape from the house late at night and do that first, most dangerous part of the journey in the dark; fortunately she knew every inch of the ground from having ridden over it since she was able to sit in the saddle.

From Wetherby to Leeds was another twelve miles, and she would have to follow the road, not knowing the fields beyond Wetherby. Some passing carter might pick her up and give her a ride; but in any case she would have all day to do it. All day, as well, for those searching for her from Morland Place to overtake her. She must get as far as she could as quickly as she could, and find somewhere to hide up during the day. And she must take food with her, too, for the stage journey, for she would not be able to spare her precious funds to buy anything to eat.

A half-moon was all she needed, and on the day chosen she made her preparations. She had her bed still in the nursery; from there the nursery stair, a stone spiral staircase, led straight down to the back door. This was always kept locked, for the bridge across the moat from it was unsafe, but Lucy knew where the key was kept in the butler's room, and during the day she made excuse to wander in there to talk to Oxhey, and while his back was turned she lifted it neatly from its hook. She found a moment during the afternoon to slip along to the door and oil the lock with a feather so that it should not creak and betray her. After she had gone to bed, she rose silently and padded about the nursery on bare feet, packing the things she would need into a cloak-bag: the clothes she had selected, Morgan's instrument case, the little sock-purse that held her precious money, and her medical books. She hid the bag under her bed, and got back under the covers to wait.

By midnight the house was still. She rose, dressed herself in her boy's clothes, and, barefoot, went down by the nursery stair along the passage, and out into the herb garden. It had been her intention to slip into the kitchen by the door of the servants' hall to collect some food, but to her horror, she found the door had been locked. She had not counted on that, and was nonplussed. The door led only to the herb garden, whose other access, the back door, was always locked – so why should anyone worry about it? She stood still in the shadows of the garden, thinking. She could go back to her room and come down to the kitchen by the normal method, through the house, but she doubted she could do that without waking someone; yet the thought of thirty-six hours, at the least, without food horrified her.

There were storehouses opening onto the garden, and she knew one of them contained boxes of apples, which would be better than nothing. She took half a dozen, and then, without much hope, opened the door of the bakehouse, which also led off the garden. Luck was with her. On a shelf she found a stale loaf, which had been overlooked, set aside for the swans' breakfast. She took it gladly, and hurried back up to her room.

She took out the cloak-bag, put in the loaf and the apples, picked up her shoes and the back door key, and was ready. She took one last look around the room, and it was useless to pretend that she did not feel a pang. She had left a note for her mother upon her pillow, but she knew she would be upset all the same, perhaps angry or afraid for her; and she was leaving home, after all, the place she had known all her life, for unknown places, sights, and an unknown destiny. But it was not for ever, she told herself sternly: she would come back one day, and everyone would be so proud of her.

She went silently down the staircase – no wooden treads to give her away, she thought gladly – and opened the back door, and, leaving the key in the lock, stepped out on to the bridge and pulled the door closed behind her. Though the crosswise planks of the bridge were rotten and unsafe, the thick outside timbers were strong enough to take her weight, and she had a good sense of balance. Bag in one hand, shoes in the other, she walked carefully across, sat down on the bank the other side to put on her shoes, and with no more backwards glancing, set off across the fields towards Wetherby.

The sky was taking on the first greyness of dawn by the time she came to the edge of the town, and she was already very tired and cold. It had taken longer than she had expected, for the ground looked different to her on foot from her memories of it from the saddle, and she had had to pick the best way she could to avoid the boggy places, for the weather recently had been mild and wet. The moon went down in the early hours of the morning, leaving her to find her way in the complete dark, when she was already far enough from home for the ground to be less familiar to her. Stumbling along in unfamiliar shoes in the darkness carrying a bag was more tiring than she had thought, and she was almost ready to give up the whole adventure.

A pause in the shelter of a haystack to eat an apple and some bread revived her a little, and she thought how simple it would be to give up now. Visions of the glory ahead of her as a ship's surgeon danced before her eyes, and following them, she dropped off to sleep, her head cradled in the hay, and dreamed huge and horrible dreams of battle-injured sailors, waking with a violent start at the sound of a terrible groan close by her. For a moment she did not know where she was; her heart pounded sickly, and her hands clenched, and the moan was repeated, resolving itself to her fluttering relief into the lowing of a cow, which was standing a few feet away looking at her doubtfully with lowered head.

Lucy sat up, and gave a laugh of relief. It was growing light, and her short sleep had refreshed her. The next part of her plan had to be carried out now, and would be difficult to do herself, but it could not be put off any longer: she must cut off her hair. She had Morgan's surgical scissors, though she disliked to use them for such a purpose, and she had brought with her the little polished silver mirror from her room at home. Watched with mute interest by the cow, she propped the little mirror up in the haystack and felt behind her for the long, thick plait into which her hair was braided at night. Sailors, of course, wore their hair in plaits, and William's was not shorter or fairer than hers, and she sighed at the thought of losing it; but she must have every aid in appearing to be a boy, and the cropped hair was the best one, for no female in the history of the world had ever had it. It was harder to cut through the plait than she expected, and when the scissor blades slipped and slid without making any impression she abandoned them for a scalpel, and sliced through the braid whole. She laid it in her lap, and it felt heavy and strange, like, she thought, an amputated limb.

Changing the knife for the scissors, she turned her head this way and that before the mirror and snipped and cropped. It was terribly difficult, and at last when she abandoned the task because it was getting worse rather than better, her only consolation was that, though she looked like a hedgehog, she certainly didn't look like a girl.

She replaced the instruments in the case, looked for a long time doubtfully at the long plait, and then with a regretful sigh, buried it deep in the hay, packed up her bag, and set off on her way again, skirting Wetherby and making for the bridge on the south side of the town where she could join the road to Leeds.

Some time later, she was plodding along the side of the road, avoiding the worst of the puddles and ruts, when she heard the sound of a heavy vehicle behind her, and stood aside to be out of the way of a large brake, drawn by a gaunt and bewhiskered horse, and driven by an even more gaunt and bewhiskered old man. The cart was laden, but a tarpaulin over the load made it impossible to guess what it was. The man, to Lucy's relief, was a stranger to her, but her heart missed a beat all the same when he pulled back on the reins, halting the aged horse, and called out,

'Now then, lad!' Lucy looked up at him apprehensively. His watery eyes surveyed her, and he knuckled a drip off the end of his reddened nose, and said, 'Artow walkin' to Leeds, then? Doost want a ride? It's hard walkin' after all this rain.'

'Thank you,' Lucy said, a little doubtfully, and, feeling she should explain herself, added, 'I'm going to see my grandmother, you see. She – she isn't well.'

'Climb up, then, lad, I'll give thee a ride in t't town,' the old man said, evincing no interest in the grandmother. Lucy climbed up beside him with some relief, and the old man shook the reins and the horse moved off. It was barely faster than walking, but much more comfortable, and the old man seemed blessedly inclined to silence. It was only after some time that he said, shaking his head, 'Eh, lad, hastow cut thy hair thyself? Tha looks as though tha's been mowed wi' a scythe.'

Lucy felt herself blushing. 'Well,' she began hesitantly, 'I thought – I thought I'd better make myself tidy for my grandmother, and – and I couldn't afford to go to the barber.'

'Ah s'd think tha'll freeten the old lady to death, lookin' like

264

that. Hast got scissors with thee? Coom, I'll trim thee oop a bit.' The horse plodded on even with the reins slack, and Lucy produced the scissors again with mixed feelings and submitted her head to the old man's slow and clumsy ministrations. At last he said, 'Well, it isn't what I'd like to see, but it's better than it was. There's a chance thy grandmother might recognise thee now.'

'Thank you,' Lucy said, stowing her scissors away again.

The old man did not appear to have been looking, but he said, after a while, 'Surgeon's tools, aren't they? Where hast them from, lad?'

'I didn't steal them, if that's what you think,' Lucy said quickly. 'I was left them – by my father. He's dead now, and I want to follow in his trade.'

'Art runnin' away?' he asked quietly. Lucy looked at him in fear, and he met her eyes and shook his head. 'Nay, lad, don't look like that. It's no business o'mine. What is it, th'army or t'navy? Well, well, if I were thirty year younger, I'd run off myself. Aye, it's a great thing to be young, when a war begins. Tha wants to be an army surgeon, doosta? Aye, well, good look to thee in it. But there's no regiment in Leeds, tha knaws.'

'I was going to take the stagecoach to London,' Lucy said, thinking it no bad idea to lay a false trail or two. 'Do you know where the London stage goes from?'

'Aye, that I do. I pass right by the inn, as it happens. I'll drop thee off there,' the old man said with a thoughtful look. They spent the rest of the journey in silence, until he pulled up outside the entrance of the coaching inn, and Lucy jumped down with a hearty 'Thank you' and went inside. The old man watched her go, and then shook up his horse and went in search of a constable to whom to report a runaway; while Lucy walked through the passage that ran from front to back of the inn, out through the back yard, and into the narrow street behind, and scurried off to find somewhere to hide herself until six o'clock, when she could seek out the other inn, from which the Portsmouth coach left. She wasn't sure of the old carter's intentions, but she was taking no chances.

14

York was a large city, but it had not prepared Lucy for the sight of Portsmouth, with its stink and bustle and its press of new buildings struggling up like weeds amongst and around the old. The long, uncomfortable, and tedious coach journey had given her plenty of time to decide her plans and perfect her story, but still when she was put down in the inn-yard and strolled out onto the street, she had much ado not to gawp like a yokel at a fair. The seagulls perched on the rooftops, quarrelling, drew her attention to the most obvious difference between Portsmouth and York, and with a lift of the heart, she turned and followed her nose in the direction of the sea.

When she came to the bottom of Queen Street and out on to the Hard, she had to stop and stare, no matter what anyone thought of her, for she had never seen the sea before, and none of Morgan's vivid descriptions had prepared her for it. In the gathering dusk it stretched huge and grey and restless, touched all over with small white flecks, bearing in its bosom countless ships and boats and buoys. Above her head the gulls circled and called; the light wind carried to her nostrils the most intoxicating smell she had ever experienced. She breathed it in so deeply she began to feel dizzy, and thought she might actually become drunk on it. *Now* I understand, she thought; she only wondered that Morgan could ever have borne to leave it.

Morgan's stories had never, naturally, included instructions on how to obtain a warrant in one of His Majesty's ships, but Lucy thought in this place at least it could not be difficult, especially if Morgan was right that there was always a shortage of ships' surgeons. She must inquire at an inn, she thought; innkeepers always knew everything, and would tell her where to apply. She had never been inside an inn, not even the dear old 'Have Another' – as the Hare and Heather had begun to be called, as a result of a badly painted and warped inn-sign – where the innkeeper and his family were distant cousins of hers; but life had never treated her less than kindly, and so she had no fear of unknown situations.

She picked up her bag and, remembering to stride out like a boy, she walked along the Hard, but her head kept turning so irresistibly towards the sea that she bumped into someone walking the other way, and was set roughly aside with a profane curse and an injunction to look where she was going. Startled, she brought her mind back to the task in hand, and found herself standing outside an inn called the Keppel's Head, and the words 'Diamond, 74' caught her eye and drew her attention to a poster fixed up on the wall beside the door.

Stepping closer, she read what she knew at once was a recruiting-poster. Morgan had told her about those. It was a captain's business to man his own ship, and he used every means in his power, first to attract willing volunteers to serve aboard his vessel and later to press any seaman he could lay his hands on. At the time of a 'hot' press, Morgan told her, many seamen, knowing they were going to be taken up sooner or later, preferred to volunteer and receive the King's bounty rather than wait in anxiety to be seized roughly and for no reward by the press-gang; so the posters were not as vain a hope as they might have seemed.

The poster said that the newly fitted ship of the line, the *Diamond*, of two decks and seventy-four guns, was preparing for a cruise in the Mediterranean and would be ready to sail as soon as a few more hands were on board. An officer from the ship would attend at the Keppel's Head every evening until ten o'clock to pay the King's bounty to any man who cared to join them. There was a great deal more about the food, pay, rum, chances of glory and prize-money, and the duty of every stout heart to shew the murdering Frogs who ruled the seas, but Lucy ignored it. One ship must be the same as another to her. She walked in through the low door, along a passage, and into a parlour where a bright fire of driftwood and sea-coal was crackling, and a candle was already lit on the high chimney-piece and reflected by an old and spotted mirror behind it.

To her relief, the parlour was not crowded with seamen, which she might have found daunting. Two settles were drawn up at right angles to the fire: one was occupied by two middle-aged, steady-looking sailors in striped smocks and white duck trousers, who looked, by their uneasy stiffness, as though they would sooner have been taking their ale in the taproom; on the other lounged a handsome young man in the white breeches and a blue coat of a sea-officer. One graceful hand was curled round a pewter tankard which rested on the settle beside him; the other slowly stroked into a state of ecstasy the inn cat, an enormous silver tabby, who couched on his knees and kneaded them with alternate, massive paws.

The officer looked round as Lucy came in, and raised a languid eyebrow.

'Hullo , young'un! Looking for me?' he drawled. The nonchalance was largely a pose, Lucy could see at once, for the brown eyes under the fine, arched brows were sharp, and subjected her to a very comprehensive once-over. 'Thirsting for a life of glory, are you? Longing to go to sea? You have that look, I must say.'

'Are you the officer from the *Diamond*?' Lucy asked.

'I have that honour. Lieutenant James Weston, fifth of the *Diamond*, at your service. And who might you be?'

Lucy licked her lips. 'Lucius Proom, sir,' she said.

'The Devil you are! What damned bad luck for you,' the young man said with sympathy. 'And you have come, I imagine, to enliven my lonely vigil. Just in time, too, for this is my last night on shore persuading cocks to lay eggs, thank God. We go up to Spithead tonight, and we'll be sailing as soon as the wind serves. How old are you, lad?'

'Fifteen, sir,' Lucy said.

'You look younger. I dare say you'd like some ale, however. *Simmy!*' The last word was spoken in a bellow that made Lucy jump and propelled the cat as if shot from a gun off the young man's lap to the door, where he favoured the company with a resentful look and flounced out; but it had the effect of producing the landlord in rapid order, still wiping a carving knife on his apron.

'Yessir!'

'Some ale for Mr Proom, if you please. And – have you eaten recently, boy? No, I thought as much. You'd better fill your belly here, for it's better than you'll get on board. Bring your ordinary for Mr Proom, Simmy, and another pint for me.'

When the landlord had disappeared to fulfil the order, Weston moved over on the settle to make room for Lucy, and said,

'Now then, you had better tell me the tale, young'un. Run away, have you? Thought you'd ship before the mast and rise to be captain through extraordinary gallantry and skill? It isn't like that, you know.'

'No, indeed,' Lucy blushed. 'Indeed, you are mistaken. I came to ask if there is a position vacant for a surgeon's mate, for my – I was told there was always a shortage of them in wartime.'

Weston gave a soundless whistle. 'So that's it, is it? What skills have you, then? You are too young to be a qualified surgeon, or even a physician.'

'My father was a surgeon, and a naval surgeon, too, during the last war. I have worked with him ever since I can remember, and he taught me everything he knew about doctoring, and I have read books, too, on anatomy and diseases and physicking. But he's dead now, and I've no other family, so I thought I'd join the navy. He left me his surgeon's instruments, but nothing else, you see.' She stopped abruptly, wondering whether the story she had decided upon in the coach sounded as false to the lieutenant as it did to her now she spoke it aloud. But he gave no sign of disbelieving her. He exchanged a glance with the two seamen, and said,

'Well, you're right about there being a shortage: third-rates are supposed to carry three surgeon's mates, and we haven't any, though the loblolly boys are very experienced. In fact the cap'n was thinking of rating one of them. I should think he'll welcome you with open arms, and, in the circumstances, ask few questions.'

He met Lucy's eye penetratingly, but she kept her countenance, and said, 'Why should I mind his asking questions?'

Weston held the gaze a little longer and then smiled, 'No reason at all. Well, lads, it seems our evening here was not wasted after all,' he said to the seamen. 'These two jacks are Povey and Hudson, Mr Proom: steady lads but short on conversation. I'm glad you've come, for now I can send 'em off to the taproom, where they'll be a deal happier, I can tell you.' He dismissed the two seamen, who were grinning broadly at his sally, with a jerk of the head, and said to Lucy, 'Now I can tell you a little about the ship, for I dare say you don't know anything.'

'I don't know anything about anything, I'm afraid, except for what M-- for what my father has told me. I'd never seen the sea before today.'

'Well, the *Diamond*'s a good ship – old, but newly coppered and refitted, so she's sounder than many a newer ship. She's really an eighty, but we only mount seventy-four guns, or she's very unhandy. She's a Dutchman, you see, a prize from the last war, and they don't build their ships for heavy seas, like ours. But she has her advantages: the accommodation is much more roomy than on a British-built ship. The wardroom has a stern-gallery, as well as quarter-galleries, and that makes a deal of difference to life, I can tell you. Well, you'll see for yourself, likely enough. I dare say we shall invite you to dine in the wardroom one day.'

'You think, then, that I'll be taken on?' Lucy asked eagerly.

'Not a doubt of it. The cap'n ain't in a position to be fussy, – well, you'll see why soon enough. No sense in putting you off.'

'What is the captain like?'

'Oh, he's good man – a gentleman, not one of your tarpaulins at all events – but a bit distant. He's a fair man, and a good disciplinarian, but dining with him – we take turns, and usually dine about once a week – that's rather a trial. Not a word for ten minutes, and then the cap'n will make a remark, and we'll agree, and there'll be silence again. He keeps a good table, but I've been on ships where dining with the captain is a pleasure, rather than a duty.'

'Do tell me, if it wouldn't fatigue you, about your other ships,' Lucy begged. She really wanted to hear, but it also occurred to her that it was better to keep Weston talking than to allow him a chance to question *her*. Under his languid pose, he was a friendly and chatty young man. She put his age at about nineteen, and from what Morgan had told her, he must have had influential friends to be even the junior lieutenant on a seventy-four by that age. The minimum age for a lieutenant was twenty, but Morgan had told her that the porter at the door of the Admiralty would sell a false birth certificate to any applicant for a crown, so that was hardly a problem. Weston proved only too happy to talk about himself, and when the landlord brought her food and drink, Lucy was able to relax and enjoy it while Weston entertained her with stories of his past ships and descriptions of the personnel aboard his present one.

Lucy's first view of living quarters aboard a ship was of the captain's drawing-room, into which she was ushered by Weston after he had made his report, and she was much impressed. The ceiling was low, to be sure, but not so low as to require a man to stoop, and it was spacious enough, and well furnished, and lit with a number of candles. A large desk dominated the space, but there were also comfortable chairs, and red velvet curtains over the windows of the stern gallery made it seem very cosy. Captain Prothero was a tall, heavy-built man with a rather dark, lowering face. He was dressed in uniform, of course, and the gold buttons of his coat glinted in the candle-light; but his hair was powdered, and he was smoking a cigar and drinking his after-dinner port just like any civil gentleman, sitting very upright in one of his crimson velvet chairs.

Weston introduced her: his manner before his captain was very different, quiet and respectful, which gave Lucy the first inkling of the extraordinary power of the captain of a naval vessel. Prothero looked her up and down in silence for some moments, and then asked her a few sharp questions about her age and experience. She answered succinctly, and had no difficulty in remembering to call him 'sir': his manner demanded no less.

'Very well,' he said at length. 'I shall rate you surgeon's mate at fifty shillings per month. You'll berth aft on the orlop – Weston will show you. You've no uniform, I take it? You'd better get something from the purser, then. He'll deduct it from your salary. That's all. Mr Weston, see Mr Proom is safely bestowed.'

'Aye aye, sir.'

They retreated from the warmth and light of the captain's quarters to the dark and cold of the unlit quarterdeck. Unseen beside her, Weston said quietly, 'Well, you're in, young'un. I wish you may not regret it. I thought the Old Man would bite.'

'I wonder he didn't want to ask the surgeon's opinion before taking me on,' Lucy said. Weston snorted.

'The cap'n don't need to ask anyone about anything. He's the master here, you know.'

'Shall I meet the surgeon now? I don't even know his name.'

'Charteris is his name, but there's no point in taking you to him now. He won't be receiving visitors. Tomorrow, about the middle of the forenoon watch, he may rise to the surface again. Meantime we'd better find you a berth. Here, you, Mr Heape, this is Mr Proom, surgeon's mate. Shew him his cot, and then introduce him to the after cockpit.'

A very young midshipman – a mere child, it seemed, of about ten years – scuttled forward at the command, and with a grin at Lucy led the way below, moving so fast down the companion that she had difficulty in keeping up with him. As soon as they were below, the air grew thick and redolent with smells, so that at first she had to force herself to keep breathing it in: it seemed less like air than like a tangible substance, a soup of stinks. Added to that, it was very dark, the steps lit only by dim horn lanterns, and the area beyond impenetrably black, and there were strange noises all around, which she resolved temporarily into creaking timbers and men snoring. She was very tired from her long day's journey, and from the multitude of new sights and experiences, and she moved now with a sense of unreality as if in a dream, following the small, scuttling creature ahead of her from dark into dark, and wondering if she would ever find her way up again into the daylight.

They went on down until they were on the orlop deck, below the waterline, where the air was noticeably thicker, the bilge smell stronger, and the darkness perfect, for there were, of course, no windows or even gunports.

'This will be your berth,' the midshipman said, stopping so suddenly that Lucy ran into him. It was nothing more than a space screened off by canvas awnings, about the size and shape of a coffin. 'I'll get one of the men to swing your cot for you. Is that your dunnage? Is that all you've got? One good thing about berthing on the orlop, it doesn't all get knocked about when we clear for action. I'll shew you the cockpit now. That's where the mids and the warrant officers mess, you know, at least the older ones. The young mids mess in the gunroom, under the gunner, Mr Richardson. He's a very good sort of fellow, but I wish I were old enough to mess in the cockpit.

Cap'n won't let us until we're fourteen.' The confiding child pattered off again, and Lucy followed, bemused. 'That's Mr Charteris's cabin, right next to the cockpit, for that's where you operate, when we're in action,' he said, his eyes round at the thought of it.

'I know that,' Lucy said, feeling it was time to assert herself.

'And this is the after cockpit,' he continued, in a reverent voice. Even through the canvas screen, Lucy could hear the voices, upraised in revelry, and not, she thought in the tones of gentlemen. When Heape opened the screen, a gust of tobacco smoke whirled out from the lantern-lit room, and Lucy saw a long wooden table, around which sat a variety of men of various ages, all with their hands round tankards, many of them with pipes in their mouths. The conversation was arrested, and the man at the head of the table said, 'What do you want, child?'

'I've brought the new surgeon's mate,' the midshipman said, giving one eager glance around the dim and smoky recess that represented heaven to him, and then backed off and disappeared into the gloom of the orlop. Lucy stepped forward nervously into the lamplight and, under the unswerving scrutiny of eyes, and in the undiluted company of adult male strangers, she felt for the first time a little apprehensive. But glancing round she saw that many of the men were not much older than her, and that some at least had pleasant faces and were looking at her with more interest than hostility.

She tried smiling, tentatively, and the man at the head of the table – the president of the mess, she assumed – said, 'Surgeon's mate? A beardless boy: God help us all, when we go into action. What's your name, young man?'

'Lucius Proom. My father was Morgan Proom, ship's surgeon during the American war, and he taught me his trade,' Lucy said.

It seemed a fortunate choice of words, for at once a quiet-looking, grey-haired man looked up and said, 'Proom? Why, I knew him. He was surgeon on the dear old *Yarmouth*, that's now laid up at Plymouth, when I was master's mate, back in the West Indies. A good surgeon, too, though a trifle fond of his bottle.'

'What surgeon isn't?' said a dour voice, and there was a general laugh, though not a kind one.

'So you're his son, are you?' the grey-haired man said, looking Lucy over with interest. 'Can't say you look much like him.'

'I favour my mother, sir,' Lucy said hastily.

'Married late, did he? and what's come of him now?'

'He's dead sir, six weeks since. That's why I have decided to follow his footsteps. But I have worked with him since I was a child.'

'Did he have a practice on land, then'?

'No, sir, he was a horse-doctor,' Lucy said unthinkingly, and there was a roar of laughter. She blushed with vexation, and when the noise had died down enough for her to be heard again, she said, 'He always said to me that he would sooner trust a good horse-doctor than a poor surgeon.'

'Aye, well, so would I, lad,' said the president, wiping tears of laughter from his eyes, 'and so would you, if you'd seen our surgeon. You'll be an asset to the ship, you know.'

'Will I?' Lucy asked, pleased. The gleam in his eye should have warned her.

'Aye,' he said, gathering his audience with a grin, 'for there's nothing makes a man more careful aboard ship than knowing if he's injured he has a choice between a half-blind tosspot and a milk-sucking groom!' The ensuing gale of laughter did not quite conceal from Lucy's ears the more improper of the remarks tossed about the table, and the grey-haired man got up and pushed his way out to Lucy, took her by the arm, and led her away.

'Don't mind it, lad,' he said. 'It's after the fork, you know, and they never mind what they say after the fork.'

'I beg your pardon, sir?' Lucy said, puzzled.

'The ceremony of the fork,' the other replied. 'As soon as the first watch is set – that's eight in the evening, you see – the president of the mess – which is Mr Midshipman Godesel at the present – he sticks his fork into the bulkhead, and that's the signal for all the younger mids to leave. My name is Gearing, master's mate, by the by.'

'How do you do,' Lucy said politely, offering her hand, which was grasped in a hard, horny grip.

'By God, you've a soft hand!' Gearing exclaimed. 'But then, I suppose you need a lady's hand to be a surgeon. Now these,' he spread his own palm up, 'these are like planks of wood. I can pull on a rope, but I could not set a broken bone, or find out a swelling. I'm very glad to make your acquaintance, my boy, especially since I knew your father. You've got your work cut out on this ship, I can tell you! You'll need all your father's skills before you're done. Here's your berth – you'd better get some sleep while you can, for we slip anchor at first light.'

Lucy needed no further urging, for she was close to exhaustion by now. In the tiny confines of her cabin, she struggled out of her breeches and into a voluminous nightshirt, one of Harry's, and reflected that there were advantages to the ship: she did not have to share her berth, so her secret would be the easier to keep. She had difficulty in climbing into her cot, which seemed invested of a life of its own and a desire to escape her, and when she settled down and pulled the blankets over her, the air felt very cold, and the bedding damp. In the shelter of the harbour, the ship was moving very little, and she found the movement soporific, and she began to relax and grow sleepy, as she thought over the day and her present situation.

The hints dropped about the surgeon – Charteris, was it? – were not lost on her: he was a drinker, and not held in much respect. That might be to her benefit, but it might also be a difficulty, and she had no way yet of knowing which. But she had a friend already in Mr Gearing, and the lieutenant, James Weston, seemed disposed to like her. On the whole, she thought she had been lucky in being directed by providence to this ship; and so thinking, she fell asleep.

The next few days did nothing to alter her opinion. The *Diamond* went up to Spithead at first light, and the wind veering soon after, they sailed in the middle of the morning. Lucy found her feet very quickly, and did not suffer from more seasickness than a faint queasiness, which was fortunate, for her services were required as soon as they hit the first Channel choppiness. She was in the purser's room, seeing about some clothes, when the first big wave put the ship over, making her stagger, and a number of loud thumps were transmitted through the ship's fabric to her ears.

The purser grunted, and said, 'First big 'un always loosens

275

something. There'll be cuts and bruises too – the landmen won't have been expecting it.' His words were borne out soon afterwards by the appearance of a messenger in search of Lucy.

'Mr Proom, sir? Wanted in the sick-bay,' he said.

Lucy glanced at the purser, and said, 'Is Mr Charteris there?'

The boy looked embarrassed, and the purser sucked noisily on his unlit pipe and said, 'He'll still be in his cot, Mr Proom. He was a bit under the weather last night. Been to the sick-bay yet? Boy, take Mr Proom there.'

The sick-bay was forward on the orlop deck, and Lucy wondered at the decision to put it below the waterline, where there was no light and no chance of fresh air: but she was soon to learn that few people shared her father's belief in the efficacy of fresh air as a curative, and that the orlop was considered safer from enemy shot, and more stable than the upper decks. The sick-bay was lit with a lantern, and when she arrived she found two seamen there, one of them evidently tortured with seasickness, and bleeding fast from a gash high up on his forehead. The other, a sensible-looking, burly man in his forties, said,

'Mr Proom? I'm Huggins, loblolly boy. I think Simpkins here needs a stitch or two.'

Lucy's interest in the job in hand vanquished any nervousness she might have felt. It was just like being at home, and tending one of the servants, and she cleaned the blood off the wound with the wadding and sea water Huggins provided, and looked at the cut with relish. It was just the kind of job she liked.

'Yes, it will need stitching all right. Is the silk here, Huggins? Good – no, I'll use my own suture needles. I'm used to them.'

'Will it 'urt sir?' asked the patient, rolling the terrified eye of a bullock in a shambles towards her. Huggins growled profanely at him, but Lucy patted his arm, never having felt that suffering needless fear was good for a man.

'Not very much – just prickles, really. I'll give you a beautiful scar. The skull isn't fractured. How did you do it?'

'When that big wave come, sir, I fell over, and 'it my 'ead on summink. I dunno what.'

'The capstan, you lubber,' Huggins told him fiercely, and muttered a few more profanities. Simpkin winced at the first prick of her finest suture needle, so she asked him another question about himself, and by keeping him talking distracted his attention from his pain.

When he was finished and dismissed, Huggins, said, 'Gaw, you done him a treat, sir, and no mistake, but he weren't worth all that trouble, you know. Mr Charteris just cobbles 'em up quick. It's not as if 'e was a hofficer, and bein' a landman, 'e'll more than likely be dead before the year's out, and then all your work'll be wasted, sir.'

Lucy raised her eyebrows at this interpretation of a surgeon's duties, and said, 'Landman or officer, I don't like to do bad work.'

'Yessir,' said Huggins dismissingly, 'but you can't afford to waste all that time and trouble on the likes of Simpkins, sir.'

'Well, now I'm here, suppose you shew me round the sick-bay. And then perhaps I'd better make the acquaintance of Mr Charteris.'

But before Huggins had finished shewing her the amenities, another patient came in, a simple oblique fracture of the radius, where the man, falling, had tried to save himself with a braced forearm; and when she had finished with that, a splinter had to be removed, and what with one thing and another, the day passed, and Charteris made no appearance. Lucy made the acquaintance of the other two loblolly boys: Smith, who only had one eye, and Palter, who was spindly and so shy that he could hardly speak, and then with an atrocious stammer. She discovered the shortcomings of the sick-bay, and the alarming deficiencies of the medical chest, which Huggins hinted, without precisely saying so, were due to Mr Charteris's not having reordered. She had her dinner, and made the undesirable acquaintance of the heads, which made her realise how lucky were the crew to be able to urinate in the open air, over the side of the ship. The whole day she was below decks, and though gradually accustoming herself to the dark and the smells and the movement of the ship, she had no idea what the weather was like above, or where they were going, or even, without asking, what time of day it was.

It was when the first dog-watch was called, that Huggins came to Lucy with an inscrutable look on his face to say that Mr Charteris wished to see her in his cabin. Her first sight of her superior officer was not encouraging. The cabin was close and smelled strange, and she could not quite decide what the smell was. Charteris was evidently well enough off to afford candles, and two were burning, affording a reasonable illumination in the small space. The surgeon had a real cabin, with proper bulkheads, not just canvas screening like Lucy's berth, and it was furnished with a cot, a desk, a chair, and a large sea-chest pushed against the wall. Charteris himself was sitting on his cot. He was dressed, but carelessly, as though he had only just got up, and done it in a hurry.

He was a large, spreading man, probably in his sixties, she thought. His face was wide and loose, the jowls flowing over his neckerchief, his nose broad and open-pored, his hair scanty, but long and greasy and a faintly yellowish white in colour. He would not have been a pleasant sight at the best of times, and these were evidently not the best. His skin was cheesy white and lightly sheened with moisture, his eyes red-rimmed, with dark shadows beneath them, and his hand shook visibly as he pushed his hair back from his face in a nervous gesture.

'So, boy,' he addressed Lucy, 'you are the new surgeon's mate? By God, but you're still wet behind the ears.'

'I'm fifteen, sir, and I've been helping my father--'

'Yes, yes, I've heard your tale. You don't look fifteen to me, but what does it matter?' he said testily. 'Huggins says you've done what you should do this morning. He says you stitched a man neatly, and set an arm amongst other things. You know your business, it seems.' The words were complimentary, but the tone was not. He sounded as though he were sneering, and Lucy could not understand why.

'They were simple procedures, sir, and not more than I could manage. But I'm well aware how little I know,' she said, in case he thought she was a young know-it-all. Charteris gave an unpleasant smile.

'There's nothing like practice for teaching you what you don't know. Huggins will help you. I shall leave everything to you. Don't disturb me unless it's an emergency.'

'But sir, what if . . .' Lucy began, but he waved a hand at her, dismissing her wearily.

'Use your wits, boy, use your wits. You'd have to if I wasn't here. Away with you, away!'

Outside the cabin door, Lucy found Huggins waiting for her.

'Don't take it to 'eart, sir,' he said. 'The doctor ain't been very well of late.'

Lucy opened her mouth to make an inquiry, and then shut it again as it suddenly came to her what the extra strange smell in the cabin had been: it was opium.

Jemima looked up in faint expectation as the drawing-room door opened, and then jumped to her feet and almost ran into James's arms.

'Oh Jamie, Jamie! Thank God you are come!'

He held her tightly against him and stroked her head. 'I came as soon as I heard, Mother. Has anything been heard?'

'Nothing,' Jemima said into his chest, and then looked up into his face, and saw her own concern and worry mirrored there. 'But it will be easier to bear now you are here.'

'What is being done?' he asked, escorting her back to the fireside.

'Every man we can spare is out searching. Edward has gone to Wetherby to see if she took a coach there, for she certainly did not in York. We have put notices in all the inns and churches, and on the village crosses, for miles around, asking for information, but no-one has come forward. I simply cannot believe that she could have gone far without *someone* seeing her.'

'She's a clever little imp, and very practical. Depend upon it, she will have thought out the best way to go undetected, if that is what she wants. But why did she run away? I had no notion she was unhappy.'

Jemima produced the note from her pocket. 'She left this.'

James opened it and read: 'Dearest Mother, please don't be angry with me. I *must* become a doctor, and this is the only way. When I come back, you will be proud of me. Don't worry about me, for I shall be quite all right. Your loving, Lucy.' He looked at his mother with an enquiring look.

Jemima shrugged. 'She had this notion about wanting to be a doctor. Last year she even suggested to me that I helped her disguise herself as a boy and enter the University at Edinburgh to read medicine. I told her pretty sharply, I'm afraid, that it was all nonsense, but she must have been brooding on it all the same.'

James folded the letter again, and bit his lip. 'I'm afraid this is my fault, Mother. If I had not dressed her as a boy for the race, it would never have entered her head. It was meant to be a piece of fun, but . . .'

'Don't blame yourself, Jamie,' Jemima said, taking his hand. 'I am the one chiefly to blame, for bringing her up with too much liberty. I should have been more careful of her, but I did not want her to be oppressed, as I was when I was a child. I think I erred in the other direction, perhaps with all of you.'

James pressed her hand in return. 'Children will always find their own reasons for being unhappy, Mama; if you don't give them cause, they will manufacture one, for one needs to feel misunderstood and put-upon when one is growing up, you know,' he teased her gently, and she gave a small, distracted smile. 'So is it thought she has dressed herself as a boy and gone to Edinburgh?'

'She has taken none of her own clothes,' Jemima said, 'and Jenny thinks some of Harry and Jack's things, that were set aside when they outgrew them, are missing. But as to *where* she has gone – we cannot find it out. She has not been seen upon the roads, and she has not taken a coach from York.'

'Ah, but she would not,' James said. 'She would cover her track, you know, and not do the obvious things. We must enquire further afield, I believe, Mama.' Jemima made an indeterminate sound of distress, at the thought of her youngest child wandering far from home, alone and friendless, and James, reading her mind, said, 'Don't worry too much, dearest. She's a confiding little thing, and someone will take care of her.'

'I only fear she may be too confiding,' Jemima said in a low voice.

'Why, love, who should harm her? We'll find her, never fear, and bring her back for you to be angry with. I think I will go straight away to the Maccabees' and ask the fellows there if they have heard anything. The more people who are on the look-out for her, the better. Then we must widen our circle of enquiry.'

He stood up and went to the door, and Jemima said, 'I feel so much better now you are here, Jamie. It's almost – it's almost like having your father back.'

'Poor Mama,' he said gently, smiling at her, 'we are such trouble to you, aren't we?' A sudden thought struck him. 'Have you written to Mary? You should, you know, for I would not be in the least surprised if she had made for London. Runaways generally think they have a better chance of hiding there.'

'I'll write at once,' Jemima said, wondering how he had suddenly acquired such an intimate knowledge of the working of fugitives' minds.

Lucy woke from a confused dream to find herself being shaken by a strange man holding a tallow dip in his hand, whose madly flickering light sent the shadows swooping like bats around the ceiling-beams as her cot swung back and forth on its ropes. After a week on board the *Diamond*, her confusion on first waking was growing shorter. For only a few seconds she stared at the man and wondered why he was calling her Mr Proom; then she struggled up on to one elbow and asked what must always be her first question.

'What time is it?'

'Seven bells, sir. In the morning watch.'

Half past seven in the morning, she translated for herself laboriously. She had been asleep about six hours, after being called out at two bells in the middle watch to examine the purser's wife, who had violent stomach pains. The purser was sure it was appendicitis and Lucy had viewed with alarm the prospect of having a first death on her hands, for Charteris was reported too soundly asleep to be aroused; but the pains had turned out to be indigestion brought on by over-indulgence in roast pork, the purser and the gunner having killed one of the litter of piglets they had bought between them.

Another phenomenon impressed itself upon her. When she had retired to her bed at three bells, the ship had been close-hauled and was pitching extravagantly, with a long slow roll in the middle of the movement; it was borne in upon her now that she was level and moving regularly and much more gently.

'Why is the ship so still?' she asked the messenger.

'We're hove-to, sir, in the lee of the land. They can see the Rock from the foretop masthead, sir.'

'The Rock?'

'Gibraltar, sir', the messenger said in surprise that anyone could not know what the Rock was. He was just stupid enough not to be able to initiate conversation, and Lucy had therefore to ask him why he had woken her before he remembered to give her his message.

'It's the doctor, sir. His servant went to wake him, on the account of having to make his report when we anchor at the Rock, and he couldn't rouse him, and Huggins thinks 'e ain't well, sir, meanin' the doctor, sir.'

Lucy remembered in time not to jump from her cot. 'Go and tell Huggins I'm coming at once,' she said, and waited until the messenger had gone before getting up and dressing herself as quickly as possible. The conditions of her life aboard the ship had been ideal for not being found out. She hardly ever went topsides, spending so much of her life in the orlop in conditions of such poor illumination that it would have taken someone who knew her well to recognise her, let alone know she was not male. She messed in the after cockpit, but never stayed after the fork; and she had her rank as a warrant officer to ensure her privacy at the heads. She had close contact with no-one but the loblolly boys, who took her entirely on trust. She had been worried by the discovery that there were about twenty women on board, for she thought a woman more likely to discover her secret than a man; but the women lived lives of even more Stygian retirement than she, and the purser's wife was the first woman she had even seen.

Palter and the doctor's servant were outside the door of the cabin when she arrived and stepped aside silently to let her in, closing the door after her. In the close, dimly lit cabin, the smell was worse than usual.

Huggins was waiting for her, and raised a candle to illuminate the doctor's cot, saying, 'Dead some hours, I should think, sir. I told the boy to say nothing until you'd been and 'ad a look.'

The doctor was stretched on his back, his eyes half open, one arm slipped off the side of the cot, knuckles trailing the floor. Lucy had little experience of human corpses, but it took no medical knowledge at all to discover that the doctor was dead as a nail, for he was cold and growing stiff.

'He must have been dead already when they tried to rouse him to the purser's wife,' she said. She wondered what to do next. Huggins leaned over her shoulder to look dispassionately at his former master's face, and a spot of wax fell from the candle onto the corpse's cheek, making Lucy jump with vicarious pain.

'I knew he'd do it, sooner or later,' Huggins commented lugubriously. 'I told 'im again and again, brandy or opium, I said, but not both together – I told 'im that, sir, but 'e wouldn't listen. He ain't never been the same since we left the old *Clytemnestra*. I been with 'im eleven years, sir, and that business with that Young Gentleman on the *Clytey* broke 'im, sir, though there wasn't never no hevidence against 'im, not what would've stood up in court o'law. Cap'n Prothero took 'im on more out o' kindness, on account the doctor saved 'is leg in the last war when 'e was a lieutenant, but 'e's been at it like knives ever since we come on board, and I knew 'ow it would end. 'E'd've done better to stop on shore, and so I told 'im, but there was that many duns after 'im, they wouldn't 'ave let 'im rest, nohow. 'E's better orf out of it, that's what *I* say.'

Lucy had nothing to add to this comprehensive, if incomprehensible epitaph, and said instead, 'What must I do now? Must I report it to someone?'

'Cap'n 'll have to be told. I should go straight to the first lieutenant if I was you, sir. I'll get Jarvey – the doctor's servant – to take you. Palter 'n me'll stop 'ere with the doctor.'

Ten minutes later Lucy was standing before the captain in his drawing-room, blinking at the unexpected light as the rising sun streamed in through the stern windows.

'There's no mystery about the death, I suppose?' the captain asked.

'No, sir,' Lucy said.

'Very well. You had better make your report in writing. My secretary will shew you how. I shall do what I can about getting a replacement. We may be able to find someone in Gibraltar, as it's an emergency.'

But only two hours later, when she was still struggling with the doctor's indifferent pen and paper so damp the ink ran upon it, while Palter and Smith were laying out the body, Lucy was summoned again to the captain's cabin. Emerging on deck by the after hatchway, she found to her surprise that they were sailing westward with the Rock already behind them. Finding one of the young midshipmen, Cutler, nearby, she asked where they were going.

'Toulon,' he replied succinctly. 'You don't know much, do you?'

'Didn't we go into Gibraltar?' she asked anxiously.

'No,' said Culter. 'A boat came out with despatches, and our new orders, to proceed straight to the blockade of Toulon. Blockade duty,' he added in disgusted tones, 'and not even an hour in Gibraltar to make up for it.'

But Lucy, with more pressing problems, hurried on. Her worst fears were confirmed moments later by the captain.

'I'm appointing you acting surgeon,' he told her, 'until a replacement can be found for Dr Charteris. Frankly, it may be a long time. You'll draw full pay at the surgeon's rate for the time being, and have use of the surgeon's cabin.'

Lucy risked a protest. 'But sir, I'm not qualified,' she said. The captain's brows drew together. The King's navy did not acknowledge the existence of the words 'I can't'.

'Do your best. No-one expects miracles of you. The loblolly boys are experienced, and will help you all they can. I have every confidence in you. You may go.'

There was nothing more to be said. Outside, as she stood a little dazed in the bright spring sunshine, Weston came lounging up to her.

'Well, *doctor*?' he said. She looked up at him helplessly, and he shrugged. 'You cannot, at least, be any worse than old Charteris. The stories about him are a legion. They say he once took off the wrong leg while he was drunk.'

'But I'm not qualified,' she produced her only plea again.

'You're better qualified than anyone else on board; and you've all his books to consult. Besides, the cap'n's word is law, and if he says you're the doctor, then you're the doctor. You'll move into his cabin, of course?'

'Yes, I suppose so.'

'Of course. And you'll mess in the wardroom from now on.

I'll introduce you, if you like, when I come off duty at the end of this watch.'

'Thank you,' said Lucy gratefully. It was good to feel she had a protector on board.

'You'll need a servant, too. I shouldn't have Jarvey, if I were you – a poisonous little beast, and stupid as a slug. Shall I find you someone? There are some decent boys on board, though I dare say you don't know one from another as yet.'

'Thank you,' said Lucy again. 'You're very kind.'

'Not at all. Glad to have you aboard. The midshipmen's mess is no place for you, in any case. Though I must say you seem to have weathered it well.' He gave her a considering look, and Lucy, with a nervous smile, fled below to the safety of the darkness, wondering what exactly he had meant by that. But if he had guessed her secret, he would surely have exposed her by now, would he not? She arrived at the door of the cabin, now *her* cabin, to find that in some mysterious way the news had got below more quickly than she, and Huggins had already moved her cloak-bag and books in, and was in process of moving the doctor's things out.

'Don't worry, sir,' he said cheerfully. 'We'll muddle through all right, between us.'

'Thank you, Huggins,' Lucy said dazedly.

15

When a thing was too horrible to contemplate, Héloïse discovered that it became not only possible, but necessary to shut one's mind to it entirely. The execution of the King in January 1793 was, to a strictly brought-up Catholic, an act of terrible impiety. The Convention had voted for it unanimously, which meant that her own husband had voted for it, a thing shocking past imagining; but she had no choice but to go on living with him, and she could only do that by dismissing the memory from her consciousness.

Her father had been out of Paris at the time, for he had been sent by the Ministry of the Interior to begin cataloguing the vast accumulation of royal treasures at the Château of Chambord as a preliminary to auctioning them, the proceeds to go into the Government's public purse. Charles Nordubois was also absent, for he had been with Dumouriez all through the victorious campaign of the autumn, and had stayed with him in the army's winter quarters in Brussels. He was there when Danton visited the General in January in an attempt to placate him, for Dumouriez had complained long and eloquently that the reinforcements and supplies he had requested of the Convention were not reaching him. Danton brought back letters for Lotti from Charles, and a present of some fine lace. She was pregnant again, and feeling peevish and neglected without her husband.

Héloïse visited her frequently, and played with the children, who more and more regarded her as a sort of substitute mother. Her relationship with her husband had settled into a pattern. Now he was a deputy he was kinder to her, feeling his present status equalled what hers had been under the old regime. They dined together, though seldom alone, entertaining or being entertained by other deputies and their wives, and the new notables of Paris. They did not sleep together – had not done so since the September massacres. It seemed as though that terrible episode had placed an invisible barrier between them.

They were more like brother and sister than husband and wife, but Héloïse was glad that at any rate he talked to her, telling her about the political situation and the daily happenings in the Manège.

She could make little of it, and wondered sometimes if Olivier fully understood what went on, for it sounded as if the days were spent in fruitless, spiteful squabbling, rather than in mature debate. She gathered that the Girondins – that faction which had been called the Brissotins – were in the ascendancy, for while the war went well, they claimed the credit of having been the ones to advocate it in the first place. In opposition to them were the faction known as the Mountain, so called because they occupied the high seats in the upper tiers of the Chamber. Their leaders were the extremists – Robespierre, Marat, and Billaud-Varennes, and the leading lights of the Jacobins Club – and they had the support of the Paris militants, and, through Marat, those dark forces of the gutter and the slum suburbs.

The great mass of the deputies, however, had no allegiance to any faction, and were usually called the Plain. It was for control of the votes of this majority that the two factions battled with each other, and Héloïse gathered from what Olivier told her that for the time being the Girondins usually controlled the voting. They, who had been the extremists of the old Assembly, now viewed themselves as the moderate men, and it was they who were now proclaiming that the revolution had gone far enough and that it should be halted, before things got out of hand. It was the Mountain which was now harnessing the violent forces of the mob, as the Girondins had done before them, in order to achieve their aim of gaining power.

When Henri came to Paris on a visit in February, he added another perspective.

'Since the Girondins control the voting and supply the ministers – in effect, since it is they who are governing the country,' he told Héloïse, 'it will be they who are blamed when things begin to go wrong. I hope your husband is not too closely allied with them?'

'I don't think so,' Héloïse said. 'I know Brissot was his patron, but he has broken with him, ever since he became disillusioned with Danton's policies. His best friend amongst the deputies seems to be Saint-Just, and I don't think you would call *him* a Girondin.'

'That's as well, for the crisis cannot be far off,' said Henri.

'What crisis, Papa?'

'My love, don't you know that prices are soaring, that the *assignat* has fallen to half its face value, that there are bread riots everywhere, and that the people are arming themselves to take vengeance on the hoarders and speculators they hold responsible for the shortage of grain?'

'But, Papa, that happens every winter.'

'How calmly you accept it! But you must know that the people of the provinces are suspicious of the power of Paris, and that the people of Paris are afraid that the provinces will rise up for the monarchy. And that Dumouriez is complaining that his supplies and arms are being diverted by the Ministry of War to strengthen the Commune.'

'I knew that he was unhappy about the situation, for Charles writes of it to Lotti, but I did not know the general had blamed anyone in particular.'

'Did you know also that the members of the Jacobins societies are pillaging Brussels as hard as ever they can, apparently on orders from the mother club in Paris, and that the Belgians are beginning to think the Austrians were no such bad masters after all?'

'No, Papa, but--'

'And when matters get too bad, there will be another upheaval, and we shall have new masters, this time a little more ruthless than the last. So it goes on, child. I do not see the end of it.'

'Oh, Papa – is it so bad?' Héloïse asked in a small voice.

'Your mother once said,' he said slowly, 'that anyone seizing power must be hungrier for it than someone who has it already. Each new party, it seems, has fewer scruples than the one it replaces. I find the contemplation of it exhausting.'

'God will take care of us, Papa,' Héloïse offered him her own comfort. He tried to smile at her, but it went awry.

'Why, Marmoset, don't you know that God has been abolished by the Convention?'

In March, the situation worsened. Dumouriez, short of men, guns, ammunition, boots and clothing, wrote a furious letter to the Convention blaming its political squabbles for his military defeats, as he was driven out of Brussels and began to retreat before a revived Austrian army. The situation was very like that of the previous August, and rumours flew about Paris, that another massacre was planned. Foreigners had their windows broken, there were riots in the suburbs, and the Convention reacted by setting up an official Revolutionary Tribunal, with special powers to arrest and punish so-called 'internal enemies', while it raised troops to send to reinforce Dumouriez.

One bright day in April, Héloïse decided she could not bear the atmosphere a moment longer. She must get out, even if only for a few hours, and breathe fresh air and listen to the sounds of nature rather than of man. She dressed herself in her favourite riding habit, ordered Prestance to be saddled, and, accompanied only by a groom, rode off to the Bois de Boulogne to seek solace.

The day was blowy, the sun shining fitfully between fast-moving clouds. The air was cool, but already scented with new grass and fertile earth, and the trees were tenderly green with their budding first growth. Prestance was gay, and put in little dancing steps along the way, shaking his head and mouthing his bit as a hint to her that he wished to gallop. Héloïse tied her muslin scarf more securely round her hat, and with a sideways glance at the groom, who was idling along in a daydream with his mouth open, leaned forward and gave Prestance the office. The little chestnut gave a half-rear and leapt away, leaving the groom all aback.

Héloïse laughed with pleasure, remembering how she had escaped old Saultier in the woods at Chenonceau, what seemed like a lifetime ago. It was unsuitable for a matron to gallop in a public park, she knew, and the groom would tell tales of her, and Olivier would be angry, but just for the moment she did not care, and was only glad to be out, and free of restrictions and worries. She let Prestance have his head to the end of the ride, and then pulled him up and sat, her cheeks glowing and her eyes bright, waiting demurely for the groom to catch her up at a sedate canter.

A carriage was approaching along the cross-drive, and

Héloïse watched it idly. It had that indefinable look of a job-carriage: a little shabby, a little worn. Perhaps a nobleman's cast-off chariot, she thought, for there was a patch of a different shade of black on the door panel, as if a coat of arms had been painted out. Prestance snorted challengingly at the horses, a common-looking unmatched pair, one bay, one brown, ridden by a postilion in a drab coat. Héloïse checked him as he began to dig, and pulled him a little back for the carriage to pass, but to her surprise it halted beside her. The window was let down, and a heavily-veiled woman leaned forward and beckoned to her.

The groom was still at a distance, and Héloïse felt a small thrill of fear. She did not know the postilion, no doubt hired with the carriage. But who would want to kidnap her, she asked herself reprovingly? She edged Prestance nearer. The woman lifted her veil a little, and spoke in a low voice so that the postilion should not hear: 'Héloïse! It is I – Marie-France! Don't speak – listen!' Héloïse bit back her exclamation of surprise. Marie-France dropped her veil again, and went on urgently, 'Your father has sent me. You must come with me at once. Trust me, and ask nothing.'

Héloïse could not quite obey. 'Is he ill?' she gasped.

'No, no, he is quite well. He said to tell you, the time has come.' She made a gesture towards the approaching groom. 'Tell your groom that I am a friend and that you will ride home with me, because we wish to talk. Send him back with Prestance.'

Héloïse's heart was beating so violently that she had difficulty in speaking calmly and appearing normal to the groom when he rode up. She met him at a little distance, and told him that she had met an old friend whom she had not seen for a long time.

'We have so much to say to each other that I shall ride home in her carriage. You shall take Prestance back for me.'

The groom evidently did not like it. 'I'll ride along with you, madame,' he said. 'It is not suitable that I should leave you.'

'No, no, you must ride ahead – to tell them at home we are coming,' Héloïse improvised rapidly. 'We must have something special for dinner for my friend. Now do as I say,' she added sternly as the groom still looked doubtful; but he was too young and too recently of her service to argue further, and she was glad it was not one of the older grooms she had brought with her that day.

When the two women were safely on their way again, they embraced warmly, and Marie-France said, 'Put on this cloak over your habit. You are too fine.'

'Dear Marie-France, it is so long since we met, but you must tell me first what has happened to Papa,' Héloïse said, obeying her.

'I must tell you nothing,' her friend replied. 'Your father will explain everything to you when we reach him.'

'But where are we going? This is not the road home!'

'We are not going home. We are going to an inn. He is waiting for us there. It would be dangerous for you to go home. He sent me for you in case he should be recognised. He knew you would trust me.'

'I do, dear friend, I do,' Héloïse said, pressing her hand.

They crossed the river at Neuilly, and travelled a little way on the road towards Saint-Germain before turning off and halting at a small inn on a side road. An inn servant hurried up and let down the step for them, and paid off the postilion, so that before the women had even entered the hostelry the carriage was moving away out of the yard. The inn-servant shewed them inside to a private parlour, and as Héloïse entered the first thing she saw was her maid, Marie, sitting on her box, and the second was her father. She ran across the room, and was in her father's arms, pressed against his comforting chest.

'Oh Papa, Papa! Tell me you are all right.'

'Yes, child, I am all right. Did not Marie-France tell you so?'

'Yes, but I thought she might say so to calm me. Thank God!' Héloïse said fervently. Henri disentangled himself from her, set her back on her feet, and with a gentle hand and a wry smile, straightened her hat for her. 'Well, Papa, tell me what has happened,' she said, trying to speak steadily, for she feared the worst.

Henri bid her be seated, and said, 'The news arrived in Paris this morning – after you had gone out, thank God – that Dumouriez has gone over to the Austrians--'

'What!'

'Yes, it is true. He was so angry and disillusioned at the way the Convention has treated him, that he tried to persuade the army to march with him on Paris, dismiss the Convention, and restore the monarchy, with the Dauphin as king under the 1791 Constitution. But he could not win enough support, and deserted to the Austrians.'

Héloïse turned pale. Henri nodded seriously. 'Yes, it is true,' he added to her silent plea.

'Lotti?' she managed to ask. 'Charles – was she with him?'

'Nordubois was with him,' Henri said, his face grave. 'He behaved with criminal irresponsibility, knowing he left his wife and children in Paris. He sent her a letter with instructions to flee and meet him at the border. She was packing when the officers from the Revolutionary Tribunal came for her.'

'No, Papa, no! They have not arrested her?'

'Yes, child, I'm afraid they have. But they would have taken her anyway, you know. She hardly escaped last time, and the Tribunal is rounding up all "suspect" people, as they call them. Fortunately the governess behaved sensibly and got the children away and sent word to me.'

'But, Papa, I don't understand,' Héloïse said.   they have arrested Lotti, how can you think I would leave Paris? I must stay, until I know she is safe. You must use your influence to get her released.'

'You do not yet know everything, Marmoset. There is no hope that Lotti will be released, now that Charles's part in the conspiracy is known. He sent letters to his wife as indiscreet as Dumouriez's to the Convention, and as she is German, she is held to have been in on the plot. Yes, nonsense I know, but the evidence against her is strong. She did not destroy his letters – the officers of the Tribunal found them when they arrested her and searched the house – and she did not denounce his intentions to the Committee of Public Safety. They will say she is as guilty as he.'

'But Papa--'

'And more than that, child. You are also in danger.'

'I?'

'Yes, my love, as her most intimate friend, and as wife of Vendenoir, who was Charles's intimate friend.'

'Olivier?'

'Yes, dearest, I'm afraid your husband has been arrested too. As soon as the news was read out in the Convention, two or three deputies jumped up to denounce Charles's friends. He was arrested at once, and the order was made out for your arrest. Thank God you were not at home! Your servants behaved with wonderful loyalty. When the house had been searched, Marie, here, sent word to me, and packed a box for you, and took a *fiacre* and left the house at once. But for her, you would be forced to flee with nothing but the clothes you stand up in.'

Héloïse looked across at her blushing maid, and said warmly, 'Marie, I cannot thank you enough. When all this is over, I will find a way to reward you. I will find a way to send you enough money to make you comfortable for life.'

Marie looked up in surprise. 'Oh, but madame, I come with you. It would not be suitable for you to go without a maid. I come with you, to serve you. Yes, yes, it is what Madame de Murphy would have wished.'

Héloïse went to her and kissed her. 'Bless you, dear Marie. And thank you.' She turned to her father. 'Well, Papa, I believe I understand the situation. I am calm now. Tell me frankly, what chance is there that Lotti and Olivier will be released?'

'My love, I'm afraid there is none,' Henri said, holding her gaze steadily. 'I wish I could tell you otherwise. But the Revolutionary Tribunal has extraordinary powers, and is answerable to no-one. You know that when it was first proposed, many deputies cried out against it. "Remember September!" they shouted. The purpose of the Tribunal is to remove anyone who might oppose the will of the Convention. It is not so stated, but it is true. Lotti is a foreigner, and wife of a most reviled traitor. Vendenoir has made enemies of some of the most ruthless people in the Manège, and has repudiated the only man who might have saved him. And you are caught between the two. You must not remain in Paris a moment longer.'

'What must I do, then?' she asked quietly.

'I have arranged matters through my usual channels. You are to go to England. Two fast chaises will take you and the children straight to Saint-Valéry, where a ship will be waiting for you. The sea crossing is longer from there, but you will be safer on the sea than on land. Duncan will go with you as far as the port, and Marie will attend you all the way. In England you must go to London, to the house of the Earl of Chelmsford, who is our cousin. He has paid us a pension ever since I was born, until the declaration of war, and he will help you establish yourself. You will not go penniless – Duncan has money for you, and I will find ways to send more. Even in war, there are channels through which money can pass.'

Héloïse had listened to this with restlessness, and now broke in to say, 'But Papa, you say *I* will do this and *I* will do that. Surely you come with me? You cannot think I would go without you.'

'No, Marmoset, I am not coming – not now. I am in the middle of some very important business, which will be of great profit to me. A few months more will make a vast difference to my fortunes. When I come to England, I wish to do so in style. No, no, don't argue with me. I shall be quite safe, I promise you. I am a loyal servant of the Ministry of the Interior, and known to be a friend of the revolution, no matter who is in power, so long as it brings me profit. The most trusted man in politics, you know, is always the wholly selfish one, for you can be sure of his loyalty as long as you pay him enough.' He made a wry face. 'I shall noisily repudiate you and your husband, never fear, and in a few months, or a year at most, I shall join you in England, and we shall be so rich and fashionable that the Morlands will tumble over one another to court our favour.'

'The Morlands?'

'The Morlands of Morland Place in the county of Yorkshire: the proud, ancient, stiff-necked English family of which you and I are a side-shoot, and who refused to acknowledge you, long ago, when you were a baby, and I asked them to receive you back into the family. But never mind that now. There is just time to eat something before you leave. You should not embark on your new life with an empty stomach.'

'Very well, Papa,' Héloïse said, trying to be brave, though she could feel the tears close under the surface. 'And perhaps I had better see the children. They must be very frightened, poor little things, and in need of reassurance.'

'Yes, by all means – Marie, run upstairs and bring down the children,' Henri said. Marie curtsied and obeyed, and it was when she had left the room that Héloïse remembered something else. She turned to her father with a stricken look.

'Oh Papa – Bluette!'

Henri shook his head. 'I'm sorry, my love, we have no time to go back for her, even if it were safe to do so. Don't worry, they won't harm her.'

The tears spilled over. Somehow it was easier to weep for a little thing; leaving Papa and her homeland was too terrible a grief to comprehend.

The bright spring morning proved treacherous: the fast clouds darkened and closed together, obliterating the blue sky, the wind rose, and by mid-afternoon a chill rain had begun to spatter the windows of the carriages. As dusk came on, the rain fell faster and Héloïse, travelling in the second carriage with the two little girls, could barely see the other carriage through the murk. The plans had been well laid, however. Henri's system worked well, and Duncan was known on the road. The changes were ready for them at every stage, and they set off again each time with the minimum delay. It was, Héloïse knew, a little over a hundred miles from Paris to Saint-Valéry, and they reached it by nine in the evening.

Lotti's little girls had slept, thank God, for the last few hours of the journey, Clothide on Héloïse's lap, and Mathilde leaning against her with her feet tucked up on the seat. Karellie was with Marie and Duncan in the first carriage. When they pulled up at the last inn, and a face loomed in the light from the windows behind the streaming glass, Héloïse was sorry to have to wake them, but they were by now too bemused with weariness to remember their pain and fear with any acuteness. The door was opened and the step let down, and Héloïse stepped out to smell, behind the usual horse smell of an inn-yard, the unfamiliar tang of the sea. She helped Mathilde down, received Clothilde into her arms, and followed the inn-servant across the wet and puddled cobbles, out of the darkness into the light and warmth of the inn.

Everything was strange to her. She felt bemused, stiff and cold from the long journey, her mind a whirl of images and memories, doubts and fears. Ah, here was Marie carrying the little boy. No sign of Duncan. A strange man in a leather apron said in coarse country French, 'This way, my lady. Come and have a warm and a drop of ale.'

'Where is Duncan?' she asked, hearing her own voice strangely, as if at a great distance.

'Your man? Talking to the ship-captain, in the taproom there-away,' said the man with a gesture of the candle he was holding that made the flame dip and jump. 'Come you in here. All's right.'

A small, dark parlour, the walls yellowed with ancient smoke, and a fire of driftwood fizzing and spitting in the rough stone chimney; a wooden settle and a rug and a battered fender on which to place her damp, deathly-cold feet. The man in the leather apron pushing past her unceremoniously with two pewter tankards, placing them on the hearth, and inserting into each in turn a hot poker drawn from the fire.

'There you are, my lady, you get yourself outside of that. And you, miss. By God, I wouldn't be in your shoes tonight. It's a bad night to be taking ship. Do those children eat bread and milk? My missus can give 'em something if you like.'

'Is the sea rough? Will it be too rough to sail?' Héloïse heard herself asking.

'Lord bless you, no, it ain't as rough as that,' the man reversed with startling ease. 'It's not more than a bit choppy. You'll be safe enough with old Rouget.' There was a sound of feet in the hallway outside, and Héloïse stiffened to listen. The man in the leather apron said. 'Don't you worry, that's only my men bringing your box in. You're safe here as in your own bed – safer! I've looked after many a lady and gentleman for Monsieur Écosse. He pays me handsome, and I ain't lost one yet to the gendarmes. You take your ease, my lady. Your man'll be in soon.'

An unknown period passed. Héloïse drank the hot spiced ale, and felt stronger, but ever more remote. Marie tended the children, fed them the bread and milk brought in by a kitchenmaid, soothed them back into an uneasy sleep. The fire snapped and spurted, sending golden sparks up the chimney, and the rain smacked like pebbles against the dark window.

The dream-like interlude was broken abruptly by the sound of horses' hooves in the yard, and the entry of Duncan in a hurry.

'Gendarmes,' he said abruptly, jerking his thumb over his shoulder. 'It may be us they're after. We can't take the risk –

we must board at once.' He picked up Mathilde. 'Bring the little ones,' he said, and hurried out into the passage. Marie and Héloïse picked up the smaller children and followed him, stumbling a little in their weariness. Duncan led them out by a different door into the darkness, hearing behind them harsh voices interposed with the slower country French of the inn-keeper, and the ring of spurred boots on the flagstones. Karellie murmured something, and Marie hushed him. The rain had stopped, but the wind was brisk and cold and salt-smelling, whipping at their cloaks and blowing the women's skirts against their legs.

'There's our man,' Duncan said suddenly as a tiny glimmer of light appeared ahead. 'Rouget has his ship, the *Blaireau*, out in the estuary. There's a boat waiting to take you out to her.'

They stumbled after him through the darkness over slippery cobbles; then there was shingle under their feet, and the sound of the waves sighing and sucking at the cold shore; and they came up to a large rowing-boat pulled up on the shingle, where a man, no more than a dark shape outlined by the glimmer of his shielded lantern, waited for them impatiently. Behind him Héloïse could see the shifting flecks of white of the breaking wave-tops – the sea at last!

'Where have you been?' the man said in a low, hurried voice. 'The tide is almost on the turn. Another few minutes, and you'd have missed it.'

'I was hoping the wind would drop a little,' Duncan said, and the other growled a disgusted comment about landmen, which was interrupted by Duncan's hurried explanation about the gendarmes.

'Christ!' the dark shape ejaculated. 'Get those women aboard, friend!'

'Madam's box – where is it?' Marie cried suddenly. Duncan cursed softly.

'Back at the inn. I'll get it.'

'No time, monsieur,' said the boatman. 'We dare not lose the tide. We leave now, or never. Get aboard, I say.'

Héloïse clasped Duncan's hand, and he said, 'I'm sorry, madame. But we'll get money to you somehow, don't worry.'

'But how shall I pay this Rouget?' she asked.

'He was paid in advance. Let me help you into the boat – there is no time to lose.'

'Yes. Take care, Duncan.'

'They won't catch me,' he said, and she heard the smile in his voice. It was hard to climb into the boat, hampered by long skirts, for the side of the boat was slippery and the sea washed at the shingle under her feet. Strong, hard, cold hands grasped at her, and she was bundled over the side unceremoniously, pushed onto a seat, and Clothilde was dropped heavily into her lap. Somewhere in the distance lights became visible, bobbing, and there was the sound of voices, and heavy feet in the shingle. Someone muttered, 'It's them!' and someone else cried, 'Push off!', and after a moment of rocking and lurching the boat suddenly moved free, and Héloïse found herself afloat on the sea for the first time. Oars smacked into the rowlocks, the rowers grunted as they dug into the water, and the boat steadied as it gathered forward way and the water deepened under it. Héloïse clutched the gunwale with one hand, and with the other pressed Clothilde against her to try to shield her from the wind and spray. Her mind was too numb properly to understand that she was departing without the box containing all her worldly possessions; she could only pray fervently that Duncan would not be taken.

At last they came up to the ship, and the men manoeuvred the boat round to lie alongside her. She was only a small fishing-vessel, but the side of her towered above the boat, looking impossibly steep to Héloïse. A row of white faces gleamed above the bulwarks, ghostly in the darkness.

'Now then, madame, give me the nipper, that's right. Now step up here, and grab his hand, and when I say the word, you scramble up for all your worth.'

Héloïse found herself standing precariously balanced on the side of the boat, her hands gripped in the plank-hard ones of a sailor above her, more hands steadying her at her waist, while the boat and ship heaved out of phase with each other. Then suddenly the gap narrowed, the man behind her shouted 'Now!' and in one breathless, exhilarating moment she was pulled and pushed and went scrambling up the side, and found herself safe on the comparative stability of the ship's deck.

In a few moments Marie and the children were with her, and

298

the rowing-boat was already rushing off and heading back into the darkness.

A stout, bearded man stepped forward. 'Now, ladies, you must get below, out of the way. We must set sail at once, or we'll lose the tide. I'm Rouget, skipper of the *Blaireau*. Jacques, take the ladies below. Stand by the anchor! Ready at the braces!'

He had turned from them to bellow orders before Héloïse had had time to thank him or ask any of the questions that filled her mind; there was a rush of bare feet over the deck as the hands hurried to make sail, and the spindly youth addressed as Jacques tugged peremptorily at her elbow.

'Come on, madame, or you'll get knocked over,' he said. He led the two women and the three children down through a hatchway, by a steep ladder, into a stuffy cabin, lit only by a glimmer from a lantern turned down low. The cabin contained nothing but two bunks covered with dirty blankets, two wooden stools, and a box pushed against the wall. Though stuffy, the air was chill and dank, and the smell of fish and dirty bodies was overpowering. The ship seemed to be leaping about extravagantly.

Mathilde whimpered, and with a glance at Marie's green countenance, Héloïse managed to say to the boy, 'Do you think you could bring us a basin?' before the need to keep her lips tightly closed became paramount.

Sometimes in the hours that followed, Héloïse wished she could die. At others, she thought she probably had died and gone to Hell. They were all seasick; cold, and weary to death; disorientated, with no idea of where they were or what was happening. The children cried with misery between bouts of vomiting, and Marie groaned and called upon the Blessed Virgin to release her from her torment, and Héloïse, ministering to them as far as her own sickness and the limitations of the cabin permitted, wondered more than once whether it would not have been better to remain in Paris and face the danger.

After an unknown length of time, when the pitching and rolling of the ship, and the creaks and groans of her fabric working, seemed to have grown continually worse, the boy reappeared at the door and said: 'Cap'n says to tell you we've got to heave to.'

Héloïse roused herself. 'I don't understand what that means,' she managed to say. The spindly boy was silent for a moment, struggling with unfamiliar words.

'Weather's worsening,' he said at last. 'We must go with it for a space, 'stead of against it, or we'll break up.'

'Are we in danger?' Héloïse asked, though she was too weary and sick to feel much alarm.

'Lord, no, madame, unless we get too close to the cape. When we're hove-to, we drift down to leeward, see.'

Héloïse didn't. 'Is that in the right direction?' He stared at her, incomprehending. 'I mean, is that towards England?' He shook his head. 'Then how long must we stay – hove to?'

He shrugged. 'Until the weather moderates, madame,' he said, and disappeared before she could ask him any more difficult questions.

'Oh madame,' Marie said, speaking for the first time in hours, 'I am súre we are all going to die.' She did not sound as if the prospect much appalled her.

Heaving to moderated the action of the ship, so that although she still leapt about like an unbroken horse, the movement was more predictable, and therefore a little – just a little – more bearable. Héloïse's sickness abated just enough for her to begin to feel curiosity, and when, a while later, there came the sound of feet running across the deck above her, and she felt the ship turning into the wind again, she felt strong enough to say to Marie: 'I'm going up on deck for a moment, to see what is happening. I shall only be a minute or two.'

Marie merely groaned in reply. Héloïse pulled her cloak closely about her and made her slow and difficult way up the ladder, and lifted her head cautiously out of the hatchway, clinging onto the rim of it to keep her balance. The little ship was thrashing along with every sail taut, the deck sloping like a roof as she heeled over at a fantastic angle. She could feel what a struggle it was to keep this position, and saw in every man standing by his post the lines of tension and readiness for action. Something was happening! At the wheel, near to the hatchway, were two men, braced to keep it steady, and between them stood Rouget, the captain, his fingers resting on the wheel's rim as if it conveyed some information to him.

'Captain,' she shouted above the wind, 'what's happening?'

He removed his hand from the wheel to make an angry gesture at her. 'Get below!' he shouted. 'I can't have women on deck at a time like this.'

'Yes, Captain, but please tell me what's happening. I can't bear to be shut away in ignorance,' she pleaded.

'An English ship,' he replied economically. 'Frigate on blockade duty. Nearly ran into her. If she didn't see us, we can lose her in the darkness.'

'Surely, we have nothing to fear from an English ship?' Héloïse cried, the wind whipping the words away from her lips.

'You may not,' he shouted. 'Damned if I want to spend the rest of the war a prisoner, and my ship a prize. Get below!'

But Héloïse was so excited at the thought that deliverance from the *Blaireau* might be at hand that she dared to disobey, lifting herself a few more steps until she was high enough out of the hatchway to look astern. She gasped as she saw the gleam of the frigate's canvas, towering, it seemed, over the little fishing vessel. The captain looked too, and cursed comprehensively. The frigate had certainly seen them, and was pursuing. Héloïse saw something else, too: that the sky, to the east, was lightening. Dawn was approaching: no chance now to lose them in the dark.

Suddenly she saw a flash of orange light from the frigate. She was puzzling what it could be when there was the sound of a flattened boom, and overhead a whining noise: the frigate had fired a warning shot at them. The captain cursed again; one of the quartermasters ducked instinctively, losing his hold on the wheel; there was a horrible cracking noise from somewhere below, and the wheel spun free, knocking the other quartermaster off his feet.

'Tiller rope's gone!' someone shouted.

'Hands to the braces!' the captain yelled. Héloïse did not understand what was happening in those minutes that followed, except that there was great danger, not only from the frigate looming up, her gleaming tower of sails making nothing of the weather that was threatening the *Blaireau*. Without her rudder, the *Blaireau* wanted to yield to the pressure of the wind; she began to turn, and there was ominous creaking from every part of her, and with a sound like a rifle shot her jib burst and was thrashed instantly into ribbons. Another boom, as the frigate fired again, and the captain tore the speaking-trumpet from its beckets and howled a mixture of defiance and curses at the English captain, in between bellowing orders at his crew.

Then the ship jarred violently, flinging Héloïse out of the hatchway, rolling her against the mast, which she grabbed instinctively as spray burst over her in sheets. She heard someone shout, 'We're struck! English bastards!', and someone else cry, 'No, we're aground! It's a sandbank!'

With a noise like the end of the world, the main mast split half-way up, and fell away over the side of the ship. She was still now, leaning at a preposterous angle, the white water pounding at her, safe for a precarious moment as the hanging mast counterbalanced her. Someone was seizing hold of Héloïse, dragging her to her feet.

'To the boats!' he shouted, hauling her by main force along the steep deck.

'Marie – my maid – the children!' she gasped. The remains of a wave broke over the bulwark, drenching her, making her gasp.

'Get in the boat,' the man howled, then, urgently, 'I'll get them. Go! Don't waste time!'

Brawny arms helped her into the boat, which was swung at once over the side, dangling for a sickening moment on its davits, a moment during which Héloïse was able to see the frigate, very close now, hove-to and also lowering a boat. Then the boat lurched violently as someone cut it free, flew through the air, and struck the water at an angle, sending sheets of spray up into the air. Héloïse, clinging like a monkey to anything that came within grasp of her fingers, was pitched into the bottom of the boat, and someone fell on top of her, treading on her hand and making her cry out in agony. She could not breathe, the breath was being crushed out of her by the weights on top of her, and she struggled feebly for what seemed like a lifetime before suddenly she was free, and someone helped her up to sitting position, and she found the boat was free on the water, and two men already rowing her away from the wreck of the *Blaireau*. There were about a dozen of them in the boat, one clutching a hand to his cut face and another cursing and raving like a drunkard, but the others sitting silent, numbed by disaster. Héloïse clung to the side of the boat with one hand, the other lying swollen and throbbing in her lap. She was so cold that her feet burned with pain, and her face was stiff, and her teeth chattered uncontrollably; but, like the others, she was too numb to think or fear.

That came later when she found herself at last on the deck of the frigate, the *Crescent*, and a rough but kindly sailor came forward to fling a blanket about her. A young man in uniform said to her in French so English that she had difficulty in realising for a moment that it *was* French, '*Je suis le capitaine*, John Shilling. *Soyez tranquille, madame, vous n'avez rien à craindre.*'

Héloïse was chilled to the bone, soaked through, exhausted, and in some pain from her wounded hand. She had lost everything she possessed, except the clothes she stood in. She had no idea how many of the *Blaireau*'s crew had survived, or of the fate of Marie and the children. She was exiled from her land; her husband and her best friend were in prison facing execution; she did not know if she would ever see her father again.

All this whirled through her weary mind; but something remained to her – something in her blood, perhaps, or bred into her by her convent upbringing, or perhaps something simply in her own nature – which made her draw herself together for one last effort before she could collapse. Her tongue seemed leaden, but she forced it to frame her words in English.

'Thank you, captain,' she said. 'I am the Lady Henrietta Louisa Stuart, cousin of the Earl of Chelmsford. I am fleeing the revolutionary government.' One thing more was necessary. She was swaying with weariness now, and the captain's surprised, kindly face seemed to surge strangely, now near, now distant. 'The men of the *Blaireau* took to sea to help me escape. I wish you will not make them *prisonniers de la guerre*.' Aware that her English had escaped her, she tried again. 'I wish that you will have them released.' She shook her head, but the darkness clouding her brain was claiming her, and she wanted most of all to yield to it. She stretched out her hand – the wounded one – in a kind of mute appeal, and the last thing she knew as she slid down the long, easy slope into darkness was the arms of the sailor grasping her round the middle, and his voice ejaculating mildly in her ear, 'Blimey! There she goes!'

16

Mary Morland and Louisa came into the blue saloon, followed by a footman laden with parcels, to find Jemima there, sitting by the window, chin in hand, staring out at the April sunshine lighting St James's Park.

'What, mother, back so soon?' Mary said briskly, stripping off her lilac French gloves. 'Yes, put them all down there, Biggs, and then you may go. Stay, is my lady at home?'

'No, madame. My lady was driven out at eleven by Sir Arthur in his curricle, madam. I believe Mr Hawkins anticipates her return at any moment, madam.'

'Oh, well let me know when she comes in, will you', Mary said, dismissing him with a wave of the hand. When he had gone, she turned to her mother with a laugh. '"Mr Hawkins anticipates", indeed! I think Biggs is looking for preferment. I shouldn't be surprised if he didn't approach Louisa's John asking to be the new Anstey butler.'

Jemima managed to smile, not at the footman's presumption, but at the easy way in which Mary called John Anstey 'Louisa's John'. She had been very glad of the match, for Louisa's sake, for John was kind, and it would mean Louisa could stay close to her childhood home, but she had not been sure, until she saw with her own eyes, that Mary had no regrets in the matter. Louisa, she thought, was positively blooming with the approach of her wedding-day, looking almost pretty, and Mary had entered with great enthusiasm into the business of buying Louisa's wedding-clothes, a task which Flora was only too pleased to turn over to her.

'I see you have plenty of boxes there,' Jemima said, nodding at the heap on the sopha. 'Have you found anything pretty?'

'Oh yes, the most ravishing hat,' Mary said, pulling off her own hat and giving her long curls a shake. 'That's the box, there, Louisa, the blue one. Shew mother your hat. I really think I might steal it from you, it is so becoming! And the pairs and *pairs* of gloves this girl has got! I will say that John does everything "very handsome", just like his father.'

Jemima glanced sharply at her daughter, wondering if the comment was at all sarcastic, but Mary's face shewed nothing but good humour. Louisa, with more animation than Jemima ever remembered in her, took off her old hat and tied on the new one in the mirror over the fireplace, and then turned to Jemima for her approval with a look almost of complacency.

'There, Mother, what do you think?' Louisa asked.

'I think you look beautiful, my love. You positively have dimples – wherever did you get them?' Jemima said, smiling. It was not the moment to reprove her, however gently, for calling Jemima 'mother', as she had done since her babyhood. Flora was addressed, most properly, as 'mama', but Jemima was so afraid the older, more affectionate term would slip from Louisa's lips in Flora's presence, and hurt Flora's feelings. 'I wish Allen could see you now, dearest. He would be so proud of his little girl,' she added, stepping up to tweak the ribbons into a better bow, and kiss the newly rosy cheek above them. 'Now tell me, Mary, who is this Sir Arthur who has taken Flora out in his curricle?'

Mary laughed. 'It's Flora's latest beau,' she said. 'Yes, isn't it shocking? She has gone back to all her old, bad ways! He's Sir Arthur MacArthur, would you believe, a colonel in Horace's regiment, and quite old enough to be her father, but as dashing as a cornet, and as fine as fivepence in his regimentals.'

'He wears the most horrible corsets,' Louisa said in shocked tones. 'You can hear them creak when he bows!'

'She has such a following now amongst the regiments,' Mary went on gleefully, 'she says it is quite like the old days. Charles laughs at her immoderately, and calls them the military papas, but she says that now all her naval officers have gone to sea she must have someone to drive her in the park and take her to the opera, and the young officers are never sober after three in the afternoon.'

'Mary, really! Such talk!' Jemima reproved, but with a smile.

'Oh, you know it's true, Mother. Horace's regiment, the Prince of Wales's own, is stationed out at Hounslow, and they exercise there in the morning, and then all the officers ride in to dine in town and spend the rest of the day drinking and gambling at White's, or taking up boxes at the opera and leaning out and ogling all the young women. Horace has taken to using a quizzing-glass – it is so droll to see him! But they have caused quite a sensation. Town is full of mamas with daughters to shed, on the catch for an Honourable in scarlet!'

'Horatio says his regiment is going down to Brighton for the Prince's birthday,' Louisa said. Brighton was where John was taking her for their honeymoon, because he felt 'abroad' was unsafe at present, and she liked to mention the town as often as possible, since she was not quite bold enough to mention the word 'honeymoon'. Mary chuckled.

'Lord! That will be a sight to see, the 10th Dragoons at Brighton, rows and rows of white tents and handsome young officers in scarlet, enough to make a young woman swoon. If Flora has any sense, she will get Dr Williams to recommend sea air for Amelia. Let her take her there in August and she'll get her off within a fortnight.'

Jemima shook her head. 'I can see that mixing with all those naval officers hasn't improved your language, Mary dear.'

Mary dimpled. 'You talk as though I spent my evenings gaming in Fladong's, Mother!' Then her face grew serious. 'But I shouldn't be so light. I guess from your being back so soon that you have no news?'

'Nothing,' Jemima sighed. 'I cannot believe that she can have disappeared from the face of the earth like that, without trace. *Someone* must have seen her. Someone must know where she is.'

Mary touched her hand and said gently, 'Mother, it has been two months now. I think you ought to resign yourself--'

'No,' Jemima interrupted her hastily, and then said with an apologetic smile, 'Please don't say it, Mary. It's unlucky.' Mary looked contrite. 'I know it's what everyone thinks, but I am sure she's alive somewhere – and Jamie thinks so, too.'

Mary reserved comment, thinking it more likely that James pretended to think so, in order to support his mother's spirits.

'He is being such a rock,' Jemima went on. 'He has left the militia, you know, to be at home with me, and to help Ned and me with the search.'

'Yes, I know. I don't think it was much of a wrench to him to leave, though.'

307

Jemima smiled faintly. 'He says if he had stayed on longer, he'd have been caught by some ravening mama with a plain daughter. He also says that he bribed Lucy to run away so as to give me something to worry about, and stop me finding a match for him.'

'James always did like to shock,' Mary said. There was a sound of horses in the street outside, and she went over to the window. 'That must be Flora returning. Yes – oh Mother, do come and look at Sir Arthur! You never saw such a macaroni! His curricle is bang up to the mark, as well, all primrose and black, and the horses so shiny you would think they had been waxed! Wait, there's someone else, too – oh, it's Horatio, just arrived! I wonder if he will stay to dinner? Charles and John are dining here today, so we should be quite a party.' She turned back to the room. 'Come, Louisa, we had better go down to the drawing-room. Flora will take Sir Arthur there, and it wouldn't do to slight him, even if he *does* creak.'

Captain the Honourable Horatio Morland, taken aback to find an elderly colonel at the door beside him, declined to take a nuncheon with the assembled party, claimed a pressing engagement with his tailor, and left again at once; but since Lord Chelmsford and Mr Anstey stepped in a few minutes later, his company was not missed. An ample display of cold meats, fruits, and cakes was spread on the round table in the drawing-room, so invitingly that Colonel Sir Arthur MacArthur had difficulty in refusing Flora's invitation to stay and eat of them; but the earl's sardonic eye and the memory of Miss Mary Morland's clever tongue were enough to rout him, and he bowed his magnificent way out.

The remaining party gathered cheerfully round the table to hear John Anstey's good news.

'I had a letter this morning from my father,' he said, 'to say that he has arranged the match between Lizzie and Arthur Fussell. They're to be married in June, when Louisa and I return to Yorkshire.'

Louisa met his eyes for a moment and then lowered them, blushing. Mary did not join in the congratulations of the others.

'But John, Arthur Fussell is such an odious, vapid, conceited little donkey! How can you condemn poor Lizzie to marry him?' she protested vigorously. John received it good-humouredly.

'Oh, he's not so bad as he used to be, you know, and marriage will steady him down. He's not a bad sort underneath, and he'll inherit a pretty property – it's a good match for Lizzie. She'll have a good dowry, but she is the youngest – and as she's the youngest, it's easy to forget that she's nearly twenty-five and still unwed.' He realised as he said it that it was tactless, for Mary was four years older and single. He hurried on, 'It's Lizzie's idea, you know, Polly! She thinks she can make something of him, and ever since she first visited Valentina Fussell at the new house at Fulford, she has had a secret desire to own it. Now Valentina's getting married, she would have no excuse even to visit it, if she didn't take Arthur.'

'She could visit Charlotte,' Mary said.

'She was never a particular friend of Charlotte's' John said, and went on teasingly, 'I confess we were holding Lizzie in reserve for James, after Cissy failed with him, but he doesn't look like coming up to scratch, and if we keep her much longer she'll go over, and then no-one will have her. So it must be Arthur Fussell, I'm afraid.'

Everyone laughed at this outrageous talk, except Louisa, who looked from her fiancé to Mary and back with round-eyed admiration.

'Well, I think we should drink a toast to them, anyway,' Charles was saying, when the door opened to admit the butler, with a letter on a silver tray. 'Yes, Hawkins?'

'This has just been delivered by hand, my lord, from Hunstanton House. I thought it might be urgent, my lord.'

Charles took the letter and waved Hawkins away, and said, 'Hunstanton House? It must be from Lady Hunstanton to you, my love. Why should Hawkins think it might be urgent? It will be an invitation to a rout or a card-party, I don't doubt.'

'It is addressed to you, my love,' Flora smiled patiently, pushing the letter back at him. 'You don't suppose Hawkins would be so simple, do you? He is not in his dotage yet.'

'I don't even *know* Hunstanton – he's one of *your* sailor friends,' Charles grumbled, taking the letter back and breaking the seal. He read the contents in silence, but a smile of mixed amusement and perplexity quivered on his lips, and when he had finished, he looked around the assembled company and said, 'Well, here's a thing! I think I am about to be dunned, but it will be done most charmingly, if the language is anything to go by.'

The letter was in a very foreign hand.

'Sir Earl,' it said, 'the Lady Henrietta Louisa Stuart desires her humble duty to milord, and begs leave to advise him that she has escaped the enragement of the Revolutionary Government in France, and is needful of begging immediate succour until her affairs shall be settled. She desires to do herself the honour to call upon milord and milady in the tomorrow forenoon, if it shall be perfectly convenient.'

'I love "enragement",' Flora marvelled. 'It sounds so terrifying!'

'And the "perfectly convenient",' Mary added with a smile. 'Such a nice emphasis. But the "Sir Earl" puzzles me a little, I confess.'

'She was thinking in French,' Jemima said absently. 'She thought "*Monsieur le Comte*" and then translated it.'

'Yes, of course,' Flora said, 'but who is she, Charles? Lady Henrietta Louisa Stuart? It sounds like something out of a history book.'

Charles looked a little uncomfortable. 'Papa told me about it when I came of age and he was explaining the duties that went with the title. He said that we had a pensioner in Paris – some sort of relative, I believe, but with a bend sinister – who had been guaranteed a competence by his father – my grandfather. This lady must be his daughter. Of course, when war broke out the pension ceased, and I must confess I had forgotten all about it. I hope she has not been forced to flee by hardship or penury.'

'You are forgetting the enragement,' Flora said soothingly. 'Well, we shall see her tomorrow. I am all agog! And after Horace teased me that I did not have a tame *emigré* like other fashionable ladies! But shall you help her, Charles? It might be a great nuisance.'

'I think I shall have to, but I don't know to what extent. She says "until her affairs are settled" as if she does not mean to be a permanent drain on my estate.'

'She probably said that to allay your fears,' Mary said. 'Once you have accepted her into the house, you'll have her for ever. But what is this *Lady* Henrietta she uses? Is there a title?'

'It's from her grandmother,' Jemima said, 'who was given an earldom in her own right. And *her* grandmother was the old Countess Annunciata. They are – a bastard branch of the family.'

'So she is a cousin of ours – of all of us?' Mary exclaimed.

'Yes, a sort of cousin,' Jemima said steadily. Charles looked at her with a faint frown, and she went on, 'Your father told me about it too, Charles. It's too complicated to tell you why. But I should like to be here to receive her with you tomorrow, if I may.'

'Oh, we all die to see her, Mother!' Mary exclaimed. 'If you do not receive her, Charles, I shall never speak to you again.'

Jemima happened to be crossing the hall the following morning when the Hunstanton carriage arrived at the door, and in pardonable curiosity she ran up the stairs to the safety of the half-landing and watched unseen as Hawkins opened the door to the pensioner. Jemima's first thought was that it was not a lady at all, but a child dressed up, for she was so tiny, a minute figure in a smart pelisse and a hat with tall feathers, entirely dwarfed by Hawkins' magnificent bulk. Jemima could not see the face, but she heard the voice quite clearly, saying with an enchanting French accent:

'Oh, but you are Hawkins, I know! for Lady Hunstanton has told me to expect you, and the maid she has so kindly lent to me has told me that in England a butler is a most important person, and must be greatly respected. So I wish we will be friends. I am the Lady Henrietta Louisa Stuart, and milord the Count of Chelmsford shall be expecting me, I think. But no, I am wrong! In England it is "earl", I must remember, not "count".'

Jemima, to her vast amusement, saw Hawkins put his gloved hands behind his back, as if he feared this volatile person might offer to shake one of them, and drawing himself up more massively than ever, he said, 'Yes, your ladyship, you are expected. If your ladyship would be so kind as to follow me, my lord and lady are awaiting you in the library.'

Jemima sped up the stairs to reach the library ahead of them. 'She is here,' she said as she shut the door behind her. 'She has mortally offended Hawkins already by wanting to be friends with him!'

Charles looked startled, but there was no time to say more, for already the measured tread of Hawkins could be heard in the passage, and it was necessary to compose oneself. The door opened, he announced the visitor ponderously, and stepped aside, revealing the tiny figure who came forward exclaiming, 'Ah, *la bibliothèque*! When your butler mentioned *la librairie*, I was puzzled! My English is not yet so good. My lady, my lord, I am enchanted to meet you, and so very grateful that you receive me.' And she went down into a curtsy, as taught her by the nuns of the Visitation, which rendered Charles and Flora speechless for a moment. She rose and looked about her, and Jemima had the opportunity to study for the first time the daughter of a man who had haunted her thoughts for a long time. She saw a long, dark face framed with a profusion of glossy black ringlets and curls; a long nose, a wide mouth, and over-large, sad dark eyes, which together added up to a Stuart likeness that was almost a caricature of the royal portraits of that unlucky family, familiar to anyone who had ever visited a palace or noble house.

Relief flooded Jemima, and she was aware for the first time of what she had feared from the meeting. But there was no likeness to her father. The face, not beautiful but with a strange attractiveness, bore a strong resemblance to portraits Jemima had seen of the Countess Annunciata as a young woman; but otherwise it was not like any Morland.

Charles and Flora gathered their wits and stepped forward to shake the visitor's hand and perform the introductions. 'And this is our cousin, Jemima Morland, of Morland Place.'

'Morland Place in the county of Yorkshire,' the visitor murmured. 'I have heard of it.'

'Welcome to England, my dear,' Jemima said, shaking the narrow hand and smiling as kindly as she could. 'I hope your sufferings have not been too severe. You are amongst friends now, and have nothing more to fear.' Why, she's only a child after all, she thought, seeing under the brave exterior and the marks of fatigue and trouble, the upraised eyes of a child seeking reassurance. She smiled more freely, and was rewarded with a brief but ravishing smile which quite transformed the dark face.

'How do you come to be staying with Lady Hunstanton?' Flora asked when the introductions were over and everyone was seated.

'Ah, she has been so kind, so kind! But I have no claim on her, and cannot be a burden to her longer than is quite necessary. I escaped, you see, on a fishing-boat from Saint-Valéry, but we came upon an English frigate, the *Crescent*, and when the fishing-boat sank, I was taken onto the frigate, wet to my skin, almost drowned, and with nothing but the gown I wore. Oh but it was so cold! And I was so sick! And I had lost my maid, also, which grieves me very much, and the children too, and I do not know what became of them.'

'Your children?' Flora asked.

'Oh no, the children of a friend which I had rescued from Paris, from the Tribunal, for she was my best friend and she had been arrested at the same time as my husband, so Papa made me flee. The captain of the *Crescent* was very kind, but he could not leave his post because he was on the blockage . . .'

'Blockade?' Flora offered tentatively. Héloïse smiled.

'*Pardon* – the blockade, yes! And so then there came another ship, but very, very small, which carries messages between the ships, and I am put upon it and taken to the fleet, and there I am put aboard another frigate, the *Phoebe*, and oh, such a storm blows! And I am sick again! But no-one can be spared, of course, to bring me to England, so I must stay with the fleet, and then Lady Hunstanton hears of my presence.' Héloïse clasped her hands. 'She is so kind, almost a saint! She was in the man-of-war ship, the *Tribute*, of which her husband, Sir Henry Hunstanton, was captain, and she sent to say a frigate was not at all *comme il faut* for a woman, and sent a boat to bring me to the big ship, and there I had a cabin – so small! but a cabin at all events – and she provided me with clothes and shared her maid with me, and when we came to Gibraltar she and I came on another ship to London and to her house and she has given me more new clothes' – she spread her hands to indicate the gown she was wearing – 'and allowed me to stay until I stopped being ill and could present myself to you, which I did yesterday, in my letter. She wished to write the letter for me, but I was sure it was more proper that I should write it myself, for I did not wish to offend in any way. I did not offend, I hope?' she finished anxiously.

Charles, remembering the letter, smiled. 'Not in any way, my lady, I assure you.'

'Oh, you are most kind. But Papa says we are cousins, of a sort, and therefore I think you should not call me my lady. I am always called Héloïse, since I am a little child. Will you call me "cousin Héloïse"?'

'Yes, indeed, and you must call me "cousin Charles".'

'Cousin Charles! That is so agreeable! I have never had a cousin before. There was only Papa, and Tante Ismène, who was not really an aunt at all. It is *très, très agréable d'avoir des parents, enfin*.'

Charles spoke for everyone when he asked her, if it would not fatigue her too much, to tell them about the events in Paris which had driven her to flee, which she did, as well as she could, for tiredness and emotion sometimes tripped her tongue into French. They listened in silent amazement and pity, wondering at the experiences this little creature had undergone by the age of sixteen; and when her voice ceased at last, no-one could immediately break the ensuing silence.

Héloïse looked around her, from face to face, anxious, afraid, and inwardly exhausted: from Monsieur le Comte, an indolent man, she guessed, and much in love with madame; to madame herself, once a beauty, and dressed in the height of fashion; to madame's daughter, plain and still the child, but madly in love with her fiancé; the fiancé himself, worthy and serious; and the older madame, whose face had great distinction, and who had listened to the story with more emotion than one would have expected from a stranger; finally to Mademoiselle Mary, whose beauty commanded one's admiration, whose *chic* demanded one's respect, and whose evident intelligence made one a little nervous. Héloïse's hands clenched together in her lap as the silence extended. If they refused her help, what then? She could bear it no longer – she must speak. She turned her face towards Charles and commanded her voice not to tremble.

'Such is my story, monsieur *mon cousin*. Milady Hunstanton has been all that is kind, but it is not proper that I place myself further in her debt. Papa was sure that you would help me; and it will be for a time only, for he will find some way to send me the--' She could not think of how to say 'the means by which to live' in English; she faltered, and stopped, and had to bite her lip, for she could feel tears close to the surface. Flora jumped up and came to her, and took her hands.

'Of course we will help you! How could you doubt? Charles, tell her! You must stay with us as long as you wish--'

'Indeed, you must,' Charles said easily. 'Lady Hunstanton is very kind, no doubt, but as you say . . .'

'Oh, and how she does *talk*!' Flora exclaimed, making even Héloïse laugh a little. 'Poor child, you shall come here this very day. I shall have a room made up for you at once, and you must consider it your very own, and we shall drive over to Lady Hunstanton's this morning and explain matters and collect your belongings.'

'But I have none, milady, except what she has given me,' Héloïse said, the ghost of a smile appearing at the corners of her mouth.

'Never mind, that shall be remedied. Mary will go out and choose things with you. She has much better taste than I, and loves shopping, while I consider it a little of a chore.'

Héloïse turned her head to meet Mary's shrewd and considering eye.

'Clothes are all very well, dear ma'am,' Mary said, 'but I think our cousin had far rather you asked amongst your naval friends for news of her maid and the children. Is it possible, cousin Héloïse, that some other ship may have picked them up?'

'That is a very good idea, Mary,' Flora said approvingly. 'I wonder I had not thought of it. I shall send Biggs round to the Admiralty this afternoon with a note for the First Lord. And meanwhile, I think we should put our cousin in the damask room, don't you, Charles? It has a very pretty aspect over the park, you know.' she added to Héloïse.

'No, I don't think,' Charles said, laughing. 'The damask room is like a ballroom, and sombre as a church. You forget, my love, that our cousin was brought up in a convent until very recently, and I imagine her tastes are quite simple. I am sure she would be much more comfortable in the small yellow bedroom.'

'Oh Charles!' Flora began reproachfully, and it was evident that an argument was about to begin, fascinating to Flora and Charles, but to no-one else. Héloïse smiled with what she hoped was diplomacy and said, 'Me, I am contented wherever you choose to put me; and I am so glad to be able to stay in your beautiful house. I shall hope that you will be so very kind as to shew me all over it.'

The members of the party scattered, to meet again at dinner. Flora ordered the town chariot, and drove with Héloïse and Louisa to Hunstanton House, which was in Hanover Square; John and Charles walked off to their respective clubs to read the newspapers; Mary went to her room to write letters; and Jemima went for a walk in the park to try to revive her jaded spirits and to wonder how much longer she dared stay away from home.

After dinner, the younger ladies had an evening engagement at Lady Carstairs', and Flora asked Héloïse to go with them, saying that she knew Lady Carstairs very well and was quite positive she would welcome Héloïse as a valuable addition to what seemed likely otherwise to be a very commonplace gathering; but Héloïse begged to be excused. She was very tired, and would be glad to retire to her newly appointed room (the yellow bedroom) and go to bed early.

Jemima spent the evening by the fire with a book, and retired early to bed, but as she was walking along the passage to her room, she passed the door of the yellow bedroom, and hesitated, and then tapped lightly upon it. If the child was asleep, it would not disturb her, she thought: but if she was awake and lonely, she might like someone to talk to. There was no response from within. Jemima was about to go away when she heard from within a stifled noise which a mother of seven children could hardly help recognising. She opened the door quietly and went in.

Héloïse, in her newly-acquired nightgown, was sprawled face-down across her bed, her tousled head in her arms. Two wet handkerchiefs beside her bore mute testimony to how she had spent her evening, and she had reached the stage of sniffing and hiccuping – that was the sound Jemima had recognised. She walked across to the bed, and gently stroked the massy black hair, pushed some wet strands away from the hot cheek, and inserted into Héloïse's clenched fingers a clean handkerchief. After a moment Héloïse sat up and blew her nose heartily, after which Jemima sat down on the edge of the bed and drew the younger woman into her arms and on to her lap. Married woman and survivor of the 'enragement' she might be; but she was small and light and thin enough to be cuddled, and enough of a child still to need it.

After some time, when the frail body in her arms was still and relaxed, Jemima said softly, 'I understand a little of what you feel, my dear. I know what it is to be parted from a loved one, and to be worried for the safety of one dear to me.'

'Yes, madame. Milady told me in the carriage about your daughter,' Héloïse said shyly. 'I am so sorry.'

They were silent for a while, and then Jemima said, 'I knew of you before this, you know. My husband visited your father in Paris many years ago, and met you there. You were only five years old at the time, and probably do not remember it, but--'

'Oh, but yes, I do!' Héloïse cried, lifting her head from the comfortable shoulder. '*Monsieur le Chevalier de Morland* – it was he, was it not? I do remember him. And he was your husband, madame? *Tiens*! And shall I meet him again in England?'

'I'm afraid he is dead, my dear,' Jemima said steadily. Héloïse's enormous dark eyes gazed into hers sorrowfully. She could see that Madame had loved the *Chevalier* very much; and she offered her as a coin of the same currency,

'My mother died when I was very young. She is with the Holy Virgin now, and so also must be monsieur, and they will be very happy, and we should be glad for them.'

Being comforted by this minute scrap of humanity was too much for Jemima's steadiness. She hugged Héloïse convulsively with something between a laugh and a sob, and said, 'Oh, my dear! When things are a little more settled, in a week or two, would you like to come home with me, to Morland Place, and live there? I should like you to regard it as your permanent home, if it would please you.'

'But, madame,' Héloïse said, pleased but perplexed, 'it would be delightful, but I have no claim on you, not even as much as on Monsieur le Comte.'

'Yes, yes you have. Listen, Héloïse, there is something I must tell you. I think you must know that your father is descended from the same family as the Earl of Chelmsford on his mother's side; but the identity of his father was always kept a secret. I do not think even *he* knew who it was.'

'I never heard him speak of his father, it is true, madame,' Héloïse said slowly. 'But do you mean--'

'Yes, *I* know. My dear husband told me, for reasons I won't go into, and it concerns me very nearly, as does your welfare. Your father's father, though it has always remained a secret, was my father.' Héloïse stared at her. 'Your father, in fact, is my half-brother. No-one knows that, but you and I – not even your father – but you see--'

'Madame,' Héloïse interrupted, her face lighting with hope, 'it means, *en effet*, that you are my aunt!'

Jemima laughed, 'Yes, *en effet*, I am your aunt.' Héloïse's face was radiant with wonder.

'Oh, but this is much, much better even than cousins! A real aunt! Oh madame, you cannot think how it overjoys me to have an aunt. Please, may I call you aunt? Or would it be improper?'

'Not at all, love,' Jemima said. 'I do not think there can be any purpose served in continuing the secrecy. I shall be proud to acknowledge you. My own brothers died when I was a little girl – like you, I had few close relatives. By all means call me aunt, if it pleases you. But until you go your own way in the world, I should be glad if you would regard me more in the light of a mother.'

'I don't remember my real mother,' Héloïse said. 'I lost her when I was very little.'

Jemima did not say, 'And I have lost my daughter,' but the fear of it was in her heart, and she hugged Héloïse no less gladly than Héloïse hugged her.

Promotion to the ward-room of the *Diamond*, together with being on blockade duty around the great seaports of Toulon and Marseilles, added further difficulties to Lucy's life. Though she was not presented with any horrifying battle casualties, something about which she had worried from time to time since she had been placed in sole command of the medical facilities of the ship, the monotony of blockade gave rise to short tempers amongst the crew, and consequently to fights and injuries. Several times she had to deal with knife-wounds and broken bones, once with a skull fracture where one exasperated jack had lammed another over the head with a belaying-pin. There were the usual day-to-day injuries – ruptures, bruises, broken bones and strained muscles – to deal with, though now the ship was away from port, the crew was healthy and not troubled too much by vermin. On one occasion she had to certify two men as fit to be hanged – they had been discovered in homosexual practices, for which the penalty was death – which upset her a great deal, for she had thought to be a doctor was to practise the saving of lives. Several times, too, she had to minister to the wounds of a victim of a flogging, which made her wonder if there might not be a less wasteful way of enforcing discipline upon serving sailors.

But she enjoyed her work tremendously, and was learning fast, and her curiosity being both strong and practical, without sentiment, she was in a fair way to becoming a good ship's doctor. The social side of her life gave her more trouble. The wardroom occupied the stern of the ship immediately below the captain's quarters, and was therefore well lit from the stern galleries, quite a different prospect from the gloomy orlop deck. The wardroom consisted of a central space in which the wardroom officers dined at a long table, with some ceremony, each having his servant in attendance, standing behind his chair throughout the meal, until the drinking of the King's health, after which the servants withdrew to leave the officers alone with their port and cigars. Whenever she dined in the wardroom, Lucy was the most junior officer, and it was therefore always her task to propose the toast. The other officers drank it with difficulty, crouched under the inadequate headroom, but Lucy was small enough to drink it standing upright, a circumstance which afforded her some amusement.

Down the side of the central space were the lieutenants' cabins, tiny compartments, the smallest hardly bigger than a coffin, all opening into the wardroom, but affording a privacy highly prized on a crowded ship. The final touch of luxury to wardroom life was that the two quarter-galleries had been converted, as was customary, into heads for the use of wardroom officers only – the five lieutenants, the master, the captain of marines and his two lieutenants, the purser, and the surgeon, for the *Diamond* had sailed without a chaplain, owing to a shortage of these gentry at the time.

Morgan had told Lucy that the character of each wardroom was different, depending on the type of officer it contained, but that it generally reflected the character of the captain, who, after all, was responsible for selecting the officers from amongst the possible candidates. Thus there were gentlemanly wardrooms, aristocratic wardrooms, 'tarpaulin' wardrooms, Irish, Scots, Welsh, those addicted to gaming, those keen on sporting activities, those whose sole purpose seemed to be eating and drinking as sumptuously as possible. Fortunately for Lucy, the *Diamond*'s wardroom was gentlemanly, though not particularly wealthy. Its members were obliged to pay out of their salaries for their wine and delicacies, unless they were content to dine off ship's rations. In some messes, she had been told, the subscription was as much as sixty pounds a year; but on the *Diamond* it was three pounds six shillings a month – affordable, since Lucy's monthly wage was five pounds.

A sociable child, used to the company of her older brothers, Lucy enjoyed dining in the wardroom and listening to the officers' conversation, though she rarely spoke herself. But she was aware that this continuous social contact threatened her secret, for naturally, from time to time, the other officers asked her questions. The fact of blockade duty added to her problems, for sea officers were always hospitable and gregarious, and the boredom of blockade, added to the fact of being in one place and close to other ships, meant that there were boats to and fro between the members of the squadron every day, bearing captains and selected bands of officers to dine aboard each other's ships. Her brother William, she knew, was somewhere in the Mediterranean, captain of the *Antigone*: it must only be a matter of time before her presence aboard the *Diamond* became known to him, and that would be the end of her adventure.

The end, when it came, came suddenly, for Lucy, toiling

away in the darkness of the orlop, remained largely unaware of the comings and goings in the squadron, and though she heard the guns which signalled a new arrival joining the blockade, she was not enough interested to ask the questions which would rapidly have informed her that the newcomer was the *Antigone*. Later that day Admiral Hood hung out what had become almost a weekly 'all captains' signal, summoning them to dinner aboard the flagship. Soon the gigs were bobbing away across the bright April water, bearing the captains: Morton of the *Squirrel*, Nelson of the *Agamemnon*, Hamilton of the *Glory*, Morland of the *Antigone*, and the rest. Captain Prothero donned his best uniform, called away his gig, and we went to dine in the great stern cabin of the flagship, where he found himself seated next to Captain Morland, the newcomer; a great privilege, since the others already knew each other's conversation inside out.

At some point in the course of dinner, the conversation came round to the difficulties of manning, a perennial subject amongst captains.

'And it isn't just the men,' Prothero complained. 'I've had to sail without a chaplain, and as my secretary, unusually enough, isn't in orders, I have to read the damn' services myself. And I'm a lieutenant short, and I've got a boy of fifteen for a surgeon.' Captain Morland murmured polite regrets. 'Yes, my surgeon drank himself to death off Gibraltar, and there wasn't a qualified man to be had, so I had to promote the surgeon's mate. Mark you, he seems to be doing remarkably well. Not qualified, but he's the son of a travelling horse-doctor who used to be a ship's surgeon in the American wars, and he seems to have learned a good deal from his father.'

The circumstances were curious enough for William to ask the horse-doctor's name, and the answer electrified him.

'Proom? Morgan Proom. But – I knew him, sir, very well indeed. I was not aware that he had a son. A fifteen-year-old?' The thought came to him, absurdly, horrifyingly. He swallowed an obstruction in his throat and managed to say, 'The name, sir, of your young surgeon? Would you oblige me . . .?'

'Lucius Proom, he calls himself,' Prothero said, cocking an eye at his colleague. 'Something wrong, Morland?'

'I'm afraid there may be, sir. Might I have a word with you in private after dinner, before you return to your ship?'

Lucy was taking the stitches out of a seaman's forearm that had been laid open in a knife-fight the week before.

'There, that looks very nice,' she said, tweaking out the last piece of silk. 'You've got good, healing skin, Glover, I'll say that for you.'

'You've done it real nice, too, sir, thanking you kindly. Much better with the needle an' palm than the old doctor, that's what we say below decks. He used to cobble you up any old how.'

'Well you don't deserve it,' she remembered to say sternly. 'I've got enough to do, without self-inflicted wounds. Keep your knives for cutting your meat, and quarrel with your tongues if you must quarrel.'

The sailor grinned, shewing her all-but-naked gums with a few brown sentinel teeth here and there.

'Lord love you, sir, I ain't a quarrelsome man, not even when I've had me grog, not like some of 'em. I didn't move fast enough when old Taffy came at me, that's all. He's always on a short fuse, sir, after up-spirits.'

'You mean he cut open your arm for no reason?' Lucy frowned. The grin widened.

'That wasn't nothing, sir. He was aiming for me face.'

They were interrupted at that moment by Huggins, who waved Glover away imperiously, and then said, 'Passing the word for you, sir, from the captain. You're to go to the captain's cabin immediate.'

'Very well.' Curiosity got the better of her. 'Know what it's about, Huggins?'

'No sir, 'Cept the captain's got another captain with him, out o' the new sixty-four what joined the squadron this morning, sir. The *Antigone*, sir, Captain Morland, I believe it is, sir.'

'Oh,' said Lucy, her heart sinking. She looked around at the now familiar, dark and crowded surroundings and sighed. 'Clear up here, will you, Huggins.'

The news that the boy-surgeon was in fact a woman spread quicker than fire around the ship. It was the biggest and best scandal most of the ship's company had ever encountered, and it was in anticipation of this that William had insisted, despite Prothero's protests that he needed her services, that Lucy should go back with him at once to his own ship, to remain there under his care and chaperonage until a way could be found to transport her to England. His anger at what she had done, and his shock at the impropriety, and his worry over how badly her and the family's reputations would be damaged, were tempered by his admiration for her courage and ingenuity, and his amusement when he remembered the first sight of her, coming into the captain's drawing-room in her white breeches and plain blue warrant-officer's coat, with her hair cropped short and her cocked hat under her arm in proper naval fashion.

'How could you even *think* of doing such a thing?' he said for the third or fourth time as his gig bore them away over the water towards the bulk of the *Antigone*, looming in the gathering dusk, and already shewing her station lights. 'It's bound to get out. You'll be ruined – no-one will ever marry you now, you know. And Mother's been almost mad with grief.'

Lucy, facing him, looked longingly over his shoulder at the diminishing shape of the *Diamond*, which seemed, the further she got from it, more and more like home. Her sadness was mitigated by the memory of the firm handshake she had had in farewell from Lieutenant Weston.

'You must always have known it could not last,' he said to her sympathetically, standing at the door of her cabin watching her pack her belongings into the cloak-bag. He had come to find her deliberately to say goodbye in private. She straightened up and looked at him curiously.

'You knew, didn't you, from the very beginning?' she discovered. Weston smiled.

'Oh yes, from the very beginning, in the Keppel's Head. Oh, it's all right, it *was* only me. No-one else suspected.'

'But you didn't give me away,' she wondered. 'In fact, you *helped* me.' He nodded. 'Why?'

'I admired your pluck,' he said frankly, and then he grinned. 'Besides, I've always thought it must be perfectly dreadful to be a woman, especially if you've got any kind of "go" in you! Condemned to needlework and playing the piano! And when I saw you, with a desire to be a doctor, doing this perfectly crazy

323

thing, I just wanted to help you, even though it couldn't last. But it was fun, for a while, wasn't it?'

'Yes, it was,' she said, and she held out her hand to him, her eyes bright. 'Thank you for helping me escape for a little while.' And that was when he clasped her hand, so firmly and warmly that she thought she felt it tingling still in her fingers, as the *Antigone*'s gig bore her away, back to the prison of womanhood.

17

Louisa's wedding duly took place on 23 April 1793, and was a very glittering occasion. She was married from Chelmsford House, as her mother's residence, and her stepfather, the Earl of Chelmsford, gave her away in her father's place, which Jemima, whose memory could sometimes be inconveniently long, thought just a little ironic. The wedding took place in St. Margaret's, Westminster, and both the Prince of Wales, representing the King, and the Duke of Clarence were there.

Flora's maid, the stern and superior Mrs Philips, dressed Louisa that morning, which was meant to be both a treat and a compliment; but the ungrateful Louisa begged to be allowed to have Jemima with her, too, and when Mrs Philips left the room for a moment, Louisa flung herself into Jemima's arms and cried.

'Now, now, hinny,' Jemima said, petting her like a child, 'you mustn't cry, or you'll make your eyes red. We all want you to look beautiful today.' She raised Louisa's head for a moment and saw with concern how white she was, and pinched about the mouth.

'I feel sick,' she said, confirming Jemima's fears, and then shut her lips very tightly. Jemima was equal to that. She put her hand in through the slit in the side of her dress and took out of her pocket a little bottle.

'I thought you might need a little stiffening this morning, chick, so I came prepared,' she said pouring the contents into a glass. Louisa looked at it doubtfully. It was a deep, ruby red in colour, and smelled delicious. Jemima anticipated the question. 'It's port and brandy – my sovereign for nervous queasiness. Drink it down, child, and you'll feel as right as ninepence in no time.'

Mrs Philips came back in while Louisa was in process of tipping it down her throat, and gave them both a look of such astonished disapproval that Louisa choked and Jemima had to bite her lips to prevent herself from laughing. Things went on a little more merrily after that. Louisa was dressed in her wedding gown, which was largely Mary's choice and, Jemima thought, very well chosen too. Louisa's colouring was not vivid enough to bear white or the usual pale blues and pinks, and green was considered unlucky for weddings, so Mary had chosen a beautiful primrose yellow silk, with a very unusual amber-coloured satin sash to raise the waistband, and a three-quarter overgown of Brussels lace which Jemima knew must have cost Charles a small fortune. Still, she thought in her thrifty way, lace you can use again and again. It is in the way of an investment.

Mrs Philips dressed Louisa's hair, taking it back and up to the top of her head whence it hung in a cascade of curls, yellow ribbons, and white roses – artificial ones made of silk, which Jemima thought a shame, but it was only April after all. Louisa did, however, have real flowers to carry: a wonderful sheath of mimosa, which the Prince of Wales had sent for her from Kew, and which scented the air for feet around so that the bride seemed to move in a cloud of perfume.

Finally two maids brought in Flora's upright mirror from her bedroom so that Louisa could see herself, and there were almost tears again, but Jemima hugged her – carefully – and told her she looked beautiful, and that John would love her very much and be a good husband to her.

'Oh I know *that*, Mother,' Louisa said. 'I'm only afraid I won't be all he wants in a wife. I know he really loves--'

Jemima stopped her by placing a finger on her lips. 'He chose you, my dear, of a free will. The past is all forgotten.' But she was surprised to discover, all the same, that quiet little Louisa was in love with her husband-to-be, and wondered how long it had been going on, and how she could have been so blind to it before.

The day was sunny, though a little windy, with some fast-moving clouds. Louisa went to her wedding in the dress chariot, resplendent with its bullion-fringed hammercloth and the Chelmsford arms painted on the door panels. It was drawn by six white horses – hired for the occasion, for Charles had no white horses in his stable – with postilions in gold-frogged jackets, and on the footplate behind hung two footmen in the cherry-red Chelmsford livery, with powdered wigs and gold-braided hats.

Amelia had long before been chosen as bridal attendant, and in rose-pink satin she was torn between pique that Louisa was marrying before her, and smugness that Louisa was only marrying a son of a baron, and a new creation at that. Her companion at the bride's heel was John's sister Elizabeth who, when Louisa's wedding was over, would be choosing her own bridal clothes. Louisa, out of kindness, had asked Héloïse if she would like to be a matron of honour, but though touched, she had begged to be excused. She did not yet know the fate of her husband or her father, and was still, under her calm exterior, deeply shocked by her experiences and the loss of her maid and the children. She sat very close to Jemima all through the ceremony, not only because she did not know the order of a Church of England service, but because she drew great strength from the presence of her '*nouvelle maman*', and would otherwise probably have cried immoderately.

The wedding-feast was held at Chelmsford House, and then Louisa changed from her wedding-dress into a very smart travelling-gown of grey-blue cambric – Mary's taste again – and she and John and Amelia set off in John's new chariot for Brighton; while the rest of the party finished off the occasion with a ball in the great ballroom of Chelmsford House, whose innumerable long windows looked out over the gardens, and which was said to have been designed by King Charles II himself.

The news that Lucy had been found safe and well preceded her to London by many weeks, arriving, in fact, in time to allow Jemima to enjoy Louisa's wedding. The arrival of the news, and the wedding, were in such close proximity that it was only when the latter was all over that the family was able to find the leisure to be astonished, shocked, scandalised, and worried over what was to be done with the miscreant.

'I must say, though,' Mary said, 'that I do admire her spirit, even though it was misdirected. She did what she wanted to do.'

'Just as you have always done,' Jemima murmured.

'Ah, but she is only fourteen,' Mary smiled. 'Just think what she may achieve when she reaches adulthood.'

'I dread to think,' Charles shuddered. Flora looked disapproving.

'You take it very lightly, Charles, but it is the most shocking scandal. When it gets out – as it is bound to do sooner or later – everyone will be talking about it. Just think: she has not only dressed as a boy, but lived in a ship with hundreds of men, unchaperoned, for months! She is ruined!'

'I should have thought her breeches a very good chaperon,' Charles said.

Flora gave him a cross look. 'Don't be frivolous. And think what she has been doing: cleaning men's wounds and sewing them up and – ugh!' She shuddered. 'Things not fit for a woman, let alone a gentlewoman.'

'But the courage,' Mary said. 'I should never have had the courage when I was her age, to leave home and travel all that way alone, and take on that task with no one to advise me.'

'Yes,' said Jemima, 'she is a strange little girl. But she has always been different. She always had such a *practical* sort of kindness. When most of us would shudder at the sight of blood, she would simply look for the best way of staunching it.'

'I think it's unnatural,' Flora said. 'I don't think she can have any normal human feelings at all. I think she must be quite heartless.'

'All the same, when she does reach England, we shall have to think what to do with her,' Jemima said.

She had been intending to go home to Yorkshire immediately after Louisa's wedding, but she remained in London now partly to be on hand for any fresh news of Lucy's progress towards England, and partly to support Héloïse's spirits. There had been no word from her father yet, and to add to the anguish of her husband's and Lotti's probable execution was the dread that he had been taken up because of her escape. The Prussians had joined with the Austrians in declaring war on revolutionary France, and were therefore now allied with the English, and Charles had sent letters not only to Leipzig, to inform Lotti's brother Ernst of what had occurred, but also to various friends in the occupying army in Flanders in hopes of tracing Charles Nordubois. One of these letters was carried by John Anstey's brother Benjamin, who, having been bought a commission by his father, was on his way to join the Duke of York's regiment in Flanders. He stopped at Chelmsford House on his way, and looked very fine and starry-eyed in his new scarlet regimentals. He and Horatio eyed each other with mutual suspicion – as Charles put it mockingly, 'the toy soldier and the real one' – and wished each other luck; and privately each put the other down as a fool.

May brought changes. Charlotte Fussell died suddenly with violent stomach cramps after dinner one night. There was, as usual in such cases, a lot of loose talk about poisoning; which, however, so upset Sir John that he suffered a stroke and within a fortnight followed her to the grave. The double bereavement put out of the question a June wedding between Lizzie Anstey and the now Sir Arthur Fussell, and poor Lizzie, her wedding clothes only half-finished, had to go home to York to revise all the plans.

Horatio, on the other hand, astonished everyone by announcing his engagement to one of the most sought-after young women who had been brought out that season. She was the Lady Barbara Rushton, daughter of the Duke of Watford. Though not of ancient lineage, the Duke had made a large fortune from the slave and cotton trades, and had married a very beautiful sugar-heiress from the French West Indies, Joséphine de Montceau. Her mother's fabled looks, together with her extremely handsome fortune, were quite enough to have Lady Barbara pronounced a beauty at her *début*, and since she was good-natured and not particularly vain, she was soon also pronounced a sweet girl and very clever; and Horatio was well pleased to have captured her.

For her part, Captain the Honourable Horatio Morland was well-known to her as dashing, handsome, and extremely eligible, for since Flora and Charles had been married now for eleven years with no signs of a pregnancy, it was generally accepted that Horatio would be Earl hereafter. In addition, Lady Barbara had two elder sisters, Cornelia and Frances, who in the years of their respective comings-out had mooned and giggled over Horatio, tried to captivate him, and eventually gone off to equally eligible but less exciting matches; and while Lady Pauncefoot and Lady St. Giles now declared they pitied their sister to be marrying such a rake, Lady Barbara knew that underneath they were jealous, and was quite content.

Charles and Flora were happy enough with the match, for since they had both long ago resigned themselves to Horace's becoming seventh Earl one day, they were more or less indifferent to the future of the earldom, and cared only that he should not disgrace them. Lady Barbara at once asked for Amelia to be her bridal attendant, which though she probably meant it kindly, was somewhat galling to Amelia, who, though she was the same age as her future sister-in-law, had already been out a whole year without 'taking'. Since, however, once married, Lady Barbara could take Amelia about, and would certainly prove a more exciting and more useful chaperon than Flora, Amelia accepted with grace.

And in the midst of this excitement came the news that Lucy was at Gibraltar and would be coming home on the packet in the company of a very respectable elderly lady who had agreed to chaperon her. She would be at Portsmouth at the beginning of June, and the question of what to do with her now became urgent. It was Mary who solved the problem.

'I think it would be better for her to spend the summer in some retired place, until the talk has died down. In London or at home, she's bound to be talked about and stared at,' she said.

'Oh dear, do you think so?' Jemima said. 'I do so long to go home – and I'm anxious to take Héloïse home, too. I know she wants to be on hand for any news, but London is pulling her down, and she's looking so pale and worn, poor child. I want to get some good Yorkshire air into her lungs, and some good, wholesome, Morland Place food into her, and make her well again.'

'Then why don't you go home?' Mary said equably. 'I can perfectly well take care of Lucy.'

'You, Mary?'

'Yes, me! Don't look so astonished, Mother. I'm not a green girl, you know. I'm almost thirty years old, and quite elderly and respectable enough to chaperon my sister, even if she is a young hoyden. She'd exhaust you, mother, you know she would. I rather admire her – though, don't worry, I won't tell her so. I shall be as strict as you like with her, but what she needs, I'm sure, is plenty to do, to distract her. I can take her out places, riding and exploring and so on, which you could not do, with all your worries.'

Jemima looked at her with weak longing. 'Oh dear, I don't know,' she said. 'It sounds all right – but where would you go?'

'I've thought of that – Bath!'

'Bath?'

'It would be the very thing – quiet enough for her not to be stared at, but lively enough to provide things to do. And the country around is perfect for riding and visiting. I can take her to Wells, and Stourhead, and Stonehenge and so on.' Seeing Jemima still hesitate, Mary smiled winningly at her. 'Please, Mother, for my sake! Otherwise I shall have to go to Brighton with Flora and Charles and Amelia, and that would drive me to despair.'

Jemima laughed. 'You mean to tell me, you unnatural girl, that you don't want to go to card parties and musical evenings at the Pavilion, and dance with handsome young officers and visit the camp?'

'Extraordinary to say, I don't,' Mary smiled. 'I really must be in my dotage.'

Thus it was decided, and James once again came into his own in making all the arrangements in the most helpful way. He went first of all to Bath to rent a suitable house for Mary – 'Not in Laura Place, James, please. Somewhere at the top of the town, and make sure it has a good stable near by, for if we are to stay the whole summer I do not mean to make do with job horses and shabby carriages' – and then made all the travel arrangements. He was to go to Portsmouth to wait for the packet, meet Lucy, and escort her as far as Reading; Mary and Jemima would go down to Reading, so that Jemima could at least see her miscreant daughter before she went into retirement, and then Mary would take over the charge of her, and continue on to Bath, while James escorted his mother back to London to collect Héloïse, and thence home to Yorkshire.

The meeting with Lucy was an emotional one, but in a way Jemima hardly expected. She had thought she would be angry with Lucy, that Lucy would be angry too, and defiant. But when Lucy walked into the private parlour of the inn where they would stay the night, looking so much more grown up than when she went away, her face having lost, in those few weeks, its baby chubbiness, and having gained an adult firmness beyond its years; her boy-cropped hair beginning to grow out with a new curliness that became her; her mien both self-assured and hesitant; Jemima felt suddenly a little shy of her. She faced her mother calmly, accepting what was to come to her, but without shame or fear, and Jemima found herself thinking, absurdly, 'Why, she has grown quite manly!' And then love and the memory of almost having lost her rose to the surface, and Jemima held out her arms, and Lucy ran to her, and they embraced, and laughed and cried in a very female manner.

'I'm sorry I upset you, Mother,' Lucy said at last, brushing away tears with her knuckles.

'It's all forgotten now, love,' Jemima said, dabbing her eyes with her handkerchief. 'You must put all this behind you, and make a new life for yourself, like a normal young woman.'

And James looked from one to the other, and smiled inwardly, thinking it very unlikely that his sister would ever be like normal young woman, and hoping his mother would come not to mind too much.

They dined together at the inn, and a very lively dinner it was, with Lucy telling stories of shipboard life which had them all so absorbed and amused that they had not time to be shocked.

'It's hard to remember you're only fourteen,' James said at one point, refilling his glass. 'What a life you've had already, Luce!'

'Well, this cousin Héloïse of ours is only a year older than me, and look at what a life *she's* led,' Lucy said calmly. 'Is she really a cousin of ours, or only of Charles's?'

'She's your true cousin,' Jemima said. 'Her father was my half-brother, though it has always been kept secret, and is not now, let me remind you children, to be gossiped about.'

'As if we ever gossip, Mother,' James said reprovingly. 'Besides, Mary and Lucy will be too busy enjoying themselves in Bath. I have rented a famous neat house for you, girls, in Brock Street, quite small, but very elegant and comfortable, with a stable just around the corner in Circus Mews – Durban looked them over and pronounced them just what you want, and you know Durban knows everything about stables. So you will be sure to enjoy your exile. I quite envy you, really.'

Lucy looked at Mary and said shyly, 'It is very kind of you, Mary, to go with me to Bath.'

Mary smiled. 'Oh, don't let Jamie's talk of exile trouble you. I am very happy to go – in fact you are saving me from a fate considerably worse than death, for I'm sure Horace only offered for his poor young woman to make me sorry I refused him. The idea of him parading her around Brighton and talking of 'the Prince' in that odious way he has makes me feel quite tired.'

The next morning the party split up, and James and his mother posted back to London, arriving at Chelmsford House at nine in the evening, to learn from Hawkins that my lord and my lady had dined early and gone to the opera, and would be going on afterwards to Lady Tonbridge's.

'But Lady Henrietta is in the blue saloon, madam,' Hawkins added.

'Alone?' Jemima asked, stripping off her gloves.

'Yes, madam.'

'Oh, poor child, how infamous! Come, Jamie, we must go and see her at once. Of course, you have never yet met her, have you?'

'I have that pleasure still to come, Mama,' James said drily, remembering the description he had been given of her – 'small and thin, like a child, not really pretty, though to be sure she has gone through such terrible sufferings she can hardly be in her best looks' – and wondering what pleasure the meeting would bring to either of them. Jemima led the way up to the blue saloon, and, opening the door, revealed Héloïse sitting alone by the fireside reading a letter.

For a moment, before she became aware of them, James saw a tiny, dark creature, small-made as a fairy, simply dressed in white muslin with a violet sash, a profusion of dark curls falling loosely down her back. Then she looked up, her face lit, and she jumped up and ran to Jemima, crying, 'Oh *Madam ma tante*, news, news! There has been a letter from Papa, brought by some smugglers, hidden in a brandy bottle. Papa is alive and well! and, madame, Lotti was not executed but sent into exile, so she has gone to join Charles, not dead at all!'

'My dear, I am so very glad for you,' Jemima said. 'And your husband? Is there any news of him?'

The light was quenched for a moment. 'I think he is dead, madame. Papa says something at the foot of the page about his execution, but the ink has run so, that I cannot read it properly. I am a widow, me.' She looked down at herself. 'I suppose I must put on black. It is very sad and horrible, but only what I expected, and . . .' the sun came out again in her face, 'I am so very happy about Lotti, that I can only be thankful. Is it wicked of me?'

'No, little one, not wicked,' Jemima said, taking her hand and turning her towards James. 'But you must let me introduce to you my son James, of whom I have spoken to you. James, Lady Henrietta Louisa Stuart, your cousin Héloïse.'

James came forward to take the tiny, slender hand that was offered him, while Héloïse lowered her eyes, not coyly nor coquettishly, but with genuine modesty as she performed her convent-taught curtsy. But as she straightened she looked up into his face with her frank gaze, to see what he was like. With the periphery of his senses, James noted the long nose and wide mouth and broad cheekbones of a face that was 'not really pretty'; but his attention was seized by the great dark eyes, dark as water, sad in their depths, yet at the surface full of laughter, as dark water may sparkle with reflected sunshine. They met his, and a strange shock, deep inside him, made itself felt, as if he had recognised her from some other time, long ago. He saw her eyes flinch, as if she had felt it too, and then she smiled, and he wanted to cry and shout and laugh all at once, though he did not know why.

Héloïse looked at her handsome, blue-eyed cousin, and was devastated. Her English abandoned her entirely, and she could only murmur, '*Je suis tres hereuse de faire votre connaissance, mon cousin,*' which she knew was a ludicrous understatement. As for James, he had neither English nor French, nor words of any sort. He could only lift her hand in a gesture he had only ever employed before in frivolity, and lay his lips upon her fingers in silent dedication.

On arriving in Bath, Lucy underwent a kind of reaction to the mental and physical strain she had been undergoing. Mary had plenty to do in establishing and arranging their little household, and was quite content to leave her be for a day or two, to sleep late, eat enormously, and lie about on sophas with books in an aimless sort of way. The house, as Jamie had promised, was neat and comfortable, perfectly plain-fronted, three-storeyed, and part of an older terrace which stood between the new and very fashionable Royal Crescent and The Circus.

There was a very pretty breakfast parlour which got all the morning sunshine, and Mary decided that they would use it as their principle sitting-room, for the drawing-room, though of a good size and elegant shape, was on the cold side of the house, and rather heavily furnished. It connected by folding doors to a small but adequate dining-room. Above, there were three very pleasant bedrooms, and servants' rooms in the attic. When the position of every piece of furniture had been slightly altered, all the mirrors and shiny surfaces re-polished, and fresh flowers arranged at every vantage-point, Mary thought it would do very well indeed.

James had hired servants for her – a footman, two house-maids, and a cook – and with Mary's own maid, Farleigh, to supervise them and take care of the ladies, they promised to be very comfortable. The horses arrived from Morland Place on the second day after their arrival, and the news of this was enough to jerk Lucy from her lethargy. As well as Lucy's and Mary's own riding horses, and Mary's favourite groom Josh with his own horse, they had been sent four carriage horses and one of the young coachmen to drive and care for them.

'Oh, Edward has sent the York bays!' Lucy exclaimed, reading the note Josh had brought over Mary's shoulder. 'I am so glad – they were the ones I'd have chosen, but I was afraid he'd send those chestnuts you like, and they have not enough bone for all the hill-work they will have to do here.'

'Just what Mr Ned said himself, Miss Lucy,' Josh said, pleased. 'Josh, he said to me, I'm sending the bays with the white socks down to Bath, for it's what Miss Lucy would choose if she were here, and she'd not have those chestnuts upon a bet, he said. And I said to him, I said—'

'Yes, thank you, Josh. I'm sure you're right,' Mary said quickly, rolling her eyes at the thought of the genealogical discussions that would ensue if Lucy and Josh were allowed free rein. Durban, via James, had persuaded her that it was not sensible to have carriages sent from Yorkshire for the summer, and had hired local carriages for their stay. Mary had had some misgivings, but James had said that the jobbing stable in Circus Place was very good, and now Josh was able to add his approbation, and say that the barouche and the phaeton Durban had chosen were newly painted and very smart.

'Not but what you'd much better stick to the barouche, Miss Mary, and let Timothy drive you. I don't like to see my young ladies driving themselves and getting covered in dust and flies, and Bath roads are very dangerous when you don't know them,' Josh said.

'In that case,' Mary said firmly, 'I had much better drive myself, for I have been coming to Bath every year with Lady Chelmsford for as long as I can remember, and as far as I know, this is yours and Timothy's first visit.'

Bath had gone past the great frenzy of its popularity, and was now frequented by the quieter sort of people. There was much interest in the two young ladies, and several older friends of her mother's and of the previous Lady Chelmsford's paid formal visits and offered to chaperon them. Mary's affirmation that she was quite old enough to chaperon Lucy herself did not cut much ice with dowagers who regarded forty as the age when respectability began; but Farleigh's forbidding aspect and evident determination not to let the ladies out of her sight allayed their worst fears.

Lucy had never been to Bath before, and Mary occupied the first week or so with shewing her around and trying to arouse her interest in such feminine matters as miliners' shops and drapery stores.

'I know you're only fourteen, Lucy,' she said, 'but you are no longer a child, and it would be foolish to pretend that you can ever go back to being one now. I think it would be much better if Mother were to treat you as two or three years older, and bring you out early. It wouldn't hurt for you to be married in a year or two. You've always been ahead of your age.'

Lucy made a face at the thought of getting married, but Mary was firm on that point. 'If you choose right, it will be the best thing for you. You must have an establishment, you know, and if it is a good enough one, you can do pretty much as you please. Look at Mother, for instance--'

'Mother's different, and you know it. Morland Place was hers, and she was always in love with Papa,' Lucy said. 'Look at you, on the other hand. You've never married. Why should I?'

'I've been lucky in having dear cousin Flora and Cousin Charles to take care of me and shew me the world. Without them, I assure you, I would have been forced to marry years ago, just in order to get away from Morland Place.'

'Well I don't particularly want to get away from Morland Place,' Lucy said stubbornly. 'I may just as well stay there and help Edward, who lets me, as marry someone I don't know, who might want me to sit on the sofa all day long and sew.'

Mary had to admit, though not aloud, that there was some sense in this, so she did not press the argument. Instead she said, 'Very well, but you should learn how to dress yourself to advantage. You could be very pretty, you know, Lucy. With a little care, you could be the beauty of the family.'

Lucy's innate honesty surfaced. 'No, no, Polly, that will always be you. It isn't just your looks, but your –' she waved a hand – 'everything. You always make other women look unfinished.'

Mary looked pleased. 'I'm glad you think so – but that, at least, is something you can learn, just as I did. I should be glad to teach you, if you'd like?'

Lucy did like, and it was the beginning of a pleasant time, and a lasting friendship between them, for each recognised the similarities and the differences between them, and respected them. Mary taught Lucy how to dress with her own particular brand of chic: 'You can never be too plainly dressed, if the materials and the cut are of the finest'; and 'when you ornament, let the ornamentation be singular, in every sense'; and 'Get the colour right, and everything's right.' These were the maxims she taught Lucy, and as they walked about the shops of Gay Street and George Street together, she discovered her younger sister was an apt pupil, with as good an eye for line in clothes as in horses.

For the rest, they took out subscriptions to the library, paid a few morning calls, and went to the concert evenings; and otherwise spent most of their time riding on Primose Hill and over Weston to Dean Hill and beyond; and going out in the carriage to explore the famous beauty spots and places of historic interest within reach of Bath. A month passed quickly and pleasantly, and they were never bored or out of sorts; and if Mary ever missed her old friends, she had only to think of Brighton to count herself fortunate.

One day in July they were sitting in the breakfast parlour by the open window, beyond which the day promised to be punishingly hot. They had taken their exercise early, and now were preparing to amuse themselves quietly until it grew cool enough to think about dinner. Brock Street was very quiet, so quiet that the sound of footsteps walking along it briskly from the direction of The Circus aroused Lucy's interest. 'Now who can this be?' she said aloud, leaning out to get a better look. 'Not the usual residents, for they never walk so fast, and besides, it is too hot to be out. Oh, they are coming here!'

'Who was it, did you see?' Mary asked, her curiosity aroused. Lucy turned to her with her face unaccountably rosy.

'It looked,' she said hesitantly, 'like two sea-officers, but I could not see their faces.'

Their curiosity was not long stretched, for a moment or two later the door opened and the footman announced, 'Captain Harvey and Captain Haworth, Miss.' If Lucy looked a little disappointed, Mary at least rose with a ready smile and an outstretched hand which shewed that there had been one part of her that was not fully occupied.

'Captain Harvey, I had no idea you were in Bath,' she said.

Hannibal Harvey crossed the room to take her hand, looking quite unchanged at first glance, still with his lithe walk, his swarthy, gypsy good looks, his long lovelocks, his amused and caressive eyes. At second glance, however, Mary could see that he was pale and strained under his weather-tan, with deep lines either side of his mouth. He bowed over her hand and laid his lips to it in the old, mocking salute, and replied:

'I had the greatest difficulty in discovering that *you* were in Bath, Miss Morland. I sought you in Laura Place, and waited for you in vain at the Assembly Rooms and at the ball. And now I find you sequestered in quite the wrong part of town, and perfectly withdrawn from the world – though not alone, I see.'

'My sister Lucy,' Mary said briefly, watching his face to see if he had heard anything of the scandal.

Harvey's face remained unmoved, however – though it was not beyond him to conceal what he did know, as she was well aware. He bowed to Lucy, and then said:

'May I have the honour of presenting to you a very dear friend of mine, Captain George Haworth? Haworth and I have known each other for ever – we were mids together, and he saved my life once when we were lieutenants in the *Achilles*.'

Mary turned with a smile and gave her hand to the other captain. He was perfectly undistinguished in his appearance, being short, barrel-shaped, and balding, as well as shewing all the threadbareness of a sea-officer with no private means and no wealthy patron. Mary shook his hand and returned her attention at once to Harvey.

'I am very glad to see you, of course,' she said, 'but I cannot think what you can be doing here in time of war. Why aren't you – both – at sea?'

'Nothing in the least exciting, I assure you – in fact, you will probably hold us in the greatest contempt when I tell you that we are both convalescing. Just when England needs us most, I must needs contract a very lowering sort of fever--'

'Yes, I thought you looked very pulled-down,' Mary interrupted anxiously. 'I am so sorry. You are progressing favourably now, I hope?'

'Since entering this room, I swear I feel the most amazing improvement,' Harvey said, and when Lucy snorted with an irrepressible giggle, he turned pained eyes on her. 'My dear young lady,' he said solemnly, 'if you doubt the therapeutic effect of one glance from your limpid eyes, let me tell you that until I entered this room, George had serious doubts of my surviving until the end of the week. We came in fact to say our farewells--'

'Oh, stop!' said Lucy, choking with laughter. 'You are too absurd! But what did you have, Captain? I'd say from the look of you it was the putrid fever. You must be very careful of your diet, you know: it can leave the stomach weak for some months afterwards. Camomile tea is very good in this hot weather – I recommend it.'

Mary was making frantic faces at Lucy to stop her, and Harvey, intercepting them, smiled and said, 'My dear ma'am, be easy. I am well aware that advice of this sort from Miss Lucy Morland is worth the heeding.'

Mary coloured, mortified. 'Oh, then you *have* heard,' she said. Harvey raised an eyebrow, his face a polite blank.

'Heard what, Miss Morland?'

Mary did not know what to do or say, and Captain Haworth rescued her with a good-natured laugh.

'Pay no attention to Harvey, Miss Morland – he likes to talk nonsense and tease people. Pray allow me to sit beside you and discourse with you in a reasonable way--'

'Oh yes, do, George, while Miss Lucy and I talk of naval matters over here,' Harvey said quickly, taking his place beside Lucy. Mary was now perfectly confused, as Harvey meant her to be, as to what he knew, and as he engaged Lucy in an animated but low-voiced conversation, she had no alternative but to give her attention to Captain Haworth.

'Captain Harvey said that you were both convalescing,' she began desperately, for want of a subject. 'I hope you have not had the fever too?'

'No, ma'am, I'm afraid it was nothing so romantic. A perfectly foolish accident, just as I was about to embark for the Mediterranean – I slipped and broke my leg.' Mary made sounds of sympathy. 'Thank you, but it is quite healed now. I was waiting for a commission, when Harvey discovered I was still beached. He's a restless creature, even when ill, and begged me to go with him for a few days to Bath. He said he had acquaintance here, but I had no idea it was with Miss Morland of Morland Place.'

Mary looked at him shrewdly. 'That sounds like the very grossest form of flattery, sir. I cannot believe that you had heard of me before.'

Haworth smiled, and she remarked to herself what beautiful eyes he had, as well as a very attractive, melodious voice. 'I would not be so foolish as to offer counterfeit coin to one who has received so much true gold. Indeed, ma'am, I had heard of Miss Morland long before Harvey mentioned you.'

'Lady Chelmsford, of course, is known to many in the naval world. It is as her companion that you have heard of me.'

Captain Haworth only smiled, just as if he were saying 'Have it that way if you will,' and after a moment changed the subject. 'When you were in Town, Miss Morland, did you happen to hear Mr Haydn's new work?'

Mary's face lit in delight at discovering another music-lover, and their talk became so animated that the visit extended far beyond the usual quarter-hour. When the gentlemen rose to go, Captain Haworth said, 'Have you visited Stourhead yet, Miss Morland? No? You really should go while this fine weather lasts. The gardens there are quite, quite magnificent.'

'I had planned to take Lucy--' Mary began, and Captain Haworth took up the cue in his warm, gentle voice.

'If you would permit Captain Harvey and myself to escort you tomorrow, it would give us the greatest pleasure.'

'Two hours and a half in the carriage should take us there,' Harvey went on briskly. 'If we were on the road at ten o'clock tomorrow, we should be there in time to bespeak a dinner at the Eagle before we take our walk around the gardens.'

'Or what do you say to a picnic?' Haworth added, watching Lucy's face. 'We could choose a spot by the lake.'

It was arranged thus, and the gentlemen bowed and left.

'What were you and Captain Harvey talking about, Lucy?' Mary asked when they were alone.

'Oh, this and that,' Lucy said vaguely, kneeling on the window-seat to watch them walking away down the street. 'Improvements that could be made to the medical facilities on board ship, mostly.'

Mary looked grave. 'Then he must have heard about your . . .adventure.'

Lucy shrugged unconcernedly. 'I suppose so – but he would never admit it, so it doesn't really matter, does it?'

The outing to Stourhead was a great success. They went in the barouche, with Captain Haworth driving, and Lucy beside him on the box, while Mary and Harvey occupied the seat, and the picnic basket occupied the footplate behind. Harvey was at his most amusing, but Mary found her attention straying from time to time, to try and hear what Haworth was talking about with Lucy. He drove quietly and well, without any flamboyance, and when they were out of the town, he let Lucy take the reins, and even at one time appeared to be taking a lesson from her. It was very good-natured in him, she thought, to treat Lucy so kindly, and as if she were an equal.

Mary had been to Stourhead before, with Flora and Charles, but there is always something fresh to be seen in a great garden, and she had as much pleasure in walking about it as Lucy did. The four of them made good company, although Mary did occasionally feel just a little left out, when the other three chatted like equals about naval matters. She was more sure than ever that Harvey knew about Lucy's adventure, for he talked to her as if she were a brother officer. But whenever she began to feel at odds with the company, Captain Haworth was bound to notice, and in his kind way change the subject to include her.

When they parted at Brock Street at the end of the day, it was arranged that the gentlemen should call for them the next morning to walk with them down to the Pump Room. When the appointed hour came, however, it was Captain Haworth alone who presented himself at Brock Street. Mary tried very hard not to look disappointed, but the mild and shabby captain was no substitute for the handsome and flamboyant Harvey.

'Captain Harvey begs me to bring his deepest regrets and apologies, Miss Morland, but finds himself too unwell to keep his appointment,' Haworth said. As Mary met his eyes, she received the sudden conviction that Harvey was not in the least unwell. She recollected Flora's indiscretion about the two ladies of mature charms in Bath with whom Harvey had long carried on a disgraceful liaison. The name *Mrs Montague* quivered on her lips, and as if he knew what she was thinking, Haworth gave his head a tiny, admonitory shake. 'I'm afraid it will be a disappointment to you, ma'am, to have only my very unexciting company instead. I shall quite understand if you wish to cancel our engagement,' he went on.

Mary blushed furiously, and lowered her eyes from his kind, too-perceptive gaze.

'By no means, sir,' she said, struggling desperately to recapture her poise. 'I am sorry that Captain Harvey should be indisposed, but I assure you I – we – shall be more than happy to be escorted by you.'

'In that case', he said, bowing, and offering an arm to each of them. Lucy at once began questioning him closely on Harvey's symptoms, and Haworth answered good-humouredly, inventing whatever she seemed to require of him; and Mary, smiling inwardly at his tact, began to feel quite comfortable again, and as they started down Gay Street she even felt that they did not miss Captain Harvey's presence at all.

18

Héloïse loved Morland Place from her first sight of it.

'Oh, but it is a real castle!' she exclaimed. 'With a . . . *fossé*?'

'Moat,' Jemima provided. 'It does look pretty, doesn't it, with the sun shining on the walls? It makes them quite honey-coloured.'

'*Et les cygnes – qu'ils sont beaux*! Do they belong to you?' she went on as an adult pair and their juveniles drifted by on a leisurely circuit.

'No, in England all swans belong to the King. We merely look after them for him,' James told her, smiling. She clasped her hands.

'Oh, but that is so romantic! And your castle – is it very old? When you said Morland Place, it sounded small and cosy, and I thought it would be a cottage with a straw roof. No, don't laugh at me – how was I to know?' She added as James went into peals of laughter. 'How old is it? Have you always lived here?'

'The date is over the door, look,' James said, pointing to the white stone panel, on which was carved '1450 – *Deo Gratias*'.

'And what is the little animal carved above?' Héloïse wanted to know.

'That's the white hare – the badge of the first mistress of Morland Place, and beside it the sprig of heather, which is the Morland badge,' Jemima answered her. 'The Morlands have lived here for three hundred and fifty years.'

Héloïse looked in silence for a moment, and then turned grave eyes on Jemima. 'It is a very great thing, then, to be mistress of Morland Place. And,' she added, her irrepressible smile breaking out, 'it is a very great thing to be a Morland, I think, even if I am not a proper one.'

Jemima put an arm round her and kissed the top of her head. 'You have been adopted, remember. You are a proper Morland from now on.'

Héloïse, arriving at Morland Place full of love, found plenty of people to give it to. As well as loving the house, she loved all the servants and all the animals, the villagers and tenants, and especially, most especially, the family. She met Edward, 'the Master', and found him a plain, simple, kind-hearted, hard-working man, what she called to herself '*un vrai chrétien*'. James Chetwyn was there on a visit, and when she saw them together, Héloïse nodded wisely to herself and said that she had seen many young men like that amongst the *Philosophes* in Paris: young men who were too much in love with Ancient Virtue to have anything to do with the gross, worldly business of marriage and procreation. Jemima found it a great comfort that Héloïse saw nothing either strange or vicious in their relationship, and realised then that she had already formed a great respect for the little girl's practical and level-headed judgement.

Jemima, of course, Héloïse loved deeply and dearly as her new mother, and in her quick way she soon found little things she could do about the house to ease Jemima's burden. Jemima had always suffered from a lack of female companionship, and found herself surprisingly quickly relying on Héloïse, as she had never been able to rely on Mary, and had not yet had a chance to rely on Lucy.

'If I had had a daughter-in-law,' she said once, 'it might have been like this. But my sons all seem devoted to the bachelor state.'

'But surely James – is he not interested in women?' Héloïse asked. Jemima sighed.

'He is interested in *all* women, that's the trouble. The troubles we have had . . .!'

'Then all is well,' Héloïse said with a satisfied nod. 'He will choose one, one day, and settle down.'

Héloïse wanted to see all over the house, and Jemima was glad to have such an appreciative and attentive audience. She was very impressed with the chapel, and the fact that there was a resident chaplain at Morland Place. 'You are a devout family – I like that very much. In France, I am afraid that the revolution is destroying the Church. They closed the convents, you know – that was why Papa took me out and married me to Olivier – and now that the priests are made to swear an oath to

345

the government, they are no longer truly Catholic priests. It is very dreadful.'

It was James who took Héloïse around the estate. Finding she loved to ride – she told him all about her dear Prestance, whom she had had to leave behind in France – he found her a suitable mount, one of the Morland chestnuts called Goldfinch, and thereafter took her out every fine day to see the country. Jemima was astonished, and almost uneasy, at how quickly James had taken to his little cousin, for even during that long coach journey home he had chatted to her as if he had known her for years. He never seemed to mind how much trouble he took over shewing her whatever she had a fancy to see, and in the evenings at home they would lean their heads together and talk, as she had seen Edward and his Chetwyn do, creating a world of their own, almost oblivious of their surroundings.

'She's like a new little sister for him', Edward said to her one day as they all sat in the long saloon, and James gave Héloïse a guided tour of the family portraits. Jemima looked at Edward questioningly.

'Do you think that's it? That he regards her as a sister?'

'I think he may have been missing Lucy,' Edward said, which was clearly an evasion. Then, meeting his mother's eyes, he said, 'Well, it isn't the way he behaves towards other girls, is it, Mother? The only . . .'

'Yes?'

'The only other woman I've seen him talk to like that,' Edward went on reluctantly, 'was Mary Skelwith.'

'But he didn't regard her as a sister,' Jemima said, shocked. Edward wrinkled his brow.

'I know. I only meant – well, anyway, Mother, there's nothing improper about it, I'm sure. Cousin Héloïse was very strictly brought up.'

James, meanwhile, was at the far end, having got half-way round the paintings and having reached the horses. 'This is Barbary, painted in 1674 – he was the Barb stallion from which all the Morland blacks are descended. And this is Prince Hal, about fifty years earlier, from whom all the chestnuts are descended. And this is the famous stallion Landscape, about fifty years later – well, you probably wouldn't have heard of him, but he's very famous in England. He won all the races there were to be won.'

'What a lot of horses!' Héloïse exclaimed politely.

'Oh, we have lots more than that. Most of the pictures of horses are downstairs in the dining-room. I'll shew you them another time.'

'Ah, this one I like – she has such a kind face. Who is she, please?'

'That's Mary Esther Morland – she was mistress of Morland Place in the time of the Civil War – with her dog. It's a Van Dyck, supposed to be very fine. And this one next to it – this is her husband Edmund Morland when he was a child, with his mother, who came from Scotland. Her name was Douglass Hamilton. The picture's by Hilliard.'

'She looks very proper, very *comme il faut*,' Héloïse said, studying the severe beauty of the mother. 'I like that.'

James gave her an amused smile. 'Do you? Well, you won't like this next lady, then, because she wasn't at all proper.' They had turned the corner of the room now, and were before the large portrait hanging over the fire. 'This is Annunciata, the first Countess of Chelmsford, our common ancestress, with some of her children. We call this portrait "the Turkish", because she's wearing a turban. She was a very wicked woman, by all accounts, though she certainly raised the family's fortunes.' He looked from the picture to Héloïse and back. 'You have a little of the look of her. That's the Stuart blood, I suppose. She was the daughter of King Charles's cousin.'

Héloïse studied the picture for some time in silence, and then they passed on to the other end of the room. Suddenly her attention was seized by the portrait of a very forbidding young woman with red hair.

'But who is this? I know this face, though I cannot think from where . . .' Héloïse said.

'That's Arabella Morland, another of the mistresses of Morland Place. That's her husband, Martin, over there. There was some mystery about her, but I don't remember what.'

'Oh please – do remember,' Héloïse said eagerly. James gave her an amused smile and called Jemima.

'Mother, come and tell us about this lady – my cousin seems unusually interested in her.'

Jemima came down to see what they were looking at, and said, 'Oh yes, Arabella. She was the daughter of the Countess Annunciata, over there, and apparently a very wild and rebellious young woman. She married the heir to Morland Place, but it was a short-lived marriage. She bore him a son, and then ran away, and was never seen again.' Jemima sighed. 'I'm afraid we do seem to be given to running away in this family.'

Héloïse stared and stared. It *must* be the same, she thought. The resemblance to the miniature Uncle Johann had shewn her was extraordinary; and she had red hair; and Uncle Johann had said that no-one knew where she came from, but that she had spoken of her girlhood in England, where she had lived on a farm where they bred horses. It must be the same person! She was about to say something, when a second thought bid her be cautious. She must think about it first, before she told Jemima, in case it caused complications. But if it were true, it meant that Lotti – dear Lotti – was a sort of distant cousin of hers. That would be delightful. She had by no means exhausted her appetite for family yet.

In early June news came of events in Paris which made Héloïse anxious again for the safety of her father. Apart from that one, hastily scrawled note, she had heard nothing from him, nor received any money for her support from him, and she was forced to conclude that he was being more closely watched than he had anticipated, or that he was unable to communicate for some other reason. But the news reached England that on the second of June the leading men of the Mountain, Marat and Robespierre, had denounced the Girondin party and all who had been associated with Dumouriez as traitors, and demanded that they be taken before the Revolutionary Tribunal to answer for their guilt. Twenty-two Girondins, including Brissot and Vergniaud and all their close friends, had been arrested; and already it was accepted that being taken before the Revolutionary Tribunal was but one short step from the guillotine.

Héloïse waited in trembling for each new bulletin, and James, grave and concerned for her, went back and forth to York, and to the Maccabees' Club, to bring her the very freshest news and the most recent newspapers. It soon appeared that

Danton had not been amongst those arrested. Even before she had left Paris, there had been a rift between Danton and the Girondins, fostered by the Rolands, who were jealous of him. Now it appeared he had finally broken with them when Vergniaud refused an overture of peace from him, and had gone over to the Mountain before the 'purge' of the second of June had been put in hand.

This meant, Héloïse concluded gratefully, that her father was probably still safe, for he was known to be Danton's friend, though he had once been associated with the Brissotins. She hoped that what he had said before she left was true, that he was a faithful servant of the Minister of the Interior, and known to be without political bias; but she prayed even more fervently that he would leave France before it was too late, and join her in England. She longed to see him, and hoped that his desire to increase his fortune would not make him delay beyond what was safe.

One day in July, James returned from York, and after enquiring of the servants, he sought out Héloïse in the rose garden, where she was cutting flowers for the house. Her face lit when she saw him, and he wondered briefly how anyone could ever have described her as 'not at all pretty', when in fact she was perfectly beautiful.

'I have something here that will make you glad to see me,' he greeted her.

'I am always glad to see you, cousin James,' she said calmly. 'How could anyone not be?'

'Oh, in my wild youth, my father often wished me at the – a long way away, for I vexed him extremely with my wickedness,' James grinned.

Héloïse tilted her head gravely. 'I can't imagine you vexing your father. You are so gentle and thoughtful – and you do such beautiful drawings.'

James blinked at this description of himself, and then frowned slightly. 'How do you know about my drawing?'

'Your mother shewed me some of your sketches. They are so very good, cousin! You should have an exhibition.'

'Oh, I just scribble, it's nothing,' James muttered, looking confused in a way that would have surprised his mother and some of his older friends if they had seen it. 'But you are straying from the subject – look, I have a letter for you.'

She blanched. 'From papa? Is it from Papa?'

'No, not quite – but almost as good. It is from Leipzig. It must be from your friend's brother, what was his name?'

Héloïse took it from him without a word, and opened it with trembling hands. James watched her in silence as she scanned the page, and then could not wait any longer.

'What does it say? Is she safe?'

Héloïse looked up at him blankly. 'I don't know. It's in German – I can't understand a word.' They stared at each other for a moment, and then began to laugh. It was a strange, almost hysterical laughter on Héloïse's part, and ended in tears, which James dealt with in the best way possible, by taking her in his arms and stroking her head until she had calmed a little.

Then he said, 'We'll take it to Father Thomas, of course! He knows a little of all languages, enough to translate your letter for you, I'm sure.'

Héloïse released herself from his arms, and wiped her tears away carefully with her handkerchief, to give herself time to recover. 'I'm sorry, cousin,' she said after a moment.

'That's all right – I rather enjoyed it, to say the truth,' James said. She met his eyes for a moment, and then lowered hers, confused. It was the first more-than-cousinly thing he had ever said to her, and it made her feel shy.

Father Thomas proved to have more than a little German, and translated the letter without difficulty. It was from Ernst Finsterwalde, and the news was both good and bad. Lotti, the letter explained, and Olivier Vendenoir had both been found guilty of treason, and had been condemned to death; but Danton had intervened on Lotti's behalf, saying that as a woman she was bound to obey her husband, and had managed to have her sentence commuted to exile. She was now safe in her brother's house in Leipzig, but her experiences, and the hardships she had endured in prison and during the long journey from Paris, had ruined her health, so that she was still not well enough to rise from her bed, or even to write to Héloïse, though she sent her love and her deepest condolences.

Charles, the letter said, was still with the Austrian army, but had been advised of his wife's whereabouts and condition; and there was more news, too, also mixed. Marie, Héloïse's maid, had not been drowned. She and the children and some other survivors had been taken up by a fishing boat, which had then been blown down the channel by the storm, but had at last managed to make a landing at Alderney. They had all been very ill, and little Clothilde had succumbed to a fever and died; but after several weeks they had been picked up by a Dutch privateer and carried to Ostend, and from there by stages they had made their way to Leipzig where they were now reunited with Lotti.

James watched Héloïse's face closely through the recital of the letter, and when it was finished, he asked anxiously, 'I hope the news has not disturbed you too much?'

Héloïse turned her damp handkerchief in her hands and said unsteadily, 'Thank you cousin James. It is dreadful – about – poor little Clothilde. I helped at her birth, you know. But it is always better to know than not to know. And Marie is safe, dear faithful Marie.' She was silent a moment, and then, 'I know I should be grateful, but it does make me feel so – so far from home. It is a lonely thing, to be an exile.'

Her voice wavered on the last words, and James took her hands and pressed them and said eagerly: 'You must never feel alone. We are your family now. We all love you, and will take care of you.'

She only nodded, not trusting herself to speak.

Life seemed to Henri to be shrinking around him, closing in on him like a prison. In the old days, before the revolution, he had ranged far and wide, sampling the life of Paris in all its rich variety. He had been at home in Versailles and at the gaming tables of the Palais Royal, in the *hôtels* of the nobility and in their country châteaux, in the houses of the *nouveaux riches*, and, in his other persona, in the salons and cafés of the *bourgeois*. Now he was in retreat, spending much of his time in the little dark house in the rue de Saint-Rustique, listening for footsteps outside.

He was being watched, he knew. When Duncan had returned from Saint-Valéry with the news that Héloïse had had to take ship with nothing but the clothes she stood in, Henri had hastened to send her money, gold, by way of one of his agents in Antwerp. He had sent with the money a message that she should not try to acknowledge receipt of it, but now he wondered if that gold had ever reached her. He had not dared to send more than one brief and cryptic message, and it was proving so difficult to move his vast accumulation of wealth out to safe places that he was having to do it very slowly and gradually, and wondered more than once if he might not have done better to leave with Héloïse, taking with him what he had to hand at the time.

He did not like the way things were going. Danton, the only man he felt he could trust, was losing his grip on affairs, and being edged out of the central arena. True, he still had influence – enough, at least, to save Lotti; and it was true also that Vendenoir had not yet been executed, but was lingering on in prison. But Henri had the feeling that Vendenoir was there not because Danton was saving him, but because Robespierre was hoping to use him one day to implicate Danton in the Dumouriez business. Danton was tired, had fought long and bloody, and now wanted peace. His wife Gabrielle had died – she who had always reminded Henri of his own dear Madeleine – and he had married a new and pretty wife, and wanted to spend time with her and on his farm, watching things grow and smelling the warm earth and grass. Things of the flesh distracted Danton; but no fleshly cares would ever divert Robespierre's energies from the task in hand. Robespierre cared for one thing only – the revolution; and desired one thing only – the power to shape the new society his way.

And that power was slipping from Danton's hands to Robespierre's, slowly but surely. It was Danton who had initiated the setting up of the Committee of Public Safety, and its spearpoint, the Revolutionary Tribunal; but by the middle of July it was Robespierre who controlled it. With the expulsion of the Girondins in June, Robespierre had removed the last stronghold of resistance. The murder of Marat by a tall, buxom virgin from Caen gave him the excuse to begin the systematic elimination of all who opposed or might oppose his view of republicanism, and slowly at first, but with increasing vigour, the guillotine began its work of 'purification'.

Little by little, as slowly as the hands of a clock move around its face, Henri converted his wealth into portable jewels, and moved them out of public view. He was still employed by the Ministry of the Interior to catalogue and auction the contents of the former royal residences, and this gave him opportunities, though he knew he was being watched, and had to be careful. The house on the rue Saint-Anne was in a curious kind of limbo, for though Vendenoir was a condemned criminal, the house and contents belonged to Héloïse, and as yet she had not been impeached. Henri visited it, casually, as often as possible, making it look as though he were merely making sure it was being looked after. He could not move any large pieces of furniture, but the smaller articles gradually disappeared.

As for his social life, he had none; for such of his former acquaintances who had not fled or been imprisoned either avoided him or were avoided by him as unsafe to be with. Danton, absorbed with his new wife with whom he was in love, retreated into a fog of domestic bliss which Henri did not care to try to penetrate; and with Héloïse gone, there was no love for Henri in Paris, except in Madame Buffon's upstairs rooms. He visited Marie-France often that summer and autumn, took what comfort she could give him, and played with her little son. Morland Cotoy was growing fast, and Henri, who had had little to do with his other children in their early life, found himself fascinated by the child, and growing dangerously attached to him. With his own hands he encouraged the child to stand and take his first steps; Morland's first words were learnt from Henri's lips; and when Henri came to the house, the boy would totter forward, grinning like an imp, and saying 'papa, papa!' with a delight that turned Henri's heart over in his breast. He bought clothes and toys and new shoes, and promised that young Morland should learn to ride as soon as he was old enough, and have a pony of his own. It was a little like having Héloïse back: even Bluette was there, playing with Morland as she had played with Héloïse, for Marie-France had taken the little dog in when Héloïse fled.

Winter began to close in, and the dangers increased. In September a new law was passed – called the Law of Suspects – which gave the Committee of Public Safety power to arrest and try anyone thought to be an enemy of the revolution; and,

353

worse, anyone who had not received a certificate of good citizenship from his local Section committee. From now on, no-one was safe. A man whose neighbour coveted his goods or did not like his face, might find his certificate withheld, and his name on the list of suspects. In October the Queen was guillotined, taken to her death in a common tumbril, with her hands tied like a criminal – the King had at least been allowed to make that last journey by carriage – and in November the Girondins, imprisoned since June, were finally tried and executed. In the same month, the Committee of Public Safety, which until then had been elected on a monthly basis, was made permanent, and it was mooted that anyone who questioned its decisions should be regarded as a suspect.

It must be, Henri decided, his last winter. In the spring, he must leave Paris, and join Héloïse in England.

'May I come and disturb you? Your servant said you were alone,' said Captain Haworth, putting his head round the door of the breakfast parlour. Mary looked up and smiled. Since that first day in July when the two sea officers had walked up to Brock Street, Mary had seen Captain Haworth almost every day. At the end of the fourth week, Hannibal Harvey had been recalled to his ship, but here it was, almost September, and Captain Haworth had still not been commissioned. Though she was sorry for him, in one way, Mary was glad in another that he had not been called, for the more she saw of him, the less willing she felt to dispense with his company and services. At any moment, she knew, his word might come from the Admiralty – and then what would she do? For he walked with her, sat and chatted with her, danced with her at the Assembly Rooms, sat through concerts with her, drove with her, and altogether made Bath agreeable for her.

'Yes, of course, do come in,' she said, putting the book she had been reading under the sofa cushion. 'Lucy is round at the stables, giving Lady Carlton's little boy a riding lesson. I hope I do not do wrong, allowing her to spend so much time at the stables, but she is so happy there, and she gets on so well with the child. And after all, Sophy – Lady Carlton – is a cousin of ours, and Lucy must get out into the fresh air sometimes. She spends such a lot of time at her books, now that you have got all those medical volumes for her. It was very good of you, but I wish she may not ruin her eyes.'

'And how did you get on with the book of essays I brought you yesterday?' he asked, sitting beside her comfortably.

'Oh, I finished them last night,' she said. He smiled at her teasingly.

'And shall I tell you what you thought of them? You found them interesting, but superficial.'

'If you are going to read my mind,' Mary laughed, 'we shall have nothing to talk about.'

'I can't imagine that we should ever run out of things to talk about. It has not happened yet, has it?'

'But we do not yet know all of each other's tastes. Once that happens . . .'

'I shudder to think,' he smiled. 'What were you reading when I came in?'

Mary blushed. 'Nothing, nothing at all.'

He leaned back to look at her. 'But this is delightful, Miss Morland. This surely must herald some absorbing new topic of conversation.'

'Well, you will laugh at me, I know,' Mary said defiantly, drawing out the book, 'but I find such things refreshing between serious study. It is the *Castle of Wolfenbach*.'

'Mrs Parson's latest work!' He took it from her. 'Now I must say, Miss Morland, that it is very unkind in you to keep this to yourself. I have been to the library every day asking for it, but they continue to tell me it is out. So it was *you* who had it all the time!'

Mary was laughing at his expression of affront, but incredulous. 'Now, Captain Haworth, you cannot mean to tell me that you read such mysteries.'

'Indeed I do! I love anything really horrid! I read the *Castle of Otranto* when I was still at school, and that was just the beginning. Then I read *Vathek*, and *An Italian Romance* . . .'

'Oh, I love Mrs Radcliffe's books. Did you read *The Romance of the Forest*?'

'Yes, I liked it extremely, and I hear she is writing another, which will be coming out next year, and will be the most horrid thing yet.' He surveyed her with satisfaction. 'I cannot tell you how glad I am to discover that you are frivolous after all, Miss Morland. It must be living at Morland Place – surely as Gothic and horrid a place as anyone can wish.'

Mary laughed. 'Well, really, you know, one would not think so, to live in it. But there are things . . .'

He pretended to shudder. 'Tell me!'

'There is a priest's hole somewhere,, though no-one can remember where, now. Anything might be hidden in it – a skeleton, or anything. And there is *one* ghost that people see, though I have never seen her: a lady in a white robe, with wild hair, who walks down the chapel stair and out through the great door. They say it is the ghost of a poor mad lady who was shut up long ago, and drowned herself in the moat.'

'I'm sure you are making it up,' he said, enjoying himself.

'No, no, I assure you! And then there is the old statue of Our Lady in the chapel – the servants say that if trouble is coming to the house, she weeps real tears. *I've* never seen it – but perhaps I am not frivolous enough, yet.'

He was laughing heartily. 'Oh, Miss Morland,' he said, and then, fixing her with his bright blue gaze, he said, 'Do you mind if I ask you a very impertinent question?' She could hardly say 'No', so she said nothing, and he went on, 'Miss Morland, why did you never marry?'

She felt herself growing hot, and turned her face away from him.

'I'm sorry, I have offended you,' he said quickly. 'I didn't mean to – but you see, I have heard of you for ever, as the beautiful Miss Morland, who has refused offers from all the most eligible, rich, and handsome men in England. They talk of you, you know, Miss Morland, as one of the three most beautiful women in London.' She returned her gaze to him, and then wished she hadn't, for once she had met his eyes she found it difficult to look away. His voice was gentler as he continued: 'Until I saw you, I thought they exaggerated; but now I see they told only half the truth. They omitted to say that you were also intelligent, witty, and charming, and that something shines out from your eyes which is an even greater beauty within you--'

'Please, Captain Haworth, I beg you will not . . .' Mary said with great difficulty: she felt as if she could not breathe.

He gave himself a little shake, and said: 'I beg your pardon, Miss Morland, I'm afraid now I have been guilty of something a great deal worse than impertinence. Pray forgive me. Shall we talk of something else? Shall you go to the concert tonight? I think you will like it: there are to be some Italian songs, and a piano concerto and a symphony by Mozart. Whenever I hear Mozart, I am reminded for some reason of the architecture of Wren. There is a sort of divine inevitability about them both, don't you think?'

She stood up and walked across to the window, and stood there with her back to him, and there was silence in the room for a while.

He stood too, and looked at her back with concern, and asked at last, quietly, '*Have* I offended you, Miss Morland? I am truly sorry.'

'No,' she said, in a muffled voice. 'No.' She turned at last, and her eyes were very bright. 'How could one be offended by such – compliments?'

'Praise, however sincerely meant, is not always acceptable,' he said steadily. 'It depends upon who offers it. And you, who have declined the hands of the highest of our society . . .'

'Can you think me so petty?' she asked impetuously. 'You asked me, Captain Haworth, why I never married. I will tell you. It was not from pride that I refused those offers. I considered them all carefully, by some I was even tempted – but in the end, I could not see that I would gain anything by accepting. I have always enjoyed my single life, and I came to the decision in the end, that I would not marry until and unless I was asked by a man who . . .' She had difficulty in continuing. He waited, his eyes on her, steady, friendly, but without hope. She gripped her hands together, and went on, forcing herself to breathe slowly, 'I decided I should only marry a man who made me feel that life without him would be – not impossible, it is never that – but impossibly dull.'

'Yes, I see,' he said. 'I honour you for that, Miss Morland.'

He would never ask her, she could see that. He was too modest, thought too little of his own worth. He was modest, and kind, and gentle, and amusing, the best friend she had ever had; and more than that, he took her breath away. She remembered with astonishment how on their first meeting she

357

had thought him negligible. How could she not have seen the strong, calm beauty in his face? His eyes, his smile, his voice – why did not others notice these things? She knew, when she walked with him along the street, that people's eyes passed over him, or that if they noticed him, it was to wonder what she, beautiful and smart, was doing with a nondescript, barrel-shaped and shabby sea-officer.

And that was how he saw himself, and he would never ask her; and she dug her nails into her palms with frustration and misery, for, however independent and strong-willed she was, she could not bring herself to do the asking. She simply *could not*, and to her horror, tears burst past the barriers she had put up against them, and she gave an audible sob.

He was all concern, taking a step towards her, and checking as he wondered if it was his fault.

'Oh, please – my dear Miss Morland – what is it? Please don't cry! Tell me what is the matter.'

She knew that if she spoke she would sob, but in the end, it didn't matter. She said, 'You will go away. A letter might come any day, and you'll go away to sea, and then I will never . . .' She choked. He came a step closer, looking at her with incredulity, but a little, just a little, hope.

'You will never *what*, Miss Morland?'

He was very close to her now. She pushed frantically at the tears which would keep seeping out of her eyes, and said, 'I will never see you again. Oh . . .'

Somehow she was weeping on his shoulder, his broad, comfortable shoulder which, owing to his not being very tall, was at just the right height for her. She felt him patting her back very tentatively, and it made her want to laugh, which was confusing.

'Miss Morland, can it mean anything to you, not to see me again? I don't know if I am being impertinent, or very stupid. Oh please, if you possibly could, do stop crying, Miss Morland, and tell me.' She nodded, face down in his shoulder. He walked backwards with her to the sofa, and sat down, and held her, bewildered and still not quite believing, until her sobs declined. She groped out with a hand for a handkerchief, and he pulled his own from his sleeve and put it in her fingers.

'Have mine,' he said. 'It's bigger.'

She sat up and turned her face away from him to blow and mop. 'I shall look dreadful,' she said.

'I don't think so,' he said tenderly. 'You haven't had the practice.' This made her laugh, and eventually she turned to look at him, shyly, more like a girl of nineteen than a woman of twenty-nine; and his face looked so dear and so unthreatening that if she had not already been committed to him in her heart, it would have happened then. He gave her a slightly crooked smile, and seeing that it was now up to him, he said,

'Dear Miss Morland, dear Mary – may I call you that? I don't quite know if I am dreaming, or if I have gone mad, but whichever it is, I think I must take advantage of the moment, or it may never come again. I have loved you since the first moment I saw you, but I never thought – dreamed – that you could care for me. But if you can . . . if you would . . .' He cocked his head a little, looking puzzled. 'I would be mad to ask you to marry me, wouldn't I? *Would* you marry me?'

'Yes, yes please,' she said. He laughed, a joyful laugh this time.

'But then *you* are mad! Miss Morland – Mary – you are beautiful, intelligent, independent, with money of your own! I am a poor sea-captain with nothing to offer. I'm not handsome or rich – I'm forty years old, you know! I'm not a distinguished captain, nor even a dashing captain like Hannibal Harvey. Just an ordinary, bread-and-butter old seadog. But I do love you – God, how I love you!'

'I told you the man I would marry,' Mary said, smiling at his description of himself. 'There are probably lots of perfectly nice agreeable men I could live with quite happily – but you are the only man I've ever known that I couldn't live without.'

'Then you will marry me?'

'Yes.'

He was not laughing now. He looked grave – almost reverent. He put his arms around her and held her against him for a moment, and then put her back from him, asked for and received permission from her eyes, and kissed her. Mary had been kissed before, once or twice, but it had never been like this. She understood the meaning of the word '*bliss*'. Everything inside her seemed to be melting and yielding, and she was seized with a fierce longing, though for what she did not know. She kissed him, and held on to him and when after a long time they paused to draw breath, she said, with her lips only a hair's breadth away from his, 'I love you. Oh, I love you.'

Something strange seemed to happen to time then, as they sat together on the sofa and in love. A very long time, or perhaps only minutes, later, Captain Haworth asked, 'When shall we be married?'

'Soon,' Mary said, pressing her cheek against him with an abandon which would have surprised most people who knew her had they seen it, and truth to tell rather surprised her. 'I must marry you as soon as possible. How quickly can it be done?'

'I could post up to London for a special licence, and then it could be done straight away, as soon as I returned. But--'

'A day to go and a day to come back – that's the soonest?' He smiled at her affectionately. 'This haste is very flattering, Miss Morland, but surely you will wish to have a proper wedding, with all your family around you?'

'Oh, there is no time for that. You may be recalled at any moment. The letter may be on the road at this very minute,' she said, looking over her shoulder as if she expected to see it winging its way across the room like a bird of ill omen. 'I must be wed to you while I can.'

'But won't you want to ask your parents – your family . . .?'

She laughed. 'I am of good age, sir. I need no-one's permission. Of course, I will *inform* my family, and Lady Chelmsford – I know what is due to them. But my marriage is now my own business, I'm glad to say.'

'But surely . . .'

Mary sat up straight and looked at him sternly. 'If you object any longer, I shall think you have changed your mind about wishing to marry me, sir.'

He lifted her hand to his lips. 'Not I. I am happy to marry you as quickly as ever you wish, before *you* change your mind about *me*.'

Another long silence later, they heard the sound of brisk steps on the stairs.

'Lucy,' Mary said, sitting up again. 'Back already?'

'Do we tell her?' Haworth asked.

'Of course,' Mary smiled. 'Won't she be surprised!'

'Everyone will be surprised,' he said in a low voice, not as if the prospect pleased him much. The door opened and Lucy burst energetically in.

'Oh – good morning, Captain Haworth. I didn't know you were here. Mary, have you--'

'Captain Haworth and I are to be married, Lucy,' Mary said, firmly enough to capture her sister's attention. Lucy's eyes stopped wandering round the room only for long enough to bestow a quick smile on them.

'Oh good,' she said. 'You've got that sorted out, then? But have you seen my *Materia Medica*? I made sure I had left it in my room, but it isn't there. One of the maids must have moved it.'

Haworth began to laugh at Mary's indignant face. 'Never mind, my dearest, I'm sure we shall surprise everyone else. You may come to be glad of Lucy's response in time.'

BOOK THREE

The Book

My hopes are with the Dead; anon
My place with them will be,
And I with them shall travel on
Through all Futurity;
Yet leaving here a name, I trust,
That will not perish in the dust.

Robert Southey: *His Books*

19

Surprise was not the only reaction aroused by the news of Mary's acceptance of Captain Haworth. Flora was shocked and dismayed.

'What can she be about? Can he have forced her in some way – coerced her? It surely cannot be of her own free will that she has agreed to marry this unsuitable sea-captain?'

'My dear,' Charles said genially, 'you have read her letter. Mary has fallen in love at last.'

'But she *cannot* have – not with him! He is nobody. He has no position, no wealth – he isn't even handsome! He is completely--'

'Unsuitable,' Charles finished for her, and began to laugh. 'It is delicious, quite, quite delicious. When I think of all the rich and handsome and eligible men who offered for Mary, and languished after her, and wrote poems about her beauty, and she would have nothing to do with them. And then, when she does finally fall in love, it is with a man no-one else can see the point of. Mary's Unsuitable Sea-captain!'

'I wish you will not, Charles,' Flora said crossly. 'If you begin to call him that, the name will stick. You know how these things do. Oh, what can Mary be about? She will make us laughing-stocks.'

'Not she! She will make falling in love fashionable,' Charles said. 'When a woman as beautiful and rich as Mary weds, no-one can think she was brought to it from lack of choice. Everyone will be forced to the conclusion that there is more to this Haworth than meets the eye.'

'How can you be so simple?' Flora exclaimed. 'She wants to wed him in such a violent hurry, and after being retired from society for months – people will think the worst.'

Charles stopped laughing. 'Flora, my dear, I am shocked at you. You cannot think – you know that it is impossible that she should--'

'Of course I know,' Flora said impatiently, 'but that is the way other minds will work.'

'Then we shall have nothing to do with them,' Charles said firmly. 'If such people there be, they are beneath our notice – far beneath. Mary has fallen in love, and since she is fortunate enough to be in a position to please herself, we should be glad for her.'

'You don't think we should stop her?' Flora asked, subdued.

'We could not – and if we could, I'm very sure we should not,' Charles said, putting an arm round her. 'Come, love, this isn't like you. Why do you mind so very much?'

Flora allowed herself to be comforted, and shed a tear or two on his shoulder. 'When I think of Lord Tonbridge – the wedding she might have had – the houses, the carriages! Such a waste of her beauty. Oh Charles, I shan't even be able to go to her wedding!'

'Never mind it, dearest,' Charles soothed her, concealing his own amusement. 'You must simply let yourself go on Horace's wedding to Lady Barbara. Now *that* will be as grand and luxurious as ever you could wish.'

'Yes,' she said, mollified, 'I must say Horace has done better for himself than I expected. To think that Mary once turned him down, too – however,' she checked herself, 'I mustn't think of that any more. As you say, one ought to be glad for her. But oh' – it burst from her in one last spasm, 'I cannot *bear* to think how Horace will laugh!'

The surprise caused at Morland Place was the less because since no-one there knew Captain Haworth, no-one knew precisely how Unsuitable he was. Mary's letter said that she had fallen in love, and that since Haworth might be recalled to his duty at any moment, she was marrying him at once. That Mary should fall in love at all was astonishing, but Jemima knew the effect of a red coat on women, and assumed that for someone more mature and sensible, the more subtle effect of a naval reputation might work the same way. She imagined someone handsome and dashing – like Hannibal Harvey, in fact – distinguished in his profession and possessed of private means. It was fortunate for her peace of mind that there was no-one on hand of whom she could enquire; but some natural concern for her daughter, who had never behaved so unreasonably like a young woman before, made her send James as fast as he could post to Bath, to make sure all was well.

He returned after a few days with the corners of his mouth curling upwards.

'Well?' Jemima demanded as he came into the long saloon. She and Héloïse were working one on either end of the Four Seasons tapestry, darning some moth damage. How to repair tapestry was one of the things Héloïse had learned in her excellent convent, and she had been shocked to discover that Jemima was intending to send the work out.

'No, no, *ma mère*, it is too valuable to trust to anyone else. Let me only shew you, and you will see we can do it ourselves very easily,' she had said, and Jemima had been glad to agree. It was only one of the ways in which Héloïse was a great help to her. Having been head of her own household, and in France where matters were much more strictly ordered, she soon won the respect of the servants, who liked her appreciation of things 'done proper', and always worked better for someone on whom poor or careless work could not be imposed. She also took from Jemima's shoulders the burden of making herself understood by M. Barnard, the cook. When Barnard discovered that Héloïse was French, he clutched her hand and poured out his heart to her, and thereafter worshipped her only a little less than Our Lady, produced delicacies for her so exotic and elaborate that they would make a strong man weep, and flew around his kitchen with a flamboyant and joyful energy that was quite as awe-inspiring to the other servants as his previous incomprehensible rages. Following his example, the servants quickly began to refer to Héloïse simply as 'Milady' – Jemima, though she was Lady Morland, had always been 'the Mistress.'

'Well,' Jemima said now, 'did you see them? What is this Captain Haworth like? Is Mary well? Is she really in love?'

'You are smiling like a sphinx, cousin James,' Héloïse said sternly. 'Please tell us at once.'

'Yes, Mary is really in love,' James said, lounging gracefully against Héloïse's chair and looking more cat-like every moment. 'It really is the most marvellous joke. When you think of all the men Mary refused, from John Anstey onwards and upwards – that she should finally be conquered, and so completely, by Captain Haworth, is a most beautiful irony.'

367

'But what is wrong with him? Is he not proper?' Héloïse asked anxiously. James grinned at her use of her favourite word.

'Oh, he is perfectly *proper* – quite *comme il faut*, I assure you, cousin. In fact, I like him extremely, and I think she may have got herself a better bargain than anyone will ever think. But he is . . .' He paused.

'For heaven's sake, James,' Jemima said crossly, 'say it out! What is wrong with the man?'

'Nothing, nothing at all. It's just that we all thought Mary was saving herself for a great match, a man who was young, handsome, rich, distinguished, powerful, and probably a duke into the bargain. And Captain Haworth is none of these things – he's just a very ordinary, nice, poor sea-officer. But Lucy says they tumbled into love with each other the first week of their acquaintance, and it only surprised her how long they took to come to an understanding.'

'Lucy likes him, then?' Jemima asked.

'Oh yes – as indeed do I. I don't think you could *dislike* him. But Lucy says Flora wrote the most amusing letter, a mixture of fury and pleading, saying that he was Unsuitable – with a capital letter – and that Mary would make the whole Morland family a laughing-stock.'

'I do not think this sounds an amusing letter, me,' Héloïse said severely. 'I think cousin Mary must have been very upset by it.'

'Not really,' James said, smiling at the memory. 'Mary is so blissfully happy with her husband, I think very little impinges on her. She is prepared to be defiant about him when he has gone back to sea and she has to rejoin the bosom of her family, but I don't think she repines, or ever will. Come now, ma'am,' he added, seeing Jemima's face still drawn in a frown, 'look a little pleased. You wanted Mary to wed, and she has. Perhaps she'll present you with some sea-puppies from her sea-dog, by way of grandchildren.'

'Really, James, your language!' she reproved him automatically. 'Well, if she really is happy, of course I am glad for her. But she always set so much store by position – she refused John Anstey in the beginning because he was only a merchant's son, and she wanted a title.'

'Mary is very different now, Mama,' James said, his expression softening as he looked at Héloïse. 'She has learned to value other things besides rank and fortune. I think she will be very happy with her "Unsuitable" man.'

September was a month for marriages: Mary's to Captain Haworth began it quietly, Lizzie Anstey's to Sir Arthur Fussell made quite a local stir in York, and Horatio Morland's to Lady Barbara Rushton reached a pinnacle of fashionable splendour. There was also the news that Amelia had become engaged very creditably to Captain the Honourable Gordon Bellingham, youngest son of the Earl of Rothbury, who had come home from Flanders to recover from a slight wound, and had fallen in love with her at a ball given at Chelmsford House just before Horatio's wedding.

At the end of August, Toulon had rebelled against the revolutionary government of France, raised the white flag of the Bourbons and declared for King Louis XVII, and opened it gates to English troops. Everyone was convinced that this was the turning-point of the war, and all efforts were to be concentrated on Toulon, with the result that Captain Haworth was recalled, given command of a seventy-four – the *Cressy* – and sent to reinforce the squadron there towards the end of September.

'So we shall have Mary back – and Lucy,' James said to Héloïse. They had taken advantage of the fine autumn weather to ride out to Marston Moor together, for Héloïse having been told of those Morlands who had died in the battle, fighting for the King, had expressed a desire to see it. They were sitting together on the dry, warm grass of Cromwell's Plump, holding the reins of Nez Carré and Goldfinch, who were grazing with the usual fervour of stable-kept horses, as if they hadn't been fed for a fortnight. 'There will be a lot of people glad to have Lucy back. She was always loved by the village people. They used to bring their ailments to her much more readily than to the doctor or the apothecary. Such a pity she was born a girl – she'd have made a fine physician.'

Héloïse nodded, looking out across the sun-baked moor, marvelling at the expanse of open sky and the fresh, wild scent of the air.

She clasped her arms about her updrawn knees in a very unladylike way, and James glanced at her sideways and smiled, and said, 'Did you always wish to be a boy when you were a child?'

'No, not really. I never thought about it.'

'Ah, you were always a good, docile child, I imagine, doing just what was expected of you,' he said.

She smiled broadly. 'Oh no, not always! The good sisters thought me a very troublesome charge. I remember how Sister Martin once said I looked like a little dark monkey, and was just as much trouble, too.'

James looked at the sad, dark eyes, and saw the resemblance, and laughed.

'But Papa said I was more like a marmoset,' she went on. 'Do you know these? They are like monkeys, but with bushy tails like squirrels, and the rich ladies have them sometimes as pets. But it is a little of a joke, for in French *marmot* means also naughty child.'

She gave him an engaging grin, and he said, 'Yes, just like a marmoset. May I call you that, too?'

'Of course, if you wish. It will be as though Papa--' She could not finish the sentence. Her concern for her father coloured all her happiness. No word had reached her, and no money had been sent from Paris. Charles, the earl, had most generously agreed to continue to pay her the pension which had stopped at the outbreak of war, so that she was no burden on Morland Place, and money was not a problem, but the news from France was of increasingly arbitrary government and savage methods of imposing it. She bit her lip, and James reached over and took her hand, and pressed it comfortingly.

'Don't be afraid,' he said. 'I'm sure that hearing nothing is to the good, in this case. I'm sure you would have heard if anything had happened to him. He is lying low, that's all.'

'Lying low?' she puzzled.

'Keeping himself safe, not drawing attention to himself, until he is able to get away. One day you will have a letter from London saying that he has arrived safe and sound and wants to see you.'

'Do you think so?' she asked, looking earnestly into his face. 'Do you really think so?'

'Yes, of course. Try not to worry,' he said, holding her gaze steadily to convince her of his sincerity. After a moment, the

370

quality of their gazing changed. A little colour touched Héloï-se's face, her lips parted, and James began, almost involuntar-ily, drawing her to him. At the last moment the enormous dark eyes closed, and their lips touched, and he felt a shudder run through her. It so moved him that he tightened his hold, and began to kiss her passionately, but she drew away from him then, and said, 'No, cousin, we must not. It would not be . . .'

'Proper?' he supplied wryly. She cocked her head.

'Not yet,' she said, and then, pressing his hands, she added, with a light of laughter in her eyes he had never seen before, 'When we are married, we shall do *everything*.'

He was so enchanted by the thought of her *everything*, and by the fervour with which she said it, that it was a moment before he registered the beginning of the sentence. Then he said, 'Are we to be married then? You and I?'

She looked puzzled. 'But of course. Do you not wish it? I thought . . .'

He thought: of having her beside him always, his companion and friend; and of having the right to hold her, and kiss her, and sleep with her in the warm dark cave of the night, and make love to her, and give her children. He said, 'Yes, I wish it.' They looked at each other in silence for a moment, and then he said, with a wicked smile, 'But you know that I have not been at all proper in my youth?'

'*Ça se voit*,' she said, shrugging. 'But you will love me better for having had the practice.'

He laughed aloud. 'What a delightfully practical way you have of looking at things, dear Marmoset! I promise you I shall be very proper once we are married.'

She smiled, and kissed his hand, in a way that made his bones melt. 'Yes, I know. I shall love you so much you will not wish to be anything else. But you know, too, that I have been a married woman? You understand that?'

He nodded. 'Did you love him?' he asked, feeling strangely shy about it.

'A wife must love her husband – it is her duty,' she said, looking away from him, into the hazy distances of the warm afternoon. 'But I was not what you call *in love* with him; nor he with me. We were married to each other for reasons of convenience, and we lived together more as friends than as man and wife.' She was silent for a moment, and then said, 'I met him for the first time when Papa took me to visit at the Château of Chenonceau. It is the most beautiful château in the world, like something out of a fairy-tale. I remember the visit so well, as if it were the last thing that happened in the old world, before the revolution came and changed everything. That world came to an end, and we – Papa and I and those we had known – we were left over from it, and somehow did not fit in the new world. But Olivier, my husband, he was there in the old world, and did not fit. He belonged in the new world, even then.' Another silence. James still had hold of her hand, and stroked it gently, not to distract her. She went on at last, 'He was like the bridge for me, which should have taken me from one to the other. But I could not keep my footing. I suppose,' she sighed, self-condemningly, 'that I did not want to.'

Her voice stopped, and there was only the sound of the bees working away amongst the wild thyme and chamomile. Nez Carré had gone to sleep, resting one hind hoof, his lower lip hanging and quivering slightly with his breathing, but Goldfinch was still determinedly grazing at the limit of his reins, tearing at the short, springy turf, the sound of his ripping teeth interspersed with the musical ringing of his bit. James felt he could have remained there happily forever, looking out over the peaceful land, with Héloïse's small hand clasped in his.

It was she who broke the silence at last by saying cheerfully, 'We have spoken of marriage, but really, we should ask *Maman* first, for perhaps she will not like it. Will she not desire you to marry someone rich?'

'You know perfectly well,' he said, amused by her unconcerned tone, 'that she will be delighted. She has almost given up hope that I will ever marry, and she regards you as a daughter already. No, no, madam, you can't get out of it so easily. You have said you will marry me, and marry me you will!'

She turned to him, laughing, 'I do not wish to get out of it, as you say! But truly, dear one, does she not have other plans for you? You see,' she grew serious, 'I know that it seems certain your brother will not marry, so all of Morland Place will go to you and your children at last, will it not?'

'Ah, now I understand – it is for Morland Place that you wish to marry me, not for myself. Well, madam, you shall be fitly punished! Don't you know I have another brother older than me, to say nothing of my sister Mary?'

She jumped to her feet. 'Pooh! Your brother William, *Maman* says, will never marry either, for he is wed to the sea. And in England as in France, daughters and their children do not inherit estates.'

James stood up too. '*Pooh*! to you too – Morland Place is not entailed, and Mother may leave it exactly how she likes, to Mary's children or anyone else. Now, do you marry me for love, or not? Confess, madam, or I shall force it out of you.'

'No, no, James, do not! You are frightening the horses! No, James, please, do not tickle me, it is not proper! It is not at all *comme il faut*! Yes, very well, I do love you!'

Nez Carré was snorting like an outraged dragon when James stopped tickling Héloïse and took her instead into his arms. Goldfinch carried on eating regardless, but the big horse watched with ears pricked as his master kissed his new fiancée very thoroughly, and the fiancée this time made no coherent objection.

Héloïse insisted that James apply properly to his mother for permission to marry, rather than merely telling her he was going to, but as he had known, Jemima was delighted with the idea, and agreed without hesitation.

'I know she has no portion, but I am so very glad you will be marrying at last, and the more I think of it, the more I see that with you it would have to be love, or you would never settle. I am so glad, dearest Jamie! She is like a daughter to me already, and she will make an excellent wife. Bring her to me now.'

James fetched Héloïse from outside the door, where she had been waiting, and Jemima merely held out her arms, and Héloïse ran to them.

'Oh, now you will be my true mother,' Héloïse said, hugging her, and Jemima returned the embrace, and could not speak for a moment.

'Well,' said James at last, 'that seems all very satisfactory. When shall it be? As soon as possible, I suppose, like Mary's, for there is nothing to wait for, is there?'

Héloïse looked shocked. 'But I must ask for Papa's consent, too! I must write to him at once.'

'But that could take months,' James frowned. 'You don't know if your letter would even reach him, or if he would be able to reply. Surely you don't need his consent?'

'I must ask him,' Héloïse insisted, looking anxious. Jemima intervened.

'My dear, as he sent you to cousin Charles, I am sure he could act in your father's place, and give his consent, if you feel it is needed. But you have, after all, been a married woman. Surely now you are able to decide for yourself?'

Héloïse turned to her. 'That is another thing, *ma mère*. I am a widow, and still in mourning. I could not marry until that period is over. I must be in mourning a year before I could marry again. It would not be proper otherwise.'

Nothing James could say would move her from that, and Jemima did not feel it her business to try. In the end he agreed to being betrothed to her, and she agreed to marry him at the end of her year's mourning, whether or not by that time she had succeeded in obtaining a reply from her father.

'April,' he grumbled. 'Wait until April, she says, as if it were next week! Mary had the right idea, with her captain.'

Héloïse smiled lovingly at him. 'It will be good for us to wait,' she said innocently. 'It will give you time to change your mind, if you are not sure.'

Because of Héloïse's circumstances, there was to be no great celebration of James's betrothal, but Mary's return home as Mrs Haworth meant a number of formal calls to be made, and she undertook to take Héloïse with her and to announce the engagement at the same time as her marriage.

Jemima was glad to have her back, and glad to have the opportunity of seeing how very happy she was in her marriage, though naturally she was also very unhappy at being parted from her husband. Lucy, too, had changed for the better, being much more grown up than when she went away, quiet, self-disciplined, and grown, through Mary's influence, into such a young lady that any parent would be glad to own. But underneath she was the same Lucy, and plunged at once and with enthusiasm into her old interests, trying to persuade one of the housemaids to let her pull a troublesome tooth for her, and joining with James in his plan for a new rig for Héloïse, to be his betrothal present to her.

'It must be different, very smart, just right for her, and draw all eyes,' he stipulated, and he and Lucy got their heads together over a large number of sheets of paper, and between them designed a dainty and delicate-looking park phaeton, which every enterprising young woman in Yorkshire would envy and covet.

'And there must be a matched pair to draw it, Jamie', Lucy insisted. 'Something eye-catching – greys, should you think?'

'No, I have a better idea. I know exactly what I want, and where to lay my hands one one – it will be matching it that will be the problem. But if I can get hold of the right pair, you will school them for me, won't you, Luce?'

'Won't Héloïse want to school them herself?'

'I don't think so,' James smiled. 'She rides very well, and drives quite nicely, but she's very much a lady, not a reformed hoyden like you.'

Lucy smiled. 'Poor James, how dull for you, to have to marry a *lady*.'

He laughed. 'You forget, infant, it's a wife I want, not a sister.'

Meanwhile, Héloïse was accompanying Mary on her round of formal visits in the small town-coach. They visited John and Louisa at the Anstey house on the Lendal, and Lizzie, now Lady Fussell, out at Fulford, and Mrs Crosby Shawe, formerly Valentina Fussell, at Bishopthorpe. Mrs Shawe, having offered all the suitable congratulations, and made enquiries after the rest of the family, and modestly admitted her own high hopes for a young olive-branch, said casually, with her eyes upon the cup of tea she was pouring:

'Have you heard, by the way, the news of old John Skelwith? He passed away last week, very quietly, in his sleep.'

'I had not heard,' Mary said after a moment.

Valentina, with a glance at Héloïse which confirmed that she knew nothing untoward about the name Skelwith, went on evenly, 'I thought I had better tell you, in case you had intended

375

to call upon Mary. You would not want to come upon her unaware.'

'No, indeed. How is she?'

'She takes it very well, upon the whole; but it must be hard for her, all the same, with a young child to care for. But I believe her husband left her very well off.'

The conversation went another way after that, and Mary, leaving at the end of the accepted time, thought that it was kind of Valentina to give her the warning like that. It was evident that Héloïse knew nothing of any past attachment between James and Mary Skelwith, but Mary wondered whether James knew that his former mistress was now free, and whether she ought to tell him. Would it be wise to stir up old fires, she pondered; on the other hand, if he were still in love with Mary Skelwith, and wished to marry her, better he disappoint Héloïse now than later. So far few people knew about the engagement: if he broke it later, when it was better known, it would be much worse for all concerned.

'Do you mind if we return home, cousin?' she asked Héloïse abruptly. 'We can finish our visits another day, but I have a little of the headache.'

'Of course, whatever you wish,' Héloïse said, brightening at the prospect of going back to James early. 'I hope you do not feel very unwell, cousin Mary.'

'It's a trifle only. I shall let down the glass this side, and the fresh air will soon make me better,' Mary said, feeling uncomfortably like a traitor.

It was not until after supper that she managed to get James alone, and even then it was with difficulty, for he spent most evenings drawing an endless series of portraits of Héloïse, and was even, now, in process of being persuaded by Jemima to do the thing properly and paint her in oils for the family collection. There came at last, however, a moment when he left the room, and Mary, excusing herself a while later, waylaid him on his way back and dragged him into her bedchamber for privacy.

'Now, Polly, what is all this?' he asked good-naturedly. 'Sharp's the word, dear girl. I want to be back to—'

'Listen, Jamie,' she interrupted urgently. 'John Skelwith is dead.' He stared at her and his face seemed to grow slowly whiter, but he said nothing. She grew nervous. 'Do you understand what I'm saying? Mary Skelwith is a widow.'

'Yes, I understand,' he said tonelessly. 'Why are you telling me this?' She made as if to touch him, and then withdrew her hand, unsure whether he was upset or angry.

'I had to be sure you knew. I hope it makes no difference, but if it does – well, don't you see, better that you find out now than later?' Still he said nothing. 'For God's sake, Jamie, you've been in love with Mary for years, and if you are going to change your mind about marrying Héloïse, it must be before everyone knows about the engagement, or there'll be another scandal.'

'Yes, all right, Polly, don't fret. I understand,' he said at last, with a curious gentleness. 'Leave me alone now, will you? I'll join you in a moment. I want to think.' She turned away, and he added quietly, 'Say nothing about this.'

She went back to the long saloon, feeling shaken, wondering if she had done the right thing. When at length James came back in, he looked to her as though he had been sick, but it seemed no-one else noticed anything untoward.

October the fourteenth was St. Edward's Day, which was also Founder's Day at St. Edward's School. It was a Morland, long ago, who had orginally endowed the school, and the Morlands had always maintained a special relationship with it and its pupils. Founder's Day began with a special service of dedication at the church, after which the main ceremony took place in the school hall. The children assembled there with the school staff and governors, and the Morland family were the guests of honour. The children entertained with songs and musical performances, and there were speeches, and prizegiving for outstanding scholars. After that the children lined up and came one by one to the dais to give Jemima a single white flower and to receive from her the Founder's Day Penny.

After that came what was probably the highlight of the day for the children: the Founder's Feast, a lavish dinner for all, provided by the Governors, but in fact largely contributed by the Morland family. When the Feast was over, the children had the rest of the day for a holiday, and the family went home to prepare for what had become in recent years the traditional ball.

The Earl of Aylesbury had timed his visit to Edward to coincide with the Founder's celebrations, which he had enjoyed in other years. He was also agog to see Lucy again and hear her adventures from her own lips, and, having heard all about Captain Haworth from Flora, he was also interested to see Mary and discover from her own lips why it was she had fallen in love with him. On the morning after the ball, he and Edward rose early and went for a long walk together to Clifton Ings and along the bank of the river, in order to have the privacy to catch up with each other's news.

When they reached a favourite stopping place – a place where a tree growing right on the river's edge had slipped and grown crooked, so that its lower trunk was horizontal, and made a comfortable seat, shaded by the higher branches – they sat down together, and after a short silence, Chetwyn fetched a sigh that made Edward say, 'Is something troubling you?'

'Yes – not something new. An old trouble, which I ought to have attended to long ago, and which is only growing worse for being neglected.'

Edward was alarmed. 'You aren't ill?'

'No, rest easy, Ned, I'm as strong as a horse. No, it's something I ought to have done when my Governor died and I took the title. And now . . .' He sighed again. 'It's getting desperate, my dear. I really have to think about marrying.'

Edward was startled. 'Marrying? Marrying a *woman*, do you mean?' Chetwyn gave a shout of laughter.

'Of course a woman, you idiot! Do you think I meant a horse?'

'Oh, hush! You know what I mean. I had never thought – I mean, what brought this on?'

'You of all people ought to know that. Hasn't your mother told you again and again to get married? Well, not of late, I grant you, but you have brothers, which I have not. Also Morland Place isn't entailed, and you have no title. But, Ned, though I've no mother to nag me about it, it's been on my mind a lot recently. I must marry and get an heir, and frankly, my dear, the idea appalls me.'

'I should think it would,' Edward said sympathetically. 'Have you someone in mind?'

'Well, there is one possibility – the daughter of a mill-owner in Lancashire. He's one of these what-you-may-calls, a Cotton King, and as rich as Croesus, and his daughter is his heiress, and will have everything. Now I can't pretend that the estate couldn't stand a little extra money pumped into it, and the Cotton King – Hobsbawn is his name, – is dead set on having a title for his daughter. So I suppose it would be a good thing. But . . .' He grimaced.

'But?' Edward prompted.

'Oh, *you* know! The idea of marrying a completely strange woman, of having her around the house all the time, filling up the rooms with clutter and women's smells and women's ailments – female servants – tea-drinking parties. And then having to – having children. Lord! I'd have to get myself as drunk as a wheelbarrow before I could touch her, and then – who knows? And if she turned out to be a shrew, Ned? If she didn't like my coming here to see you and my second mother? If she--' He did not go on, but Edward knew what he meant. He thought of shrill-tongued contumely and insult being poured on his friend by a woman who did not understand his delicate nature. Edward patted his hand sympathetically.

'Yes, I know. It's dreadful. Isn't there anyone else?'

'Oh, I dare say there would be, but what then? It will be all the same, whoever I marry. All women are the same. You know I could never tell one of them apart from the others. But I must marry and get an heir – it's my duty, and one must perform one's duty, however disagreeable.'

Edward nodded, thinking how lucky he was to have brothers, and then how it was a pity that one couldn't marry one of one's own sisters, who at least knew all about one. And then he had his Great Idea. His face lit, and he seized Chetwyn's wrist so fiercely that it made him wince.

'I have it! I have the solution!'

'Yes, Ned, maybe, but don't break my arm,' he chided gently.

'Oh – sorry! But listen – why not marry Lucy?'

'Lucy? Your sister, Lucy?'

'Of course – it's the perfect solution! You know how much

you like her – we've always got on together, the three of us. She's good fun to be with, and not at all *missish*. She wouldn't fill the house with clutter – she likes horses and hunting and suchlike much more than fashion and gossip and those women's things – and she's sensible, and since she ran away to sea, she talks like a man, and has plenty to say for herself. You wouldn't be dull.'

'No – but look, Ned, what about an heir? It's all very well having Lucy as a friend, but what about the other business?'

'Well, don't you see, that'd be all right too! She knows all about us, and would never mind coming to visit here, and she wouldn't expect you to be in love with her. And for the physical side – well, she's helped with foalings and so on since she was a little girl, and she knows all about breeding, and she's been used to doctoring people so she's not at all squeamish. She'd go about the whole thing in a businesslike, sensible, practical way.'

'Ye-es,' Chetwyn said slowly, thinking about it. He liked Lucy enormously, and could see that with someone who regarded the business as something purely medical that had to be gone through, someone who wasn't an innocent, fluttering virgin, but who knew all about it, at least from a theoretical point of view . . . 'Yes, but would she agree? I mean, why should *she* want to marry *me*? I should think it would be the last thing she'd want.'

Edward grinned. 'Not the last, my dear. Leave that to me. I think I know of a few reasons to put to her, that she would see the point of. Well, is it agreed? Shall I ask her for you?'

'If you really think she would . . .'

'I do. And if she wanted to, I'm sure Mother wouldn't stand in your way.'

'Well, I do think it would be much less dreadful marrying Lucy than any other woman. And the three of us could go on being jolly together, just as we have done here.'

'I'll talk to her then, as soon as we get home.'

To Lucy, Edward used many of the same arguments. She listened to him in silence, and then said, 'Yes, Edward, I see what you are saying, and I do like Chetwyn very much – but why should I want to be married at all? I can't see why I shouldn't just go on living here with you for the rest of my life.'

Edward shook his head sadly. 'I never thought to hear you speak so unadventurous. You, who ran away to sea! I'll tell you why, Lucy: because if you married Chetwyn you would have an establishment of your own, and you could do what you liked with it. You could set up your own stud, for instance – you'd like that, wouldn't you? – and try out all your own pet theories for breeding and schooling. No-one could stop you doctoring your own horses. You'd have a whole household of servants to doctor, too, and if anyone dared to frown at you for it – why, you'd be a countess! You could frown them down with no difficulty.'

'Hmm,' she said, with dawning interest. He had another idea.

'And you remember what you were saying yesterday at St. Edward's? About how it was wrong that there should be such schools for boys but not for girls? Well, you could start up your own school if you wanted. Lady Aylesbury's School for Gentlewomen – I can see it now. Or you could found a hospital, or anything. With a title, and wealth, it wouldn't matter so much your being a girl. Think of all the good you could do! You could begin to change the way people think.'

'Yes,' she said, her eyes beginning to shine, 'yes. I see!' A sudden doubt. 'But wouldn't Chetwyn mind? Would he let me do these things? Wouldn't he want a proper female for his countess, the sort that giggles and vapours?'

'Don't be silly,' Edward said.

Lucy and Chetwyn looked at each other cautiously, even a little shyly.

'You'd let me do what I liked?' she said. 'I mean, what Edward said: start a school for girls, for instance, or breed horses, or doctor my own servants?'

'Of course,' Chetwyn said. 'I shouldn't mind – it would be jolly. I could help you.' He coloured a little as he went on, 'But we'd have to – there'd have to be some children. You know, an heir.'

Lucy was brisk. 'That's all right – we could do that. In fact, if we had a lot – well, several – we could try out different ways of bringing them up and educating them. I'm not at all sure some of the things we do are right.'

Edward grinned triumphantly. 'I told you it would be all right,' he said, putting his arm across Chetwyn's shoulder. 'Now we only have to talk to Mother. You'll be my brother, James – won't that be good?'

When Jemima had got over being astonished, she began to like the idea, and the more she thought about it, the more she liked it.

'Lucy a countess!' she said. 'What a marvel! She'll astonish the world from that position of advantage. But, Chetwyn, are you sure she's what you want for a countess? I mean, she may not do you much credit in society – though she has improved beyond measure since Mary took her in hand. But I'm afraid she's still a sad hoyden.'

'Oh, Mother,' Lucy said crossly, 'of course I'll do the polite when it's necessary. I'm not such a child as all that.'

'I think she's exactly what I want ma'am,' Chetwyn said, smiling affectionately at Jemima, 'especially as she brings for her dowry the person I've always wanted for a mother.'

'Oh yes, dowry,' Jemima said, ignoring all this. 'Well, of course, I shall have to give her something – and there's a little money which Allen settled on her in his will. I should think she may have ten thousand.'

'I don't want money, ma'am,' Chetwyn said. 'She's treasure enough in herself.'

'Well *I* want money,' Lucy said firmly. 'When you get over being polite to me, and start to come the ugly, and tell me I can't have this and that, I want to have money of my own so that I can stand up to you.'

The young men shouted with laughter, but Lucy stood firm, and Jemima, smiling, agreed with her. 'It's a great thing to have a little independence,' she said. 'Take the ten thousand, Chetwyn, and settle it on your bride.'

'It can be her running-away money, in case she takes a notion to join the army and fight the French single-handed,' Edward said.

'Then it's agreed?' said Chetwyn, looking from Jemima to Lucy. Lucy nodded and looked at her mother.

'If you are both happy, then I am. But, Chetwyn, she's not fifteen until the end of the month. When were you thinking of taking her?'

'Whenever you say, ma'am. She's young, but very grown up for her age. But it will take me a while to arrange things, legal things, and to get the house ready to receive a bride.'

'Well then, what do you say to next spring? April or May next year? Does that suit you both? Then I can take a little time to teach Lucy the basic things she should know about running a house, for I'm afraid, for all her medical knowledge, she's as ignorant as a butterfly of domestic science.'

'Yes, next spring will do very well,' Chetwyn said, and Lucy nodded. Jemima looked at her with affectionate astonishment. Lucy a countess! she thought. She had never expected to get her off so creditably, especially after her adventure, which, indeed, she had thought had prohibited her from ever marrying respectably. She remembered Lucy as a pretty, chubby baby, always dirty and dishevelled, running after Harry and Jack, but with a smile and a hug for every living creature. She was growing tall now, and after Mary's summer school she had learnt how to hold and dress herself. Her cropped hair was growing curly, and she had the makings of a fine and handsome woman. She might make Chetwyn a better countess than any conventional debutante, after all. She put an arm round Lucy's shoulder and kissed her rosy cheek.

'Allen would have been so pleased,' she said.

20

Paris, the Convention, and all of France, was ruled by the Committee of Public Safety, with Robespierre at its head. Henri was at times amazed to see twelve such diverse characters – sometimes called, not without irony, the Twelve Just Men – acting with such apparent concord; amazed, too, to find Robespierre, a man of iron virtue, working hand in hand with such amoral characters as Collot d'Herbois and Hérault de Séchelles and Billaud-Varennes, and yet still talking about the basic goodness of Man. What united them was an at least spoken belief that the revolution was good and that everything else was by definition evil. Saint-Just, that coldly handsome young man that Vendenoir had so admired, summed it up in a public speech: 'What constitutes the Republic is the complete destruction of everything that is opposed to it.'

One of the things to be destroyed in the November of 1793 was Christianity. The calendar was suppressed, with its Christian echoes of Sundays and feast-days, and in its place a new system was imposed, with a ten-day week, the months named after the seasons, and the years numbered from the Republic instead of from the Incarnation. It was a signal for the more unruly elements of society to sack the churches, rob them of any remaining wealth, and put up statues of Rousseau and Voltaire in place of those of the saints.

One of the thorns in Robespierre's side was Hébert, editor of the *Père Duchesne*, a revolutionary newspaper whose language was violent and whose invective was of an unparalleled salacity. Hébert was influential in the Commune, and had inherited the gutter kingdom of the murdered Marat, which demanded a yet more extreme, violent and popular revolution. Henri watched with wry amusement as Robespierre, now with all the power he wanted, became the one to say 'The Revolution stops with me,' and to deplore the extremism of the Hébertists. The Hébertists wanted Christianity completely banned, and forced the Bishop of Paris publicly to abjure his faith and demanded of the Convention that there should be no worship in France but that of Liberty and Equality.

And it was the Hébertists who organised the Festival of Reason in the cathedral of Notre Dame: a Greek temple was built of cardboard in the nave, the religious embellishments of the cathedral were removed, and an actress from the Opéra was enthroned as the Goddess of Reason. Revolutionary songs were sung, and the worshippers dancing grew wilder and more abandoned, until men and women were whirling about half-naked, screaming like mad creatures, and reeling away to couple like beasts in dark corners of the sacred precinct.

The affair shocked and disgusted the ordinary, quiet citizens of Paris. That this blasphemy was performed in their name sickened them, as did the violence of the punishment meted out to those towns in the provinces which had rebelled against the revolutionary government. In September, when the Vendée, Lyons and Toulon had rebelled, the Convention had declared that 'Terror is the order of the day'. The army marched in and suppressed the rebellions, but in its wake came the officers sent out by the Committee. In Lyons, the guillotine did not work fast enough for Collot d'Herbois. He abandoned it for mass executions by firing-squad, and then had citizens lined up by the hundred before ditches, and mowed down with cannon. In the Vendée, Carrier despatched the victims in mass drownings in the Loire, and had several thousand peasant children assembled in a field and shot.

'But what can anyone do?' Marie-France said in a low voice when she and Henri discussed these things. He took his dinner with her and the child most days now, and the simple food and *petit bourgeois* surroundings reminded him of his life with Madeleine in the early days. He probably talked to her more freely because of it.

'However much we hate these things, we dare not speak out against them,' she said. 'Hébert rules the Commune, and the Commune rules the Sections; and it is the officials of the Section committees who decide who shall be put on the list of suspects for having insufficient revolutionary fervour.' She sighed. 'I don't understand anything any more. It's as if the world had gone mad.'

'Only a little while longer,' Henri comforted her. 'Just until spring, then we'll leave.'

'You'll take me with you?' she said in sudden panic, catching at his hand.

'Of course, of course. Don't be afraid. There is still Danton. Danton will hold things in check for a little longer.'

It seemed, indeed, as though he would. He had been out of Paris, visiting his farm, but when he returned in November, he began a campaign against the terror. In December, Toulon fell to the revolutionary army, thanks in great part to the skill and initiative of the young officer in command of the artillery, a Corsican called Buonaparte, and Danton stood up in the Convention to demand an end to the atrocities and a new rule of clemency.

'Perhaps the Terror had its place, when the Republic was in danger; but now those emergencies are over. Open the prisons! No-one wishes to see an individual treated as a criminal because he does not display sufficient revolutionary vigour.'

Danton's friend Camille supported him, writing in his column in the newspaper *Vieux Cordelier*: 'Love of country cannot exist where there is neither pity nor love for one's fellow countrymen. Release the two hundred thousand suspects who are imprisoned! In the *Declaration of Man's Rights* there is no house of suspicion, only houses of arrest.'

But however the great silent majority of the Plain might have welcomed a rule of clemency, they were too afraid to come to Danton's support. His speeches were listened to in silence, Camille's diatribes in the *Vieux Cordelier* were read avidly as they came off the press, but in secret. In January, Fabre d'Églantine was arrested, and soon afterwards Hérault de Séchelles, the only member of the Committee friendly to Danton; and members of the Convention began to fear being seen with Danton, and crossed the road to avoid him.

Mary had been resigned to having to pretend to enjoy Christmas, but the loss of Toulon and the withdrawal of the squadron from its harbour resulted in the *Cressy*'s being sent home to England, and a fortnight's leave for her captain. As soon as he was able to leave his ship, Haworth threw economy to the winds and travelled post up to Yorkshire. Mary was sitting in the drawing-room, reading without much interest, when the door opened and Lucy came in looking excited.

'Mary, guess who's here!' she exclaimed, but had no time for more, for she was almost bundled out of the way, and a whirlwind passed her, and Mary and her husband were in each other's arms in the middle of the room.

'What are you doing here?' she managed to say, though he was holding her so tightly she had trouble drawing breath.

'Leave,' he said succinctly in between kisses. '*Cressy*'s in dry dock – sprang a timber off Spithead. Only just got her in. I came post – Oh, Mary!'

'Oh, my darling!'

'This is all very well, you know,' Lucy said at last, 'but you haven't even met the rest of the family.'

Mary broke away from him in a hurry, and said, red-faced, 'Go away, you abominable child!'

Haworth laughed and slipped an arm round her waist. 'No, no, Lucy's right, this is very poor behaviour. Come, love, let's do the pretty. Where is everyone?'

'Mother's in the steward's room doing accounts with Edward,' Lucy said, 'and Jamie and Héloïse are out riding, but they should be back soon. I say, did you really come post from Portsmouth? It must have cost you a fortune! If you'd only gone to London, you could have come up tomorrow with Lord and Lady Chelmsford. They're coming for Christmas, to Shawes. We're going to have a splendid Christmas this year, except that William and Harry and Jack won't be here, but Mother says we can't look for them until the end of next year. I'm glad you have come, though. Did you know I am going to be married?'

'Oh Lucy, do stop chattering,' Mary said, leading her husband to the door. Lucy hopped in their wake, continuing as if she had not spoken.

'I'm to marry Edward's friend Chetwyn – you remember I told you about him in Bath? He's the Earl of Aylesbury really, so I shall be a countess – isn't that a joke! He's coming for Christmas too, you'll be able to meet him.'

387

'I'm very glad to hear it,' Haworth said, smiling at her. 'And my hearty congratulations on your good news.'

'Thank you. Mother's pleased, and I think Mary's relieved more than anything, for she was sure I would never marry at all after running away to sea.'

'Oh Lucy, why can't you forget that awful incident? If you keep talking about it, people will never forget it,' Mary said.

'I don't want them to forget it,' Lucy said stoutly. 'I said I'd be a doctor, and I was, and a very good one, too.' They reached the door of the steward's room, and she dropped back. 'I'm going out to the stables, Captain Haworth. If you'd like to see the horses when you've said hello to Mother, do come out, and I'll shew you round.'

'Thank you,' he said gravely, and Mary grimaced at her, and opened the door. The steward's room presented a cosy aspect on a gloomy December afternoon, for there was a huge and spitting log fire in the chimney, before which Edward's dogs, Leaky and Brach, were toasting their bellies and paws, and several working-candles to brighten the room. Jemima, with paper cuffs over her sleeves, was at the table with the account books open in front of her, and Edward stood behind her, leaning over her shoulder with his head against hers. He had pushed her cap awry, giving her a very human look which made Haworth smile.

Jemima looked up as they came in, and then, realising who Haworth must be, stared with more honest curiosity than politeness. The 'Unsuitable Sea-Captain' presented himself to her gaze as a shortish, roundish man in a shabby blue uniform coat whose buttons were only too obviously not real gold. The front and top of his head were bald, though what hair he had was thick and brown and inclined to be curly. His face at first glance was plain, at second distinguished by a sweetness of expression, a firm and beautiful mouth, and a pair of very humorous blue eyes. Jemima was reminded of her husband Allen, and after a moment realised why: it was because he looked *kind*. Kindness would be this man's guiding principle in all things, she thought, and liked him instantly, and was glad for Mary.

'Mother,' Mary was saying unnecessarily, and with a touching shyness, 'I should like to present my husband, Captain Haworth.'

Jemima rose and went round the table to give him both her hands. He took them and met her eye with perfect understanding, and she smiled and offered him her cheek, too, to be kissed, so that he would be sure of his welcome.

'I am delighted to meet you at last, captain,' she said.

'And I you, ma'am. I'm sorry I married your daughter in such haste, without coming to see you first, but the fortunes of war make matters so uncertain.' He gave a sidelong grin at Mary. 'Besides, Mary was so insistent, I dared not defy her. It would take a stronger man than me to resist her, once she had her mind set on something.'

Jemima laughed. 'If you understand that, you will be happy! My eldest son, Edward.'

Edward shook hands, surveyed the captain and decided he liked him, and said, 'How goes the war, sir? Losing Toulon must have been a blow, I fancy?'

'It was very smart work on the part of the French, I have to say,' Haworth replied. 'I won't pretend it wasn't a blow, but we'll lick 'em in the end. If what we hear about the cruelties that have been going on is true, their own people may well rise up before long, and save us the trouble of toppling their government.'

'Do you stay long, captain?' Jemima asked. 'Will you be with us for Christmas?'

'If you'll have me, ma'am. I have leave of two weeks.'

'Good, then stay, and welcome,' Edward said. 'Do you hunt? We have very good hunting here about, and I can easily find you a horse. Perhaps you'd like to look around the place? I dare say Mary will have told you something about it.'

'She has,' he said, his eyes twinkling, 'I am in great hopes of seeing the ghosts and finding the hidden treasure.'

'Ghosts? What ghosts?' Edward said, puzzled.

'I think he's teasing you, Ned' Jemima discovered. 'Come, shall we go into the drawing-room and have some tea? I dare say the captain could welcome a cup, after his long journey. Or perhaps you'd like something stronger?'

Haworth further endeared himself to Jemima by joining in with a good will with the Christmas celebrations, beginning by going out on Christmas Eve with Edward, Chetwyn and James to fetch in the Yule log. It was lit with the usual carols and prayers, and Héloïse watched it all with round eyes, wondering that anything so obviously pagan could be celebrated in such a Christian way. Later in the evening the heavy curtains were drawn against the cold and dark outside, and the drawing-room glowed with firelight and candlelight, and Mary sat down at the old harpsichord, which she could make sound sweeter than anyone else, and they sang all the old traditional carols together. Captain Haworth proved to have a very strong, clear, true voice, and led the singing, standing beside the instrument with his eyes never leaving Mary's face.

On the sofa, James and Héloïse sat as close as they could get to each other, black head and foxy head leaning together; and Lucy, Edward and Chetwyn shared the other sofa and put in harmonies, laughing when they went wrong. They were a trio, Jemima thought, like three brothers, as close as triplets: perhaps it would start a new fashion in marriages! Father Thomas looked around him indulgently, and beat the time on his knee, humming tunelessly; and the dogs snored on the hearth, their paws twitching, dreaming of the roast goose to come. It was a good scene: a warm, safe, family scene, and for a moment Jemima could almost believe she felt Allen's presence in the empty place beside her. Sleep well, my love, she said in her thoughts, all's well.

On St. Stephen's Day there was the traditional hunt, and the party from Shawes came over for the meet, as well as other friends and neighbours, and those who did not actually hunt spent a happy day inside Morland Place by the fire, drinking hot punch and exchanging gossip. Charles and Flora had a large party at Shawes, for as well as Horatio and his new bride, and Amelia and her fiancé, there was also Sophia, Lady Carlton, with her husband and two sons, and Charles's cousin from Northumberland, Maurice, Viscount Ballincrea, with his son Lord Rathkeale and his daughter Helena, a dashing young maiden of fifteen who was longing to hear Lucy's story.

In the evening there was the hunt ball, held at Shawes, in the great ballroom which had been modelled on the Galerie des

Glaces at Versailles. Héloïse, standing in the first set for the first dance with Jamie, found it all too French. She looked along the line of dancers, their soft, pretty-coloured clothes reflected many times in the long, gilt-framed mirrors; she looked at the hundreds of candles glittering in chandeliers and sconces, and the older folk and chaperons watching from the side, sitting on the spindly-legged gilt chairs around the walls; and she found tears coming to her eyes. James, sensitive to her moods, took her hand and led her out of the set.

'What is it, love?' She looked at him with her dark eyes swimming with misery, unable to speak. 'Homesick?' he guessed, and she nodded. 'My poor darling,' he murmured, with vast but helpless sympathy.

Héloïse swallowed hard, 'This made me think of Versailles, and the poor King,' she said. 'And my first ball, at Chenonceau – I had such a beautiful dress, James, cream silk and pale pink in stripes, and the most beautiful new c-c-corset.' He pressed his lips together, knowing he must not laugh, but she did not notice. 'And Papa gave me a necklace to go with it, pink shells and coral, and I loved it so, I swore I'd never part with it, but I left it behind in F–France.' She ended with a choked-off sob, and two tears welled over onto her cheeks. James could say nothing to comfort her, only offer her his handkerchief.

He waited until she had emerged from it a little more composed, and then said, 'It is very hard, I know, but if you had not left France, I should never have met you. And I do love you, so very much.'

She gave him a wavering smile. 'Yes,' she said. 'I love you, too.' In a little while she was dry-eyed and smiling again, and he led her back to the set. She was, after all, only sixteen, and this was a ball.

Later she danced several dances with Lord Rathkeale, who told her a great deal about her new-found family. He was a sort of cousin of hers, too, for he was the great-grandson of Maurice Morland the composer, who had been brother to Aliena, Héloïse's great-grandmother. Lord Rathkeale was handsome and charming and a great flirt, and Héloïse learned something else from him: that she was no longer a little dark monkey-child, as she had grown used to thinking of herself, but an attractive young woman.

Later, when James came to reclaim her hand, he said sternly, 'I'll have you know, madame, that I intend to be a very jealous husband. If you insist on dancing and flirting with handsome noblemen, I shall be forced to take up duelling, which I have always considered an unpleasant and wasteful business.'

'Lord Rathkeale was telling me such interesting things,' Héloïse said.

'I know exactly what he was telling you, and I'm not surprised you found it interesting. But in future, if anyone is to tell you you are as beautiful as an angel, it is to be me, do you understand?'

'Yes, James,' Héloïse said demurely. 'Would you like to shew me the orangery? *Maman* says it is most interesting.'

James gave her a wicked grin, and tucked her hand under his arm. 'I think I had better, in case Lord Rathkeale offers.'

Mary and Captain Haworth were sitting in a shaded corner of the orangery with their arms round each other, and Mary sighed and dropped her head onto his shoulder.

'Hmm?' he enquired gently.

'The time passes so quickly,' she said. 'I hate to think you will soon be going away again.'

'It's my duty,' he said.

'I know. I knew what to expect when I married a naval officer, but . . .'

'No, dearest,' he corrected gently. 'I am a sea-officer. A naval officer is one of those dockyard officials who makes life miserable for sea-officers.'

'Well I know that,' Mary said with spirit. 'Don't quibble.' He laughed at her change of mood, and she settled on his shoulder again and said, 'How long have you got?'

'I really ought to leave on the second,' he said. 'There will be a great deal to do, and I ought not to leave it until the last moment.'

'Only a week?' she said, dismayed. He pulled her closer, and kissed her brow.

'I know. I feel the same. But listen, dearest, I know it is a great deal to ask, but would you come with me to Portsmouth? We could take a room at an inn, and then I'd be able to see you until the last minute, right up until we sail. I hate to ask you but'

'Oh, you fool! Of course I'll come. Why would I not?'

'I didn't think you'd like it. Portsmouth in January is not pleasant, and you would be much more comfortable at home.'

'Home is where you are. And what does comfort matter? All that matters is to be with you,' she said. She lifted her face to his and he kissed her, and they were so absorbed with each other that they did not notice James and Héloïse enter a few moments later. The young lovers looked at them with indulgence, and tiptoed away to the other end of the orangery, so as not to disturb them.

On the morning after the ball, James unveiled his portrait of Héloïse, finished at last. Everyone exclaimed over it, and called it a 'speaking likeness'.

'It's not near as good as the drawings were,' James said with a frown. 'Somehow when I began painting I lost it. Perhaps I should try something smaller. I might try my hand at a miniature.'

'I think it's very good,' Jemima said loyally. 'It shall have a place of honour in the long saloon – that picture of Prince Hal can go into the dining-room to make space for it.'

'If you are serious about trying a miniature,' Haworth said, 'could I perhaps commission you to do one of Mary? I should love to have such a thing, to take with me to sea.'

James looked doubtful. 'Well, I suppose so, if you like. But when do you go back? I don't know if I could get it ready in time.'

Lucy clapped her hands. 'Oh do, James, it would be the very thing! You've a whole week yet, plenty of time. You could go into York this morning and get what you need, and start right away.'

James allowed himself to be persuaded, provided, he said, he could get a suitable bit of ivory. He took the opportunity of calling in at the coachmaker's to see how the phæton was coming along, and then went to the supplier he patronised in Stonegate. Then, since he was so close, he decided to drop into the Maccabees' Club, which was on the corner of Stonegate and Little Stonegate, to read the newspapers. While he was still there, Charles strolled in.

'Ah, bent on the same mission as myself!' Charles said. 'Anything of interest in the Chronicle?'

'Here, I've finished with it,' James said, passing it across. 'It was a splendid ball yesterday, by the by.'

'I'm glad you enjoyed it. I saw you leading your fiancée away – she looked rather upset. Nothing serious, I hope?'

'She was homesick. The ballroom reminded her of Versailles.'

'Ah, yes. Poor little thing. It's a bad business. Nothing from her father yet? No, I thought not. Between you and me, James, I wouldn't be surprised if he hadn't got into trouble, the way things are going over there. Wouldn't do to say so to her, of course, but . . .'

'Yes, I've been thinking so myself,' James said. 'But one has to keep cheerful for her sake. Well, I must be off – I only came into York to buy some odds and ends.'

'Something important?'

'I came to get a bit of ivory. Haworth wants me to do a miniature of Mary, to take with him to sea.'

'Commissioned you, eh?' Charles looked thoughtful. 'I wonder – how would you like some more work of that sort, James?'

'Portraits?'

'No, not that – wall paintings. You know the panels in the great hall at Shawes – the alcoves to either side of the pilasters? Well, I've been looking at the original plans, and they were meant to have paintings in them, you know, what-you-may-calls . . .'

'*Trompe l'oeil?*'

'That's the thing. Pastoral scenes, nymphs and the like. The countess never got 'em done, but Flora and I have a fancy to get the thing finished. How would you like to do the job for us?'

'I'd like to very much, if you're sure it's me you want.'

'Oh, quite sure. Much better keep it in the family. Besides, I'd like to have something of yours. Tonbridge showed me a very clever cartoon you did, of King George and the Whigs. Is that agreed, then?'

'Yes, by all means. Thank you.'

Charles grinned. 'It will give you something to think about, until your marriage comes off! She's a fetching little thing, I must say. Strange to see her at last, after paying her a pension all these years. I hope you hear something soon, about her father,' he added civilly. James thanked him without optimism.

He had left Nez Carré at an inn on the corner of Grape Lane, and when he had collected him he rode through the back lane and emerged into St. Sampson's Square, and almost bumped into Mary Skelwith, holding her child by the hand, and followed by a maid. She was in heavy black mourning, with a half-veil over her hair, but even so he could see how pale and drawn her face was. They both stopped dead, staring at each other, and then James, with an effort, raised his hat and bowed slightly from the saddle.

'I hope I see you well, ma'am,' he said stiffly. She looked up at him, and then gave the child's hand to the maid, and told them to go and wait a little way off.

When they were alone, she said, 'Is it true?' her voice was so low he had to lean down from the saddle to hear. 'Is it true you are to be married?'

'Yes, it's true.'

'I didn't believe it when I heard. After all you'd said. But you did not even enquire after me, so I suppose I should have known.'

He looked puzzled. 'I don't understand. I thought you did not want to see me again. That last time in Scarborough, you said . . .'

'I said I loved you,' she said painfully, raising her eyes to his.

'But you said you would never wed me, not even if – if he died.'

'It's different now!' she cried. 'That was then – now it's different! How could I tell what it would be like? But you said you loved me, only me.'

'Mary, please don't.'

'It's not too late – you aren't married yet. You could change your mind.'

'I can't,' he said, low and anguished. She drew a sharp breath, and then let it out slowly, staring at him.

'You don't want to,' she said flatly.

He returned her gaze steadily. 'No, I don't want to. I love her. I'm sorry, Mary. It's too late – everything's changed.'

'Too late,' she replied dazedly. Then she seemed to shake

herself, looking round the square as if she had not been sure where she was, and drew on her dignity like a garment. 'Please have the goodness to forget this conversation, Mr Morland,' she said harshly. 'I wish you – good day.'

She turned away abruptly, hurrying across the square, caught her child's hand and almost dragged him away, disappearing down Davygate with the maid scurrying behind her. James rode on slowly, turning Nez Carré's head into Feasegate almost without noticing where he was going. His heart felt sore and he wished with all his might it had not happened. He had wanted Mary so long, that it tore him, however sure he was that he now loved Héloïse. And he was sure. Yes, he had been right to refuse Mary. Even taking into consideration the child, he was sure he had been right.

Charles went back to London on the second of January, partly because he had some business to transact, but mostly out of his good nature, so that he could offer transport to the Haworths. Mary was so used to sharing Flora's life, that she made nothing of it, but the captain thanked Charles with a thoughtful look which proved he understood how much money the earl was trying to save him.

His business done, Charles dined at his club, read the papers, and then, declining a game of picquet with the First Lord, walked home to Chelmsford House. Hawkins the butler opened the door to him looking ruffled, proof enough to Charles that something untoward had happened.

'My lord, there is a young person here, demanding to see your lordship. I informed her that your lordship would be away all day, but she insisted on waiting.'

'A young person?'

'A French young person,' Hawkins elaborated with muted horror.

Charles was intrigued. 'A lady?'

'A lady's maid, I should say, my lord, if I ventured to guess. I put her in the business-room.'

'Very well, I'll go and see her. It's all right, you needn't wait. I don't think I shall be in danger, even if she is French.'

In the business-room, a small dark female in plain travelling-clothes sat very neatly on the edge of an upright chair, her hands in her lap and her portmanteau at her feet, as if she had been sitting like that a very long time without moving. When Charles entered she rose, surveyed his face comprehensively, and then gave a deep curtsy.

'Ah, at last, you are *milord*! Monsieur le Comte de Chelmsford.'

'Yes, mademoiselle. What can I do for you?' Charles said politely.

'I seek madame. I wish to see my lady.'

'Madame la Comtesse?' Charles said, puzzled. She frowned.

'Pardon, *milord*, my English is not good. I wish to see *my* lady – Madame Vendenoir. One told me she is here.'

'Ah, Héloïse, you mean!' Charles exclaimed, the light dawning. 'You are Héloïse's maid, the one who went missing.'

'I am Marie, *milord*,' she said, evidently not understanding all this. 'Is my lady here?'

'No, she is in Yorkshire. But what are you doing here?' Marie looked pained, and he grinned and sat down on a chair opposite her. 'Tell me everything, slowly, from the beginning. *En français*, if you prefer. If it's slow enough I should manage,' he added to himself in a mutter.

The express arrived for Héloïse at Morland Place on the morning of the fourth. The family watched her open and read it, but so many different expressions seemed to flit across her face, that they could not tell if it was good news or bad. At last she looked up.

'It is from cousin Charles. My maid Marie is with him. But Lotti is dead – my friend, Lotti.'

The tale was unfolded. Lotti had never recovered her health after her flight from Paris. Ernst had written to Nordubois to tell him she was dying, and Nordubois had gone at once, arriving in time to be with her at the end. Ernst had offered to keep the children, but Nordubois had taken them away. He had asked Marie if she wished to stay in his service, but she had said what she really wanted was to rejoin her mistress in England. Nordubois had undertaken to send her, and on arriving at Antwerp he had been to visit one of Henri's agents, to see if there was any message Marie could carry to her mistress. It was lucky he arrived when he did, for a message and another consignment of money had just arrived, and Nordubois, judging from the agent's behaviour, guessed that neither would have gone any further had he not intercepted them.

He had put Marie on a ship at the first opportunity, and sent a message back down the line that Frankel was not to be trusted any more.

'Cousin Charles writes that a large sum in gold has been put with a banker for me, and I can draw upon it as I like,' Héloïse was still reading.

'Oh, excellent!' Jemima said. 'Just in time – you can buy your wedding clothes with it, and have the pretty things you want.'

But Héloïse did not appear to have heard. She was staring straight ahead of her, her face pale. James caught her wrist.

'What is it, Marmoset? Is it bad news? Tell me!'

'Papa,' she said, and had to wet her lips before she could go on. 'Papa is well, and safe. He will be leaving Paris in the spring, and coming to England. Papa will be here in the spring!' Her eyes went from one face to another, far too bright, and as the exclamations of pleasure and congratulations began, the shining tears slipped over, and she was crying and laughing all at once.

21

Spring came early to Paris in 1794: a spring of extraordinary beauty, of tender budding, of lambent skies, of sparkling, crystal light. Hope revived in Henri's heart: the world was too beautiful to believe the worst could happen. He went out of Paris at the beginning of March to the Touraine to complete his work at Chambord, and the further he went from Paris the less he could believe in the blood and the terror and the hatred. France was his country, his home; all he was, was of her. If he left France, he would be nothing. It was one thing to send Héloïse to the safety of England, for she was a child and could make her life anywhere; but for him, exile would be like a living death. He gulped as he realised that he did not want to go, that his feeling was so strong that it seemed at that moment that death would be preferable.

He had promised Marie-France that he would be back in Paris for Morland's second birthday, and he arrived back in Paris on the sixteenth of March, bearing a present for the little boy which he knew would please him and his mother: a toy horse on wheels that had belonged to Louis XV in his childhood. He left his horse at home and walked to the rue Papillon, and was let into the house by Jean, who grinned and shuffled and jangled the keys, and finally admitted that his mother had gone to market, but said that he thought it would be all right to let Henri in. Henri restrained his impatience, knowing that if he tried to hurry the boy it would confuse him and perhaps lead him to refuse entry altogether.

Then he was running up the stairs; the door was opened, and little Morland saw him and came running across the drawing-room, arms out, not solely to balance him, crying, 'Papa! Papa's come home! Come and see, maman!'

Henri swept the child up, lifted him to the ceiling, and then swung him round in his arms, and Morland gripped a handful of Henri's hair and crowed with laughter. Marie-France appeared from the room beyond, pinning up her hair, and laughed too, and came forward to share the embrace.

'Henri, listen,' she said at last, wriggling free a little breathlessly, 'good news! Madame told me this morning – it is all through the streets that Hébert and his supporters were arrested last night.'

'What!' Henri cried.

'Yes, yes, it is true. Twenty of them, they say. Hébert guessed it was coming, and tried to get the Commune to support him, but no-one would speak for him, and the Committee made out the warrants last night, and they were taken during the hours of darkness. Isn't it wonderful, Henri? It must be Danton's influence, Danton and Camille. It is the beginning of the reign of clemency.'

Henri pressed his son close against him, and closed his eyes. 'Thank God,' he said. 'Thank God they are coming to their senses at last.'

When he met up with Duncan later on that day, the latter was not quite so sanguine. 'I've been around the city, talking to people,' he said. 'You know that Hébert's friends on the Committee were not taken?'

'Collot d'Herbois and Billaud-Varennes, you mean? Well, perhaps they are being protected by Robespierre,' Henri suggested, unwilling to abandon his joy so easily.

'Probably,' Duncan said. 'But sir, don't you see what it means? This is not a proof of Danton's influence, but of Robespierre's. The Commune would not stir to help them, because it was afraid. Robespierre has the Committee and the Jacobins Club behind him. Now there are vacancies in the Commune – and are you willing to bet that those vacancies will not be filled by Robespierre's men?'

Henri laid his hand on his friend's arm. 'You may be right, Duncan – I'm not saying you aren't. But the fact that Robespierre has struck down these bloody butchers is surely a sign that he is ready to support the move for clemency. Otherwise, why would he not have continued to use them?'

Duncan shook his head. 'I'm worried, sir. I think we should leave as soon as possible. Now you have finished at Chambord, there's nothing more to wait for, is there?'

Henri shifted his gaze away. 'No,' he said thoughtfully. 'No, not really. We'll think about it, shall we?' Duncan stared at him, aghast, but Henri allowed him no further opportunity to argue, sending him out to buy some hot supper for them both.

On the nineteenth, Danton appeared before the Convention, and made a speech which seemed to herald the beginning of a new era in the revolution. He demanded that all resentment and suspicion be put behind them, and that from now on men should be judged only by their actions. It received a standing ovation of such enthusiasm that Duncan's dark prognostications seemed groundless. Danton went on to seek a reconciliation with Robespierre, and some of the friends who had been avoiding him since Fabre's arrest gathered round him again.

On the twenty-fourth, the Hébertists were executed, before a crowd which was almost in festive mood, and yelled with a savage joy as Hébert himself screamed with fear at the sight of the knife. A few days later Henri was surprised to receive an order from his ministry for the seizure of the house on the rue Saint-Anne and its contents for the government. Duncan was thrown into the deepest gloom, and Marie-France fluttered, but Henri would not abandon his hopes.

'See, it says merely that emigrants cannot be allowed to own property in France – nothing about Héloïse or Vendenoir being traitors or anything of that sort. And, see again, I have been given the office of clearing the furniture. Now they wouldn't do that if I were in danger, would they?'

'I don't know,' Duncan said. 'It could be a joke – a nasty sort of joke, like the executioner the other day letting the blade of the guillotine dance on old Hébert's neck, to please the crowd.'

Henri patted Duncan's arm. 'You're letting your imagination run away with you. I'll tell you what this is – it's a reward for my loyal service. They're giving me the chance to recover this furniture, which otherwise would just have to lie there and rot. It's a very clever scheme. We'll be able to send Héloïse's stuff back to her. Furniture like that would be worth a fortune in England. That *bonheur du jour*, for instance . . .'

'Oh sir, be careful,' Duncan said. 'Let's get out while we can, before it's too late.'

'All right, don't worry, we'll go. There's still plenty of time. We'll make our plans and then be off,' Henri said evasively.

It was two nights later, on the thirtieth, that Henri was working late at the rue Saint-Anne, and on leaving the house and strolling down to the rue Saint-Honoré, he saw that there were an unusual number of lights still burning in the Tuileries. The Committee was meeting late – and what did that portend, he wondered? As he watched, someone came out, and hurried along the road towards him, and he recognised by the stiff gait old Rühl, a member of the General Security Committee, who came from Alsace and was a friend of Danton's. As soon as he saw Henri, he tacked towards him, seized his arm and pulled him back into the shadows.

'What's the matter, sir?' Henri asked, startled. Rühl's grip was hurting his forearm.

'Listen to me – they're going to arrest Danton.'

'What!'

'That was an emergency meeting of the two committees. Saint-Just read out the accusations and demanded the arrest of Danton and Camille, but it was Robespierre's work, everyone knew that. They all signed of course, except Lindet – he said it wasn't his business to send citizens to their death.' Lindet was the member in charge of supplies.

'And you, sir?' Henri said, still bewildered. Rühl made a face.

'I refused, of course. You don't think I would – but listen, boy, there's no time to waste. You must go and warn Danton at once. You're twenty years younger than me, and faster on your feet. Go to him as quickly as you can and tell him he must flee. It'll take them a little while to get the mayor's signature on the order, enough time for you to get to the cour du Commerce.'

'But surely they won't go there tonight?'

'You young fool! Don't you understand the nature of our government yet? Saint-Just wanted Danton arrested in front of the Convention – until Collot pointed out that if they did not arrest Danton at once, they might be arrested themselves. That is the whole philosophy of this Terror of theirs. Now waste no more time – go, for pity's sake, before it's too late!'

Henri went then, hurrying through the dark streets and across the river to that place he knew so well, the *apartement* just across the courtyard from the one he and Madeleine had occupied so many years ago. Danton's new young wife let him in, looking startled. Danton himself was sitting in a chair before the fire; he looked up as Henri came in, and nodded a vague greeting, and then looked down again. He continued to stare into the fire as Henri told him what Rühl had said, and then he sighed.

'I can't go,' he said, and his voice sounded dull and listless.

'But you must,' Henri said urgently. 'You must flee the country at once.' Even as he said it, he was conscious that he was playing Devil's advocate: how often had Duncan urged him to flee? Danton gave a curious little smile, more like a grimace.

'No, my friend. One does not carry one's country on the soles of one's feet. I grew out of the soil of France – you cannot uproot me from it, and expect me to live.'

'Well, then, counter-attack,' Henri suggested urgently. 'Even the members of the Committee saw that it was you or them. People are tired of this business – they'd rally to you. You could--'

'No, no, Henri, don't go on. Don't you see, it would only mean the shedding of more blood, and there has been enough shed already. How can I tell people I am preventing bloodshed by spilling it? Better in the end to be guillotined than to guillotine.'

There was a silence. The fire fell in a little with a soft sound, and Danton leaned forward to stir the embers. He looked tired, Henri thought, not just an ordinary tiredness, but a sick tiredness. It had all become too much for him: it was not for this that he had fought.

'That golden country of equality and justice is further away now than it has ever been,' he said in a low voice. 'We longed for an end of tyranny, and we have made ourselves a tyrant worse than any king.'

'But what will you do?' Henri said, looking down at him with a feeling of helplessness.

'Wait,' he said, staring into the fire. 'Just wait. I shan't go to bed. I should not like them to take me from my bed. I'll sit here by the fire until they come.'

'Oh God . . .' Henri said. Danton looked up at last.

'You had better go, my friend. Why have you not fled the country? You should go – I would not want any of my friends to suffer because of me. And we have been friends, have we not, Henri?'

'Yes, Georges, friends,' Henri said, comforting him as one comforts the sick or the dying.

'You remember the old days, you and your Madeleine, and me and my poor Gabrielle? Those supper parties, companions around the fire, good wine, good talk? Everything was before us then: it all looked so – so *possible*.' He smiled into the embers, remembering. 'Thank God they are not here to see it, eh? They would not be able to bear it.'

There were sounds below. Louise came running in, her face white with fear. Danton stood up and drew her against him. 'They are coming for me,' he said gently. She burst into frightened sobs, clinging to him, and he kissed her forehead and smoothed her hair tenderly. 'Don't be afraid, my darling, they won't dare to hurt me,' he said, and, still holding her close, he said to Henri, 'Go up the stairs to the next landing and hide there until they have gone. It would not do for you to be seen here.'

The day was well advanced when Henri went back to the house on the rue de Saint-Rustique. After the arresting officers had gone, he had had to comfort the weeping Louise and, unable simply to leave her there, had taken her back to her parents; her father was a clerk in the Admiralty. Duncan greeted him with relief.

'Thank God, sir – I thought you had been arrested. You know they have taken Danton and Camille?'

'Yes, yes I know,' Henri said wearily. 'Boil up some water, will you, Duncan? I must shave and have a bath, and some clean clothes. I feel as though I have been in these for a week. And then some breakfast. You can bring me coffee when I'm in the bath. I'll have something hot for breakfast, I think – mutton cutlets, or a steak. See to it, my friend.'

Duncan looked at him oddly, and went away to carry out his instructions. Henri shaved, and bathed, and then dressed slowly, taking time over the tying of his cravat, listening without appearing to to the footsteps that went by up and down the narrow street. Then he went down to the parlour and Duncan

404

served him with mutton cutlets and fried onions, and fresh bread, and more coffee. 'It's a pity it's only March,' Henri murmured as he sat down and shook out his napkin. 'I should have liked some fruit – grapes and peaches and an apricot or two. Well, there it is.'

He ate slowly and with relish, and while he was drinking his last cup of coffee, he called for paper and a pen, and wrote quickly, one ear cocked towards the street. When he had finished the note, he folded it, and at that moment there was the sound of marching feet without. He gave a little quirk of a smile. 'Ah, just in time.'

'My lord!' Duncan cried, forgetting himself, hurrying into the parlour white-faced.

'Yes, Duncan, they have come for me. I was expecting them. You know what to do. Do not linger here. Make sure Héloïse's furniture is on the road, and when you get to England, take her this letter from me, with my love. She will reward you, as far as money can reward loyalty, for all your service to me.'

'My lord, please--'

'No, Duncan. I can't run. It's too late. All our plans have been made, and I look to you to see them carried out, or all this has been for nothing. Open the door to them, Duncan,' he added as the thunderous knocking began. 'And – Duncan' – his man turned back, wide-eyed – 'God bless you, dear friend.'

Moments later the tiny parlour, which Aliena had furnished so long ago with the simple tastes of a nun, and which had never been altered since, was filled with men and the smell of their nervous sweat.

'You are Henri-Marie de Stuart? I have a warrant for your arrest,' said the officer.

'Henri-Marie Fitzjames Stuart,' he corrected with a faint smile. 'Yes, I am ready.'

The trial began on the second of April, before a jury of only seven men, hand-picked as enemies of Danton. Danton, Camille, Henri, and the others accused of political crimes were not the only men in the dock – in fact, they occupied the rear benches, while the front benches were filled with men accused of fraudulent dealings in the East India Company scandal. The purpose was clear: any uninformed member of the public entering the courtroom would assume that Danton and his colleagues were implicated in that business. The whole of the first day's proceedings were occupied, moreover, with the reading of the report on the East India Company. At the end of the day the prisoners were taken back to the Conciergerie without having had a chance to speak. Camille was inclined to be tearful – since his arrest he had occupied his time in writing long impassioned letters to his wife Lucile, whom he loved to distraction – but Danton slapped him on the back and told him to be cheerful.

'We'll make a fight of it yet, don't worry. We must reach the ear of the People. We'll see what these bastards look like when I'm through with them!'

The second day of the trial began as the first had ended, with the East India Company scandal, until Danton stood up and demanded to be heard. Herman, the president of the court, rang his bell energetically to try to drown Danton's voice, but he only roared louder, lowering his head like an enraged bull.

'Don't you hear my bell?' Herman cried in frustration.

'A man fighting for his life laughs at bells! Proceed with the case. I demand our case is heard.'

At last the accusation was read. They were accused of having plotted with Dumouriez to 'murder Liberty and march on Paris with an armed force in order to destroy the republican government and restore monarchy'.

When he heard the accusation, Henri looked across at Danton. It was that old business again – and he feared that, as he was evidently here because he had been a friend of Nordubois and his wife, Danton might be here by contamination. But Danton shook his head and whispered,

'No, friend, it is the other way about. You are here because you were my friend.' And then he answered the accusation, and it was as if a dam had burst, and the flood of his eloquence thundered out. He was magnificent, a huge presence, just as he had been in the days when he stood for the people, when they saw him as a safe bulwark against evil and oppression. All his lethargy had left him, and he spoke toweringly, denying the charges with contempt and demanding that those who had initiated the charge should appear and speak against him publicly.

'I am in full possession of my faculties when I summon my accusers to come forth. I demand the right to pit my strength against theirs. Let them shew themselves, the vile impostors, and I'll tear away the mask that protects them from public chastisement!'

He spoke for an hour, ignoring all attempts to silence him, and when he finally ceased there was a spontaneous outbreak of applause, and the atmosphere in the room was so evidently favourable to Danton that the jury began to look anxious, and the president had no alternative but to adjourn the trial until the next day.

On the fourth of April, the others accused with Danton were given the opportunity to speak, and all in turn refuted the charges and, following Danton's example, demanded that the witnesses be brought forth. Some of the charges were vague in the extreme. Philippeaux, for instance, was accused of nothing more concrete than having criticised the Government in his writings. Henri, as he had expected, was accused with Danton of having been a friend of Dumouriez, and of having plotted with him to restore the monarchy.

'Everyone who knows me knows that I am not a political man,' Henri said in his defence. 'I have been a loyal servant of the Ministry of the Interior, and have never entered into, nor even listened to, any plot against the Republic. Let those who say I have come forth and say it before my face, for they lie abominably.'

The continued demands for the witnesses to be summoned became harder to ignore or refuse, and Herman and Fouquier, the Public Prosecutor, were seen to exchange nervous glances as the trial began to get out of hand. Finally, Fouquier declared that he was again going to suspend the trial. 'I am going to write to the Convention to demand what its wishes are. Those wishes shall be carried out to the letter.' And he hurried out of the courtroom. When he returned some time later, it was with a satisfied grin on his face, and a sheaf of papers in his hand, which he waved triumphantly as he hurried back to his seat.

'I have here a letter which reveals the existence of a plot on the part of Danton and Desmoulins and these other wretches to assassinate the members of the Revolutionary Tribunal and all loyal patriots who supported it. Desmoulins' wife has been stirring up resistance ever since her husband's arrest. The details of the plot are unfolded in this letter which I will read to you.' He read aloud the letter, which purported to come from a prisoner in the Luxembourg, where Danton and Camille had first been imprisoned. The reading was received in blank silence, the entire assembly of jury, prisoners and spectators appearing to be dumbfounded by this blatant travesty of justice. At the end of the letter, Fouquier continued, 'And here is a decree from the Convention, to whom this letter has just been read, which says that every accused person who resists or insults the National Justice shall be forbidden to plead. The very resistance of these wretches is proof of their guilt – no further evidence is needed!'

Danton rose to his feet, and seemed to go on rising. 'You are murderers!' he bellowed. 'Murderers! Look at them! They are hounding us to our deaths!'

Camille clutched at his coat-tails, fainting with terror. 'Lucile!' he shrieked. 'They are going to murder my wife!'

Danton did not seem to hear him. He swung his massive head round like a goaded bull, seeking some face in the shadows. 'Vile Robespierre!' he cried suddenly. 'You too will go to the scaffold. You will follow me, Robespierre!'

'The debate will now end,' Fouquier proclaimed, and Danton turned his terrible eyes on him.

'How can it end?' he bellowed. 'It has not begun. You have not read a single document! You have not called a single witness! You are condemning us without a hearing!'

There was uproar, and Herman rang his bell as though his life depended on it. Fouquier demanded that the prisoners be removed while the jury considered its verdict and sentence was passed, and the guards stepped forward to take them away. Camille began to scream again, clutching at his chair so fiercely that it took three men to unhook his fingers and drag him out. Surrounded by armed guards, they were marched back to the prison of the Conciergerie, and there they sat in stunned silence, awaiting their fate. Danton appeared strangely cheerful, and Henri thought he understood: he had made his last stand,

and now it was out of his hands. His responsibilities were over, and there was nothing more he could do.

'By God, I shall be leaving a mess behind me,' he said suddenly. 'I wish I could leave my legs to that cripple Couthon, and my balls to that eunuch Robespierre!'

'For God's sake!' Camille cried out quaveringly. Danton patted his knee.

'Now, now, friend, death is not so terrible after all. What does it matter if we die? I've warmed my hands by the fire of life. I've caroused, and spent lots of money, and loved lots of women. Now it's time to sleep.'

'It's all right for you,' Fabre moaned. 'Posterity will do you justice, but what about me? What about my new play? I know that villain Billaud-Varennes will steal it, and have it published as his own work. It's better than anything he can do. It's got such beautiful verses in it. I make such beautiful verses!'

Danton stared at him in astonished contempt. 'Verses? Before the week is out, my friend, you'll be making beautiful worms!'

They had little time to wait. Very soon the clerk of the court arrived to read the sentence of death to them, and they were ushered into the ante-room of the courtyard where the tumbrels were waiting, where the executioner, Samson, and his assistants, stood ready to *faire la toilette*, as it was called. Each prisoner in turn was sat upon a wooden bench while his shirt collar was cut open at the back, his hair clipped to leave the neck bare, and his hands bound behind his back. Camille became hysterical, and resisted all Danton's efforts to soothe him. When he saw the scissors he began to scream, and the assistants had to tie him to the bench before they could clip his hair. When it was done, and his hands were tied behind his back, the assistants came to strip him of any valuables. He always wore a locket around his neck which contained a lock of Lucile's hair, and when they came to take it off, he sobbed and begged Samson to allow him to hold it until the end.

'Well, I don't know . . .' Samson began.

And Camille went on, 'And when I'm dead, will you take it from my body and send it to my wife's dear mother?'

'Oh, very well then,' Samson said, and turning away, gave a wink to his assistant which Henri intercepted. He doubted if that locket would go very far. But Camille at least was comforted, and turned to Danton, who had not yet been bound, bidding him to take off the locket and put it into his hands.

'Now, citizen, let's have you. Are we going to have to bind you down as well?'

Henri jerked back to the present, and found one of the assistants beside him, grinning, though, he thought, it was probably a nervous habit rather than real malice. He was a fat man with a coarse, dark complexion like a southerner, one of the men from Marseilles, perhaps, a Sicilian or Corsican. Henri shook his head and sat down on the bench. It was horrible to feel the cold metal of the scissors against his skin; it made him realise for the first time exactly what was to happen. He clenched his hands together between his knees, and tried to think of God, tried to pray. But his mind was filled with a succession of unrelated images: of Ismène's hands as she poured coffee from the exquisite gold-rimmed pot; of a boat containing a man fishing, drifting under the arches of Chenonceau; of Héloïse laughing as she cantered Prestance along the path in the Bois de Boulogne; of little Morland pushing his wheeled horse across the faded carpet of Madame Buffon's upstairs room.

His hands were pulled behind him roughly, and he felt the harsh touch of the rope binding them, jerking at him as the knots were pulled tight. He thought of all the victims that had gone before him to the scaffold, and wondered at all the rope that had been used. Did they remove it from the bodies afterwards, or was it wasted? He shook his head to try to concentrate his mind, but it would not stay still, wandering here and there like a restless ghost.

He thought of the glorious sunrise on the day his grandmother died. He thought of Madeleine serving him with lentil soup in their *apartement* in the cour du Commerce, and the taste of bacon in it which had made her lentil soup special. Now they were being ushered out into the yard, and the air smelled fresh after the closeness of the prison. There were three tumbrels waiting – eighteen of them to fill them. They had to be helped up, for their hands were bound behind them. Henri was pushed up into the first tumbrel with Danton, Camillle, Fabre, Hérault de Séchelles and Philippeaux. The sun was low in the sky, and shone into their eyes.

'What o'clock is it?' Danton asked, of no-one in particular. 'It must be three o'clock, I should think.'

The cart started off with a lurch that threw them off balance. Henri landed against the solid bulk of Danton, and recovered himself, and the two men exchanged a look of sympathy. Surrounded by armed *gendarmes*, the three carts left the cour du Mai and crossed the Pont Neuf, and turned into the rue Saint-Honoré. These streets, Henri thought, as they passed by, he had known since his childhood, every stone, every corner, every smell. He had ranged like a cat over this city. From his new vantage point, he got a fine view of it. They passed the end of the rue Saint-Anne, and he turned his head to the right. Ismène's house, Héloïse's house. At least it had never been Vendenoir's house. Where was he, Henri wondered? Dead, by now, or still rotting somewhere in prison? Crowds lined the streets for this last journey, but Henri hardly noticed them; only once, when he caught the eye of a young girl with a market-basket over her arm. She was pretty, with the prettiness of youth, and looked frightened, as though she did not much enjoy this kind of public occasion. Their eyes seemed to lock as the tumbrel passed. Henri wondered what she had in the basket. He thought of peaches, and wished he could have one, taste one this last time. Then he thought it was strange to be thinking about fruit at such a time.

They passed the house where Robespierre lodged, its windows shut tight, as though to hide its occupant. Danton lifted his head, and bellowed loudly enough for his words to be heard inside, if anyone was listening:

'Vile Robespierre, you will follow me within three months! Your house will be levelled and the ground where it stands sown with salt!'

Now they turned into the place de la Révolution, and they saw the scaffold for the first time, and the huge crowd gathered round it. Camille was taken with another frenzy. 'Citizens, they have lied to you, they are duping you! They are sacrificing your servants!' he shrieked to the people.

Danton nudged him, and shook his head. 'No, no, be quiet,' he said. 'Leave that vile rabble alone. They don't hear you.'

Samson and his valets helped the men down from the carts and lined them up at the foot of the scaffold. The sun was westering, and Henri guessed that it was past four o'clock. Here the King had died, and the Queen, and so many others. He looked up at the guillotine, and it was dense and black in the afternoon light; beyond it the sky was pale and sweet. He tried to imagine he could smell grass and warm earth; he did not want to die with thoughts of horror in his mind. But there was so little time. Hérault was taken by the arms, to go first. He tried to turn to say goodbye to Danton, to embrace him, but Samson hurried him away up the steps.

'Wretch!' Danton muttered. 'You will not stop our heads meeting in the basket.'

Samson and his men worked with the efficiency of abattoir attendants: they had eighteen heads to take off before dark. A long plank was before the guillotine, leaning at an angle. Hérault was stood before it, and then Samson and an assistant took an arm each, while the other assistant seized his feet, and with a deft movement he was flung onto the plank face down, and the plank was dropped horizontal, and thrust forward under the blade. There were three thuds: the first of the plank falling into place, the second as the neck-clamp was slammed down, and the third as the blade fell.

Hérault's head dropped into the basket. Briskly the executioners dragged the body aside and tumbled it over the side of the scaffold into a straw-filled cart placed ready. The head landed beside the body with a thump, and they were coming down the steps for the next victim. The efficient heart-lessness of the butchery sickened Henri far more than the thought of death: to be dispatched with no more feeling than a veal-calf seemed a denial of humanity that . . .

But they had taken his arms, they were hurrying him up the steps. He did not want to die. His feet dragged, though one part of his mind told him he must not appear a coward; he wanted to look round at the sky and the tops of the trees, the only living things he could see, but there was no time. His feet flew out from under him, and his chin hit the plank with a thump that made his eyes water, and he cried 'Wait!'

They left Danton to the end, and it was growing dark by the time they escorted him up onto the scaffold. Trapped in the crowd near the railings of the palace, Marie-France was facing westwards into the dying sun, and the scaffold was a flat black cut-out against the red sky. Beside it was the bulk of the huge plaster statue of liberty, black and shapeless. With as little ceremony as the others, Danton died, and the crowd began to thin at the edges and drift away. Marie-France found herself able to move at last, and turned away to go home, heading northwards and eastwards, keeping to the back streets as much as possible, not from fear, but because she did not want to meet anyone or speak to anyone.

She was alone now. Duncan had come to her to try to persuade her to leave Paris, but she would not – could not, she said, while Henri lived.

'Go to England,' Duncan had urged her, growing angry at her resistance. 'Your friend Héloïse is there. Think of the child – *his* child. You owe it to him to keep the child safe.'

'He would not leave,' she said in the end. 'I understand now. He belonged here, and so do I, and so does Morland. He could have run away, and taken me with him, but when it came to it, he could not go.'

'You're a fool,' Duncan said bitterly. 'If you stay, I cannot help you.'

'No, I understand that. It's all right, Duncan, you have done all you need. I shall take care of Morland in my own way. We belong here.'

So he had left. At the last moment, he had told her that he would come back for her, if he could, when he had done what Henri had instructed before his arrest; but she did not think he would come back. She was alone now, for good.

Jean was waiting for her in the doorway of the house, and when he saw her, his idiot face lit with pleasure, and he called over his shoulder to his mother that Madame was back. Madame Buffon came out from her little room with Morland on her shoulder, his head drooping sleepily against her lace-edged cap.

'He was crying, madame, so I took him in.' Her sharp eyes surveyed Marie-France's face. 'It is all over, then?'

'Yes,' she said.

'Ah, you must be worn out, poor dear,' said Madame Buffon. 'Come, let us go upstairs, and I will put little Morland to bed, and then I will make you a nice hot cup of tea, to make you feel better.' Madame Buffon regarded tea as a medicine, and though she hated the taste, she prescribed it for most ills, and drank it herself for her health. In the upstairs *apartement* she took Morland away, while Marie-France sat down in a chair by the window and stared at nothing, too numb to think or move. When Madame Buffon came back, she said,

'Ah, Madame, he has gone to sleep like an angel. Poor little boy. He is an orphan now.'

Marie-France looked up, dazed. 'You knew – that Monsieur Morland . . .'

'Of course, my dear. I am not such a fool. But that was your business, and none of mine. But don't you fret now, my dear, we'll take care of you both, Jean and I. It's what he would have wanted.'

'Madame, I must tell you – I have no money of my own. Everything I had came from him. I do not know how I shall be able to pay your rent. I must find work, I suppose . . .' Marie-France said, trying to rouse herself from her lethargy with the use of a counter-irritant. But Madame Buffon folded her hands over her stomach and smiled.

'Don't you worry, madame, that's all taken care of,' she said.

'What do you mean?'

'I mean that Monsieur Morland – as we shall continue to call him, eh? – left me instructions about what I should do if anything were to happen to him. Oh, that was months ago! He was a cautious man, and did just as he ought. And he's left money for you, and for the little boy, enough to keep you, if you stay here with me, until little Morland is able to go out and work to support you. Yes, I have all the money safe and sound, so don't worry about anything. And now I'm going to go and get you that cup of tea, my dear.'

She went to the door, and turned back with an unearthly smile as she opened the door, to say, 'Just you trust me, madame! I know all about you, you see.'

Even to Marie-France's dulled senses, the glitter in Madame Buffon's eyes was obvious, and was not all made up of sympathy.

22

In the middle of March 1794, Mary, looking younger and gentler than anyone ever remembered her, announced herself to be pregnant. Jemima cried.

'I'm sorry,' she gasped, 'I know it's foolish, but I can't seem to stop.'

'Oh, Mother,' Mary said fondly. Edward gave her his handkerchief, and Brach trotted across to her to lick her hands, interested by the puppy-noises she was making.

'It's just that . . .' Jemima said when she had got to the sniffing stage, 'I had come to the stage where I did not think it would ever happen, I'm nearly sixty-two, you know. I should have been a grandmother long since.'

'Well, now you've started, there'll be no stopping you,' Lucy said. 'Once James and I get into our stride . . .'

'Don't be shocking, Lucy,' Mary reproved. James only watched in silence, upset by the sight of his mother crying.

'You don't understand, children,' Jemima said. 'I have a great responsibility to Morland Place. There have been Morlands here for three hundred and fifty years, and since none of my children would marry, it looked as though I would have no-one to leave it all to. Now, at last--'

'This little one will be a Haworth,' Mary reminded her. 'No use to you, mother.'

'Don't be silly, darling,' Jemima said briskly. 'I'm sure your husband wouldn't mind what the child was called, in such a case. After all, Allen saw the necessity.'

Lucy was to be married from Morland Place at the beginning of April, and Héloïse asked James to postpone their wedding until after Lucy's, because there would be so much to do.

'Besides, Lucy's will be so grand, it will be better if ours, being small and quiet, should happen afterwards,' she said. James smiled.

'My love, arrange it however you like. I don't care a bit about the wedding – all I want is to be married to you. We can just slip downstairs one morning and have Father Thomas tie the knot, if you like.'

Héloïse frowned. 'It would be nice,' she acknowledged, 'but I do not think it would be quite fair. After all, you are the heir presumptive to Morland Place . . .'

'What big words you are learning, my lady!' he laughed at her. 'Who taught you that?'

'Mary did – now hush, James, and don't laugh at me, for I cannot think properly! What was I saying? Oh, yes, that I think we cannot marry only to please ourselves, if our children will one day inherit all this. There must be some ceremony, though I think it should be quiet, as I am a widow.'

'And a foreigner,' James said, taking her in his arms. 'If this were a hundred years ago, the villagers would think you were a witch, and had thrown an enchantment on me.' He smoothed her hair back from her face. 'Perhaps it's true. I feel as though I were enchanted, all tangled up in you, snared like a rabbit.'

She smiled up at him contentedly. 'Such pretty things you say, dear James. I sometimes wish you were not to inherit Morland Place, that you were poor and outcast, so that I could prove how much I love you!'

His sense of humour, never far buried, rose to the surface, and he laughed heartily. 'Oh, you'd wish that on me, would you? Perhaps you'd like me a helpless invalid too?'

'No, James, hush, do not say so. It is unlucky!' she said, putting her fingers against his lips. He kissed them and said,

'Well, if you like, love, I'll tell Mama to leave everything to Mary's child instead.'

'She is pleased, isn't she?' Héloïse smiled.

'Yes – I am too. I'm very glad for her, that she's fallen in love at last. I was never very close to Mary, when we were children – we were too different. I was always romantic, a dreamer. Mary was practical. I suppose all women are, really – level-headed and practical. They have to be.'

'Your mother said, when you were little, you lived in a world of your own,' Héloïse said.

'I was the odd one out,' he said. 'Mary was always with Edward and John Anstey, and the twins had each other. Lucy and Harry weren't born, of course. I belonged to none of them. I had to learn to be satisfied with my own company.'

It had been a lonely childhood in some ways, he reflected. His mother and father were always busy – and besides, it was not then fashionable for parents to notice their children much. He was brought up by nursery maids, and Flora had been the adult who paid him the most attention. But he had lived, for the most part, in a world of his own making, and that habit of withdrawal had been a hard one to break. He had never known the easy camaraderie that other little boys had with one another; he had found it easier to get on with adults than with other children. Flora made a pet of him, and Father Ramsay, the previous chaplain-tutor, had made a friend of him, and to neither of them had he revealed much about himself, looking at them out of his eyes like a wild animal inside a cave. What they knew of him was what he wanted them to know, which again was what he knew they wanted him to be.

Perhaps that was why, when he had fallen in love, it had been with Mary Loveday, as she then was, who was older than him by several years, and a serious-minded, quiet girl. He had never been at ease with young women, any more than with young men. He had flirted with them outrageously, teased them, made superficial love to them, for that way he had never needed to reveal anything about himself; but no-one, not even his mother, had ever guessed that that was why he did it. But with Mary he could talk sensibly, for she did not expect to be flirted with. Afterwards, when she had married old John Skelwith, the relationship had changed, and he had never perfectly understood why. Perhaps she needed his physical reassurance; perhaps her inaccessibility had made her more attractive to him. Now, with the warmth of his real feeling for Héloïse for comparison, he thought that he had never really loved Mary; that they had clung together because each of them had some unfulfillable need, and there was no-one else to turn to.

But Héloïse was different. Héloïse he really loved. She was so strong, and so brave, having been through so much, without having become hardened. She was quick, and intelligent, and loved to laugh; he could say anything to her, and she would not be censorious; she was beautiful and passionate; and with all that, she was vulnerable, and needed him. Most of all – perhaps it was all of the argument after all – she loved him, completely, and uncritically. He was safe with her, safe to come cautiously, inch by inch, out of the lonely cave he had chosen for himself.

He loved to see how quickly she had been absorbed into the family, how easily she mixed and adapted, how the servants respected her and the tenants loved her. With the approach of Lucy's wedding, she spent a great deal of time in the kitchen with M. Barnard, poring over receipt-books and discussing astonishing delicacies; and with Oxhey in the butler's room, shewing him new and better ways of polishing glass and silver; and in the linen room with Mrs Mappin, making minute and delicate repairs to napery and listening with rapt attention while Mrs Mappin told her stories of the Morlands' history, on which she accounted herself an expert. He was always coming across her, scurrying from one place to another, with her tiny, child-sized form enveloped in a huge apron made for some buxom Yorkshire serving-maid, and the sight of her, and the glad, radiant smile she would fling at him as she passed, would make him want to cry.

He longed so to give her things, to make her life comfortable and beautiful, but everything he did for her seemed only a gift from her to him, for it was he that was enriched by it. She lived, it seemed, to radiate love: whatever was poured in, poured out again, multiplied a hundredfold. Every moment they were sitting still together, he drew her, almost obsessively, for his skill with the pencil seemed to him the only thing he possessed of any worth that even came near to hers. He tried again and again to capture her on paper or in paints, and she would look at the finished work, and her face would light with love and admiration, and she would cry, 'Oh James, you are so clever!' And once again it would be *she* who had given riches to *him*, not vice versa.

Lucy was his ally, however – Lucy, who had not a scrap of sentiment in her, who never shuddered at the sight of blood, in whom the sight of suffering roused no desire to cry or tremble, but merely, practically, to help. She never spoke of such things as feelings, nor so much as hinted that she understood James's helpless desire to give Héloïse something worthy of her; but despite the busyness of the time before the wedding, she laboured with James in every spare moment to perfect the thing he had decided upon. That, he felt, was typical of Lucy:

had she been forced to encapsulate her philosophy in words, she would have said an ounce of help is worth a peck of words; but being Lucy, she would never have said it.

So it was a few days before the wedding that James brought Héloïse out to the step of the great door, stood her in the centre of it, facing the courtyard, and bid her keep her eyes on the arch of the barbican.

'But what is it, love?' she asked. 'M. Barnard is having trouble with his marzipan and I should not really leave him.'

'Hush – wait! Watch. M. Barnard was making marzipan before you were born. He only likes to pretend he needs your help. Look, here it comes!'

Lucy drove in through the barbican slowly, turning into the corner of the yard and pulling up before the step. She drove well, holding the horses up so that they stepped high and showily – and indeed, they were a showy pair, part of the smartest outfit that had ever graced the yard. The phaeton which James had designed with Lucy's help was small and perfectly balanced, a delicate spiderweb of arched woodwork poised gracefully above the wheels as though it were floating there. The wood had been rubbed down and rubbed down until it was smooth, and finally waxed so that its own pale golden colour shewed through. The upholstery was coral-coloured velvet, and there was a tiny seat slung behind for the groom.

The horses made it perfect. They were pony-sized, but they were not ponies but perfectly formed small horses, Arabians, with all that breed's slender elegance and strength. They were the colour of thick cream, with darker streaks in their manes and tails – James had seen one of them locally, and decided at once it was perfect for Héloïse's rig, but it had taken him months to find a match for it, and he had had to make enquiries of breeders all over the country. But the result was worth it: they were beautiful, long-maned, long-tailed, gazelle-eyed, and, thanks to Lucy's schooling, perfectly in step with each other.

'It's for you,' he said to Héloïse, 'so that you can drive yourself around the estate, or into the village, or to visit friends.'

She turned to him with her lips parted and her eyes bright. 'Oh James – I've never seen anything so lovely, in all my life.'

'Lucy's been schooling the horses, and she says they are well-mannered and easy to drive. The near horse is six, and the off is seven, so they've all their lives ahead of them.'

'I haven't given them names,' Lucy said from the driving seat. 'I thought you'd want to do that. They are nice little things, very gentle and friendly. I've enjoyed working them. The phaeton was James's own thought – don't you think it's come out well? He has a good eye, I will say: the balance is just right, though the coachmaker worked from James's own drawings. Why don't you jump up and try them? Come on – just round the house a few times.'

Héloïse, pink-cheeked, was stepping down to do so when Jemima, who had disappeared indoors a few moments ago, came out saying, 'Wait, I have something here – the final touch. Look,' she put into James's hands a pair of bridle ornaments, gold discs from which hung fine gold chains threaded with coral beads. 'There's only a pair – they were made for a riding-horse – but you can put them on the outside.'

'Oh Mother, they are lovely. Just what it needs to make it special,' James said gratefully.

'Why have I never seen them before?' Lucy asked. 'You've never used them, have you, Mother? What a waste! Héloïse, jump up here and take the reins, while we put them on. You do that one, Jamie, and I'll do this. You'll have to undo the cheek-strap and slip it up from the bottom. Make sure you get the buckle back in the same hole when you do it up again, or the bit won't lie right.'

'Teach your grandmother to suck eggs, Luce,' James said good-naturedly.

'They're very old,' Jemima was saying, rubbing the horses' soft cream-coloured noses while Héloïse settled herself in the driving seat. 'Heirlooms, really. They've survived mostly because they weren't valuable enough to sell, when all the plate and jewels went. Of course, we don't tend to decorate our riding horses that way any more, but there's no reason not to decorate driving-horses.'

When the horses' heads were released, they tossed them up and down as horses do, and the ornaments shook and caught the sunlight and looked very pretty.

'Now try them out,' Lucy commanded.

'You must come too,' she stipulated. 'Maman, come sit beside me.'

'No, no, I've too much to do. I'll let you take me out some time. You go, children.'

So James got up beside her, and Lucy climbed into the groom's seat, and Héloïse drove her pair very carefully out through the barbican and three times round the moat, and the horses lifted their feet high and stepped together, their muzzles touching and their bridle ornaments winking in the sunlight.

'I shall have to buy myself some new clothes to drive in,' Héloïse said. 'My blue habit will not do at all.'

'You can get something when you get your wedding clothes,' James said.

'What a thing to worry about!' exclaimed Lucy.

Lucy's wedding took place on the second of April, in the chapel at Morland Place. It was enormously well attended: all the family, the Chelmsford family, and friends and neighbours of the Morlands and of Chetwyn's were there. Lucy looked very lovely in a high-waisted, long-trained dress of cream silk, with an overdress of ecru lace, fastened all the way down the front with pearl buttons. Her hair was still quite short – Flora told her that in London it was becoming fashionable for women to crop their hair *a la guillotine*, as they called it – and she wore a long veil of gauze held in place with a simple circlet of white daisies.

Chetwyn looked like a fairy-tale prince in pale blue satin and white breeches, and a waistcoat embroidered with gold thread. Edward attended him, looking as though he was going to laugh, and Héloïse attended Lucy as matron of honour. Afterwards they went to M. Barnard's feast, which was all laid out buffet-style in the great hall, because there were too many guests for them all to sit down at the table. The hall was decorated with white flowers, blue-and-white ribbons, and the Morland and Aylesbury achievements of arms. The display of delicacies was so beautifully laid out and decorated on the long tables that it was quite some time before anyone could bring themselves to broach it. The centrepiece was an enormous cake, three feet in diameter, covered in white sugar-paste, decorated with sugar flowers and coloured marzipan fruits, little silver vases holding fresh spring flowers, and white candles in silver holders. In the end, it was Héloïse who broke the deadlock over the feast by making the first onslaught, and since she had had the most to do with it, apart from M. Barnard himself, she was the only person present who would have dared.

After that there was dancing, during which the family gathered to see Lucy and Chetwyn off to Wolvercote, where there would be more ceremonies, welcoming the new countess to her home. Mary was to go with her to help her settle in, and they were to return in three weeks for Héloïse and James's wedding. Lucy for the first time shed a tear or two, and clung round her mother's neck as they said goodbye; but once she was in the carriage her spirits revived, and she scandalised Mary by hanging out of the window and waving wildly until the carriage was out of sight.

'Well, that's that,' Jemima said to Edward as they went back inside the house. He put an arm round her waist, and she leaned against him comfortably. 'I think they'll be happy, don't you?'

'Oh yes, I expect so,' Edward said. 'And in a few years, we'll be having their children here, running about the house. Lord, that will be strange!'

'You don't mind, do you, Ned?' Jemima asked cautiously. He grinned.

'Of course not, foolish. Why should I?'

Two days later Héloïse and James went down to London with Flora and Charles, for Héloïse to buy her wedding clothes, and also so that she could be presented at Court. It was Charles's idea that she should have a formal presentation at one of the Drawing-Rooms.

'It isn't essential, but it could be useful to you in future. All our girls have been, and Mary was, and Lucy will be when she has finished her honeymoon.'

'But then, Lucy is now a countess,' Héloïse said.

'So will you be, one day,' Flora pointed out, and Héloïse smiled and shook her head.

'I don't think King George would recognise a title given by King James,' she said.

She enjoyed her time in London. The spring weather was lovely for walking in the Park and driving along the Row; and she enjoyed the quiet evenings they spent at Chelmsford House, with Flora's naval friends dropping in for a chat and a hand of picquet. They were invited to a great many parties, and went to a few, for Flora would not allow her to be stared at 'like one of those poor lions at the Tower' by people she hardly knew.

Héloïse also enjoyed the shopping, for her years of sewing in the convent, and her stern, housewifely soul made her much fiercer with the mantua-makers and warehouse proprietors than Flora would have dared to be.

'You could easily afford his prices, you know,' she said once when Héloïse had stalked out of a Bond Street shop in disgust. 'Your father did send you quite a large sum.'

'I don't wish to spend it all,' Héloïse said reasonably. 'One never knows when it might be a very good thing to have some money at hand.'

She was intending to make most of her clothes herself, and haunted the silk-warehouses in Spitalfields, and Harding and Howell's, the drapers, just along from Chelmsford House, where she bought exactly the right trimming with which to refurbish one of Flora's court dresses; for it had been decided that, as she was intending to live in the country, it was not worth the expense of a new court gown for the one occasion.

One morning, when they had been in London a few days, Héloïse came down to breakfast early, to find Charles and James alone, reading the papers: Flora rarely rose before ten. The gentlemen looked up as she came in, and their faces grew grave, and when James held out his hand to her, she knew that there was bad news.

'What is it?' she asked. 'Tell me.'

'You had better sit down, my dear,' Charles said kindly, pulled out a chair for her, and folded the newspaper and laid it before her. The sunlight slanting in through the window fell across it and across the well-polished mahogany of the table, and made it difficult to read. Héloïse found herself looking at the dancing dust-motes in the golden stream, and knew it was because her mind did not want to understand what was in that paragraph of black and white. She forced herself to read. It was an account of the execution of Danton; her father's name was there in the list of those executed with him.

She read it through, and then began again at the beginning, and was reading a third time, like some dumb creature on a treadwheel, when James's hands laid upon her shoulders made her start. She looked up, but his face was strangely misty. She felt she should say something to comfort him. Someone near her was hurt: she could feel their pain.

'I'm so sorry, my dear,' Charles said. 'It must be a terrible shock for you.'

She supposed it must be; but in another way, it seemed something she had always known. Her mind kept setting up the image of the scaffold, her father mounting the steps . . . And then the picture would be shut off abruptly, only to resume: the scaffold, her father mounting the steps . . .

She reached up for James's hand on her shoulder, and held it hard. She wanted to be in his arms, but did not know how to get up. The men were talking above her, saying the names: Danton, Camille . . .

'It was Camille who led the mob to storm the Bastille,' she said suddenly. So long ago – could it be only five years? And Danton, the mob's darling, so vital, forceful, with his battered face and huge appetites and enormous laughter. 'They were at our wedding,' she said, 'Danton and his wife, Camille and Lucile. They dined with us.'

'It is Robespierre's doing,' Charles said. 'It's all here in the paper. What kind of a monster can he be? And this man Saint-Just – they call him 'the Angel of Death'. Anyone who gets in their way – they simply kill. They must be monsters, inhuman monsters!'

Saint-Just, fair and Grecian-beautiful, with his flowing tie and his gold earring – how Olivier had admired him!

'No, they are not monsters. You don't understand. They think they are doing things for the best.' She heard herself speaking, and was surprised, and went on doing it. 'Papa and I, we saw it from the beginning, how every time there was a change of government they would be more and more ruthless, do things that only a few months before would have horrified them. But they all thought the end justified the means, and that when things got to a certain point they would be able to stop. But they didn't understand that you can't do evil that good may come. The means create the end, and if you do evil,

424

only evil can come of it, and then you can't stop, or what you have created will devour you too. As it is devouring France now. France – my country!'

At some point she had slipped into French, and she looked up at the two men and saw that they had not understood her. There were tears on her face, and she put up her hands to wipe them, and then held them out for James, needing him to touch her. He stepped closer, and she buried her face in his waistcoat and wept, and they stood in grave silence, unable to come near to comprehending what her loss must be – not just her father, nor even her country, but a whole world destroyed, an innocence.

In the carriage on the way to St. James's Palace, Héloïse said suddenly, 'Now I am an orphan, me, and a widow. And a countess, but not in England,' she added. Charles smiled.

'We'll see,' he said cryptically. The two women looked at him, and at each other and shrugged. He had been dropping sidelong remarks for days now. It was not a Drawing-Room they were going to attend, because Héloïse's mourning made it impossible for her to have a formal presentation; but Charles had been invited to bring her to tea with Their Majesties, which Flora said was a great deal better, as it was treating her like a friend.

'But don't be nervous,' she advised. 'No-one will expect anything of you, and you probably won't be expected to say more than 'yes' and 'no'. You call the Queen 'ma'am' and the King 'sir', and when in doubt, curtsy.'

It all went as Flora had described at first. Héloïse was presented by the senior Lady in Waiting to the Queen. She approached, curtsied deeply, and kissed the Queen's hand, and the Queen smiled kindly at her and bade her be seated. A small, round table was placed beside the Queen, and her tea and bread-and-butter were placed on it, and the company sat on gilt-and-brocade sofas around the room and drank tea; though they were all at too great a distance from the Queen to hear what she said to her closest companion, and since no-one could speak unless the Queen spoke to them, the conversation was not a feature of the occasion.

After a while the King came in, and then everyone had to stand up, moving out from the centre of the room to stand in small groups and wait until the King came round to speak to them. The King soon beckoned Charles over to him, and they had quite a conversation before Charles brought him over to where Flora and Héloïse were waiting. The women curtsied deeply, and the King raised Flora first and kissed her cheek – he kissed only peeresses and peers' daughters – and said:

'Lady Chelmsford. Good to see you again. Quite well?'

'Yes, thank you, sir,' said Flora. Then Charles presented Héloïse, who was about to curtsy again, for good measure, when the King leaned down from his great height and kissed her cheek too.

Héloïse was so surpised she stood for a moment with her mouth open, as the King said:

'Welcome to our country, madame. Sorry to hear about your father – Charles was telling me. A bad business that – bad business.'

All Héloïse's English had fled. All she could manage was to say 'Sank Your *Majestie*,' – the last word being definitely the French version rather than the English. The King surveyed her with his pale protruberant eyes, and then turned to Charles.

'Never mind, we'll lick 'em – won't we, Charles? Have you told her? No? Do so, then, by all means. Well, ma'am – I hope to see you again. Chamberlain'll be writing in the morning.'

He went on his way, leaving the women confused, and Charles with a smug smile. When they were alone again, he explained at last.

'I've persuaded the King to recognise your title,' he told Héloïse. 'Not that he needed much persuading, for he's a kindly old fellow. So you are now Countess of Strathord, and you can use the title in this country, and pass it on to your children. The Lord Chamberlain will send you the official document. Isn't that splendid? Oh, now, for heaven's sake, don't cry – not in the Drawing-Room! It wouldn't do at all.'

The wedding had to be put off again. 'I must wear black for Papa for six weeks,' she told James firmly. 'It is only what is proper.'

426

James rolled his eyes. 'Another six weeks! I know what it is – now you are a countess, you are having second thoughts about marrying a mere commoner! You are growing too high for me.'

'But James, if I am a countess, you will be a count, *non*?'

'Non,' he grinned. 'Nor even an earl. In England, love, husbands do not share their wives' titles. Even a queen's husband would be only a commoner.'

'*Tiens, que c'est étrange*! Shall I then reject the title, and be common with you?'

'Not at all. We shall be Mr James and Lady Henrietta Morland. *I* don't mind.'

'You will not be jealous?'

'Not of words, Marmoset. Only of people,' James said, kissing her on the forehead, both eyes, and the lips. She put her arms round his neck and kept him there.

'You will have no cause to be jealous of people. Kiss me again, James, I like it.'

The wedding was to take place at the end of May, and Flora persuaded Héloïse to remain in London a little longer, 'For now you are a countess, you must have more clothes.' James, however, went back to Yorkshire, for Edward had written to say he could not manage without him any longer. He was very reluctant to leave Héloïse.

'Oh, don't be such a wet Monday, James!' Flora said indignantly. 'Let the poor creature have a little fun, before you lock her away for ever in the country. My dear, are you sure you want to marry this man? He seems to be turning into a perfect bear.'

'It is entirely up to her how long she stays away, ma'am,' James said with dignity. Héloïse looked stricken, and Flora laughed.

'Now that really *is* unfair! Tell her you don't mind, and then go away with a good grace, or she won't stay at all.'

'Very well, I'll send Mother down in my place. She likes a jaunt, before the weather gets too hot.'

'Yes, very good, and we can all go out to Wolvercote later on and visit Lucy, and then we can leave Jemima there to travel up with them in comfort.'

But even with Jemima, Héloïse did not like London half so well without James, and Flora, with some amusement, saw she was not going to be able to keep her there, and decided a trip to Wolvercote was the only card left for her to play.

'But I have all the things I need, cousin Flora,' Héloïse said. 'I can make up the gowns as well in Yorkshire as here.'

'Of course. Far be it from me to keep you from your pressing engagements in Yorkshire. I'll write to Lucy and ask if we can visit her earlier than expected. It would be monstrous to interrupt the honeymoon of any other couple, but in the case of Lucy and Lord Aylesbury, I don't suppose it will make any difference.'

'If I know Lucy,' Jemima said, 'she'll want to shew us the improvements she's made in the stables.'

'If not the hospital she's set up in the small dining-room,' Charles added with a grin.

On the eve of their departure for Wolvercote, Hawkins' monumental calm was once again, inexcusably, ruffled. They had dined early, and Charles was on the point of leaving for his club, where he promised to stay only an hour, when there was a distant sound of commotion in the hall, and Charles and Flora exchanged a puzzled look.

'Now what could that be? Not visitors, surely. Didn't you tell everyone we were leaving early tomorrow?' Charles said.

'Well, not *everyone*, Charles, be reasonable,' Flora said, listening. 'But it doesn't sound like a visitor. It sounds as though Hawkins is having trouble.'

'Oh well, Hawkins can take care of himself,' Charles said, 'so I shall wait until all's quiet before venturing down. I don't want to get embroiled in whatever it is.'

'That's my brave soldier,' Flora teased.

Some time later, when Charles was beginning to think it must be safe to leave, Hawkins came into the drawing-room and said, 'I beg your pardon, my lord, but there is another French person here.'

'*Another* one? How infamous!' Charles cried. Flora gave him a reproving look and said,

'Is it something to do with her ladyship, Hawkins?'

'I could not undertake to say, my lady. The person seems to speak no English, and I could not find out what he wants. I would have sent him away, my lady, thinking at first that he was drunk, but he seems to be in some distress, my lady, and I thought if he *did* turn out to be asking after her ladyship, he might have a message or something of the sort.'

'In distress, you say? Is he ill?'

'I think – yes, my lady.'

'Well, bring him up, then, man,' Charles said.

'I beg your pardon, my lord, but I had him taken to the kitchen.'

'What on earth for?'

Hawkins appeared uneasy, and his eyes actually wandered from his master's face as he answered. 'The person, my lord, is in a condition of – in short, my lord, his apparel is not suitable for – the kitchen seemed the best place, my lord,' he said at length in agonised tones.

Héloïse jumped up in alarm, and without further ado headed for the door.

'Shew me to this person *at once*,' she said. 'If he is ill the doctor must be summoned.'

'My lady, I don't think--' Hawkins began, and she actually stamped her foot.

'Who else is to talk to him, *imbécile*, if he speaks no English? It may be à friend of mine or my father's. Excuse me, please, ma'am,' to Flora.

'I'll come with you,' Jemima said, and the two women hurried out, with Hawkins struggling to keep up with them without impairing his dignity.

The kitchen at Chelmsford House had never yet been honoured with a visit from a ladyship, and the consternation there was extreme, far more than had been caused by the intrusion of the tattered foreigner. He was shivering with fever, emaciated, dirty, with lice in his hair, dressed in rags which were quite inadequate to cover him, even dragged together by his thin hands. His feet bore the signs of having walked a very long way without the aid of shoe-leather, and apart from the fever, he seemed to be in some great mental distress, which, as the second housemaid said to her next underling, was hardly surprising when you thought what a shocking heathen country France was, and what terrible things had been going on there.

Héloïse and Jemima came in to find him crouching in a chair

by the kitchen fire, shivering and panting like a hunted animal. As they went towards him, he looked up, and Héloïse stopped so abruptly that Jemima bumped into the back of her; the foreigner stretched out a claw-like hand to her, and let loose a flood of, to Jemima, incomprehensible French. But it was French, at all events – she had not supposed Hawkins would know the difference between one foreign language and another.

'Do you know him, my dear?' she asked Héloïse. There was a moment's silence, during which Jemima felt a shiver of foreboding, before Héloïse answered in a flat voice, devoid of all expression:

'*Oui, madame. C'est mon mari.*'

23

Marie and Héloïse, with the aid of two junior footmen, took Vendenoir upstairs, stripped him, washed him, cut his hair, and put him to bed. The doctor, hastily summoned from two doors down, opined that the fever was neither putrid nor infectious, but caused by exhaustion and fear.

'Sleep, rest, and good food will put him right,' he said to Héloïse, who stood nearby, her hands clasping and unclasping, sole outward sign of her inward turmoil. 'Poor devil, who is he? Another poor *émigré*, I suppose, fleeing the Terror?'

Héloïse assented to this proposition. Some instinct of self-preservation must have made her speak French in the kitchen: so far only Jemima knew who the stranger was. How – even whether – that would help she did not know, but fear and secrecy are inseparable twins.

'Should I give him food now?' Héloïse asked, but the doctor shook his head.

'I think sleep is what he needs more. I'll give him a few drops of laudanum, and when he wakes in the morning, he should feel a lot better. You may feed him then – a low diet, madam, of course, until he is stronger.'

Vendenoir was already almost asleep, lulled by the warmth and cleanliness as much as by the comfortable bed, but he took the drops docilely, and in a few moments was heavily asleep, and Héloïse went slowly back to join the family in the drawing-room.

For a long time they sat in silence, not looking at one another. That it was a disaster no-one tried to deny; and in the silence every mind revolved about the possibilities, finding them all impossible. At last it was Charles who spoke.

'Anything that money can do, you may depend upon me for,' he said. Everyone looked up at him. He bit his lip. 'It occurred to me,' he said hesitantly, 'that he might be induced to divorce you.'

'Divorce is not possible,' Héloïse said in a flat voice.

'In England it is. It needs an Act of Parliament, but--'

'You forget: I am not English. Also, we are Catholics. There can be no divorce.' Flora tried next. 'Perhaps, if some retired place could be found for him – out in the country, perhaps, where he might be persuaded to go for his health's sake . . .?'

'And what then?' Héloïse said in a low voice. Flora looked unhappy.

'There can be no necessity for you to live with him,' she said.

Héloïse only said again, 'And what then?'

They all thought. Every possibility they considered turned out to be a closed door. Eventually, Charles said:

'I think we had all better go to bed. It can do us no good to worry about this now. In the morning, things will seem better, and I'm sure some answer will present itself to us.' They all rose, eager now to get away from one another. 'I think it will be best, for the moment, not to tell the servants,' Charles added as they parted at the door.

Marie was waiting for her in her room. As always when alone together, they spoke in French.

'Oh, madame, what is to be done?'

'I don't know, Marie. We must go away, I think.'

'Will monsieur be able to travel? What did the doctor say?'

'He says that monsieur is only exhausted, and that sleep and good food will revive him.' She sat down on the edge of her bed and thought, deeply, for a long time, while Marie stood near, watching her. At last Héloïse looked up, and smiled, a little bleakly, at her maid.

'How patient you are, and quiet, like a little dog! Marie, I cannot take you with me.'

'But madame, why?'

'Because we shall be very poor. I must go away in secret, and tell no-one – you will see the necessity. I shall have to find a cheap lodging somewhere, and work of some sort. I could not afford a lady's maid – and I would have no suitable work for you to do anyway.'

'But madame, I don't want to leave you!'

'Marie, good Marie, you won't be abandoned! I know that

432

her ladyship will find you a place – perhaps she may take you on herself. She will do this for my sake I know.'

Marie knelt beside her and took her hand. 'Please, madame, let me come with you. It was not to be a lady's-maid that I begged to come to England – it was to be with you. I can be a *bonne-à-tout-faire* – I can be useful to you. I can do anything: I am strong and clever. And as for wages – pooh!' she snapped her fingers. 'Only feed me from your plate, and shelter me under your roof – it is all I ask. But don't leave me behind.'

'Oh, Marie!' cried Héloïse, and embraced her, and they both wept a little, and felt better for it. 'Very well, if you wish it, I shall be very glad to have you with me. Listen, this is my plan: we shall say nothing to anyone about leaving, but tomorrow you must go out and find us somewhere to live. There is a place to the west, near Kensington, called Brompton, where I have heard all the poor *émigrés* live. You must go there and find us lodgings. I will pack our belongings secretly, and we will leave in the night, as soon as you have found somewhere.'

Marie looked apprehensive. 'But madame, how shall I get to this Brompton? Is it far? How shall I know the way?'

Héloïse patted her cheek. 'You will take a hackney coach, of course. Don't fret, Marie. I have still some of the money Papa sent, enough to keep us for a while, until we find work. But the lodgings must be the cheapest you can find – let them only be clean and decent.'

'Yes, madame. And what about monsieur?'

'I will tell him when the time comes, and we will smuggle him out in the night-time, and have a coach waiting to take us to our new home,' Héloïse said. Her eyes were brighter now, now that she had decided what to do; and it seemed, safe and comfortable as they were just then, a sort of adventure, which might even be enjoyable.

The hardest thing was to persuade Olivier, who could see no reason for leaving the comfort of the Chelmsford's home.

'Let your rich cousins support us,' he said more than once. Héloïse could not, would not, tell him about James. She argued quietly and continuously that they must leave, that their presence was an embarrassment, that they had no claim on the

Chelmsfords, that she neither could nor would ask them for help. Fortunately his exhaustion and the low fever made him a little confused, so that eventually, without having given a specific reason, she was able to convince him that they must leave in secrecy, and at night. All the same, she realised that they must go quickly, before he recovered enough wits and enough English to argue the case out for himself, or spill the secret to his hosts.

Marie returned at the end of her first day's search to say that she could find nowhere fit for madame to stay. Her eyes were round with indignation.

'It is a very low place, madame. A poor quarter, not at all the sort of place you are used to.'

Héloïse realised that she could not leave such a task to Marie, and resolved to go herself the next day.

'We must leave tomorrow night,' she told her maid. 'We dare not stay any longer, or it will be impossible to get monsieur out of the house. I shall go myself and find a place – no matter if it is low, we can look for somewhere else once we are there.'

It was easy enough to get out of the house the next day, by saying that she wished to take some fresh air in the park. She left Marie with Olivier, put on her cloak, and walked quickly across the park to Birdcage Walk, where she hailed a hackney coach, and asked for Brompton.

'Where in Brompton, lady?' the jarvey asked, cocking a curious eye at her. He looked a kind man, and she determined to ask his help.

'I have heard that the poor *émigrés* live there,' she said. 'As you see, I am French, and I must find some lodgings – cheap ones, for I have very little money.'

He eyed her clothes doubtfully, and she spread her hands with a rueful gesture.

'I possess what I stand in, monsieur. When these clothes are worn out, I shall have no more new ones.'

'Hop in then, mam'zelle and we'll see what we can do. It's a bad business that, ain't it? How do you mean to keep yourself in Brompton? Giving French lessons, I suppose, like the rest of 'em – though why anyone wants to learn French I don't know – no offence, you understand. But it ain't a tongue what any decent man can get to grips with, now, is it?'

Héloïse, less dainty on her own behalf than Marie could be, managed to find two rooms up a stair near the King's Road with the jarvey's help. They were partly furnished – which was to say there was a bed in one room, and a very battered sofa, a wooden table and two wooden chairs in the other. They were very dirty, and smelled unpleasant, but Héloïse supposed it would be easy enough to clean them. The house was owned by a woman of indeterminate age who lived on the ground floor. She probably looked older than she was, on account of having lost all her teeth, and being dressed all in rusty black; her dark rooms, and she herself, smelled powerfully of tomcat.

'Frenchy, aren't you? Well, I've nothing against Frenchies. Got to live somewhere, I suppose. A month's rent in advance, my lady, I'll have right away if you please. They're nice rooms, them, though I says it myself – get the sunshine up there, and your own entrance, nice and private.' She nodded towards the rickety wooden staircase, clinging despairingly to the outer wall of the house, which gave access to the rooms. 'Do what you like, so long as you make no noise and no disturbance. This is a decent house, and we're decent people hereabouts, so none of your nasty foreign ways here, my lady, that's all. You keep your nose clean, and you won't come to no harm.'

The jarvey, who had waited for her, pretended tactfully not to have seen her tears.

'Where to now, miss?' he asked. 'Back to St. James's?'

'Yes, please,' Héloïse said, and sniffed dismally, and then blew her nose firmly, determined not to give way.

'Don't you mind the old termagent, mam'zelle,' he said genially. 'She don't mean nothing by it, the mangy old cat.'

Héloïse decided he was kind enough to be trusted, and asked him if he would come back that night and collect her. He looked doubtful, eyeing her with a small bright eye, his head cocked a little, so that he looked rather like a magpie on a window-sill.

'Dead of night? What's all this then, miss? Are you in trouble? Not running off with someone's silver are you? I don't want nothing to do with nothing criminal.'

'No, no, I promise you, I have done nothing wrong. But there are reasons – personal reasons – why I must leave secretly. I swear to you it is nothing against the law.'

One of the letters was addressed to Jemima, and they brought it to her early in the morning while she was still in her bedgown and wrapper.

'Dearest madame,' it said. Jemima noticed that the second word had been altered from '*maman*', and it tugged at her heart. 'I am sorry to leave like this in secret, but I know if you think carefully you will see it is necessary. I know what my duty is, but I know also that dear James, in his love for me, will try to persuade me to do other things. Already, you see, my cousins have talked of divorce, and of leaving my husband, and how much more eagerly would James press these actions? I must do what is right. He must not be allowed to know where I am – and if *you* know, dearest madame, he will find it out from you some time. So you can tell him with a clear conscience that I have gone away with my husband, and that you do not know where. Tell him to forget me. And for you, madame, my dearest, dearest love, and thanks. Adieu – Héloïse.'

'Poor child,' Jemima said. 'Poor child.'

'We must find her,' Charles said. 'She mustn't be allowed to wander off like that.'

'But if you find her, what then?' Jemima said. 'She is right – she must do what is right. You must not try to persuade her to leave her husband.'

'Very well, but we can help her, can't we? Pay her a pension? How will she live, how will she support herself and him?'

'Perhaps that is her husband's business,' Flora said suddenly. Charles snorted in derision.

'That thing? He isn't capable of supporting anyone.'

'Not now, perhaps, but he will recover his strength.'

'Well I am going to search for her,' Charles said firmly. 'And I'm going to find her. Poor misguided child, she should have trusted me. I wouldn't have forced her to do anything she thought wrong.'

'Perhaps not,' Jemima said sadly, 'but James would. She is right about that. I hope you find her, Charles, and that you will be able to help her, but if you do, don't tell me where she is. I could never convince James I didn't know, if it wasn't true.'

The other letter was for James, and it was Jemima who deliv-

436

ered it to him. She went straight home, leaving Charles and Flora to break the news to Lucy and Mary that there would be no wedding to come to Yorkshire for; travelling post, for it was only right that James should be told as soon as possible. It was a hard task, to tell him; Jemima knew how badly he would take it. He raged, not only against fate, but against himself.

'Why did I go away and leave her? If I had only been there, I could have done something!'

'What could you have done? Be sensible, James.'

'I'd have killed him. I'd have made sure she was a widow,' he said, his lips white. 'I'd have smothered him with a pillow while he slept.'

'Don't, James, don't talk like that. Please – things are bad enough.'

'Why didn't I marry her before? Why didn't I *make* her marry me, while I had the chance? What a fool I was! Dear God, what a fool!'

'But it would have been bigamy, Jamie. It wouldn't have made any difference, except it would have been worse when her husband really turned up.'

'Why did you let her see him, any of you? God I wish I'd been there! A pack of fools, helpless, stupid fools, to let her go down to the kitchen! Once she'd seen him, of course it was too late.'

'Darling, we had no idea who he was! No-one could have guessed.'

It was useless to reason with him. He raged, and raved, and cursed, threatened all manner of violence, was for posting straight to London and finding them, and murdering Vendenoir with his bare hands; and Jemima was glad to be able to say truthfully that she did not know where they were.

But when the rage passed, she almost wished it back again, for it was so hard to see his naked, wounded grief; harder to see him weeping helplessly like a child, than grinding his teeth in a rage against fate. He read her letter over and over, so often that the paper, wet with tears, began to fray and tear.

'My dear James,' it said, 'I cannot tell you how sorry I am that things have happened this way. But my husband was not dead, and he is here, and I am going away with him. I ought to wish that I had never supposed him dead, and never fallen in love with you, because of the pain we will now both feel. But I cannot. I am glad to have had the joy of your love. Now you must forget me, and I you. We will not meet again. You must marry someone else – you owe it to yourself, and to your family. We have nothing to blame ourselves for – we did no wrong. But it is the end now. Adieu – Marmoset.'

'There was nothing else she could have done, you know,' Jemima said late that evening, when they were sitting by the last of the fire in the steward's room. 'There was nothing anyone could have done.'

'I know,' said James, his head in his hands, his hands on his knees, and the endless tears running down his fingers and wetting his cuffs. 'I know. But that only makes it worse, don't you see?'

For a week Jemima watched helplessly as his grief tore through him. He had fits of fury, when he would beat his fists against the wall and shout his frustration and anger, and fits of wild crying, and long spells of sullen silence, when he would not answer when spoken to, or even acknowledge the presence of anyone near him. But after a week, he began to come out of it. He began to eat normally, and respond when spoken to, though he remained withdrawn, and absented himself from the house for long periods, going for long, solitary walks, or taking Nez Carré out alone, returning late with the horse all but done-up.

The Aylesburys and Mary arrived. James looked at them strangely and said: 'There's no wedding, didn't anyone tell you? There was nothing for you to come here for.'

Lucy was brisk. 'Don't be silly, James – even if you don't want us here, I'm sure Mother and Edward do.'

After a moment James nodded, stiffly. 'Yes, I suppose so. I'm sorry. There's no news, I suppose?'

'News?' Lucy said vaguely.

'Surely someone is trying to find her? Surely Charles is searching for her?'

Lucy took him a little to one side, holding his arm tightly to ensure his attention. 'Listen, Jamie – you know I always give you good advice, don't I? Then my advice to you is: put her from your mind. I know it's hard – I know you loved her. But she's gone from you for ever. Charles will try to find her, so that he can make sure she has enough to live on. But there would be nothing you could do, if you did know where she was – and if you went to see her, it would only make her burden heavier. You don't want to do that, do you?'

'No, No, I don't. I just want to know she's all right, that's all. I know you're right – I've thought it through, over and over, this last week. But if I could just know she was safe, and taken care of. I can't bear to think of her hungry, cast out, destitute. Oh why did she run away!' He cried out in agony. 'Why didn't she trust us?'

Lucy patted him kindly. 'I expect she was too upset to think clearly – just as you were when you first heard, I've no doubt. Come now, dear brother, let's go and get some tea. I haven't even taken my hat off yet.'

'Oh Lucy – tea!'

'Life has to go on, you know,' she said, linking arms with him and turning towards the drawing-room.

Lucy did him good; Jemima was glad to see him gradually become more normal as the days passed. He had one last out-burst of pain, when he met Lucy driving the new phaeton and pair across the drawbridge one day. He jumped to the horses' heads and stopped them, annoying Lucy, who cried:

'Don't do that! Really, Jamie, you almost had us over, apart from jagging their mouths.'

'What are you doing in that phaeton?' he cried furiously. 'Who gave you permission to take it out?'

'No-one *gave* me permission,' she retorted with spirit. 'Humby asked me what was to be done with the cream ponies because they needed exercise, but no orders had been given about them. He wanted to know if they should be turned out, but I thought that would be a shame, after all the work I put in on them, so I told him to put them to in the phaeton. Now be reasonable, James, they must be exercised, and I don't want their mouths and their manners ruined by some heavy-handed groom.'

He glowered at her sullenly. 'I don't want anybody driving that rig – not you, or anybody.'

'Very well, I'll have them put to in a training phaeton.' James did not answer standing still in her way. The cream Arabs nuzzled him, and one of them scraped impatiently at the ground with a flint-hard hoof.

'Would you like to have them?' he asked at last, with evident difficulty. 'It's true, they shouldn't be wasted. Would you like to take them home with you?'

'Oh, Jamie, surely . . .'

'If you don't, I'll just have them turned out,' he said harshly. 'No-one else shall drive them.'

'Well, in that case, of course I'll have them, and gladly. And what about the phaeton?'

'No, not that. I'll have it put away somewhere. Not the phaeton, Lucy.'

On his orders the phaeton was pushed into a space in the back of one of the coach-houses, its axles blocked up, its upholstery covered in Hollands; and when Lucy took the Arabs out, she had them harnessed in tandem to a very old cabriolet that Humby had unearthed for her.

One evening Jamie came in to the drawing room and wandered over to where Edward and Chetwyn were playing chess on the old rosewood-and-ivory board.

He watched them in silence for a while, and then said abruptly, 'Who was that cotton heiress you were thinking of marrying, Aylesbury?'

Chetwyn looked up. 'What? Oh yes, the daughter of Joseph Hobsbawn, the Cotton King – Mary Ann, I believe her name is. She's his only daughter, and will inherit everything.'

'And it's quite an everything, from what I hear,' Edward grinned.

'Do you still have contact with him? Is she still unwed?' James asked.

'I have no idea,' Chetwyn said, surprised. 'Why? I haven't heard anything of him or from him for months.'

'But you could renew contact, I suppose?'

'I could, but why should I? Why the sudden interest in Hobsbawn?'

'I thought, if she was still unwed, this heiress, I might offer for her,' James said, elaborately casual. There was a short, startled silence, and he went on, a touch defiantly, not meeting anyone's eyes: 'Well, I must marry – I owe it to the family, since Ned isn't going to make any little heirs for Morland Place.

And if she's rich, I daresay we can find ways of using some extra money.'

'Well, of course we can,' Edward said. 'I'd like to pull down Twelvetrees entirely and build a whole new stable there. I've been drawing plans for years, but we have never been before enough with the world to afford it. And the moat needs draining and cleaning out, and the servants' attics need completely rearranging, and then there's the stock--'

'Yes, yes, we get the picture, Ned,' Chetwyn said, 'but first land your fish, before you eat it. Hobsbawn may not fancy the match. James is only the third son, after all.'

'That's where your help would be needed,' James said, 'to explain to him how things are here – that Ned and William will probably never marry, and what a good match I would be. I'm sure you could persuade him, with your silver tongue.'

Chetwyn shrugged. 'Possibly I could – who knows? But James, do you really want to wed this girl, whom you've never ever seen? You know nothing about her.'

'She's rich – what more do I need to know' James said harshly. 'If one must marry, for duty's sake, one ought to marry as well as possible – as you were going to, need I remind you, before Ned suggested Lucy.'

'Yes, but that was different.'

'Was it?'

'Of course. *I* wasn't – I mean, I hadn't thought of . . .' Chetwyn stopped, realising there was no unhurtful way of ending the sentence. He met James's eye, and James returned his gaze steadily. At last Chetwyn shrugged. 'Well, if it's what you want, James. I'll write to Hobsbawn on your behalf and suggest the match. But only if you're sure. I've let him down once already, I shouldn't like to do it again.'

'I'm sure,' James said, and turned away with what sounded like a sigh. 'Yes, I'm sure.'

A while later Lucy came in and said, 'What on earth is wrong with James? He's tearing up all his sketches of Héloïse and burning them on the steward's-room fire.'

Edward told her. Lucy listened in silence, and then nodded approvingly.

'That's good – it's the best thing for him, really. Once he's safely wedded to someone else, and producing children he'll have too much to think about to fret over the impossible. Do get on to it straight away, won't you, Aylesbury?'

'But why *her*?' her husband complained, and she tutted impatiently.

'Really, husband, what does it matter who it is? If he likes the idea of the cotton heiress, let it be her. Don't for heaven's sake, start arguing with him, or you'll put him off the idea altogether.'

Héloïse returned home to find Vendenoir, still in his dressing-gown and unshaven, sitting beside the fire.

'Really, Olivier, a fire in this weather!' she exclaimed. He frowned at her.

'It's all very well for you – you haven't been ill for a year and more. I feel the cold, and I'm sure this place is damp.'

'But we can't afford the coals – I mean, coals are so very expensive, we ought to make economies,' she corrected herself placatingly, knowing he hated to be crossed.

'Oh, very well, we'll put the fire out, and then when I get pneumonia and you have to pay a doctor's bill, you will see where your economies take you,' he said petulantly.

'Oh no, my dear, I didn't mean – of course, your health must come first,' Héloïse said hastily, untying her hat.

'Why don't you ask your rich cousins for money for coals?' Vendenoir said nastily seeing he had won the point. Héloïse flushed a little, but made no answer. There had been times, many of them, when he had said he would die rather than accept charity from bloated aristocrats like the Chelmsfords; there were other times when, perversely. he blamed their present discomfort on her unwillingness to lower her pride and ask them for help. At first she had put down his perversity to his not being well – for a year in a prison cell had left him a chronic invalid, and very nervous – but recently she had come to think he was perverse for the sheer pleasure of tormenting her.

She tried now to cheer him up, placing her basket on the table, unpacked it, saying: 'We have a little something extra today – look, Olivier, peaches! Aren't they fine? Very small, of course, not like we used to have at home – but all the same, only smell!'

She advanced with a peach in each hand, but saw by his scowl that he was not to be pleased today. Perhaps she should not have mentioned home.

'Where did you get those? I thought we were going to have to make economies – or is it only I who must go without things?'

'I did not buy them, indeed – I was given them,' she said hastily. 'Madame Sotterley gave them to me from her garden.'

'Who is Madame Sotterley? What a name!' Olivier said.

'You know who she is,' Héloïse said patiently. 'She is the lady whose little girls I teach the piano. Tuesdays and Thursdays, Madame Sotterley – you *know* that.'

'Why should I remember the name of every miserable *bourgeoise* you hire yourself out to? One is much the same as another to me – they are all foreigners. I don't like you taking charity from such people.'

'It wasn't charity, it was a present. She gave me the peaches as a gift, nothing more,' Héloïse said. I will not cry, she told herself sternly, biting the inside of her lip, I will not cry again. It will only annoy him. But Vendenoir had turned, with the restlessness of an invalid, to another grievance.

'Where's Marie – why is she always so late? Why do I have to wait until this time of day for the newspaper? It is absurd.'

'Because it is too far for her to bring it back to you and get to work in time. Please, Olivier, don't make a fuss about it. She does so much for us – I can't ask more,' Héloïse said wearily, and this time he said nothing, only leaned forward and stirred the coals irritably, and stared moodily into the flames.

The fire was the only bright thing about the room. When Héloïse had supposed it would be easy enough to clean it, she had not considered how hard it is to wash things thoroughly when the water has to be fetched from a common pump out in the street; or how little effect damp bread has on old, thoroughly engrimed wallpaper; or how dust rises from old floorboards and seeps in through ill-fitting window frames. A carpet on the floor had clearly been a necessity, but second-hand carpets and furniture always look grubby and depressing, and both Héloïse and Marie had to go out to work all day, and had therefore little time or energy to spare for making their two rooms more pleasant and cheerful.

Marie worked as a sewing-maid at a coaching inn at Tyburn

Corner. It was a long walk there and back every day, but she was given her dinner at the inn at midday, and since she spoke little English she could not get a better job. Héloïse taught French and piano-playing to the children of the rich middle-class who lived on the fringes of society and who, while they could not afford full-time tutors, liked their children to have the social graces which would mark them out as superior. From time to time she would also be asked to teach a young girl just about to come out how to dance, or to curtsey or to behave in Court circles, and for these things she would charge a little extra.

Héloïse would not have minded her new life very much, in spite of the rudeness of some of her employers, had it not been for two things: Olivier's continuing illness and irritability, and her great loneliness. She had expected to be unhappy, heart-sore, and she was : she did not allow herself to think about James and Morland Place, but sometimes the thoughts would come unbidden, and refuse to be expelled. But she now had no-one in whom to confide, no-one for company. Olivier would not be kind to her, and his attitude cut them off from the society of the other *émigrés* who otherwise would have taken them into their close-knit community. But the *émigrés* liked to sit about each other's hearths at night and share a bottle of wine when it could be got, and talk about the old times in France, supporting their spirits with nostalgia for the *ancien régime* and optimism for the restoration of monarchy which would one day allow them to go home.

Olivier would have none of this. Despite the fact that he had been imprisoned by the revolutionary government and, when released from prison, had been forced to flee for his life from it, he remained obstinately a republican, hated England and the English, and used 'aristocrat' as the worst perjorative he knew. He had told Héloïse only a little about his experiences after her flight – for which he blamed her bitterly, for he claimed that her flight incriminated her and, by association, him. He had dwelt on the horrors of long imprisonment with-out offering her any explanation of why he had not been executed, and she had never been able to understand why he had finally been released. He had told her only that he had been released after Danton's execution into house arrest, but that warning having been conveyed to him that he would soon be arrested again and executed immediately, he had fled Paris. He had had to walk a good deal of the way to the sea, and though he had managed to secure a passage to England on just such a boat as the one which had taken Héloïse, he had had to walk from the coast of England to London, and had only once been offered a ride on a market cart.

'But why did they let you go after so long?' Héloïse asked again and again. 'And why, if they had let you go, did they want to arrest you again?' But he would never answer, only grew angry and changed the subject. In vain, also, did she ask him for information concerning those left behind in Paris: Marie-France, her father's servant Duncan, Camille's and Danton's wives. He claimed to know nothing, and considering that he had spent only two days out of prison, both under house arrest, she decided he probably did know nothing.

He was difficult to live with. Nothing pleased him, he was irritable and suffered continually from ailments for which he blamed her, because it was her fault in the beginning that he had been imprisoned.

'I should never have had anything to do with damned aristocrats!' he would say. 'I should have spat in your father's face when he offered me your hand in marriage.' Héloïse knew he said such things at least partly to provoke her, but it was hard not to react to them all the same. 'I protected you and him from being imprisoned or exiled – and now what thanks do I get? You ally yourselves with a parcel of filthy traitors, and it is I who get imprisoned, while you all get off scot-free!'

'Papa died!' she cried out once when he said that. 'He and Danton and Camille died!'

'Serves them right, the traitors,' he snarled. He was very bitter against Danton in particular, though Héloïse could not understand why.

'They weren't traitors! They had nothing to do with Dumouriez's plot. They were his friends in the past, that was all. You know that!' But it was no use arguing with him. Hatred seemed to be the only thing he had left with which to warm the fires of his heart, and in the end she decided it would be cruelty to him to take it away. She was glad that he insisted on sleeping on the sofa in the living-room. At first she had intended Maria to sleep there, while she and Olivier took the double bed in the smaller room; but there was no fireplace in the bedroom, and Olivier felt the cold so much that he had insisted on sleeping in the living-room, leaving Héloïse to share the big bed with Marie. She did not *think* that, if they had shared a bed, Olivier would have wished to have intercourse with her, but she was grateful not to have to find out.

Leaving her husband to poke the fire, Héloïse went through into the bedroom to change out of her 'decent' clothes, which she brushed carefully and hung up inside a Holland bag from a nail in the wall. She had to appear well-dressed and respectable for her work, and so she was extremely careful with her two good dresses. At home she changed into a skirt and bodice of strong calico, with a cotton apron over the top. She tidied her hair, and went back into the living-room to start preparing their supper.

Marie came in at last, dusty from her walk and very tired, bearing the master's newspaper, and the bottle of cheap port-wine he had bid her bring back. The doctor they had consulted when they first moved into Lincoln Street had said that port-wine would be beneficial to Olivier's health and nerves, and he had taken to the advice with more fervour than Héloïse could have expected, considering the doctor was an Englishman. Héloïse poured him a cupful and gave him the newspaper, while Marie took a bowl of cold water into the bedroom to wash the dust from her face and hands and arms. She came back into the living-room, red-faced and shiny, just as Olivier discovered something in the paper which made him give vent to a string of curses.

The two women clutched each other for a startled moment, before Olivier flung the paper at them in disgust, and they were able to discover the cause of the outburst. It seemed that the English fleet under Admiral Howe had won a battle against the French fleet off Ushant. Twelve French ships had been dismasted after fierce fighting, and seven of them had been captured. Eleven English ships had also been heavily damaged, but it was still being considered a glorious victory for the English: the excitement was perhaps tinged with relief, Héloïse thought wryly, since it was the first victory at sea since the war began. The newspaper was calling it 'The Glorious First of

June', and Black Dick Howe was a hero, to whose name every virtue was being attached.

Olivier was raving about the perfidious English, about their lying cowardice in calling such a battle a victory, about how someone must have betrayed the French fleet, about how the French ships which had been allowed to escape, because of Howe's pusilanimity, would soon return and wipe the English fleet off the face of the waters; but Héloïse was reading the detailed report which followed the exclamatory opening paragraphs. She was looking for news of her kin – and she had a number of relatives and friends to be concerned about: William, Harry and Jack in the *Antigone*, Captain Haworth in the *Cressy*, Hannibal Harvey in the *Orient*, Collingwood in the *Barfleur* to name but a few. Olivier was asking her something, but she could not attend to him until she had ascertained that none of these was reported as dead or wounded.

'Why should you care about them?' he sneered. 'These Morlands – who are they?'

It was meant to be a rhetorical question, but she was nettled. 'They are my kin. Naturally I am concerned.'

'Kin? The most distant of cousins, that is all.'

'No, they are closer than that. They would have been my . . .' She stopped abruptly, seeing Marie's alarmed face.

'Your what? Closer? What do you mean?' She said nothing, and he lost his temper. 'Answer me, you sullen bitch! Don't you dare to use dumb insolence on me! I am your husband!'

She should not have spoken, but somehow, to be called bitch by him was one thing more than she could bear. She told him, in a fury, that had she married James, as she ought, these Morlands would have been her brothers. She told him that she had thought him dead, and wished she had not had to revise that opinion. She told him she wished he had never come to England. Then Marie pinched her – hard – and she stopped abruptly just before telling him she wished he would die now.

He stared at her, white almost to greenness, except for one red spot high up on each cheek, and a red gleam in the depths of his eyes.

'So, you had made yourself a widow, had you? You didn't wait long, did you? Couldn't wait to get yourself into bed with another man, you rotten aristocrat whore. God, that I ever

447

soiled my hands with touching you! When I think of being married to you, I could – but I got my revenge on you, and your aristocrat father! Oh yes! You didn't know that, did you? Didn't even guess! It was I who sent him to the guillotine – yes, me! I gave the evidence that condemned him, *and* Danton and all his filthy crew.'

Héloïse was staring at him now, her eyes wide with horror; conscious of Marie close to her, her arm round her waist as if to support her. Her husband raved like a mad thing, hardly seeming to know what he was saying. 'That's why they reprieved me – and a year I spent in prison, God rot them, waiting for them to close the net on Danton and his friends. A year! A year in a cell hardly bigger than a coffin! Robespierre's doing – he said he'd release me when I'd given them what they wanted, but he didn't tell me it would be year before I was let out. And then, when I was out, they made a new warrant for my arrest. They betrayed me! They never meant me to live – the cheating, lying bastards! Well, I shewed them, I got away, and they'll pay for it one day. The dogs will drink their blood one day, you'll see!'

Now he was weeping. Héloïse turned and fled, stumbled blindly into the other room, found the window with her out-stretched hands, and leaned against the pane, trembling and sick, and hollow inside, as if she had been emptied out and scoured like a basin. Her lips moved soundlessly. Oh Papa, Papa! Her father, whom she had loved, betrayed to his death by the husband to whom she had given her loyalty, even at her father's expense!

To Héloïse, loyalty was an absolute, something so fundamental to life that to abandon it threatened the foundation of existence. For her it had been not the least of the Revolution's horrors that she had been forced into a conflict of loyalties between her husband and her father, her father whom she loved, her husband whom she did not. Love went deep in her, but some things went deeper than love, rooted so far down in her soul that she could neither uproot them, nor believe that those she cared for were made any other way. The black horror that seized her now was not only at what Olivier had done, but that *he* had done it. A cold nausea filled her, and darkness ebbed and waned before her eyes, and for a long time she could only cling to the window-frame with whitened fingertips, while her soul cried out with wild grief for this last and most dreadful loss, this final betrayal.

Some unknown time, moments or aeons later, she became aware of Olivier calling for her querulously from the other room. The nausea had passed, and she felt only cold and faint and empty, as though her heart had been cored out like an apple; but as she moved automatically to answer the peevish call, she found that there was still something left, something that remained to her from her earliest upbringing, to sustain her. When all else failed, there was still duty; even in the waste of hopes destroyed and trust shattered, one still knew what had to be done.

She straightened her shoulders and smoothed her hair with an automatic hand and turned towards the other room; and discovered, as she passed through the door, an unexpected lightness, which made her pause for a startled instant to analyse it. He had freed her. Her duty lay with him; she must stay with him and care for him for as long as he lived; but she did not love him, had never loved him, and now she no longer needed to feel guilty for it. He had freed her from that.

24

After the initial enquiries by Lord Aylesbury, all the negotiations with Joseph Hobsbawn were undertaken by Edward,
who travelled to Manchester to meet Hobsbawn. On his return,
he found his mother in particular eager to hear all about it.

'Well, what is he like, this cotton king? Is he agreeable? Did
you meet the girl?'

'Ring for some wine for me, Mother, and I will tell you
everything,' Edward said, sitting down opposite her in the
other chimney-chair. James was sitting at the table nearby,
reading, and did not raise his head from his book. Edward
looked at him, and decided that he was only feigning not to
listen, and addressed his commentary equally to the top of
James's head as to Jemima's eager face. 'Well, Manchester is
an up-and-coming place, and no mistake! I never saw so many
fine buildings going up at once. Cotton has certainly brought
prosperity. Think of it, Mother: only twenty years ago it was
just a village by a stream! Now it's a city, with civic buildings,
assembly rooms, and as many fashionable people and elegant
carriages in the street as you'd see anywhere. Of course, it
hasn't the style of York – it's a new town, after all – but there
is certainly plenty of wealth there.'

'And Hobsbawn – is he an elegant man?'

'Well, I don't think you'd call him elegant,' Edward said
hesitantly. 'Forceful is more the word he suggests. But he has
an enormous new house, all built of stone, with Roman col-
umns at the front door and a ballroom at the back as big as the
one at Shawes.'

'Good heavens!'

'Oh yes, he's as rich as a nabob, there's no doubt about it.
He seems a nice enough fellow, however, and eager to please.'

'Eager to please you?' Jemima asked with a smile.

'Oh yes – once I'd told him about Morland Place, and how
ancient our family was, and that we lived in a moated castle,
and had a coat of arms. He was a little worried at first about

our not having a title – though he had asked about us and found that we are related to the Chelmsfords. He'd like a title for his daughter, you see.'

'Not really,' Jemima said. 'How did you get over that difficulty?'

'I explained about the religious difficulties we'd had in previous generations, and that persuaded him. They are Roman Catholics, you see – probably he has found out by now that most of the peerage wouldn't take a Papist, however rich, into the family. But I said we didn't mind – we'd had them before, and it was close enough to our religion not to trouble us.'

'Did you see the girl? What was she like?' Jemima asked. James lifted his head, but it seemed only to scratch his ear, before returning to his book.

'Yes, I met her. She seemed nice enough.'

'Pretty?'

'Pretty enough. Very quiet – likes reading – but that might be because she's an only child, with an oldish father. No-one her own age, you see, to chat to. Mother's dead – has an old nurse to be her companion. Anyway, she seemed happy enough about the match, and Hobsbawn and I came to a pretty good understanding. He's offering a good dowry with her, on the understanding that we make a settlement of the same amount on her, and she'll inherit everything from him, provided her children inherit our estate.'

'It must have been quite difficult to make him understand the situation here,' Jemima said thoughtfully. Edward shrugged. 'It was one of the things we talked about. He wasn't convinced I wouldn't marry myself, but I persuaded him in the end. I told him that I couldn't afford to be distracted from the business of running the estate, and that it took up all my energies – he seemed to understand that. He sighed and said he thought his wife had had a lean time of it while he was building up his empire, for he never saw her from one week's end to the next.'

'Didn't he think it odd that James did not come with you?'

'Well, strangely enough, he thought that was a point in his favour,' Edward grinned. 'I think he saw James as a dutiful, obedient boy who was allowing his family to choose his bride in the old-fashioned way. I didn't disillusion him – though he wants to see you, Jamie, before he'll sign the girl over.'

Now James really looked up. 'I don't want to go there,' he said.

'You must, old chap, or the deal is off. I expect he wants to make sure you aren't a hunchback or a dribbling idiot or something. You'll have to go and do the pretty, and tell him how much you'll be honoured to have his daughter. The sight of you ought to clinch it – you look so much more the gentleman that I do.'

'Nonsense, Edward, you are a gentleman to your toes,' Jemima said severely.

'Ah, maybe, but James is prettier, and Hobsbawn will want to be sure he's getting his money's worth, since we've no title. He really is astonishingly rich! These cotton mills must be worth their weight in gold.'

'Did you see the mill?' Jemima asked eagerly, 'Your father and I once visited a mill in Derbyshire – do you remember, Ned? It was most interesting.'

'No, I didn't see them, actually – they're in a different part of town from where rich folk live – but he told me about them. They use steam power, you know, not water power. Think of it! Manufactories don't need to be sited by streams any more – they can have them anywhere they like now. They burn coal in a furnace, which heats water into steam, and the steam passes through a narrow outlet with such force that it can drive all the machinery they want. Amazing! No more worrying about drought for the cotton kings! They even work looms off this steam power, Mother, and Hobsbawn says the shuttles move so fast you can hardly see them!'

Jemima marvelled. 'It wouldn't do for our woollen manufacture – the stress would break the thread,' she added, and Edward said:

'He thinks one day they will be able to modify the machinery even to do that. But we've come to a nice little arrangement in the meantime: he is to take a whole supply of our pauper children off our hands. They need children for the mills to take the bobbins off . . .'

'Yes, I know, I saw it all at Cromford,' Jemima said. 'Well, it isn't a bad life for them, and it teaches them a trade.'

'Yes, and it solves a problem for us, of what to do with them, the foundlings and orphans,' Edward said. As governor of the workhouse, he had a perennial worry over what to do with the flotsam and jetsam of humanity. 'So all we've got to do now is to dress Jamie in his best and drive him over to Manchester, and the deal is made.'

They persuaded him without much difficulty. Since he was determined on the course he saw that it must be done.

'I just wish you had seen the mill, though,' Jemima said as they went in to dinner. 'I'd have loved to hear your description of it.'

The *Cressy* was one of the English ships which was dismasted during the battle of the Glorious First of June, in consequence of which she had to put in to Plymouth to refit. Mary travelled down there for the chance of seeing her husband again. Replacing a mast was not a difficult task, like replacing a sprung timber, not requiring that the vessel be put into dry dock; but all the same, *Cressy* was in Plymouth harbour for ten days, and Mary was able to see Haworth at least briefly every day. He was delighted by her pregnancy, thrilled at the thought of becoming a father, and concerned for Mary's safety.

'Don't worry,' she said more than once. 'I shall be perfectly all right. It is the most natural thing in the world, after all.'

'A *dangerous* natural thing,' Haworth frowned.

'My mother had seven children, and look how healthy she is,' Mary smiled.

'True – and as long as she is looking after you, I shan't worry too much. Promise me you'll go back to Morland Place when I sail again, and stay there until the baby's born? No more gadding about – I'm sure it can't be good for you, in your delicate condition.'

Mary laughed at that. 'What can you know about it, pray? And as for my delicate condition – I ask you, do I look delicate?'

He looked at her with admiration. She looked strong, and bright, and healthy, and indestructible, carrying her pregnancy easily, and managing to look quite elegant in a special gown she had designed herself.

'You look . . .' he began, and found that words were not adequate to describe what he thought about her. There was a long and very satisfying silence, after which Mary sighed, rubbed her cheek against his, and said:

'What would you like the baby to be called? Have you thought of any name?'

'Not yet – I shall give it some thought during the long days of my next spell of blockade duty,' he said. 'Something plain and wholesome if it is a boy, and something pretty and different if it is a girl. I shall put my mind to it.'

'I hope you do go back onto blockade duty,' Mary said severely. 'I think it most unkind in you to enter into a battle the moment my back is turned.'

'What, madam, you would condemn me to boredom – and obscurity – and poverty? If there are no battles, there is no glory, and precious little prize-money.'

'Never mind. I want you safe, that's all,' Mary said. 'If a French man o' war heads towards you, you run away!'

'Would you prefer me to leave the navy, and get myself a safe job, in a bank, perhaps?' he enquired ironically.

'Oh no, I would not wish to interfere with your chosen career, sir,' she said demurely. 'That would be most improper!'

When the *Cressy* had sailed, and Mary had watched from the Hard until not even she could believe the ship was still in sight, she went back to the inn and told Farleigh to pack her clothes.

'We shall go to London and see Flora and Charles, and then to Wolvercote.'

'You promised the master you'd go back to Morland Place,' Farleigh said, looking mulish.

'How can you know that? Have you been listening at doors?' Mary demanded.

'Of course not! As if I would!' Farleigh said hotly. 'The master told me so himself. He gave me a crown for myself, and told me to keep my eye on you, and make sure you were careful, and didn't go gadding about.'

'And I suppose if I do go gadding about – for if I want to, you will have no way of stopping me, will you – you'll feel you have to give the money back?'

'That's right – and a crown is a crown, after all,' Farleigh said. Mary smiled sweetly. Farleigh liked to pretend she had no affection for her mistress and only served her for gain, but Mary knew better.

'Well then, I'll give you a crown, and do as I like, and it will be all the same to you, won't it?'

Farleigh picked up the gown she had been folding and brushed it with her hand. 'You always did do as you liked, from a girl,' she grumbled, avoiding the question. 'Your father should have whipped you when there was still time to mend your ways.'

Mary regarded her affectionately, and then said suddenly, 'He will be all right, won't he?'

Farleigh gave her one of her rare smiles. 'Aye, Miss, he'll be all right. The Dear One will look after him, don't you fret, and when he comes back you'll have a pretty bairn to shew him.'

'Nothing,' said Charles. 'Absolutely nothing. I didn't realise before how easy it is for someone to lose themselves in London, if they really want to. I've made enquiries, even advertised in newspapers, but she seems to have vanished off the face of the earth.'

'And she's never contacted you,' Mary mused. 'That, surely, must be a good sign? I mean, don't you think she'd come to you, if she was really in need?'

'I don't know – she was determined not to be found out,' Charles said doubtfully. 'I think she might starve to death before she asked me for anything.'

'Yes, but she wouldn't let Marie or her husband starve, would she? No, I think she must be managing, or she'd come to you. She's a capable, practical sort of girl, after all.'

'Perhaps you're right. I hope you are, anyway,' Charles said, putting a cheerful face on it, for he felt very bad about Héloïse's having run away like that, without asking his help. 'So your husband has gone back to the fleet? I dare say he's hoping for some more action like the First of June.'

'And I'm hoping for some nice, safe blockade duty for him,' Mary said. Charles smiled.

'That won't do any good. Flora will tell you, the sea's a far more dangerous enemy than the French, and beating about on lee shores and dodging shoals is just as hazardous as fighting battles.' He realised too late that this was not very tactful, and hurried on, 'Well, you can be thankful, at least, that he has no

West India experience. Look at poor William, sent off to convoy troops to attack the sugar islands; and from what Pitt says, it's going to be a long campaign. All the West India veterans are being detached and sent out there – Harvey's gone, you know, in the *Orient*.'

'I don't suppose he minds,' Mary said. 'He always used to tell me the West India station was the best for prize-money – and I happen to know he has a very handsome widow in Antigua whom he longs to visit.'

Charles grinned. 'Oh, you know about her, do you?'

During her visit, several old friends walked up to Chelmsford House to pay their respects, and to wish her well. But the talk always came round in the end to the terrible events in France, which had captured the unwilling imagination of the English. It was hard to believe that such horrors were happening just across the Channel. Paris was tearing itself to pieces: a new law had been passed on the tenth of June – or the twenty-second of Prairial, as the revolutionary style was – which speeded up the process of 'justice' by preventing the accused from defending themselves. Now when anyone was brought before the Revolutionary Tribunal, the fact that they had been accused was enough to condemn them, and a simple identification was all that was necessary before they were hurried away to undergo Samson's *toilette* and be bundled into the tumbrels.

The numbers being executed by this process had risen to horrifying heights. The guillotine had had to be moved from the place de la Révolution because the local, wealthy, property-owners complained about the terrible smell of blood. It had been removed to the place du Trône at the far end of the poor faubourg Saint-Antoine, and there the victims were despatched fifty, sixty, seventy a day, like cattle in an abattoir. Plans had been drawn up for a sangueduct to carry away the rivers of blood from the site; great pits were dug at the limits of the city to cope with the huge numbers of corpses arriving daily.

It was called the Great Terror, but it was more like a great insanity. No-one seemed to understand it; citizens were numbed with horror, and except for those whose appetite for blood was great enough to gather at the place du Trône each day for the spectacle, they crept about their business, trying not to attract attention to themselves. It seemed as though people denounced one another for fear of being denounced themselves. Many were the tales that filtered through to the outside world. People were denounced for the strangest, the most insignificant things; and once arrested, they were in a net from which there was no escape. A carelessness for human life grew up amongst the clerks of the Tribunal. Once there were two women of the same name arrested, and no-one seemed to know which was the one wanted. 'Oh well, execute them both, then,' was the order. On another occasion, twenty peasant girls arriving in Paris looking for work were gathered in and executed, without their having any idea of what was happening to them.

Charles was reminded of what Héloïse had said, about the means shaping the end. 'It's madness,' they said to each other. 'It can't last. Soon they will come to their senses.' Robespierre was popularly credited with bringing about the Great Terror, and his name was reviled throughout England. 'It couldn't happen here,' people said, and it gave a sense of holy purpose to the war.

'Thank heaven poor Héloïse got out before that began!' Flora said once.

Mary added, 'She may even come to be glad that her father died when he did, and did not live to see what happened to his country.'

Mary stayed two weeks in London, and then in response to Farleigh's urgings, went home, via Wolvercote. It was pleasant to be in the country again, and to see how the new Countess of Aylesbury was reshaping her husband's home. Lucy was settling in well, and becoming a very efficient mistress of her house. She was at present rearranging the servants' quarters along more rational and hygienic lines, and had gone a little way towards fulfilling the prophecies that she would open a hospital by setting aside a suite of rooms as a sick-bay for the servants and estate workers.

'Though at present I am not having much success in persuading them to trust me,' she told Mary with a sigh. 'They are such superstitious fools, and prefer dosing themselves with the most terrible poisons, and saying charms under a full moon, and walking backwards round goats and all that sort of black-magic trickery. It never seems to impress them that these 'cures' don't work. They go on believing in them, in the face of all the evidence to the contrary, just because they are traditional. It is very provoking.'

She was very interested in Mary's pregnancy, and, as she had read Smellie's works on midwifery, she had some good and sensible advice to offer, which Mary accepted with good grace. 'I wish I could be there to deliver the baby for you,' Lucy said, 'but I've so much to do here, I don't think I shall be able to spare the time.'

'I'll just have to manage without you,' Mary said equably. Lucy did spare the time to drive Mary round the home park behind the cream-coloured Arabs.

'Such a pity about James and Héloïse,' she said to Mary. 'They'd have been well suited, I think. Héloïse was so sensible and practical. Still, it can't be helped. At least I made him see sense about this pair – he was going to turn them out, you know, rather than let anyone drive them. Such nonsense!'

'Men are nonsensical creatures,' Mary agreed. 'I suppose they can't help it. It is a pity, though, that women aren't allowed more to do in society.'

'You wait until I open my school,' Lucy said cheerfully. 'We'll shew 'em then! I say, Polly, if your baby turns out to be a girl, can I have it? No, no – I mean, will you send it to my school, of course!'

'I don't promise anything,' Mary laughed. 'Why don't you have some of your own?'

'Oh, I will, when I have a moment. I must get everything sorted out first.'

'Do you like being married to Chetwyn?' Mary asked curiously.

Lucy concentrated for a moment on putting the pair through a gateway neatly, and then replied cheerfully: 'Oh yes, he's a trump! I've just thought – when you get back home, would you ask Edward about that filly, Mimosa? She was ready for backing when I was there last, but you know, he almost promised I could have her for myself. I should like to have the schooling of her, and I ought to have her soon, if I'm to have her at all, before someone else spoils her. Will you ask him if he'll send her down to me? Or if he can't spare anyone, I could send a groom up for her.'

'Yes, I'll ask him,' Mary said with an inward smile. It seemed unlikely that she would get any more detailed comment on married life from Lucy.

Hobsbawn House, as the stone house in Manchester was called, was a revelation to James, for he had never before been in a house which was entirely newly furnished, and which belonged to someone for whom expense was no object. Chelmsford House and Shawes were grand, to be sure, and belonged to the nobility, but they were filled with a collection of things which had accrued through the ages. Shawes he was beginning to know very well, for he had begun the wall-paintings he had been commissioned for, and he was coming to appreciate the exquisite taste which had designed, built and furnished it. It was his refuge from his unhappiness: once he had filled his brush, he went away out of the world for a space, and nothing existed for him except the small patch in which he was creating a new vista. When he had painted all he could for the time, he would wander around the house, looking into the shuttered and Holland-shrouded rooms, and feeling the peace which was engendered by the harmony of perfect proportion and clear, elegant lines.

Hobsbawn House, on the other hand, was not peaceful: exotic, exciting, colourful, perhaps, but not peaceful. It was filled with riches. Eveything that could be gilded or silver-plated was gilded or silver-plated. Carpets were thick and lavishly coloured, chandeliers were huge and so glittering they dazzled even when unlit. There were enormous mirrors everywhere, and hundreds of candles in sconces; velvet drapes with bullioned cords and tassles; marble and onyx and ebony tables with gilded legs; clocks and statues and vases and bowls on every surface. Everything that could be decorated had been carved or moulded or elaborated upon in some way. Hobsbawn himself was very fond of Chinese art, and whole rooms were done in the Chinese style. The bedroom which was assigned to James – obviously one of the best, by the pride with which the butler shewed him into it – had a bed shaped like a Chinese pagoda: circular, with a golden roof rising into dizzy spires, and ivory bells hanging from the edge of the canopy. The washstand was an elephant, bearing a bowl on his back instead of a howdah, and the numerous huge mirrors reflected a dark red-and-gold wallpaper in which mandarins and tigers stalked each other through a landscape of bare, knotty trees, summer-houses, and rustic bridges.

The cotton king moved with firm tread amongst his treasures. He was a big man with a restless energy and hands like hewn rock, legacy of the days before he made his fortune, when he had to do everything for himself. His voice was loud, used to having to be pitched against the roar of machinery, and when he caught himself bellowing, he would lower his voice abruptly, with an apology and an embarrassed smile. He knew little of the world beyond his own part of it, little about matters which did not appertain to his trade, but he was not a rough man, and his religion had brought him into contact with a beauty that was not entirely wordly. He liked music, and was pleased when he discovered that both Maurice Morland and the earlier William Morland, whose religious music he admired, were from the same family. It added the final touch to the impression James's personal beauty had already made.

Edward was doing his best by James, mentioning his education, his previous army career, his talents as a painter and his horsemanship, but Hobsbawn was more impressed when James was persuaded to sit down at the enormous new pianoforte and play. All the Morland children had been taught to play and sing, and they all performed more or less well. James knew his limits, and never attempted anything he could not finish with credit, and so he got by, but he knew he was no musician, and did not like to hear himself praised. Edward had to distract Hobsbawn's attention from James's scowl by asking about a vase standing at his elbow.

Amid all this splendour, Mary Ann Hobsbawn moved almost invisible, like a candle flame in full sunlight. She was not by any means a plain girl. She had pale, creamy skin, light brown hair that was rather thin and silky, and light brown eyes. She was tall for a woman, having inherited her father's frame, and large-boned, though she moved lightly and gracefully. But she disappeared into the background, for she was quiet, had nothing to say for herself, and had an expression of calm which was almost passivity. On this, his second visit, Edward knew no more about her than before. She made commonplace answers to the commonplace questions he put to her, speaking in a light, unaccented voice, and otherwise sat silently on the sopha, her hands in her lap, neither speaking nor smiling.

James had private speech with her only once, when the tea was brought in after dinner, and laid upon a round table away from the area where they had been sitting. Mary Ann rose and went to pour the tea, and James got up to help her. He stood for a moment watching her. She was tall enough to be of a size with him, perhaps even to overtop him a little, but she seemed unembarrassed by it – even unaware of him. Her whole attention was on what she was doing, which she did unhurriedly, every movement calm and graceful. Her clothes were over-elaborate, the colours too rich for her. They did not suit her, and, he realised, were one of the reasons she blended into her background so well.

She finished pouring a cup, and looked up at him, and said, 'would you hand this to my father?'

He took the cup from her, and continued to look at her, and then asked her abruptly, 'I beg your pardon – but – perhaps I may not have another chance to ask. Do you wish for this marriage? I should not wish to press the matter, if you did not like it.'

She regarded him gravely, and he wondered if there was not a touch more colour in her face than before? No, he must have imagined it. At last she said:

'My father thinks it a good match. I am quite content with his choice.'

James could think of nothing to say, so he bowed slightly, and took the tea to her father, as she had requested. Dull-witted, he thought. Bovine. Well, what did it matter? Any woman who was not Héloïse must be the same to him as another. If she cared nothing about the marriage one way or the other, so much the better – for neither did he.

Before the Morlands left, Hobsbawn had shaken hands on the bargain, and a date had been settled on in October. He called for wine to celebrate, and looking at his daughter over his glass, he sighed and said, 'By heaven, this house will be lonely without my girl!'

Now her face did gain a little colour, and her eyes were

bright. James bowed slightly to her father and said, 'I shall encourage her to visit you as often as possible, sir.'

Hobsbawn beamed, thinking this a piece of graciousness, but Edward knew better: that James was declaring his indifference. Catching Mary Ann's eye at that moment, he gained a sudden certainty that she knew it for what it was, too, and he hastened to add: 'And I hope you will often come to visit us, sir, at Morland Place. I know Mother would be very glad to meet you.'

'Aye, lad, I should like that very much. I should like to see the castle where my girl will be living. Think of that, love: a castle, just like in those books you are so fond of!'

'Not *quite* the same, Father,' she said, and she smiled for almost the first time.

In early August the news came that Robespierre had been toppled from power by a number of deputies in the Convention who, discovering that they were on the list for arrest, decided that their only hope was to act together, and persuade the Convention that Robespierre had better be put to death before *they* all were. Robespierre, Saint-Just, the crippled Couthon, and nineteen others of his close associates were arrested and executed on the twenty-eighth of July, the guillotine being transported across Paris to its former site in the place de la Révolution for the occasion. Whether or not Robespierre had been responsible for the Great Terror, it ended with his death. Over thirteen hundred people had been beheaded in two months, but now the power passed back into the hands of the Convention, and no more tales of horror were heard across the Channel.

The summer was hot, and Jemima felt it as much as Mary. The two of them spent long hours sitting in a shady bower in the rose-garden, enjoying each other's company thoroughly for the first time, and talking quietly about husbands, marriage, and children. Jemima had great satisfaction in gazing at this most beautiful of her children, and felt that maternity had only increased her beauty, by giving it a new gentleness.

'It will be a handsome baby, whichever sex it is,' she said once, 'and whichever parent it takes after.'

'Do you think he is handsome, then, Mama?' Mary asked, turning her head with a smile. The shifting sun-pattern through the leaves dappled her face and flickered across the hands, resting from their crochet-work in her lap. 'I thought it was only I that saw his beauty.'

'I don't know that I would call him precisely *handsome*,' Jemima said. 'But he has a face one would not tire of looking at. He reminds me very much of your father.'

'Does he? Well, that is a compliment indeed.'

'Have you decided what to call the baby?' she asked next.

'Oh, I shall leave that to him. He said he would write and let me know what he decides,' Mary said placidly, and Jemima concealed a smile at this long-delayed dutifulness from a female who would never before be told what to do.

Because of Jemima's age and Mary's condition, the planning of the alterations to the house which were necessary before it could receive a bride were left to Edward and James, and therefore were largely carried out by Edward. Jemima gave advice when asked, and Mary occasionally criticised afterwards, and Edward longed secretly for Héloïse's practical help, and outwardly wished Lucy were there to organise things. Mrs Mappin was sulking, because it was decided to move Jemima from the great bedchamber, where she had slept for over thirty years, in order to let the newly-weds sleep there. In vain did Jemima tell the housekeeper she didn't mind: James had never been a favourite of hers, and since Mary slept in the West bedroom, which was the prettiest of the smaller rooms, and Edward had moved into the North bedroom when Allen died, as befitted the Young Master, it left only the Red Room for Jemima.

'It isn't fitting, my lady,' Mrs Mappin said, more than once. 'You are the Mistress when all's said and done, and Mr James is only third son.'

'I really don't mind,' Jemima insisted gently. 'The great bedchamber is too big for me anyway.'

'But you've never liked the Red Room,' Mrs Mappin protested almost tearfully, and Jemima patted her hand and smiled.

'No, *you've* never liked it, Mappin! I always think of it as Uncle George's room: whenever I go in there, I think I smell leather and lavender water.'

Father Thomas was sulking because Hobsbawn had insisted that his daughter be married from her own house, and would not be comforted by the promise of a service of dedication when the couple arrived. The fact of the matter was that since the boys had gone to sea, he hadn't enough to do. Jemima had asked him to plan the resiting of the herb garden, which she had been thinking about for years, but now he was claiming that he had better leave it until James's new wife could be consulted, as she would probably disagree with anything he did.

'They are making this poor girl into an ogress,' Jemima sighed to Mary one day. 'Well, at least Oxhey is happy: he likes an occasion when all the family plate can be got out. It seems to feed something in him, a display of polished silver.'

'It feeds his self-consequence,' Mary smiled. 'All the same, you know, it is James who is causing all this strife. He won't interest himself in the preparations, which makes the servants feel there is something wrong with the girl.'

'I expect it will be all right once she's here. Edward says she's a perfectly nice little thing, only very shy.' She had an inward vision of a tiny, slender-built dark-haired girl, very young – very like Héloïse, in fact, she realised guiltily. 'And Barnard is happy,' she went on hastily, 'or at least I think he is. He said something to me yesterday that sounded like '*heureux*' and shewed me a book with illustrations of new ways to decorate cakes. I think he is planning to outdo Lucy's. I just hope it isn't *bigger*, only more elaborate, for I don't think the trestles will stand the weight.'

'Tell him so,' Mary suggested, fanning herself. A bee alighted on her hair, and Jemima lifted it off gently with a forefinger and placed it in the heart of a white rose.

'Oh, I don't think I'd better. I never know if he understands me when I tell him things – and if he did, it would probably only offend him. Much better to leave it to him.'

As September advanced, James busied himself with the harvests, absenting himself from the house for most of the day, and winning Edward's praise for the energy with which he was throwing himself into the running of the estate.

'It's good to have someone to help me, after all these years,' he said one evening, when he and James and Mary were lingering by the open windows of the long saloon. Jemima had retired to bed, worn out by the heat. 'I have had to carry the load alone for so long, since Mother grew less active. And after all, if it will all be yours one day, who better to help me?'

'Not mine, really, Ned,' James said cynically, lounging on a window-seat, 'but Hobsbawn's daughter's children's.'

'Well, that's the same thing, isn't it?' Edward said, refusing to be baited, or perhaps not noticing.

When he left the room a few moments later, Mary regarded her brother with tightened lips. It had not escaped her that James was staring, not into empty air as it appeared, but at the portrait of Héloïse on the wall beside the fireplace. At last she said:

'You're just like a spoiled, petulant child, aren't you? Determined to make everyone unhappy because you can't have what you want.'

'What do you know about it?' James replied with feigned indifference, still looking at the picture.

'You only fell in love with Héloïse to spite Mary Skelwith. Now, to spite Héloïse, you're going to make this poor Hobsbawn girl unhappy, and everyone else into the bargain. Why do you do it, James?'

'I am marrying, for your better information, in order to provide Morland Place with an heir,' he said with dignity, but his eyes were narrowed.

'Stuff! If that was all, why didn't you marry poor Mary Skelwith, and adopt her boy legally? At least that way you'd make a few people happy. What has this poor cotton heiress ever done to you?'

'I don't want to marry Mary Skelwith – and I'll thank you to keep your nose out of my affairs,' James said, through gritted teeth. Mary looked at him with contempt.

'You're such a romantic,' she said scathingly. 'You only want what you can't have. I wonder how long Héloïse would have kept your favour, if she had married you?'

James stood up with a violent movement, took a step towards Mary, and then stalked out, leaving her feeling a little guilty at having provoked him.

'But he deserved it,' she muttered to herself. All the same, when she saw him the next day, she apologised. 'I'm sorry if I said cruel things to you – but, really, you might think about other people sometimes.'

'What do you mean by that?' he asked curtly.

'If you are determined to marry this girl, at least shew a decent eagerness for the match. The servants are beginning to think she must be a hunchback.'

She had said that to try and tempt a smile from him, but he looked at her with a terrible bleakness, and said at last, 'Yes, I suppose you're right.'

Mary did not feel as though she had won any victory.

A letter came for her that morning from her husband, which she snatched with a girlish eagerness and bore off to the rose garden to read and relish in private. When she returned, she was laughing.

'What is it?' Jemima asked. 'Is it some joke?'

'I'm not sure,' Mary said, smiling broadly. 'I think it may be. We shall have to wait and see.'

She went into labour on the twenty-seventh of September, early in the morning. She was thirty, an advanced age to be having a first child, but Jemima was at her side, and reminded her that she had been thirty when she had had Edward.

'Don't worry,' she said, 'that's the main thing.'

'I'm not worried,' Mary panted, clenching her teeth, 'I'm just hot.'

James and Edward were out in the fields all day, and it was not until four in the afternoon that the ringing of the house-bell told them that it was all over, and with a grin at each other, they picked up their coats and raced back to the house. Jemima met them in the hall, and was glad to see for the first time in months a natural, unforced expression on James's face.

'Has she had it?' Edward gasped, out of breath.

'Is she all right?' James asked at the same moment.

Jemima pushed down the fawning muzzles of Leaky and Brach, who had been rolling in cowpats as usual, and said happily, 'She's perfectly all right – a very quick labour, all things considered!'

'And the baby?' Edward asked eagerly.

'A girl – a beautiful little girl,' Jemima said. 'You shall see her by and by, but first, will you ask Oxhey to bring up some champagne, Edward? We ought to wet the baby's head – and Mary says that Lucy says that champagne is very good for women who have just given birth.'

'If that's the sort of advice that Lucy gives,' Edward grinned, 'there really ought to be more women doctors!'

Oxhey, his face wreathed in smiles, brought a tray with the champagne and the glasses, and the congratulations of the servants.

'It's been a long time since we had a new baby in the house, my lady,' he said. 'She's as welcome as the sunshine, God bless her!'

Jemima patted his hand. 'Yes, there were times when I thought there wasn't going to be a new generation.'

'Has Miss Mary decided on a name yet, my lady?'

'She hasn't told us – I asked her, but she just laughed. She's up to something,' Jemima said with a faint frown. Oxhey smiled as he bowed himself away,

'Ah, Miss Mary always was an original, my lady. I dare say we shall find out at the christening tonight.'

The chapel was a blaze of candles, and the whole household, with the exception of Mary and her maid, was assembled to see the baby christened, and to give thanks for the first of the new generation. Jenny, the nursemaid, came downstairs with the baby, wrapped in one of the family gowns, trailing lace almost to the floor, and placed her in Jemima's arms; and Jemima carried her to the font accompanied by Edward and James. Father Thomas stood ready with the holy water in a silver basin on a tripod, and as Jemima reached him she said in an urgent hiss:

'Has Mary told you the name? The *name*, Father?'

'Oh yes – it was in a letter from her husband. If it was a boy, he was to be called Henry, after his grandfather. As it's a girl, she's to be named Hippolyta Diana Mary.'

A low snigger broke from James, which was hastily repressed, and Jemima, a little dazed, passed the tiny, red-faced scrap of humanity to Father Thomas, and realised that

that was the joke Mary would not divulge; and also, that it could have been much worse.

Flora and Charles spent September with their friend Lady Tewkesbury at Stratton Hall, returning to London in October to prepare for Amelia's wedding. When the first flurry of their arrival was over, Charles was sought out by Hawkins, with a by-now familiar look of anxiety in his eye.

'Something untoward has happened, my lord, during your absence,' Hawkins said.

'Oh dear, not *more* strange Frenchmen I hope?' Charles groaned. 'If this continues, I shall have to move house and change my name.'

'No, my lord, it was not a French person, but it was indeed something to do with her ladyship – her *French* ladyship, I mean, my lord.'

'Speak on, Hawkins I am prepared for the worst.'

'Well, my lord, it was three days ago, my lord, that a carrier's cart arrived, and the carrier knocked upon the door – the back entrance, quite properly, my lord – and said that he had a delivery for Lady Strathord. Of course, I was aware that her ladyship had taken that title, my lord, and I took it upon myself to inform the carrier that her ladyship no longer resided at this address. The carrier said he couldn't help it, my lord, and shewed me the direction on his bill – which was the Countess of Strathord, care of the Earl of Chelmsford, Chelmsford House, Pall Mall'.

'I shall definitely change my address,' Charles murmured. Hawkins bowed.

'I then enquired as to the nature of the delivery, my lord, and was informed that it was furniture.'

'Furniture?'

'Just so, my lord. The carrier was to say that it was furniture belonging to the late Earl of Strathord, to be delivered to the present Countess.'

'Did you take it in?'

'In the end, I did, my lord. I hope I did not do wrong, but it seemed to me that there was nowhere else the man could take

468

it, and if by any chance your lordship did succeed in tracing her ladyship—'

'Quite right, Hawkins, you did quite right. Where is the stuff? I had better have a look at it, I suppose.'

'I placed it in the far bedroom in the east passage, my lord, as a temporary measure.'

'Very well – it can stay there, I should think. We have never used that room, have we?'

'No, my lord.' Hawkins added other details to the story as they went up the stairs and along the passage. The goods had been sent by sea from Antwerp, after having travelled slowly, and with many hold-ups across France, but that they had passed over the French border solely on account of having a Ministry of the Interior official stamp. Charles knew from what Héloïse had told him that her father had worked for that ministry, and was in no doubt that Henri had sent the stuff off when he knew he was going to be arrested. He wondered, however, why Henri had bothered to send furniture at all – until he saw it.

'Good God, Hawkins, the room looks like a bazaar!' he exclaimed when the door was opened. The furniture filled the room, stacked high, and even what little Charles could see was obviously going to be worth quite a lot of money, when and if it was sold. He could see a boat-bed with carved and gilded ends; a suite of Louis Quinze chairs upholstered in pink brocade; rolled carpets; tapestries which, even by a single corner, he could tell were very fine, probably Gobelins; a *chaise-longue*, upon which rested a looking-glass with an ormolu frame; various tables and dressers.

'I believe, my lord, that there is quite a market for French furniture, since the late troubles,' Hawkins offered deferentially. 'Even antique furniture, as I believe much of this is.'

'Hum, yes, well we can't sell it for her, without her permission – not yet, anyway. It will have stay here for the time being. I suppose eventually, if she doesn't turn up, we may have to think of selling it, and investing the proceeds in the funds. This is a pretty writing-desk, isn't it, with the porcelain insets? Sèvres, I should think. It's a wonder they didn't get cracked on the journey.'

'And there is something else, my lord,' Hawkins said, stepping to the last-mentioned piece of furniture and opening a drawer. 'A letter, my lord, addressed to Lady Strathord.' He took out the package and handed it to Charles. It was heavy-quality paper, sealed in several places over thin red ribbon, and addressed in dark ink in a flourishing, masculine, and very French hand – Charles guessed, Henri's.

'Well, this obviously was not meant to be opened, except by her. We shall have to keep this, too. Put it back in the drawer, Hawkins – that's the best place for it.'

'Yes, my lord. Will your lordship be making another effort to find her ladyship?'

'I suppose I'd better,' said Charles with a sigh.

The wedding was over. Mary Ann, in white satin, white lace, ribbons and roses had been given by her father and united by the Holy Catholic Church to James Morland, who looked very handsome but pale and serious in a sapphire-blue coat and white silk breeches. Two school friends of the bride's attended her, and the bridegroom was attended by his brother, who looked anxious all the way through the ceremony, and kept glancing at the bridegroom as if he thought he might run away.

The bride's father sobbed unashamedly all through the service, but afterwards was very lavish in the matter of champagne, and bestowed upon the bride a handsome wedding gift of a necklace and earrings of sapphires and diamonds; and to the bridegroom an enormous clock of white marble supported by two bronze rearing horses and crowned by an eagle perching on an urn. James found it hard to find the words with which to thank his father-in-law for this astonishing gift; but his stammering did him no disservice, for Hobsbawn took it for modesty.

The wedding feast went on until two o'clock, and then the bridal party departed. Edward left in the Morland travelling-chariot which had brought him and James to Manchester, intending with several changes of horses to go straight home; but as it was a journey of nine hours or so, the bride and groom were to go only as far as Huddersfield today, stopping at the George Inn for dinner and to sleep the night, and completing the journey tomorrow. They travelled in a very pretty vis-à-vis which was another present from Hobsbawn to his daughter, but with post horses, for Edward had insisted it would have been absurd for him to go to the expense of providing horses as well, when his daughter was marrying one of the foremost breeders of carriage horses in the north. In a hired chaise behind travelled Durban, Mary's elderly maid Dakers, and the luggage.

While Durban and Dakers were getting quite comfortable and friendly in the second carriage, there was little conversation in the vis-à-vis. James began by making a few commonplace remarks about the weather and the scenery, to which Mary Ann responded politely with the minimum of words, but silence soon fell, and proved difficult to break. At each stage, when the horses were changed, James asked his wife if she would like to get out, or if she required anything, and she replied no, and that was that.

Dinner had already been ordered for them at the George, and when they arrived, welcomed by the landlord and his wife with the broad and sentimental smiles reserved for newly-weds, they were told that everything was ready for them to dine at once, when they had seen their rooms and taken a moment to repair their toilet.

'Are you hungry, ma'am?' James enquired of Mary Ann.

'Yes, very,' she replied

'Then may I suggest we dine in ten minutes?' James said. She bowed her head in consent and disappeared up the stairs with Dakers. To his surprise she reappeared in the private parlour exactly ten minutes later, having removed her hat and pelisse, washed her face and hands, and tidied her hair. James handed her into her seat, and sat down opposite her, and they were served.

It was a handsome dinner: there was an excellent pea soup, with little balls of forcemeat floating in it, a duck stuffed with oysters and chestnuts, a raised pork pie and a pike with sharp sauce; and for dessert there was a pupton of apples, a blackcurrant pudding, and butter and cheese. James attended to his bride's requirements, and was glad to see that she ate heartily, and also drank claret with the enjoyment and freedom of an only daughter brought up by her father.

He himself could eat little, though by serving himself and

haggling his portions on his plate, he made it appear that he was eating. He felt as though he were in a dream; nothing seemed real, least of all the tall, fair, serene-faced woman opposite him, who answered him so politely when he spoke and never once met his eye. The food he put in his mouth had not more flavour or texture for him than ashes, and he could only swallow it by washing it down with wine – too much wine, he knew, for his sense of unreality was growing. It was their wedding night: later, he would be expected to consummate their union. The marriage would not be legal without that, and once that was done, there would be no dissolving it – as there had been no dissolving Héloïse's marriage to that Frenchman. Did she sleep with him? he wondered, tormenting himself until he moved restlessly in his chair, making his wife look up in faint surprise.

When they had finished eating, he rose from the table while the servants cleared, and went and stood by the fire, one foot on the fender, staring into the flames. After a while Mary Ann came and sat in the fireside chair near him. He knew she was watching him, wondering about him, and in desperation he began a conversation, about hunting, which was the only subject that came to mind. At last that flagged, too; there was nothing else to do but go to bed.

They had been given two rooms with a connecting door. He escorted her to her door, and, without meeting her eyes, muttered, 'Shall I come in to you – say, in half an hour?'

'Yes,' she said, and hesitated, and then went into her room and shut the door. In his own room, Durban was sitting up for him.

'Go to bed, I don't need you,' James said harshly. Durban rose without a word. 'Stay – do you think you can get me some hot water?'

'I think so, sir,' said Durban. When it came, James dismissed him, stripped off his clothes, and washed, and then put on his bed-gown. He looked at his reflection in the mirror over the dresser. It was an old-fashioned mirror of polished metal, and the softened and dimpled reflection added to his sense of unreality. In the mirror he looked no more than a boy, with tousled hair and veiled eyes. He brushed his hair smooth, until it shone, as he might have groomed a horse to soothe it. Now there was nothing more he could do: he must go in to his bride.

He knocked on the dividing door, and opened it cautiously.

'May I come in?'

'Yes,' she said. She was in bed, hidden in the shadows of the curtains; there was one small candle still alight, on the other side of the bed. He blew out his own candle, went over to the bed, and without looking at her, blew the bedside light out, too. Easier, he thought, in the dark. He climbed in beside her, and for a long time lay there in silence, unable to go on. A cold sweat was forming along his spine; he was as aware of her beside him as of the presence of a burning brand; if he touched her, he felt, he would turn instantly to charcoal.

It was she who broke the silence. 'I'm afraid,' she whispered. He turned towards her. 'I expect it will hurt,' she went on.

'I will try not to,' he said. It reminded him that, while this was the first time for her, he had done it many times before. She was a woman, as other women, he told himself sternly. Her skin was warm and smooth, her body soft and shapely. Shutting his mind, he let his body take over, trying not to think about anything. She moved pliantly to his direction; and then at the last moment, he could not. His body simply would not obey him.

'Is something wrong?' she asked softly after some time. He was lying half on top of her, his face turned away from her and buried in his arm. 'Have I done something wrong?'

Helplesly, in the dark, he began to cry.

'What is it?' she whispered. 'What's the matter?'

'I can't,' he sobbed into the pillow. 'I just can't.'

She began to stroke his head, very gently.

'It isn't your fault – nothing to do with you. It's . . . something else,' he cried.

'Yes, I know,' she said. She put her arms round him and stroked his hair, and after a moment he turned his wet face to her, and wept like a child in her arms, while she held him and comforted him wordlessly. In the end, when he could cry no more, he grew drowsy, and fell asleep; waking an hour or two later to find himself still in her arms, comfortable, comforted.

And then there seemed no more difficulty, and the thing was accomplished at last, quietly, in the warmth and darkness, with

473

no sound but their breathing. James Morland, wed at last, he
thought; and that's that.

'Hmm?' She was almost asleep.

'Nothing,' he said. He settled himself with one arm across
her, and his cheek on her round shoulder. 'Go to sleep, wife.'

FRIENDS AND ENEMIES

Kate Alexander

The year: 1938. The scent of war is in the air.

The place: Austria. Christine Brookfield, the indulged and beautiful daughter of a comfortable middle-class household, has fallen hopelessly in love with her German ski instructor, Gunther. And when he comes to visit her family in England they realise that this is not a short-lived holiday romance but a deep and true love.

Then war breaks out.

And Christine and Gunther are forced to confront the harsh reality that they are now enemies. With Gunther a fighter pilot for the *Luftwaffe* and Christine a radar operator, dreams for each other must die, as each fights courageously and ruthlessly for national victory.

Movingly told, with infinitely memorable characters, FRIENDS AND ENEMIES is Kate Alexander at her best.

Futura Publications
Fiction
0 7088 2337 8

ESTELLA

Alanna Knight

ESTELLA
a heroine consumed by the love she sought to deny.

Ward to the eerie Miss Havisham, she passed her childhood amidst the decaying splendours of Satie House. Though born with breathtaking beauty, Estella was schooled in cruel pride. 'Break their hearts,' Miss Havisham's vengeful cry echoes forever in her ears – and she obeys . . .

Pip, the devoted admirer of her early years, is spurned. But her cruel successes turn to dire defeat, her loveless marriage brings only bitterness, pain and danger. Forced to flee, she searches for safety amongst the mill towns of Derbyshire and the gypsy camps of the open road. And she craves for love – love, deep and true, as Pip once offered her.

But Estella's dark, dark eyes hide darker secrets still. Only half-known to her, they taint her life, poison her loves and theaten to destroy her hopes.

ESTELLA
a tale of love, loss and redemption based on the haunting heroine of Charles Dickens' *Great Expectations*.

'This masterpiece of reconstruction will give you one of the best reads since the publication of the novel in which Mrs Knight's heroine first appeared.'
Yorkshire Post

Futura Publications
Fiction
0 7088 3159 1

HEARTS AND FARTHINGS

Beryl Kingston

London in the 1890s . . . a foggy city bustling with activity and bubbling with Cockney repartee.

To this alien world comes Alberto Pelucci, an early immigrant from distant Italy, dreaming of adventure and romance. Adventure enough is the verminous room of his first night's stay in London, but romance seems more rewarding when the shy Alice accepts his hand. Only on their wedding night does he realise that his bride will never share his passion for physical pleasures.

And so when Alberto meets Queenie Dawson – exuberant, sensuous star of the music halls – his ordered new life is flung into turmoil . . .

HEARTS AND FARTHINGS: the heart-warming saga of a man torn between two women, and of children born in the last, bittersweet days before the war that should have ended all wars.

Futura Publications
Fiction/Saga
0 7088 2976 7

ALWAYS A STRANGER

Margaret P. Kirk

The tranquil Yorkshire countryside in the summer of '39 offers Lallie Wainwright, adored only child of a wealthy foundry owner, blissful happiness: as long as she has her family, dogs and Neil, her childhood friend, her life is complete.

But the war brings more than upheaval – it brings Jan Kaliski, a Polish pilot in a strange land, into Lallie's home and into her heart. Then the war, and the chaos that is war's aftermath, forces them apart. Only after heartbreak and tragedy do Lallie and Jan learn the bittersweet lesson that home is not always where the heart is . . .

'a love story in the old, grand manner – heroic and emotionally charged. She deals with big themes in the stylish and deceptively simple manner of the born storyteller. Have your handkerchiefs ready. You won't just read. You'll care.'
    Sarah Harrison, author of *A Flower That's Free*

'vivid and real . . . an irresistible read of passion and heartbreak. I couldn't put it down.
    Madge Swindells, author of *Summer Harvest*

'a really heartwarming story with flashes of brilliance'
    Cynthia Harrod-Eagles, author of
    the *Dynasty* series

Futura Publications
Fiction
0 7088 2723 2

All Futura Books are available at your bookshop or newsagent, or can be ordered from the following address: Futura Books, Cash Sales Department, P.O. Box 11, Falmouth, Cornwall TR10 9EN.

Please send cheque or postal order (no currency), and allow 60p for postage and packing for the first book plus 25p for the second book and 15p for each additional book ordered up to a maximum charge of £1.90 in U.K.

B.F.P.O. customers please allow 60p for the first book, 25p for the second book plus 15p per copy for the next 7 books, thereafter 9p per book

Overseas customers, including Eire, please allow £1.25 for postage and packing for the first book, 75p for the second book and 28p for each subsequent title ordered.